Every gentleman in England wants a wife like her—beautiful, uncomplaining, and never underfoot.
There is definitely

SOMETHING ABOUT EMMALINE

Perhaps it's the fact that she doesn't exist! Alexander Denford, Baron Sedgwick, invented a gentle, subservient, never seen "wife" for the sole purpose of deterring the *ton*'s marriage-minded ladies and their infernal matchmaking mothers—thereby enabling him to enjoy his frequent late nights and lustful dalliances in peace. So imagine Alex's surprise when a stunning stranger appears in his private bedchamber . . . and brazenly announces that *she* is "Lady Sedgwick!"

This "Emmaline" has been living by her wits her entire life—and dearly desires what the dashing, much chagrined rake can provide: an entry into good society. In the meantime, she is plunging his household into chaos and, worse still, wreaking havoc with his heart. For there's something about her spirit and fiery sensuality that Alex is finding impossible to resist. But before he can make his perfect love his actual bride, he'll have to somehow become the ideal husband he never dreamed he could be.

ELIZABETH BOYLE

Something About Emmaline

An Avon Romantic Treasure

AVON BOOKS
An Imprint of HarperCollinsPublishers

AVON BOOKS
An Imprint of HarperCollins*Publishers*
10 East 53rd Street
New York, New York 10022-5299

Copyright © 2005 by Elizabeth Boyle
ISBN: 0-7394-4868-4

Printed in the U.S.A.

To the memory of Rody Burrows,
who taught me to play cribbage.
And let a kid win more times than she deserved to.
I shall never forget your patience,
your kindness or your stories.
And you will be a hero to me always.

Prologue

England, 1801

"**M**y last meal," Lord John Tremont bemoaned as he tucked his knife and fork into the thick cut of beef before him. "But at least it is a fine one."

"I suppose it helps that I am paying for all that, eh, Jack?" his best friend, Alexander Denford, Baron Sedgwick, commented dryly.

"You owe me nothing less," Jack replied between bites.

"I owe you?" Alex laughed. "Now, I'm not one to call accounts between friends, but truly I don't see how *I* owe *you*." He refilled his glass from the bottle the innkeeper had left for them. Given that it was French and very dear, he knew he'd best get a few glasses in before his friend decided to attack the rare vintage with the same fervor as the roast beef. "Now, let me see, there was that rather large marker of yours I signed for last month at White's."

"Pocket change," Jack said with a wave of his hand.

"And the lady of questionable character for whom I bought that bracelet because you feared losing her to old Ambercrombie?"

"That was a matter of honor." Jack reached for another slice of beef. "Besides, can you imagine me losing Camilla's affections to that fossil?" He shuddered, then eyed the claret.

Alex nudged it out of reach. "And what about that pair of cattle you had to have at Tatt's but you hadn't the blunt?"

Jack grinned. "Necessities, my good man. Besides, that was nothing more than I would do for you."

"The only difference is that I have the money to afford all these *necessities,* whereas you do not."

Jack's fork paused between his plate and mouth. "Sedgwick, what the devil is wrong with you? You sound like my palsy brother tonight. What has you in such a foul temper?"

"Nothing," Alex told him. "But I still don't see how I can owe you anything."

Jack grinned and leaned forward. "Have you forgotten your dear wife, Emmaline? Without me, you would never have obtained her devoted attentions. I think that leaves you utterly in my debt."

This time Alex did laugh. "You think I owe you because of my wife? Some nerve, that." He picked up the bottle of claret and poured his friend a glass. Jack Tremont was an annoying sponge, but he was also Alex's best friend. Despite his spendthrift ways and penchant for peccadilloes, a more loyal friend Alex had never known.

"I think the success of your marriage was a stroke of genius, and worthy of unending reward," Jack said, raising his glass in a mock toast, most likely to himself.

Worthy of something, Alex mused. "My marriage is successful because I have the wit and wherewithal to bring it off. If you must know, it is careful planning and intelligence that make it work. You were merely the catalyst to seeing it come to life."

His friend snorted. "Sedgwick, you are the most stodgy fellow alive. Careful planning and intelligence, indeed! Emmaline was the best thing that ever happened to you. She keeps you from being a complete dullard."

"I am not dull," Alex said, straightening his shoulders. "I'll have you know some people consider me quite the dasher."

"Who?" Jack demanded. "Ambercrombie's ancient mother?"

Alex nudged the bottle of claret back out of reach. Then he looked up at Jack and they both broke into companionable laughter.

"I will own that I am perhaps not the first Corinthian people think of," Alex admitted, "but I have my position and the responsibility of my family to consider." And what a family it was. He had no brothers and sisters, but scads of cousins and aunts and uncles who relied on his benevolence to keep them employed and housed and fed, not to mention his tenants and servants. It was a burden he took with great seriousness and pride, though there were many times when he envied his friend's situation—a third son and unlikely to inherit. Jack's legacy would mostly be a lifetime of scandalous memories and unpaid vowels.

Jack shuddered. "Gads, how I detest those words. Position and responsibility." He tossed back the claret and pushed his empty glass forward. "I propose we change the subject, for you are sounding more and more like Parkerton. It is bad enough he has summoned me home for my annual accounting. I daresay, no one can tally accounts with more excruciating detail than my brother." Jack took another bite of roast beef. "By the by, how is dear Emmaline? You don't know how many times I've kicked myself for not marrying the chit myself."

"Happily," Alex told him, "there is only one Emmaline."

"Is she in London or Westmoreland at present?"

"You know the answer to that." Alex glanced over at the door. It wasn't closed, but it was nearly shut and there seemed to be no one about.

"No, I don't really," Jack said, leaning back in his chair. "I mean when you are in London, the dear girl is supposedly happily awaiting your return to Westmoreland. And when you are home in the country, your family believes her to be living in London." Jack leaned forward. "So I pose this puzzle—where does the chit reside when you are in neither place?"

Alex laughed. "That is why you could never manage such a marriage. I'll say it again: careful planning and intelligence." He tapped his skull. "Those are the reasons why I am married to Emmaline and you are not."

"Bother both your smug assurances. Your hide is safe because your grandmother remains encamped in the north. Can you imagine if she ever decided to venture to town and discovered that Emmaline was nothing more than a figment of your imagination?"

Since that would never happen, he had no worries the dear lady would ever discover the truth.

That Emmaline Denford, Lady Sedgwick, had come to life one night five years earlier after too many hours of carousing with Jack. It wasn't that Alex drank often, but he'd been in low spirits and his friend had offered him a night away from the problems plaguing him—especially when Alex had declared he was leaving town the next morning.

Jack had protested vehemently against such a plan, for who would pay his drinks and debts if his best friend left London?

But Alex was tired of being harassed at every turn by marriage-minded mothers and their conniving daughters. It seemed that the entire eligible female population of London had set their cap to see him married that Season.

Never mind that it was a well-known fact that Sedgwick barons were rather unpredictable when it came to marriage, marrying late in life, if at all. For some it had been a case of wanderlust, like his grandfather, who spent most of his adult life in the army, having inherited his title late in his career from a cousin who'd never wed.

Perhaps Alex should have just made it a point to avoid London during the Season altogether, like his own father had, knowing too well that all anyone saw in him was the old and respected title, vast holdings in the north and the wealth to support even the most spendthrift of wife and in-laws. All that was just too tempting a lure for a mother with an unmarried daughter.

"No, there's no way around it, my good man," Jack had said. "You need to get married. That would get the cats off your back."

"Married?" Alex shuddered. He just wasn't sure he could take that next step. Certainly it was a matter of duty, but something held him back from taking that all-too-essential plunge. Besides, a wife, he was convinced, would be tempted to start reorganizing his perfectly ordered life. "I'd rather see Hubert inherit," he declared.

"Never!" Jack drained the expensive champagne with a long guzzle. "Do you think Hubert would be inclined to pay my vowels? I think not!" He paused and raked a hand through his hair. "Why couldn't you get married, but not actually take a bride? Invent one, so to say. I'd wager that if you placed a notice in the Post, *told the world you'd married, they'd all leave you alone."*

It had been that simple. Alex had always considered himself a sensible fellow, but he'd been desperate, and in a flash, Emmaline was created. With a proper and likely lineage found with the help of an old copy of *Debrett's,* they'd dashed off a notice and tipped a lad to deliver it forthwith to the paper.

And to his utter amazement, his *faux* bride had done the trick. The night after the announcement appeared, he'd been left blissfully alone, with only a few scathing glances shot in his direction from his more persistent, now former, pursuers. To the few curious who'd dared question his sudden marriage, he declared Emmaline to be in poor health and living in seclusion in the country. His stodgy reputation offered its own advantage, for then he'd give a strict, uninviting stare that cut off any further inquiries.

The arrival of Emmaline into his life had also given him the added bonus of eliminating his grandmother's nagging. Well, most of it. She'd written to him with her overjoyed blessings that he had finally wed.

When he'd returned home that summer, he'd explained his wife's absence by stating that her delicate health prevented her from traveling so far. When he'd returned the next Season, any inquiries about Lady Sedgwick were met with the same explanation—Emmaline's health prevented her from traveling to London.

And thus, the perfect wife had entered his life.

Though not everyone was convinced of the wisdom of his solution. His solicitor had warned him time and time again that a false wife was but asking for trouble. Bother the authorities, Alex had told the man, for there would be worse hell to pay if his grandmother discovered the truth. Then again, his grandmother's distaste for London was the key to Emmaline's existence, or rather lack of one.

"How is it that your grandmother hasn't discovered your secret?" Jack asked, eyeing the roast beef and the wine and in an apparent dilemma as to which to go after next. "I mean, if anyone is likely to ferret out an incongruity, it is her."

"Right you are, but then again," Alex said, tapping his skull, "careful planning has ensured my success. As it is, my solicitor's wife pens a carefully worded letter to Grand-mère every six weeks and signs it as Emmaline."

"I suppose being dull has its advantages," Jack admitted. "Why, you've thought of everything." He rose up and leaned over the table, his long arm reaching for and succeeding in gaining the bottle of claret. He filled his glass and then topped off Alex's.

Raising his glass in a toast, he said, "To Emmaline Denford, Baroness Sedgwick, the most perfect wife ever."

"To Emmaline," Alex agreed.

In the shadows outside the private dining room, a woman retreated from the partially opened door. She hadn't meant to eavesdrop, but the conversation inside had caught her ear, and she'd found herself spellbound by the revelations.

Sedgwick's wife didn't exist?

It was so unbelievable, she thought as she silently made

her way out of the inn and to the waiting carriage. Oh, this information was far too valuable, far too scandalous not to be put to good use immediately.

And she knew exactly where to start . . .

Chapter 1

For his first month home at Sedgwick Abbey, Alex found himself left in blessed solitude.

Instead of being there to greet him, his grandmother had decided to remain at her sister-in-law's estate for an additional month, most likely unable to leave until they had caught up on every bit of family gossip. Therefore, his summer began with no pestering talk of heirs, no lengthy discussions of Emmaline's continued ill health, just a continuation of his perfectly ordered life that Jack had the audacity to call "boring."

But eventually his grandmother had decided she could no longer leave him to his lonely exile and had returned home like a whirlwind, her herd of pugs trotting in her wake.

Genevieve Denford, Lady Sedgwick, had been born in France, and the sixty-odd years she'd been in England hadn't diminished her Gallic presence in the least.

His grandfather, another reluctant-to-be-wed Denford,

had taken a trip to Paris in his late sixties and had brought home (to the horror of his own heir apparent) a French wife. Given his grandmother's *joie de vivre,* Alex doubted his grandfather had stood a chance.

A lesson to all unmarried English gentlemen, he'd decided years ago. Never venture across the Channel.

Grandmère had greeted him merrily when he'd come in to breakfast and hadn't stopped talking since. "And imagine Imogene's shock when I told her . . ." she was saying from her end of the table, where she sat encircled by her dogs.

It had been quiet without Grandmère, he mused as she barely paused between bites to regale him with tales of his great-aunt's grandchildren—and, horrors, a few great-grandchildren. Heirs abounded in Aunt Imogene's world, and he knew the next few months would see no end of hinting and prodding that he and Emmaline should be doing the same as well—producing the next Sedgwick baron.

He'd have to make a note to his solicitor to have his wife's next letter from Emmaline detail a litany of female complaints that would unhappily prevent such an event. The more, the better. He hoped that would keep Grandmère sufficiently diverted through grouse season.

The door to the dining room opened and Burgess, their butler, entered, staggering beneath a large silver tray. Behind him, a footman followed with an even bigger tray, just as laden with papers and notes.

"My lord, a pouch from Mr. Elliott's office arrived this morning along with the mail," Burgess said, setting his burden on the dining table before Alex. "To be specific, there were three pouches." His bushy brows rose. "Large ones."

Alex stared up at the monumental pile, his knife and fork held in midair. "What the devil is all that?"

Burgess, being ever the diligent butler, replied, "The regular newspapers and periodicals for her ladyship, but the remainder appear mostly to be bills, my lord."

"Bills?" Alex looked at the collection again. He'd instructed his London solicitor to take care of all his outstanding accounts. Besides, that pile looked like something Jack had run up, not him.

"Unlike Elliott to be so inefficient," Alex muttered, as he began to sort through the mess. "Ah, here is the answer. Seems Mr. Elliott's wife has inherited property in Scotland and they needed to inspect the place. His clerk is attending to all his business in his absence. I'll have to speak to him when he returns—the fellow has obviously gotten my accounts mixed up with some wastrel client of his."

"What is it, my dear?" his grandmother asked from her end of the table, where she was dropping tidbits to her dear dogs.

He waved his hands over the pile of bills. "Just the London papers and such."

"The papers! Why didn't you say so?" She rose and hustled down the side of the long table, her lace cap aflutter. Before Alex could stop her, she swept aside the neatly arranged piles to get to her most favorite thing in the world—the gossip column in the *Morning Post*. Separating the pages with the skill of a farmer's wife plucking a hen, she had her quarry in her clutches in a flash and settled into the chair next to Alex to begin reading.

Hopefully not aloud, he thought as he continued his sorting.

He was rewarded with a minute or so of silence before she couldn't contain herself.

"Lady Vassar had a baby. A son, it says." She sighed and

then shot him a significant glance. "An heir is so important, don't you think, Alex?"

"Yes, of course," he agreed, his gaze stopping on one of the bills before him. Four hundred pounds for carpets. Another expenditure listed furniture for one hundred and fifty pounds. Bills for drapers, carpenters, painters, and that was only the start. Why, it appeared the poor sot for whom these notes had been intended had outfitted not only a new house, but a wife and stable of mistresses, what with the unending collection of milliner, modiste, glover, and lace bills.

"And finally a mention of our dear girl," his grandmother was saying. "Listen to this: *Lady S. was seen shopping diligently with the assistance of Lady R., who has taken her new friend under her wing. Lady S., so long from town, is a delight and sure to be the prized guest next Season.*" She pursed her lips. "About time she was mentioned. But what an odd thing to say. Why would they think her so long from town when she has lived there all her life?" She tossed aside the paper and began once again upsetting Alex's carefully wrought piles with her rustling.

"Madame!" He rose up from his seat and covered the bills with his arms to protect them from her marauding. "What has gotten into you?"

"I just want to see some more recent columns." She cocked her head and eyed the collection again. Before he could stop her, she spied her prize and caught hold of another paper, tugging it free and settling into her chair with a speed that belied her eighty-some years.

"I think you've gone mad," he muttered. Though with her nose buried in another edition of the *Post,* he doubted she heard him. "Didn't you get enough of that prattle while visiting Aunt Imogene?"

"Imogene doesn't take the *Post*," came the frosty reply.

That had to be the eighth wonder of the world, in his estimation, right behind the Tower of Pharos. He didn't know anyone more addicted to gossip than his Great-Aunt Imogene—that is, save his grandmother.

He turned his attention back to the bills at hand, tossing aside the ones that were obviously not his and the few that needed his attention.

His grandmother shook out the pages as she searched for her beloved column. "I knew it!"

And he knew she'd continue to interrupt him until he replied, so he said, "Knew what?"

"Knew she'd be mentioned again. But I don't know if I should read it to you. You'll be in a dither for the rest of the week."

Alex gave up all hope of having a decent morning meal. In peace. "Go ahead," he told her. "Or you'll be huffing and puffing until I relent."

"I never puff," she said in a voice that sounded remotely like a huff. "But if you insist: *It is a good thing there are so few people in town, for Lady S. creates a stir wherever she is seen. One wonders what the baron is thinking sending such an Original to town without his watchful eye about.*"

He held out his hands and shrugged. "And how is that supposed to put me into a 'dither'?"

She held out the paper for him as if the answer were as clear as the printed words before his eyes. "Don't you see? It's Emmaline they are talking about. Your wife. Our dear girl."

"Emmaline? Preposterous." he scoffed. "Grandmère, there are a dozen or more 'Lady S.'s' gadding about town on any given day. I assure you, that is not our Emmaline."

"And whyever not?"

"Because Emmaline would never comport herself in a manner that would be of any interest to a gossip column. 'Tis absolutely impossible." Alex had never issued a statement with more confidence.

But that was the problem with confidence, occasionally it needed to be shaken, and Baron Sedgwick was about to be rattled right down to the roots of his illustrious, as well as fictional, family tree.

"Then why does it go on to say the following? *From the amount of tradesmen seen coming and going at Hanover Square, it is said traffic has become a nuisance.*" She glanced up at him. "Hmmm. How many 'Lady S.'s' reside on Hanover Square these days, Alex? For I can only think of one." She shook her paper again and went back to her reading.

His mouth opened to argue with her, but he couldn't get the words past his suddenly dry throat.

Tradesmen on Hanover Street? Near his residence? Enough to cause traffic problems?

His gaze shot to the pile of errant bills and he grabbed up the first one he could put his fingers on.

If his throat was dry, his heart nearly stopped as he spied at the top of the bill the telltale evidence to support his grandmother's outlandish theory.

No. 17, Hanover Street.

How had he not noticed this before? Of course, why would he? Imaginary wives did not go on shopping sprees capable of beggaring an Eastern prince.

He shuffled through the notes before him, and to his horror they all had the same delivery address. *His* London address. And every single one was addressed as being the purchase of *The Right Hon. Lady Sedgwick.*

Not the gloating dowager peering over the top of her newspaper as she watched him come to the conclusion he'd pompously told her was impossible. But the current Lady Sedgwick.

Emmaline.

"This can't be right!" he said, grabbing the paper out of her hands and reading the entry for himself.

"Oh, Alex, do settle down. A lady is entitled to make some changes to her home from time to time. I've always thought that house on Hanover Square was a veritable mausoleum. If your grandfather hadn't been so tight-fisted, I would have—"

But her words fell to a stop as she glanced up and realized she was talking to an empty chair.

Alex, it seemed, had departed. *One would hope,* she mused, *for London.* Back to his wife.

"Right where he belongs," she said to the closest pug, scratching the dog indulgently.

His trip to town most likely set a record, if Alex had been of a mind to consider such things. He'd been far too occupied envisioning the scenes of complete and utter disaster awaiting him in London.

Emmaline? Impossible, he kept telling himself. But there she was in the *Post* and the *Times*.

Someone had let slip his secret. But who? It couldn't have been Elliott or his wife, or Simmons, his London butler. All three of them owed him their very livelihoods.

So that left only one suspect.

Jack.

It would be just like his puckish friend to think that bringing Emmaline to life would be a good jest.

Yet that left so many other unanswered questions. Such as, how had she gotten into the house? Simmons, having served the family for over forty years, would never allow such a calamity to sully the Sedgwick name.

Then, after that, he had to consider who else had seen this imposter. He shuddered to think if any of his extended family had come to call after seeing the accounts in the paper. Or, worse yet, had come to London and used the Sedgwick town house, as was the custom. He'd always been generous about extending the house to family during the off season and knew that his cousins and aunts and uncles often took advantage of this standing invitation.

And right now this person was living in *his* house, sleeping in *his* bed and passing herself off as *his* wife. Possibly even entertaining his family.

He buried his head in his hands. Lord, he could well imagine the type of doxy Jack would hire to impersonate Emmaline.

Entertaining his relations took on an entirely new meaning.

When his carriage turned the corner onto Hanover Square just after one in the morning, to his relief he found that his toplofty neighborhood looked much as it had when he'd left it a month or so ago. Dignified and proper. And Number Seventeen appeared just as it should, the house of a respected member of the *ton*.

Hard to believe that inside, catastrophe awaited him.

The carriage pulled to a stop and he bounded out and up the front steps, running through the list he had compiled.

First he was going to toss this imposter into the streets. After that was completed, he was going to hunt up Jack and give him a thorough thrashing.

Then he was going to get very drunk. And make his former friend pay for every bottle, if he had to pay for it with his confounded flesh.

When he got to the door, it didn't open immediately as was the case when he was in town for the Season. Since he kept only a limited staff in London during the summer months, the door was locked, even to him.

He pulled the bell, then rapped on the panel with his walking stick as if every moment counted.

Well, it did.

He heard Simmons coming up from the back. Actually it was his muttering complaints that echoed forth.

"Who is it?" Simmons called out from behind the barred portal.

"Open up, it is Sedgwick."

"Sedgwick, indeed," Simmons shot back. "His lordship is in the country. Go on with you, and play your tricks elsewhere."

And then, much to Alex's chagrin, the candle that had lit the entryway began to retreat back into the house. He pounded on the door anew. "Simmons!" he bellowed. "Open this door at once or I'll tell your wife about your Thursday night card games."

The retreating light came to a fast halt. "My lord?"

"Yes, Simmons, 'tis me. Now open the door."

There was a shuffle near the door, a rattle of the latch and then it opened wide.

"My lord, what are you doing here?"

Alex swept inside. "Why do you think I'm here? She's here, isn't she?" He knew he was bellowing, but demmit, it wasn't every day one met his wife.

And had the rare pleasure of getting rid of her.

The butler glanced up the stairs and put his finger to his lips. "Sssh, my lord, or you'll wake her ladyship. She had a rather long day and retired early."

Alex stopped, one foot poised on the stairs. He couldn't have heard Simmons correctly. For he swore he heard concern in the butler's voice.

Concern? For this imposter? Alex held his temper in check for the moment. And lowered his voice. "Simmons, you know as well as I that whoever is up there isn't my wife."

Simmons nodded. "Yes, my lord. But no one else does."

That's good news. But it still didn't explain the more important question. "What were you thinking, letting *her* into the house?"

The butler heaved a great sigh, as if untangling himself from a mighty coil. "She arrived on a Thursday night."

Alex groaned. Of course, she arrived on the one night Simmons traditionally took off.

"Thomas, the second footman, was the only one about," Simmons said, continuing his tale. "He didn't know what to do, so he went and fetched Mrs. Simmons. By the time I got home, her ladyship had been put to bed and two of the maids sent for to return to service." He leaned forward. "I could hardly put her out with everyone fussing over her like that. There would have been talk."

Alex glanced once more up the stairs. "So how many people have seen her?"

Simmons flinched. "Enough."

"What do you mean by *enough*? Or rather, *who* do you mean?"

The butler squirmed again. "If it is any consolation, my lord, your wife seems quite popular. So much so, that—"

Alex didn't want to hear another word about it. He started up the stairs. Ensconced in his house for well over a month and she'd already become popular. He wanted to groan.

There was only one solution.

This wily minx was about to make him a very contented widower.

As Simmons had said, it had been a very busy afternoon at the house on Hanover Square and Lady Sedgwick had sought her bed early, dropping into an exhausted, dreamless slumber in the secure peace of her home.

That is until the door of her bedchamber burst open. It rattled on the hinges and banged into the wall with a furious slam.

Emmaline sat bolt upright and stared at the caped stranger marauding into her sanctuary as if he had every right.

So she did what any lady of the *ton* would do when her honor was in peril. She pulled a small pistol from under her pillow and pointed it with dead-eyed aim at the intruder.

So perhaps she hadn't gotten this lady of the manor part down completely, but it was what *she* would do.

"Stay where you are, sirrah, or it will be the last thing you do."

He ignored her warning completely, coming closer. The candle he held aloft cast a circle of light around them both. His gaze fell first on her face, then like any raving midnight visitor, it strayed lower, to the opening of her lacy nightrail.

Instinctively, she used her free hand to gather it up, blocking his view.

Thus thwarted, his gaze fell to the pistol in her hand and one regal brow rose. "Put that away!"

"I will not," she said, her hand shaking. She didn't really want to kill anyone, but the way her hand was starting to tremble, she was afraid she was going to accidentally shoot the miscreant. Worse, now that he held the candle up, she could also see that he was devilishly handsome and well dressed.

Hardly some Seven Dials cutthroat.

From the imperious twist of his lips, the strong line of his jaw, to the upright, impossibly steely stance, he had to be wellborn. Gads, probably some drunken rake out to make a name for himself by seducing Sedgwick's wife.

That put his intentions in an entirely different light. He didn't look like the type of man a woman would deny easily.

Herself included. She'd always had a weakness for impossibly handsome men, especially dark-haired ones. They were as irresistible as the rustle of a new deck of cards being shuffled.

Then she stopped herself—what was she thinking? She had a reputation to uphold. She was a lady now. At least for the time being.

And as a lady, she had a duty to protect her virtue. Yes, that was exactly what she should do, she decided, as she took one last regretful look at the magnificent man before her. "Simmons! Simmons! Help!" she cried out.

"He won't be forthcoming," the villain told her.

More's the pity, she wanted to say, but still she couldn't let this arrogant lout get the best of her.

At least not without the appearance of a struggle.

She waved the gun at him again. "My husband will not take kindly to this intrusion."

The fellow just laughed, his gaze raking over her with a measure of appreciation. "I don't think he'll mind."

Well, if Sedgwick doesn't mind . . . Emmaline shook off that errant thought. "I assure you, he will kill you for this."

"I doubt it."

Smug bastard. She sat up straighter and pointed toward the door. "Get out."

Of course, when she'd pointed at the door, she'd had to let go of her nightrail, and it fell open again, giving him a generous view of her breasts.

Her order was completely ignored. Instead, he came closer until he stood at the foot of the bed. Emmaline scooted up the mattress, dragging the sheets with her, pulling them up to her chin. "When my husband returns from . . . from . . ."

Oh, demmit, where was it that Sedgwick had his ancestral home?

"Westmoreland," the fiend offered.

"Yes, thank you," she replied. "When my husband returns from Westmoreland, rest assured, he will kill you."

"Have you ever considered, Lady Sedgwick, that perhaps he already has?"

"Has what?" she asked, the pistol trembling anew in her hand.

"Returned."

It was at that moment that Emmaline Denford, Lady Sedgwick, realized she was about to shoot her husband.

The very notion startled her so much, she dropped the pistol. And then the damned thing fired for her.

Chapter 2

Alex closed his eyes and waited for his last moment. Luckily for him, it whizzed past. The bullet, that is, not his earthly existence. Slamming into the wall behind him, the lead ball sent a shower of plaster down.

"Oh, my!" Emmaline exclaimed. "This is terrible." She bounded out of bed and headed toward him.

He had to say one thing for Jack: When he'd picked out an Emmaline, he'd gotten her all wrong.

The gel was glorious.

Her blond hair fell to her waist in long, tempting curls. He wasted only a sparing glance at her breasts, for he'd already witnessed enough there. No, it was the lithe, long legs that captivated his imagination, the rounded curves of her hips, the wide and generous turn of her lips that stirred his blood.

No, indeed, leave it to Jack to get Emmaline all wrong.

The Emmaline he'd always envisioned was a slight, modest chit of decent breeding. There was something wild and disconcerting about this woman—nothing boring or staid about her—and she was heading straight for him, obviously to throw herself into his arms and plead for his mercy.

And really, what harm would there be to hold her just once? To allow her to ply him with kisses and her favors, before he tossed her out in the street?

She was his wife, in a manner of speaking.

But if he thought her concern was for him, he was in for a shock. Emmaline sped past him, as heedless as the bullet from her pistol.

"Do you see what you did?" she said, her finger pointing accusingly at the gaping hole in the wall. "Look at that! Do you have any idea how expensive that paper is?" She heaved a grievous sigh and shook her head woefully. "All my work. 'Tis ruined. Utterly ruined. The entire ambience of this room is lost." She looked about to fall into a spate of tears.

Her work ruined? She'd nearly blown his head off and she was worried about the demmed wallpaper?

He held the candle up and stared at her, wondering if Jack had found her in Bedlam. No, she looked in her right mind, albeit a furious one.

Just like any wife who'd found her newly redecorated boudoir spoiled. Sedgwick cringed and reminded himself she wasn't his wife. And this wasn't her room.

Then he glanced again at the wallpaper. The brand-new wallpaper, alongside new blue drapes, a new armoire in the corner and the list went on of furnishings and paintings and knickknacks quaintly adorning the room, none of which he'd ever seen before. Over the mantel, where before a dour Holbein of the eleventh baron had hung, there sat a lovely watercolor of Sedgwick Abbey, a dreamy, wonderful rendition of his beloved home.

"What have you done to *my* bedchamber?" he bellowed. He made a point of emphasizing the "my" part to make sure she understood that this was not her room.

"Isn't it wonderful?" She patted him on the chest, her palm warm and familiar against his jacket. "I knew you'd love it." Then she sailed out of reach and went back to the bed, catching up a lacy, frothy confection that she tossed over her nightrail. It did little to cover her, only adding to her soft, feminine wiles. "You don't mind, do you? It was such a dreary place, I can't see how we ever got a good night's rest in it before. Why, it was like a mausoleum."

In truth, the removal of the eleventh baron had lightened up the room considerably. He'd never been able to guess how his relations had ever conducted any marital business in the chamber with that dour face keeping a watchful eye over the proceedings.

No wonder the Sedgwick barons had been so reluctant to marry for so many generations. But he didn't know if he liked a stranger banishing one of his ancestors to the dustbin.

"Madame, I want you out of here," he told her, getting back to the business at hand.

"So formal, Sedgwick," she said, gliding around him like a wary cat. " 'Tis me, Emmaline, your dear wife."

"You and I both know that isn't your name."

"Ah, but it is now," she said, smiling at him. Her hands glided over her hips. "I think it fits perfectly, don't you?"

"You presume too much," he told her, his hand snaking out and catching her by her wrist before she could sidestep him. He towed her toward the door with every intention of sending her packing.

Out of the house, out of his life.

But Emmaline had other ideas. She dug her heels into the carpet.

The new carpet, he noted.

"Sedgwick, what will the neighbors think if you toss me out into the streets in the middle of the night?" She shook at his grasp. "I won't go quietly."

"You will if I tie a gag around your mouth."

"You wouldn't dare," she sputtered. "I'm your wife."

He cocked a brow at her. "Consider this the end of our marriage."

She hadn't lied to him, she wasn't about to go easily, catching hold of the doorjamb and hanging on with the tenacity of an alleycat. "Demmit, Sedgwick, this isn't funny."

"I couldn't agree more," he said, letting her go.

She straightened up and smoothed out her robe. "Now, if you will just hear me out, I believe we can—"

He wasn't listening to anything she had to say. She'd turned his perfect existence upside down, possibly brought ruin and shame to his good name, and most likely put a dent in the family fortunes that would take several generations to repair.

Not to mention whatever she'd done to the eleventh baron.

So instead of falling prey to her pretty pleas, he snatched her up by the waist, and in one quick motion hoisted her onto his shoulder. Her nicely rounded bottom sat right next to his face, with the rest of her trailing down his back.

Her breasts pressed against him, while a wild and exotic perfume assailed his senses. His body responded instinctually, clamoring for him not to throw this bounty of feminine wiles out the door, but toss her onto the bed and demand his marital due.

Luckily for him, he wasn't ruled by his senses. Family duty and obligations always came first. But for once, he had to admit the clarity of his purpose and duties wasn't as obvious and golden as it usually was.

"Oooof," she sputtered. "Put me down, you cad!" Her fists pounded on his back.

She thought him a cad? He'd never been called a cad before and rather liked it. Relishing his new role, he decided to show her just how boorish he could be, and gave her backside a nice, solid spank.

"Ouch! That hurt."

"Yes, quite my sentiment when I saw the bills for all the havoc you've wreaked on my life."

"That gives you no right to brutalize me," she complained.

"Madame, I should have you locked up and transported."

"You wouldn't dare—"

His response was another slap to her bottom. Now that he had started along the road of villainy and caddish behavior, he found it quite invigorating. He marched down the stairs, his gaze fixed on the front door. He'd throw her into the carriage and tell Henry to drive to the worst part of Seven Dials and set her loose among her own kind.

She'd probably find an entire block of tempting, redecorating vixens there to commiserate with.

"This isn't done," she said. "I am your wife."

"I doubt the courts would agree," he said, surveying the course ahead. Three more steps, then across the foyer, into the carriage and she'd be gone.

After which, he'd find Jack and kill him.

"You'll have a fine time explaining yourself, now, won't you?" she argued. "You can't prove I'm not Emmaline Denford."

He'd give her one thing, she had nerve. For she was right. He couldn't go to the authorities. But that didn't mean he was going to stand idly by while she ran up his bills and paraded herself about society.

No, the only way to end this charade was to get rid of Emmaline. Then he'd deal with the aftermath.

And while that plan seemed the best one, given the circumstances, even as his boot hit the marble of the foyer, his hopes for a quick end to his marriage faded from sight. The front door opened and while Alex looked up, thinking he was going to see Henry coming inside to inquire as to his wishes, there, to his horror, stood his cousin Hubert Denford and his wife, Lady Lilith, their mouths agape at this unseemly display.

Not Hubert, Alex wanted to groan. Of all his relations, why did it have to be Hubert and Lady Lilith who arrived in such a timely manner? The rest of his greedy cousins and wastrel relations could be happily bought off, but not Hubert.

"I tried to tell you, my lord," Simmons offered from his post near the door.

Lady Lilith clucked disapprovingly at the shocking display before her, while Hubert struggled to maintain the same dismay as his wife, though he wasn't above taking a less-than-subtle survey of Emmaline's bare limbs and her curved backside. In Hubert's eyes glowed the same avarice that went with all of his presumptions when it came to the Sedgwick barony.

Hubert was, after all, the next in line and liked to remind

everyone of that fact often enough. His cheekiness had been one of the many reasons Alex had concocted a wife, if only to keep his relation from becoming too comfortable in his tenuous position as heir apparent.

But with Hubert's eyes raking over Emmaline, Alex felt a new fury. It wasn't like the lady was indeed his wife, but Hubert didn't know that.

Dropping Emmaline to the ground, he hastily shoved her behind him. Hopefully, well out of sight.

"Cousin," Hubert began. "We didn't know . . . that is, we would never have intruded . . . that is—"

From behind Alex, Emmaline piped up. "Oh, Cousin Hubert, I told you before that dear Sedgwick wouldn't mind if you and Lady Lilith stayed with me. Family is, after all, family. Isn't that right, my love?" She placed her hand on Alex's shoulder, a gesture that sent a message of marital intimacy he didn't need right now.

Especially with her lithesome figure pressed up against him. If she thought her charms and curves were going to save her, she was wrong. Very wrong.

Just the same, he put a bit of distance between them.

"How was the opera, cousins?" Emmaline asked. "I was so distraught to turn down your kind invitation."

Cousins? he thought as he shot a glance at her. Just how long had the Denfords been in residence?

"You might have made it tolerable," Hubert told her. "Always nice to have someone along, eh, Lilith? For I don't understand most of that caterwauling and—"

Lady Lilith wasn't so toadyish. She came straight to the point. "Sedgwick, you aren't supposed to be here."

"No, I'm not," he said. "However, some new business brought me back unexpectedly."

Hubert's eyes flickered with interest. "New business? Mind sharing it with me, eh, Sedgwick? Always looking for the right opportunity."

To climb upon my back and suppose a station you are utterly unfit to assume, was the response Alex bit back.

Instead, he replied, "Nothing that I fear is likely to bear any profit." For this, he received a very unfeminine nudge in his back. He stumbled forward and Emmaline just shrugged at his cousins, as if she hadn't a clue as to her husband's discomfort.

Hubert's bushy brows knit together, suspicious and intent, and Alex knew his cousin would only strive harder now to insinuate his way into this mysterious prospect. His best hope was to find some bone of an opportunity to toss out and send the fellow off in the wrong direction.

While at the same time keeping him as far away from Emmaline as possible.

After a few more moments of awkward silence, Lady Lilith took charge. "I fear we are intruding, and we shall leave you two to . . . to . . ."

"A little midnight supper," Emmaline offered. "Sedgwick arrived just *famished*."

The way she said the word in long purring tones made it sound like the sustenance her husband was seeking would not be found in the kitchen.

"Then we should let you get to your . . . your meal," Hubert offered as he took his wife by the arm.

Lady Lilith shot another scathing glance at the pair of them, drawing her skirt close as she passed by. The daughter of an impoverished earl, Lady Lilith had the haughty reserve of a duchess. And worse yet, the ability to gossip like a fishwife.

Alex closed his eyes. Now the entire family would not only think of this woman as his wife, as his Emmaline, but would hear the tales of their supposed lascivious practices.

In the very foyer, mind you, he could hear Lady Lilith saying in a scandalized voice. *In front of the servants, no less.*

"Will we see you for breakfast?" Emmaline called after them merrily.

"I think," Hubert said, chuckling with boorish tones, "the better question is whether you and my cousin will be there."

Lady Lilith sniffed and tugged her husband up the last stair and they disappeared from sight.

When Alex glanced down at her—well, actually glowered—her brows tipped with an innocent arch, as if she hadn't the vaguest notion what had him in such a foul mood.

"Ah, hmm," Simmons coughed. Stationed as he was in the corner, Alex had forgotten he was still there. "If there isn't anything else you'll be requiring, my lord—"

"No, no," Alex told him. "Go to bed. I can settle this on my own."

The butler fled from the foyer, moving with due haste.

And once they were alone, Alex turned toward Emmaline, still very much of a mind to toss her out the door. Wisely, she'd retreated to the stairs, her hand clinging tenaciously to the post.

"Did you want a tray, Sedgwick?" She nudged her bare toe at the floor, then glanced up at him from beneath her fair lashes. "Or is there something else you require?"

"Did you see her?" Lilith sputtered as they made their way to the guest room in the back of the house.

"Yes, I saw her," Hubert answered a little too enthusiastically.

He was rewarded with a thwack from her fan. To avoid a second one, he said nothing more, but rather opened the door to their room and allowed his wife to stomp inside.

"Parading about in the altogether. Land sakes, what was Sedgwick thinking, hauling her about like some savage—for one and all to see?" Lilith yanked off her spencer and tossed it on a chair.

"Most disturbing," Hubert rushed to agree.

Lilith eyed him as if she were considering if he needed another smack. "I don't believe for a moment that they were simply seeking a midnight supper."

"I thought the same thing," Hubert said. If he had a wife as gorgeous and so obviously willing as Emmaline, food would be the last thing he'd desire.

"Dear God, this is a disaster," Lilith complained. "That woman could produce an heir. Why, that would ruin everything."

Bother, Lilith was right. Hubert hadn't gotten that far yet. He was still trying to recover from the sight of Emmaline in that negligee.

Though his cousin's marriage to the sickly Emmaline had at first seemed a boon, especially since Sedgwick hadn't shown the least bit of concern for his ailing wife, now that her health appeared to be on the mend, so was Sedgwick's interest in her.

Lilith was over at the desk, rummaging around in the drawers. After some searching, she pulled out a sheaf of paper and set up the pen and ink. "Write your grandmother immediately. She'll be able to put things to right."

Hubert knew exactly what his wife meant and nodded in

agreement. No one could sow strife in the family like Grandmère. She'd have Sedgwick and the delectable Emmaline back to living apart in no time.

Downstairs, Emmaline wanted to bite back the seductive words that had come out of her lips.

Is there anything else you require?

Was she mad? She knew men, and she knew what it meant when they got *that* look in their eyes. And right now, the hot light burning in the baron's steely gaze said only too clearly he was of a mind to demand his marital rights—from the appreciative glance that raked over her figure to the way his gaze strayed over her breasts like a hungry caress.

It wasn't like she'd never been looked at by a man, admired by one, but most of them sent the same coveting glances that seemed to be Hubert's domain. However, it appeared that Sedgwick coveted nothing. He was a man who knew what he wanted and was used to demanding it—if not just taking it outright.

Oh, bother! Where was the staid, dull man she'd heard so much about? This Sedgwick was nothing like his reputation. No, the way he looked at her said that if she was willing, the taking would be unforgettable.

One very unforgettable night. She cocked her head and gave him another once-over. Make that a night and a day, with his apparent stamina.

Steady, Emmaline, she told herself. *Remember, you are a proper lady now. A fortnight is all you need. A fortnight and you'll have the stake of your life.*

Yet her gaze strayed once again to his chiseled features, the pair of firm lips pursed in a hard line—ones that promised breathless, staggering kisses. Now, that was a way to pass the time. It wasn't hard to imagine what two weeks spent in this man's bed would be like . . .

The silence in the foyer had grown terribly uncomfortable, and thankfully he broke it.

"We are going to settle this right now." Sedgwick caught her by the arm and started dragging her back upstairs.

She pressed her lips together. Tightly. Gads, she could only imagine what wayward suggestion would come out of her mouth next—unnerved and borne by his sure touch.

Up the stairs he pulled her. Now, that was a fine sight better than out into the street as he'd promised earlier.

However, while she was here to impersonate Emmaline Denford, that didn't mean she should expand her reign as the lady of the house to the man of the house.

It would complicate matters. Utterly. Completely. She continued to convince herself of that fact as he towed her up the stairs.

Not that she wasn't going willingly, but she didn't want to seem too eager.

"Well, that just makes this a fine mess," he was sputtering, as they got to the bedchamber and he shut the door behind her. "Inviting yourself to breakfast."

"I do live here," she countered, stopping before the bed. Truly, she hadn't chosen that spot on purpose. Not completely.

Whatever was wrong with her? He was just a man, and an arrogantly noble one at that. She abhorred those types. Absolutely.

Yet why did his eyes have to be so green . . . his shoulders so broad and imposing? He quite stole her breath with all his magnificent brooding and posturing.

That is quite enough, Emmaline, she told herself. *You have a task to attend to.* Tipping her nose in the air, she said, "If I didn't arrive downstairs in the morning, don't you think your cousins would find that odd?"

"The point is that you shouldn't be here!" His glance went from her to the bed behind her and then back to her again. His jaw worked back and forth, and then he caught her by the hand and hauled her through the bedroom into the private sitting room beyond.

"And why shouldn't I be at breakfast?" she asked. "I am your wife."

Through clenched teeth he sputtered, "The point is, you are not."

"Not invited to breakfast?" she asked coyly, settling herself onto a settee. She hadn't spent a lifetime avoiding being evicted without learning how to change the subject. Besides, the key to any deception was believing utterly in your guise. And she wasn't about to drop this one—not when it afforded her the chance to leave her life of guile and deceit behind forever. "Someone has to act as hostess, and who better than your own dear wife?"

"You are not my wife."

She leaned back and tapped her chin with her finger. "Ah, now that is a problem, isn't it? If I'm not Lady Sedgwick, then where is she?"

He glowered at her. It actually made him more handsome, that fierce mien of his. "My wife is none of your business," he told her, pacing about the room, his hands folded behind his back.

"I think she is."

"Fine, have your breakfast," he offered, "but then you are going to leave."

"Tomorrow?" She shook her head. "I fear that won't work. The draper is coming with the fabrics for the ball-room."

Sedgwick closed his eyes. "Madame, there will be no more drapers, no more bills, no more of this dalliance. Your time as Emmaline Denford is over."

"I hardly think you should cancel the draper's work. He sent a note around that he found the most perfect Chinese brocades to match the new carpets."

He crossed his arms over his chest and let his sharp green gaze bore into her. "How much?"

She glanced up from her examination of her nails. "For the carpets or the drapes?"

This time, she could spy a vein in the side of his head that looked ready to explode.

"*No,*" he said. "How much are you being paid to ruin my life?" The words ground out with an impatient air.

"I hardly think a few alterations and knickknacks are go-ing to ruin your life."

"How much are you being paid?" he repeated.

Well, she'd give him one thing. He was dogged. But as much as he wanted her gone, she had every reason to stay.

"Nothing," she said. "A wife does all these things purely to make her house a home for her dear spouse."

"But you are not my wife."

"There you go again, making a bad situation worse," she said, rising from the settee and making her way toward him. "Really, Sedgwick, if I'd known you were such a dour man, I would never have married you."

"The point is, you didn't."

She smiled. "Prove it."

This time she overplayed her hand. You'd think that after so long taking such risks, she'd know when to fold her hand and run. For in an instant, Sedgwick took her in his arms and hauled her close.

"Would you like me to?" he offered. "Prove it, that is?"

Up against his chest, Emmaline found herself assailed with memories, memories of what a man with some charm and skill could do to a woman.

How could this be? Where was the dull, stuffy baron she'd been promised? For this man appeared not only quite capable, but would relish the task at hand.

No matter how tempting it was to prove her dedication to her employment, she had sworn off such temptations. They only led to ruin, and ruin was what she was trying to avoid.

Of course, she'd also sworn off gambling, drinking, and all sorts of other vices at one time or another . . .

"Oh no, you don't," she told him, pushing at his solid chest, trying to twist out of his muscled arms. "If you think you can just assert your . . . your . . ."

"Marital rights," he said, looking down at her as if he had every right, and then some.

"Yes, those," she said, struggling some. "That would hardly help your case that I am not your wife."

"Yes, but it might satisfy my curiosity."

"I wasn't paid to—"

He quirked a brow at her.

"What I mean to say is that I'm not that kind of woman."

"The kind of woman who poses as a man's wife, runs up enormous bills for clothes and other extravagances, and then refuses to make good her status as his wife?"

Much to her chagrin, he let her go.

"You make it sound as if I'm not a lady."

"And you are . . . ?"

"Here to help," she said as she straightened out her night-trail and patted the ribbons on her robe back into place. If only she could erase the way her body tingled, cried out to return to the pure masculine heaven of his embrace.

He laughed. "Help? How? By driving me straight into the same cell in Bedlam that you came from?"

She tipped her chin up in the air. "I am not infirmed."

"But that's the point," he told her. "Emmaline is. My wife is ill, infirmed, sickly, and more importantly, indisposed."

Emmaline sighed and smiled at him. "Ah, but I've been cured. Consider it a miracle."

He shook a finger at her. "I have no room in my life for miracles or a wife."

"I beg to differ." Her hands went to her hips.

"You would." He groaned again. "The point is, I want you gone and this is what you are going to do—"

"I don't see what you could possibly offer me that would induce me to leave." She planted her feet and stared at him.

"An opportunity to avoid transportation," he said, a murderous glint glowing in his eyes.

There were some things Emmaline had learned in her life, and one of them was when one's quarry was ready to deal. Sedgwick was most definitely in that position, despite his outward confidence.

He couldn't just toss her out. Not immediately. He knew it and she knew it.

That's why it was a good thing she knew how to gamble. Sitting as she was with a rather fine hand, she knew her best chance of winning was to play it right up front and unnerve her opponent before he had a chance to set the stakes.

"I can't possibly leave while the Denfords are still in residence," she said. "They would be rather suspicious if I departed so abruptly."

His brow furrowed, as if he knew that as well.

"So let us come to an agreement," she offered. "As long as they are in residence, I can remain."

He cocked his head and stared at her. "Just like that?"

She nodded.

He looked taken aback by this, but recovered quickly. "I'll have them gone by breakfast and then I expect you to follow suit."

Emmaline used every bit of demure acquiescence she possessed to lower her lashes and look ever so thankful. "If you think that is best."

"Yes, I do. And I don't want you to go down to breakfast. Send your apologies and let the servants know you are not feeling well."

"I doubt the Denfords will believe I am in ill health."

"They are my concern. Just keep to this room until they are gone." He took one last glance at her, as if weighing a choice, then shook his head. "Now I have another matter to see to," he said, before he swept from the room, leaving her once again in the solitude of the boudoir.

She grinned at the empty space.

So he thought that was it? If Sedgwick really believed Hubert and Lady Lilith could be so easily dispatched, he was in for a shock. The pair had arrived earlier in the day and it hadn't taken them more than five minutes to start fussing over her expensive changes to the house, as well as peppering her with a bevy of pointed and overly inquisitive questions.

No, that pair was up to something and Sedgwick would have his hands full disengaging them from Hanover Square.

Then again, she was also willing to wager that he was in for more than his share of surprises if he thought she'd be leaving before her fortnight was completed.

Chapter 3

It took Alex nearly four hours to discover Jack's whereabouts. He'd tried Camilla's house, rousting the lady and the gentleman in her bed from a sound night's sleep.

Only the man in her bed hadn't been Jack, but old Ambercrombie. Apparently Alex's bracelet hadn't been enough to retain the lady's affections.

Ambercrombie had been furious over being interrupted and had threatened to send over seconds in the morning until Alex explained that he had thought to find Jack in the lady's company. Then, and only then, did Ambercrombie relent—on the promise that Alex told his friend that Camilla looked well pleased.

A promise Alex made with relish, vowing to regale Jack with the tale . . . right before he killed him.

As he left the house, Camilla came downstairs and confided that she thought Jack had been sending flowers to a Mrs. Gannett on Thornton Street.

"Oh, and my lord?" she called out as Alex stormed down the front steps.

"Yes?"

The lady raised her hand and patted a few stray strands of reddish hair back into place. "Thank you for my bracelet." There on her wrist sparkled the bauble that Jack had insisted was paramount to keeping his ladylove's affections.

So she'd kept the token and traded her heart.

Smart woman, Alex conceded, as he made his way around the corner to Thornton Street.

As it turned out, Camilla hadn't been wrong about Jack. He was at Mrs. Gannett's, warm and cozy in the lady's comfortable bed.

What the pretty coquette was doing with Jack, Alex wouldn't wager. Perhaps she'd seen Camilla's bracelet. That seemed the likeliest reason, considering the way she cast an appreciative glance in his direction after his unwanted entrance and hasty introduction.

He made a note to tell the light-skirt there would be no more bracelets from his accounts. Right after he got done thrashing her lover.

Jack wasn't as pleased to see his friend, nursing the foul aftermath of a night spent carousing and a lack of sleep from the rest of his evening's active entertainments.

"Sedgwick, what the devil are you doing here?" he'd complained groggily, just before Alex caught him up by the scruff of his shirt and dragged him from the lady's bed.

"What the devil," Jack sputtered, twisting and turning in Alex's intent grasp. "Have you gone mad?"

"I would ask the same of you." Down the stairs and out the front door, Alex hauled his protesting friend.

"Come now, my good man. Just unhand me and have

Mrs. Gannett fetch us a pot of coffee. We can discuss this with clear heads. I fear I'm still a bit squiffed from last night." Jack tried again to shrug off Alex's grasp to no avail. "Is this about that wager I made with Clifton? I promised him you were good for it."

Ah, wonderful. Another vowel wagered in my name. Alex glanced up and down the street until he spied the perfect cure for Jack's self-induced plight.

The poor sot never saw it coming in his befuddled state. But once Alex tossed him into the horse trough, the elegant rake came up clear-eyed and furious.

"Demmit to hell, man!" he sputtered. "What is wrong with you?"

Alex caught him by the collar and shoved him down again. Jack came back up, spewing dirty water and curses like a Versailles fountain.

"You bastard, unhand me." His fists swung impotently as Alex gave him another dunking.

But this time, Jack didn't come up. In fact, he started to sink to the bottom of the trough.

Against his better judgment, Alex heaved a sigh and reached in to pull his friend out.

Even as he caught hold of Jack, his friend exploded in fury, catching Alex's arm and pulling him into the muck-filled water.

The two of them thrashed about, cursing and throwing fists, finally spilling out of the trough and into the street, brawling like a pair of callow youths.

Lights came on in the nearby houses, the ladies of the neighborhood opening their sashes and doors to witness the disturbance. Gentlemen fighting over a lady wasn't an un-common sight in this part of London, and if anything, it gained the object of such fury some notoriety for months to come. Therefore, everyone wanted to have their own accounting of the event.

Jack caught Alex in the jaw with a hooked shot and sent him sprawling. Mrs. Gannett applauded from her front steps, but her enthusiasm was a little premature. It was going to take more than that to stop the baron.

He staggered up to his feet, then with surprising speed landed a facer on the unwitting Jack. Now it was the other man's turn to find himself lying atop the cobbles.

From there, he heaved a great sigh. "Sedgwick, what the devil is the matter with you?"

Alex caught him by the shirt and dragged him upright. It just wasn't done to finish a man while he was down.

"My wife," he said as he punched him again.

Jack swayed on his feet from the blow. "Emmaline? What has that got to do with me?" When the next one came, he managed to dodge out of the way and had time to wipe some of the blood from his nose.

"Don't play coy with me, you bounder," Alex said, coming closer and lowering his voice. "I know demmed well you hired that doxy to impersonate my wife." He reeled back his fist to strike again, but something in Jack's befuddled expression stopped him.

"Me? Hired her?" He swiped at his bloody nose again. "Where would I find the blunt for such a thing?"

Alex's fist froze in midair, cocked back and ready to swing. *Good point that,* he realized.

Meanwhile, Jack continued his protests. "Besides, I thought you hired the gel to keep Hubert at bay. Been visiting her and making like a good friend ever since she arrived to make sure no one questioned her."

He peered through the one eye that Jack hadn't managed to blacken. "You didn't hire her?"

"No," Jack said with every bit of honesty the knavish fellow possessed.

Alex dropped his fist to his side. Then he glanced up and down the street and realized he'd created a regular spectacle of himself.

Baron Sedgwick brawling on Thornton Street. Wouldn't that make a pretty story.

Luckily, Jack never held a grudge for long. Tugging down the tails of his shirt in a halfhearted attempt at decency, he said, "Are you telling me all this was because you thought I hired that chit?"

Alex nodded.

Jack broke out laughing. "Suppose you've been hunting me all over town?"

Alex closed his eyes and nodded. "I roused Ambercrombie from Camilla's bed thinking he was you."

Jack snorted. "Hope you gave that old roué heart palpitations. Though if a night in Camilla's bed isn't enough to send that fellow into an early grave, I swear he will live to be a hundred—and make a fine cake of it stealing my mistresses."

Now Alex laughed.

Jack took a playful swing and then wound his arm over Alex's shoulder and guided him toward the curb. They climbed the stairs to Mrs. Gannett's house, where the hospitable woman provided a pitcher of warm water, basins and clean towels, and the rest of Jack's clothes. Then the lady had the good sense to leave the gentlemen to set themselves to rights over a bottle of brandy.

After they'd done the best they could to repair the obvious damage, Jack sat back in a chair and eyed his friend. "Do you mean to tell me that you didn't hire this Emmaline?"

"No!" Alex said. "Remember, I'm the one who didn't want some bothersome female interfering in my life to begin with."

"There are worse things than a female in your life," Jack said, waggling his brows up at the ceiling, where above them Mrs. Gannett's comfortable boudoir was situated. "Besides, your Emmaline is a pretty thing—and wouldn't be such a bad sight to wake up to in the morning." He grinned. "Why not keep her for a bit?"

Of course Jack would suggest such a thing. The man who never thought of consequences.

Keep Emmaline? Impossible. Wasn't it bad enough that the sight of her rising from his bed like a Venus would be forever burnished in his memory? He'd be hard put to ever walk into his bedchamber again and not recall the sight of her.

Better to get her out of his life before she had the opportunity to etch even more indelible memories upon his sensibilities.

"Really, Alex, how much damage has she done? So she's been seen around town—by who? It's summer, no one of consequence is about."

"Try Hubert and Lady Lilith."

"The devil you say?" Jack wrung out a cloth in the basin, and held it to his bloody nose. "Certainly that puts a bit of a crimp in things, but mayhap it isn't all that bad. They can't have been in town long enough to discover the truth."

"Any length of time with this chit mingling with Hubert is nothing less than an unmitigated disaster."

Jack pulled the cloth away. "Well, it will stop him from skulking about. Now that he's seen her for himself, maybe it will end all his infernal inquiries and questions about your wife."

There was some sense in that.

Reaching for another cloth, Jack dipped it in the water and handed it over to Alex. "That eye of yours looks like the very devil. Sorry about that."

"No, my apologies for thinking the worse of you," Alex told him, wincing as he put the cloth to his quickly swelling eye.

Jack grinned. "I do admit, it does seem like something I would do."

"Yes, it did have your air about it."

His friend nodded, then went back to dabbing at his nose. "Well, if you didn't hire her, and I certainly didn't hire her, who did?"

Alex glanced over at his friend. "I don't know. But I mean to find out. Right after I get her out of my life."

"Well, one thing is for certain," Jack declared. "As long as she's about, no one will call you dull."

By the time Sedgwick returned to his London house, the sun had risen and the day shone brightly.

Though the same couldn't be said of his mood. He was sodden and battered and hadn't had a good night's rest in four days.

And he still had to see to the matters at hand. First thing, the removal of the Denfords, and then Emmaline. As he started up the steps, he straightened his shoulders for the battle to come.

Jack had been right when he'd said he was in a fine pickle. He couldn't just toss Emmaline out without questions being asked.

Especially not with Hubert and Lady Lilith in town. No, the only solution was to send his relations on an extended trip, then undo the damage wrought by Emmaline's untimely arrival.

And more importantly, find out who hired her.

He strode into the house and into the dining room, where Emmaline, Lady Lilith and Hubert were breaking their fast with a sumptuous spread. The smell of ham and kippers reminded him that as well as sleep, he hadn't had a decent meal in days.

Simmons, at first taken aback at Alex's disheveled state, reverted to the safe realm of his station and said nothing. Instead, he caught up a plate and began filling it with the baron's favorites.

At least, Alex noted, some things in his life still proceeded in an orderly fashion. But even as he stood in the doorway staring at this macabre scene of domestic bliss, a shriek broke out from the end of the table.

"Sedgwick! My darling! Whatever happened to you?"

Emmaline was at his side in a thrice, staring in horror at his face. Then just as quickly, she stepped back, wrinkling her nose.

Obviously, she had caught a whiff of him, for Lord, he stank to high heavens. "Do you need a cold compress? A surgeon? *A hot bath?*"

"None of that," he said.

"Are you sure?" she asked.

"Yes, I'm fine," he told her, brushing past her toward the table. She smelled of violets and looked as pretty and bright as a summer morning. Her blond hair danced in curls down the back of her head. Her gown, simple and modest, did nothing but remind him of the lush curves and lithe limbs it managed to conceal. He glanced over at her again and winced.

Demmit! He needed to stay focused. First the Denfords, then Emmaline.

"However could this happen?" she asked, staring at the wreckage of his face.

"I was . . . set upon," he said, as matter-of-factly as he could muster. Better another small lie than the truth. The last thing he needed was it being nosed about town that he'd been fighting with Jack on Thornton Street.

Not that the ladybirds of that less-than-reputable address wouldn't be busy fluttering about with delighted titterings of the spectacle they'd witnessed this morning—but it would take a week or so before their gossip would rise to the lofty reaches of the *ton*.

By that time, he'd be well on his way back north and all this trouble would be but a distant memory.

"The villains!" Emmaline gasped, her hand and handkerchief coming to cover her mouth and nose. "Are you sure you are unhurt? You didn't kill them, did you?"

Lady Lilith cocked an elegant brow at this statement.

"No, nothing so dire," Alex said, noting that neither of his real relations appeared overly beset by his announcement. "Suffice it to say that they were dispatched and I am unharmed." Her concern would be touching if she had been his wife, but as it was, her performance only added to the drama he did not want to play out before the household.

"How frightening," Emmaline said. "How dreadful for you."

"Yes, quite frightening," Lady Lilith echoed, her horror most likely drawn from the fact that he survived his ordeal.

Perhaps that was the answer—he'd do himself in and let the Denfords deal with this impossible Emmaline.

Serve the pair of them right, he thought as he settled into his seat at the head of the table. Though he would like to live long enough to see Hubert's face when his cousin surveyed the wreckage that was her bills.

Meanwhile, Emmaline had poured him a cup of tea and was having a conference with Simmons about some matter.

"You must never fear for Sedgwick," she said, coming to stand behind his chair. "He's extremely capable when it comes to an altercation. Why, he saved me from three such wretched villains the day we met. Do you remember, Sedgwick?"

Villains? The day we met? A premonition of disaster ran down his spine. And it certainly didn't help that she now had Hubert and Lady Lilith's full and rapt attention.

No, demmit, he wanted to tell her. *Cease this immediately.*

But he soon discovered that having given her a small white lie to work with, under her obviously skilled tutelage it was blossoming into a Banbury tale that would make a Covent Garden tragedy look simpleminded.

"He saved you?" Lady Lilith asked. She set down her knife and fork and folded her hands in her lap. "How remarkable."

"Oh, yes, it was a most desperate day," Emmaline told her, her hand going to her brow.

"Desperate, you say?" Hubert asked, finally looking up from his paper. "As dire as all that?"

"Oh, yes. I hadn't been in England more than a day when

my coach was set upon by thieves. The driver and footman were overcome, and my dearest chaperone, Mrs. Woodgate, swooned immediately." Emmaline sighed and shook her head, while her hands wrung at her handkerchief as if the danger were right outside their door.

Alex, for his part, wished she *had* been set upon and therefore had saved him from ever having to listen to this bouncer.

"How terrible for you," Lady Lilith said, though her tone suggested she didn't believe a word of Emmaline's dramatic rendition.

"Terrible indeed!" Hubert chimed in, once again with more enthusiasm than his wife shared—which garnered him a dark look from Lady Lilith's side of the table.

"Yes, but as terrifying as it was, it was what brought me to my dearest Sedgwick," Emmaline said, her hands coming lightly to rest upon his shoulders. "The last thing I remember was the sight of him riding up over the crest of the hill, his pistol drawn, his great black cape swirling in the wind as he rode to my rescue."

"Sedgwick with a pistol?" Lady Lilith asked. "Why, this is quite news to all of us." She turned her skeptical gaze on him. "I didn't know you were so proficient."

"It wasn't anything," he said quite truthfully.

Not willing to yield the floor just yet, Emmaline continued. "All I remember was the sight of Sedgwick riding forth, for just then I was struck by a stray bullet and rendered unconscious. Sadly, I can't recall anything else until I woke up some time later, Sedwick's handsome visage, so filled with concern, the first thing I saw."

Hubert sputtered, as if he'd never heard such rot.

Granted, neither had Alex, but he didn't like Hubert's rude suggestion that his wife was lying.

No matter that she wasn't his wife.

But Emmaline wasn't about to give quarter to the likes of Hubert Denford. Her brow rose in a regal arch as she turned her face toward him. Slowly her hand went to her brow and she drew back the artful and fashionable curls arranged around her face.

And revealed a scar both hideous and alarming.

Sedgwick blinked and looked again. *Christ, she* had *been shot.*

Who was this elegant, delicate-looking creature, that she had such secrets? Had lived such a life?

"O-oh, gracious," Hubert managed to stammer, looking like he was about to lose his breakfast.

Lady Lilith's face mirrored her husband's shock; then, like the proper lady that she was, she glanced away. But not before her eyes narrowed with a calculated estimation.

Emmaline patted her curls back into place and her pretty mouth began to open as if she had every intention of adding to this spectacle, so Alex stopped her before she showed them anything else.

"You know, perhaps I could use a cold compress," he announced.

"If you think you need it," she said, clearly disappointed at his interruption.

"*Yes,*" he said firmly, taking her by the arm and steering her from the room.

"Oh, if you wish," she sighed.

"I do." He dragged her out of the dining room and up the stairs to the first landing, quite forgetting his plan to evict the Denfords. "I thought we agreed you were going to seek your bed today. Feign ill health." Despite his best manners, his gaze traveled back up to the line of curls at her brow.

Shot? She'd been shot? He didn't think he knew anyone who'd been shot. Not shot and lived. Glancing over at her, he wondered what trouble had beset her to meet such a fate.

Suddenly his earlier ideas of tossing her back into the streets didn't seem so well thought out. For there was something about Emmaline that touched him—not just her infuriating *joie de vivre,* but something so utterly unexpected and vulnerable in the way she'd defiantly given the Denfords a glimpse into a past that none of them could imagine.

"I fear taking to my bed was impossible," she told him, shaking loose his grasp, her hand rising self-consciously to her hairline once again.

"Impossible?" he asked. "How so?" What was there to feigning a megrim or some female ailment? Her performance just a few moments earlier proved she was a dab hand at acting.

"Sedgwick, my dear, it is a ridiculous notion. How could I feign an illness? Look at me—do I appear ill?"

She stepped back so he could do just that, look at her. And he felt himself taking her in like a tonic. Never before had he ever seen anyone or anything brighten his Hanover Square house as Emmaline did. When she smiled, her eyes sparkled, her cheeks brightened and pinked. Her vivacity was infectious, a fever of life that defied the bedridden existence he'd instructed her to partake.

There was no way Emmaline looked the least bit ill.

Which only added to his problems.

Alex leaned forward and lowered his voice. "My wife is not supposed to be of such a strong constitution."

"But don't you see," she said, her lashes dipping flirtatiously, "it was your love and admiration that helped me make a complete recovery from my maladies?"

He groaned. "That hardly fits with our agreement for your immediate removal from this house."

"Don't you think my leaving so abruptly would raise questions you don't want to answer?"

He ground his teeth together. Smart, impertinent minx.

She edged closer to him and whispered, "Keep me, Sedgwick. For the time being."

Keep her? His body tensed at the enticement she offered. She was like a blithe wind through his dusty life, and all of a sudden all he wanted to do was throw open the windows and welcome her in.

What had Jack said? *As long as she is in your life, no one will call you dull.*

"I promise I won't be any bother," she added, sweetening the temptation.

Bother? Oh, she'd be more than that. Another twenty-four hours in the house and she'd have him tangled up like a fish in a net. Have him believing that men actually had wives as beautiful and intoxicating as the one before him. And then he saw himself, waking up beside her, brushing her hair aside to kiss her rosy lips, feeling his body stir and wake and knowing that she . . .

"No," he sputtered. Good God, keep her? What was he doing even considering such a notion. Alex wasn't too sure what brought him to his senses, whether it was his still-wet clothes or perhaps the wafting odor of horse trough that finally cleaned his befuddled senses, but he knew one thing for certain. "As I said last night, the moment I remove Lady Lilith and Hubert, I want you out."

"Yes, Sedgwick," she said, like the obedient, docile Emmaline he'd always imagined. If only the sparkle in her eyes hadn't revealed her true thoughts. *Good luck in trying that one.*

Alex squared his shoulders. "I am still the master of this house. And when I tell the Denfords to leave, they will."

Again, she nodded, then leaned forward. "In truth, I can see why you would want them gone. They are dreadfully tiresome." She paused, her teeth nibbling at her lower lip. "I suppose that is unkind, to speak so ill of your relations, and I suppose if I had any—relatives, that is—I wouldn't appreciate anyone speaking ill of them. But in truth, if I possessed cousins like Mr. and Mrs. Denford, honestly, I don't know if I'd own up to having them." Then the cheeky little minx winked at him.

Despite his best effort, Alex smiled. Once again, her blithe spirit was coaxing him into her mayhem. He did his best to recover, trying to think of his loyalty to his family, but even that was impossible to muster. Instead, he told her, "I am going to seek a bath and then my bed."

She looked about to offer to help, but that kind of help he didn't need. He staved her off with a shake of his head. "Can you stay out of trouble until I arise and devise a plan to remove my cousins?"

With you following right behind them.

She waved her hand at him. "Of course, Sedgwick. I have more than enough to occupy myself until you are rested."

He didn't know if he liked the sound of that. "No more Banbury tales."

She had the nerve to appear affronted. "Sirrah, I never—"

"Yes, yes, I know—"

"It was an excellent story," she said, patting her brow again. "Far better than some dreary tale that you acquired me through a debt of honor or some other bit of dull nonsense." She turned to go back down the stairs, then stopped. "By the way, how did we meet?"

He flinched. "I offered for you after your father died. I felt it was a matter of honor."

She shook her head. "Oh, Sedgwick, you are terrible at these sort of things. How have you managed to keep me so well concealed for so long?"

"It wasn't a problem until you decided to move into my life," he shot back. The story had been adequate enough for him and the rest of the *ton*. "And far superior to that bouncer you told about being set upon and shot."

"But Sedgwick, I was shot," she said, her gaze falling to the bottom of the stairs, and once again that calculating, outlandish, storytelling light burned to life in her eyes. The warning bell inside him began tolling the alarm, so he barely heard her muttering, "Oh, bother, what is she doing?"

And like lightning, she struck again, this time throwing her arms around his neck and saying loudly, "My dearest Sedgwick, you will always be my knight errant." Then, before he could stop her, she rewarded him with the favor of her lips.

Changing his view of marital relations utterly and completely.

Chapter 4

Emmaline caught hold of Sedgwick's lapels and drew him closer. "Lady Lilith is watching," she whispered hastily as she rose up on her tiptoes and pressed her lips to his.

She hadn't meant it to be anything more than just a diverting eyeful for Sedgwick's nosy relation.

Never mind the fact that she'd spent the night tossing and turning amidst the sheets, bothered and spent by dreams of this enigmatic man. He was supposed to be dull and rather tiresome, but instead he'd ignited her passions like a match to the flame.

No, she told herself, this kiss is nothing more than a diversion for Lady Lilith's sake and had nothing to do with her misguided desires.

Yet, who would have thought the stuffy baron would take his performance so to heart?

And so thoroughly.

His lips, warm and strong, bent to hers, covering her

mouth and taking command of the situation. Not that she minded his overbearing nature in this instance—Lord knows she was in over her head with all this being a wife and a baroness—but to her credit, she did know a thing or two about men . . .

And, while Sedgwick had no talent for prevarication, when it came to kissing, his skills scorched. Gads, if she *were* his baroness, she'd stay in bed and feign anything he asked—as long as she had to spend the time burning beneath his kiss.

When his tongue ventured forth with a teasing swipe, the kind that promised so much more than a quick dalliance, her knees wavered and her mouth opened, in shock or of its own volition—she wasn't too sure which.

Then he really took command of the situation, winding his arms around her, one at her waist and the other at her shoulders, drawing her closer—not that he smelled all that great, rather like he'd been doused in a horse trough—but none of that mattered, once she found herself hauled up against his solid chest, the length and breadth of him pressed against her.

All of him.

When did barons start having the physiques of an Elgin marble? Most of the barons she'd ever met were toady little fellows with rounded bellies.

Nothing about this baron was squat or round.

Just hard and insistent. Like his mouth. And his kiss.

In the back of her mind, she thought she heard Lady Lilith's indignant footsteps retreating, but obviously Sedgwick didn't realize they'd lost their audience.

Honestly, Emmaline wasn't of a mind to enlighten him.

Besides, if the man could be enticed with a kiss, who was she to object?

Especially when he groaned and tugged her closer. His hands didn't just hold her—they moved with an explorer's ardent heart. Tracing the plains of her back, the valleys of her torso, even climbing the full hills of her . . . breasts.

As his fingers curled up over the hardened peaks, her senses exploded and Emmaline panicked. Suddenly her curiosity became too real, the risk too great. She wrenched herself free and backed away from him. Her breath was coming in ragged, short gasps and her heart hammered in her chest.

Her temple throbbed as well, like a warning bell, a dangerous reminder of the price passion could cost.

"I think we've made our point," she told him. "Mrs. Denford is gone."

"She could come back," he said, stalking closer.

"Highly unlikely," she told him. "Besides, you smell like a . . . like a trough!"

"You weren't objecting a few moments ago."

Oh, this will never do, she thought. He could kiss like the very devil *and* be astute. "I was trying to be polite, like any other wife," she told him, knowing her motives had been borne out of anything other than a sense of matrimonial obligation.

He edged closer, his green eyes glittering with wicked intent. "If you were in truth my wife, you wouldn't still be in this hallway."

If he came any closer, if he dared kiss her again, Emmaline knew her resolve would crumble. She had to be honest—she had a weakness for men, especially ones who could kiss her senseless while they stole her garters and her virtue.

Yet she'd always prided herself on knowing when to cut her losses and run rather than risk the temptation a handsome man offered. Careful planning and execution of a well-thought ruse had no room for passion.

Oh, but there was something about Sedgwick that made her feel reckless, restless and willing to play a hand that would have had her piquet-loving grandmother tossing the cards in the fireplace.

Damn her promises to keep the Sedgwick name free of scandal, her behavior circumspect. Surely that hadn't meant with the man who was purportedly her husband?

Sedgwick caught her chin and looked down into her eyes. "The point is, madame, you are not my wife and I'll not be swayed by your playacting." He then turned on one heel and marched up the stairs to the next flight.

Emmaline stumbled into the empty space where he'd been standing. *Playacting?* He thought she was playacting? Well, of all the—

When he reached the top of the stairs, he glanced over his shoulder. "Emmaline, please use care until I arise. And remember our agreement. The Denfords, and then you."

"Yes, Sedgwick," she replied to his retreating figure. He strode into the bedchamber and closed the door with a little more enthusiasm than probably was necessary, leaving her standing alone in the middle of his house.

Oh, the devil take him. He still wanted her gone. Even after that kiss. She supposed he kissed ladies like that all the time. All in a day's work for Lord Sedgwick. Kiss a few birds senseless and then take a respite. Her hands wound into two tight fists at her side. Infuriating man.

Glancing around the empty foyer, she heaved a sigh and flexed her fingers. He wanted her out, and out this very afternoon. Oh, that would never do. She wouldn't get a farthing if Sedgwick tossed her out too soon.

If only he hadn't come to town so quickly. Though she probably had only herself to blame for that. Obviously she'd taken to being Lady Sedgwick with a little too much enthusiasm—what with the mentions in the *Post,* the rather horrendous pile of decorating bills that was giving his cousin fits, along with the collection of vowels from the twice-weekly visits to the dressmakers, glovers and millinery shops in which she'd partaken.

Well, moderation had never been one of her finer skills.

What Emmaline needed was help. Or at the very least a miracle. But since she knew miracles were always in short supply, she'd have to make do. Or better yet, improvise.

Glancing down toward the dining room, she knew there would be no aid from the Denfords. Not that she'd want it.

And she couldn't expect any help from the servants. In the great houses of the *ton,* the servants owed everything—their livelihood, the very roof over their heads—to the master of the house. No, as nice as Sedgwick's help was, none of them was going to go against the baron's orders.

That she'd been able to gammon them this far was indeed perhaps indication of a miracle. Or evidence of her superior skills at prevarication.

But Emmaline soon discovered that perhaps she'd been too hasty in her estimation of Sedgwick's staff. From down below she heard a man's voice rising up the staircase. It was one of the footmen—Thomas, she thought.

"I tell you, Simmons, that new fellow at the duchess's can't be beaten." The footman was trimming wicks and changing candles in the sconces, while Simmons followed and collected the spent candle ends. Neither of them noticed her standing above them. "He won five guineas off Franklin, then turned around and pigeoned a quarter's wages off that stuffy fellow from the earl's. I say something's not right about the way he plays."

Emmaline leaned forward. Sedgwick's servants gambled? And deep, if Thomas wasn't using a gossip's inflated tongue about the amounts.

"A quarter's wages." Simmons let out a low whistle. "If I lost half such a sum, Mrs. Simmons would have my head. Not that she isn't going to ring a peal over my head for the bit I've lost to that fellow."

"That's what I'm saying," Thomas said. "We can't face them come Thursday night or they'll clean us out good. We'll be living on them candle stubs till next Season."

The butler nodded. "We'll just have to come up with an excuse not to play."

"Play what?" Emmaline asked, leaning over the railing.

Both men jumped, startled to be caught gossiping by the lady of the house.

"Nothing, milady," Simmons offered. "I'm sorry if we disturbed you."

"Oh, please, Simmons, don't fret on my account." She started down the stairs until she came to the last two steps. There she put her hands on her hips and faced the guilty pair. "Besides, you haven't answered my question. Play what?"

Thomas's gaze fell to the floor, his cheeks turning a ruddy shade, while Simmons looked close to apoplexy, given the way his brow furrowed into a deep line.

She tipped her head. "I may be able to offer you some assistance."

The butler glanced at her, his gaze narrowing and assessing.

Then it struck Emmaline. He knew. Knew she wasn't Sedgwick's wife. She'd suspected it all the while, though she'd thought her worried notions impossible—for why would he let her stay if he knew the truth?

Yet there it was—he knew the truth and had held his tongue. For whatever reason.

He glanced around the foyer and lowered his voice. "Piquet. A few of us play piquet every Thursday night."

"Piquet?" Oh, she was in luck. Or rather they were.

Don't do this, Emmaline, an overly cautious voice urged her. *You're in over your head as it is. Don't go butting into business that is none of yours. What has meddling ever done for you?*

Never mind that she'd recently sworn off meddling. Right along with cards . . . and men . . . and . . .

Thomas, obviously emboldened by Simmons's confession, spoke up. "There's a new footman over at the duchess's across the square. A regular Captain Sharp, he is, if you'll excuse me, ma'am, for saying so."

Emmaline nodded solemnly. "How patently unfair."

Simmons shot Thomas a hot glance to silence the man, then he continued the story in a more dignified manner. "We believe the duchess's butler hired this fellow while the family was away, if only to get back what they lost this past winter."

"And you say the duchess's servants aren't very good at playing cards?" Emmaline asked, trying to ignore the familiar pounding in her heart.

As much as she knew she should walk away from the servants' problems, perhaps this was a time to make an exception to her rule. Perhaps, it might even be a way to gain her stake if her gammon with Sedgwick failed.

"The duke's staff are right awful, ma'am," Thomas told her. "Always good for a few extra quid, they are. That is until this new footman arrived. Now we'll have to call off our regular night."

Emmaline came down off the steps and smiled. "Don't cancel just yet," she told them. "I think you might have found a sharp of your own."

If Emmaline thought Sedgwick indifferent to their kiss, she didn't know her husband.

He'd walked away from her in a painful state of awareness as to her charms.

She's not my wife, she's not my wife, he repeated with each step up the staircase, even as the thrumming of his blood threatened to snap the taut thread of control he could still claim.

While every bit of common sense he possessed clamored at him not to go anywhere near this imposter, when she'd caught hold of him, pulled him close and offered those rosebud lips of hers to him, he'd had only one thought.

Kiss her. Kiss her quickly and deeply and thoroughly—for he might not have another chance of it before his sensibilities gained the upper hand and managed to toss her out into the streets where she belonged.

No, this Emmaline was nothing but folly. Pure folly, he thought, recalling her kiss.

He couldn't remember the last time he'd kissed a woman and found himself so undone. So willing to forget that she wasn't his wife.

And if she were to walk through the door right this

minute, he wouldn't trust himself not to take her in his arms and finish what his hard and thrumming body cried out for. The passion and pleasure her kiss promised.

Just then there was a knock on the door, and he stopped his reckless pacing and turned toward it. He tried to speak, but found his throat dry.

Gads, this was his house. He was still the master of it. He wasn't going to be ruled by anything less than common sense. And that meant he could face this pretty imposter and her all-too-kissable lips.

"Come in," he ground out.

To his utter disappointment, as much as he was loath to admit it, it was only Simmons and a line of footmen, all carrying buckets of steaming hot water.

"Her ladyship thought you might like a bath before your respite," the butler said, leading the parade of servants into the bathing chamber beyond. One of the maids followed, carrying a tray with his forgotten breakfast.

First her kiss, now this offering. And when he'd stripped himself of his clothes and sunk into his hot bath, a comforting cup of hot tea and buttered toast nearby, he realized this Emmaline was more devilish than he'd first thought.

By the time Alex arose, the day was well spent. And despite a series of fitful dreams featuring a tempting blond vixen, he'd awakened feeling like himself again.

Sensible and ready to conquer the problem at hand—namely, getting rid of Hubert and Lady Lilith.

And then Emmaline.

He opened the clothespress in search of a new waistcoat and suddenly his senses were assailed with the soft scent of violets.

Her perfume.

And upon a closer inspection, he spied a plain brown valise tucked into the back of the armoire. *Her valise*.

All her belongings, all her secrets, perhaps even her identity might be found in this innocuous, innocent-looking bag.

"No," he told himself. "That would hardly be fair." So he closed the door. It wasn't seemly to go through a lady's private possessions.

Yet how was he to learn about her mysterious past if he didn't do a bit of investigation? Didn't he have a right to know exactly who was parading about town wearing the Sedgwick name?

His hand went to the cabinet door and he opened it.

"No," he said, closing it again. Where was his honor? His integrity?

Then he opened it once more.

He temporarily disavowed those qualities as he went down on his knees and began pulling open the ancient bag.

But if he'd thought he was going to find anything that might reveal her identity, he was sadly mistaken. Her worldly possessions consisted of a plain muslin gown, a dull gray pelisse. Unmentionables in white cotton. A pair of well-worn shoes. Some mismatched ill-knit stockings. A pair of spectacles. A battered and well-thumbed copy of *Debrett's*. And a copy of *Billingsworth's Guide to the Historical Estates of England*.

And just as quickly as he'd opened the case, he was at the bottom of it and there was nothing more. Nothing at all.

No telling inscription in the books, not even initials on the bag to give a hint as to the name of its bearer.

Nothing.

"Demmit," he muttered shoving it away, disgruntled not to have found anything, and dismayed at his own lack of principle.

"Uh-hum," came a cough at the door.

Alex cringed, then glanced over his shoulder.

There stood Simmons, gazing down at him with a frown creasing his brow and lips. "Have you lost something, my lord?"

"Um. Actually, I found it," he said, rising and holding up a hastily selected cravat. "Is there something that needs my attention, Simmons?"

"Actually, I had hoped you were up. I wanted to speak to you about Lady Sedgwick."

Alex didn't like the sound of that. "What has she done now?"

"Nothing, my lord," the butler said. "It is rather something I think you could do for her."

"For her? Simmons, don't you think the lady has taken full advantage of my largesse already?"

"She has only done what any other lady in her position would have done," Simmons protested.

Alex resisted the urge to groan. He was going to have to see about Simmons's pension—the man was rising to the defense of a lady who most likely was no lady.

The butler entered the chamber and drew back the curtains, letting the clear light of day shine into the room. Illuminating Alex's crimes all too clearly.

Simmons sniffed once or twice, then came over to the wreckage that was Emmaline's belongings poking out from the hastily closed cabinet doors. Uttering a few *tsk-tsks,* he bent over and retrieved her things, carefully refolding and replacing her meager and threadbare belongings in her valise and placing it exactly where she had left it.

Then he reached in and got out a waistcoat and jacket for Alex, laying them on the bed as if nothing were amiss.

"Perhaps, my lord, if I may be bold enough to suggest this," Simmons said, looking him straight in the eye. "Instead of demanding the particulars of her past, or attempting to uproot them," he said, his sharp gaze straying in the direction of the armoire, "perhaps if you got to know the lady. Gained her trust. Then she would be more inclined to share her confidences."

Alex supposed Simmons had a point. Why should Emmaline trust him? He hadn't done anything to gain her favor.

Other than taking advantage of her kiss and then storming away like a conceited fool.

"How might I do that?" he asked, wondering if he really wanted to hear his butler's answer.

Simmons's brows furrowed, a silent protest that said such a matter was well beyond his realm. "Perhaps that is best left to your discretion," he finally said.

Discretion and Emmaline were two words at odds, Alex wanted to tell him. Even so, he finished dressing and followed the man out of the room and down the stairs.

Everywhere he looked, he spied the changes she'd wreaked upon his house. One that barely resembled the home he'd left just a few months ago.

There wasn't a wall, corner or floor that didn't cite evidence of Emmaline's handiwork. Or at least he assumed it was hers, given that he had the recent bills to prove most of the changes.

The new drapes (green silk brocade, Leahy & Sons,

Drapers, £72), the matching elegant and graceful Grecian styled end tables under the windows on the second landing (Bradley Brothers, Cabinet-Makers, £47 apiece) and a series of watercolors for which he couldn't cite a bill.

He came to a stop before one of the paintings and realized it was of the south meadow at Sedgwick Castle. The one where the family liked to picnic in the summers.

When there had been family enough to do those sort of things, he mused. His mother had always seen to those events, merrily inviting relations and friends for the summer months and holidays . . . With his parents gone all these years, he'd all but forgotten those languid days. How quiet the abbey had become since his father passed away from a heart ailment and his mother shortly afterward from a fever. What had it been? Ten? No, nearly fifteen years.

Yet the sight of the verdant fields, the small lake, the grand oak at the far end, it sent a thread of nostalgia through him, and he could almost see his mother sitting by the water, his father fishing nearby.

"Simmons," he called after his butler. "Where did these come from?" He'd never seen any of them. And certainly Emmaline couldn't have commissioned them in such a short time.

The butler glanced at them and smiled. "The attics. I believe those were painted by your grandmother."

Alex took another glance at the compositions. *His grandmother?* He didn't know she could paint, let alone capture such magical moments. The distraction the images provided ended abruptly when a bell rang upstairs, jangling with a discordant note.

"That will be Lady Lilith," Simmons said. "*Again.* My lord, how long will the Denfords be staying this time?"

"Not much longer," Alex promised. They continued down the hall going past more new drapes (explaining the additional entries on Mr. Leahy's bill for yellow brocade and white trim), the carpet beneath his feet (something imported and expensive, if he recalled correctly) and a pair of chairs (more evidence of the Bradley Brothers' handsome work).

He shook his head. For such a petite thing, she had gone through his house like a whirlwind—transforming the once dark and drearily formal apartments into . . . well, as much as he hated to admit it, into a home.

Assembled at the doorway to the ballroom appeared to be his entire staff, besotted with whatever was taking place inside.

"Ahem," Simmons coughed.

Startled gazes turned in their direction, and then, like deer having heard the huntsman's horn, they fled back into the deep reaches of the house, bowing and apologizing as they went.

Alex stepped forward to see what was so enticing, taking a cautious peek into the ballroom. At first he thought he was in the wrong house, for the large room before him certainly bore no resemblance to the one that had been a fixture at the Hanover house since . . . well, since the square had been built.

Gone were the dark red drapes, the gilt furnishings, the endless rows of uncomfortable chairs. The Flemish wall hangings, the dark-framed paintings, the ornate sconces, all of it had been stripped away.

Simmons beamed like a proud parent. "Don't blame the staff, my lord. It is an honor and a pleasure to see her work," was all he said, before he too left to attend to his duties.

Alex's gaze returned to the chaos before him. There were tarps spread about the floor, while workmen on scaffolding labored at repainting the ceiling. He stepped farther inside and found overhead the miraculous sight of a dreamy sky that spread from the rosy fingers of dawn to the starry wonders of the night. It looked so real, one might think one could reach up and do the impossible—touch the very heavens.

Then, as if bidden by a sly, whispering breeze, he looked across the room and spied her watching him. She stood there, looking breathless with anticipation as she awaited his verdict. That she had taken it upon herself to reorder his house was incorrigible, yet what she had done left him spellbound—just as the lady herself did.

And while he didn't want to concede to her in any fashion, he couldn't help but smile. Let his astonishment at her accomplishments unfurl between them like a white flag.

She grinned back, then turned to the tradesman who was standing by with a large sample of paper in his hands.

"Mr. Starling," she began, "I asked for a chinoiserie that made one feel as if one had stepped into a summer bower. Those . . ." she said, pointing at the sample he held, "why, those birds look as if they would peck one's eyes out."

"These are some of the finest examples of wallpaper to be had in London," the man said. "My clients have the highest regard for my wares."

"Of course they do," she agreed, "but this is Hanover Square." She made it sound as if the land beneath them towered somewhere between the highest steeple of St. Paul's and the realm of angels. Shaking her head at the next three samples, she finally said, "I would like to see birds who look capable of lulling one to sleep with their sweet song, flowers that make me want to inhale deeply, and twining vines that could conceal a pair of lovers."

The man heaved a sigh and burrowed further into his portfolios. "I have a piece that may be of interest to you, my lady," he said. "My other clients found it too provincial for their taste, but it may suit your bucolic tendencies."

Alex ruffled at the man's tone, for he hadn't seen a single sample about which he didn't agree with Emmaline's assessment. The woman had excellent taste and obviously knew good wares from bad.

"Here it is," the man said, holding it up.

The moment he saw the wallpaper—with its robins and wrens, tangles of roses and arching sprays of ivy—he realized what had been Emmaline's intent with the ballroom—to make their guests feel as if they were in the midst of an elegant garden. Though it may be a chilly February night outside, and surrounded as they were by the brick and mortar of London, everyone who entered this room would have nothing but thoughts of June and romance.

He almost jumped forward to tell the man to measure the walls and put the paper up, but Emmaline was once again shaking her head.

The exasperated man held out a larger section for her to survey. "What is there not to like about this one?"

"The price, for certain," she told him. "I cannot pay that. Why, it is more dear than half the Chinese silks you've shown me—which, while you claim were painted in the East, have all the markings of east Cheapside."

The man's face flushed. "Milady, I would never—"

"Of course you wouldn't, Mr. Starling," she said, soothing his ruffled feathers. "But I don't think that shade of green will look good with the draperies I've ordered." She tipped her head and eyed it again. "No, not at all. I'm sorry, but I fear I will have to look elsewhere. Especially with so much of the room to be covered." She waved her arms around the expansive walls, while the man's avaricious gaze followed her movements.

Alex could see by Mr. Starling's squinty gaze that he was calculating the square footage to be covered and the profit to be had but for the whimsical taste of the lady before him.

"Lady Sedgwick, I think you should take another look, over here by the light. Are you sure this is not the perfect shade of green?" he asked, moving toward the window and holding the sample up so it could take advantage of the afternoon sun.

She looked again and sighed. "It's just that when we have the opening fête for next Season, which his lordship is insistent we do, I would like to be able to tell all two hundred of our closest and dearest friends that the wallpaper came from you. Especially Prinny, who I know will be most insistent on having me reveal all my suppliers. And while I make it a rule never to divulge the names of my select tradesmen, for I abhor imitation, I would be very neglectful if I didn't credit you completely for adorning our ballroom with the perfect wallpaper."

Alex watched the man's mind tallying such a disclosure. Telling the crown prince would be better than taking out a front-page ad in the *Morning Post*. Why, it could lead to a Royal Warrant! And with that added cachet, in addition to the amount of walls that needed to be covered, the man would pocket a tidy profit.

Even at half the price.

Mr. Starling adjusted his glasses. "Did I say fourteen pounds? I meant seven. But only for you, milady. And only in the strictest confidence, for I can't make such an allowance for all my clients."

Emmaline beamed. "As long as I won't see this wallpaper hanging anywhere else in London."

"Absolutely not, madame." The man nodded, basking under her smile even as he waved for his assistants to start measuring.

Smart minx, Alex noted. She'd given the man permission to copy her room in every country house in England, and it would be, once the fashion-mad *ton* caught sight of her innovations.

He was so caught up in her negotiations, much like his staff had been, he didn't realize he was no longer alone until his cousin spoke up.

"She'll spend you into debtor's prison if you don't put your foot down," Hubert said, having crept up to his elbow in his usual sly way.

Alex bit back the first remark that sprang forth. *It is none of your affair, cousin.*

However, it wouldn't do to offend Hubert. The odious fellow would stay around for weeks trying to reingratiate himself into Alex's favor. So he said, "From what I've seen, she's done nothing but improve the house by reestablishing it as the jewel of Mayfair."

Hubert's nose wrinkled as if he didn't agree in the least but wasn't so foolish as to say so twice.

"Oh, Sedgwick, darling," Emmaline called out. "There you are. I'd all but given up that you would be down in time to lend me your opinion on Mr. Starling's samples." She caught him by the arm and dragged him through the warren of scaffolding and workmen. Picking up the sample, she held it out for him to see. "What do you think? I'm worried the green is too dark and the price too dear." She leaned forward and whispered loudly. "'Tis five pounds per panel, and I know you've been quite vexed with me of late for overreaching my allowance, yet I would love to have this paper, for it is the only one Mr. Starling has that does this room to advantage." Then she showered a brilliant smile on him and one for poor Mr. Starling.

Alex was taken aback by her brass. She'd shaved two pounds off the price, yet if Mr. Starling corrected her, he risked the baron's ire and the loss of the entire commission.

And it worked like a charm, for the man just gulped and nodded in agreement—to her assessment and the new price.

Gads, if he let her stay another day, she'd have him convinced she was indeed his lawful wife.

"It looks perfect, Emmaline," he said, bowing slightly to her and then to the tradesman.

Hubert had followed close on his heels and Alex soon discovered Lady Lilith wasn't far behind. Usually he wasn't too pleased to see the pair of them descending upon him, but there was no time like the present to get rid of them.

Oh, yes, and Emmaline as well, he reminded himself. "Hubert, actually I was looking for you. I have an errand that requires your expertise."

"Whatever you need, cousin. I am always there to help you. You have but to ask and I am at your disposal. Just say the—"

"Yes, I know," Alex told him. "I would like you and Lady Lilith to travel with all due haste to . . . to . . . Cornwall and visit a property I obtained this past season. It is a matter of some importance, so if you would leave immediately I would be most obliged."

Hubert glanced over at his wife and then back at Alex. "'Fraid we can't."

Alex shook his head. Perhaps he hadn't heard Hubert correctly. "You what?"

"Can't go," Hubert said. "Can't leave town just yet. At least not for a fortnight."

"Whyever not?" Alex asked, trying to recall if there had ever been a time when Hubert had naysaid anything he'd been asked to do.

"My brother's wedding," Lady Lilith said, coming up to stand beside her husband. "I am so sorry, Sedgwick, but we couldn't possibly leave town until after the wedding. Mother is in a state over the arrangements."

Hubert nodded. "That's why we came to town in the first place."

"A wedding," Emmaline said dreamily. "I adore weddings."

From the sly tilt of her head and the mischievous smile on her lips, he realized she'd known all along that his efforts to evict the Denfords would come to naught.

Why, of all the unscrupulous, underhanded . . .

Lady Lilith, in the meantime, was picking her way through the tarps and scaffolding to inspect Emmaline's latest choices. More likely, trying to gauge the expense. She looked at the paper and sniffed. "Of course, you will be invited to the wedding breakfast—that is, if your business keeps you in town that long," she said. "You can let Mother know tonight at her supper party."

"Tonight?" Alex asked. "What supper party?"

"Mother is having a little party for Miss Mabberly, my brother's betrothed, to introduce her to a better sort of company," Lady Lilith explained. "I believe she sent around an invitation this morning when she heard you were in town. Of course, I informed her you would be there, for I knew you would never want to slight my mother."

Alex felt his control once again slipping through his fingers. "I don't think that we can—I mean to say, Emmaline's health prevents her from—"

"Oh, you can't avoid society forever, you two," Hubert said, nudging Alex in an overly friendly manner. "No one will think less of you, cousin, when they discover how truly besotted you are with your bride."

Besotted? He was no such thing. And he certainly didn't need that bit of nonsense being bandied about by whatever limited society was in town. All it would take was one gossipy matron, one spinster with a bent for chatter, a Corinthian in search of a new *on dit,* and everyone would know.

Meanwhile, Emmaline was peppering Lady Lilith with questions. All he heard were the words he dreaded. *A supper party . . . a wedding . . . a fortnight?*

Hadn't any of them heard a word he'd said?

"We are not going," he announced.

The banter stopped and three pairs of eyes stared at him.

"I've already accepted. Mother is expecting you," Lady Lilith said, her tones as haughty as her manner. "It will cause comment if you are in town and don't deign to make an appearance."

He wasn't used to being countermanded under his own roof, especially not by relations who owed their livelihood to his largesse. Yet he felt the challenge of her words right down to his toes. She was daring him to take Emmaline out into good company.

He slanted a quick glance in Lady Lilith's direction,

ready to deliver his final word on the subject, yet something in her smug smile stopped him. Right there and then he realized his cousin's sharp wife suspected something was amiss.

He didn't even want to think of the price he'd pay if Hubert and Lilith discovered the truth.

"Yes, of course, it would cause unseemly comment if we didn't attend," he said. Comment he could ill afford. "Thank you, Lady Lilith, for pointing that out."

"That's my girl," Hubert said, beaming at his wife. "Always looking out for the Denford name."

Maybe more so than Alex thought necessary.

"Then tonight is looking up already," Hubert enthused. "It will be quite a feather in Lady Oxley's hat to be the first hostess in London to present Lord *and* Lady Sedgwick together for all to see."

Alex wanted to groan. Instead, he turned on one heel and stormed from the room, fleeing before he found himself in the wedding party or hosting the breakfast.

"Sedgwick, where are you going?" Emmaline called out.

"My club."

"We are expected at eight," Lady Lilith added, a wry smile on her face.

Eight it would be then. And they'd leave promptly at half past before any further mischief could be wrought on his life.

Chapter 5

Emmaline let out a deep breath as Sedgwick left the ballroom. She'd been granted a reprieve. And she had Lady Lilith and Hubert to thank. Why, she could have almost hugged the imperious woman when she'd said that they couldn't leave. Almost, that is. Lady Lilith's pinched expression probably kept even the unruliest of small children and unrestrained dogs at bay.

Still, another day here was another day closer to the end of her career conning the *ton*. In two weeks' time, she'd pluck a passel of fat purses at the Marquis of Westly's annual piquet challenge, and then she'd retire someplace quiet and picturesque.

She could almost hear the happy jingle of gold coins in her pockets.

"What has you smiling like a cat in the cream?" came a sweet dulcet voice near the doorway. Hubert and Lady Lilith were gone, and in their stead Malvina Witherspoon,

Viscountess Rawlins, stood there grinning at her. "Why, you look like you've just made off with half the diamonds at Rundell and Bridge!"

Emmaline couldn't help wondering what Malvina would say if she knew how close to the truth she'd come.

Then again, she doubted it would bother the viscountess in the least if Emmaline *had* robbed the well-appointed jewelry store. Anything for a diversion.

Take for instance, Emmaline's unexpected arrival at Hanover Square. The viscountess had descended on Number Seventeen the morning after she'd arrived and immediately made herself a fixture in Emmaline's daily life.

"I am so glad you're here," Malvina had declared as if they'd known each other for ages. *"I hope you don't mind my presumption, but I had to call. I haven't a friend in town right now, and I am dying for some company."*

And then, before Emmaline could utter a protest, Malvina had declared her gown a disgrace and promptly called for her carriage to transport them both to Bond Street for a day of shopping to bring Emmaline up to par.

"The cats would have a field day with you, my dear, if they saw you in that wretched gown. Why, you look like someone's cast-off companion."

How right Malvina had been, not that Emmaline dared tell her the truth.

Besides aiding and abetting Emmaline's rather tenuous use of Sedgwick's credit, Malvina had also done something Emmaline would never have been able to accomplish in such short order. With the indomitable Viscountess Rawlins at her side, Emmaline had gained an instant and immediate cachet within society.

Thus was born their unlikely alliance. Though as each

day passed, Emmaline found it was less and less easy to reconcile the guilt she felt each time Malvina introduced her as her "dearest friend."

The viscountess strolled into the ballroom, studying first the ceiling, then the paper Mr. Starling had left on the worktable. "Emmaline, you have the most engaging eye. How do you do it? If you weren't so charming, I'd declare you horribly annoying to anyone who would listen."

"I haven't done anything you couldn't do."

"Oh, bother me. All I seem fit for currently is scaring small children with my great girth." She folded her hands over her enormous stomach, full with a baby that was due any day now. Because of her *enceinte* state, she and her husband, Viscount Rawlins, hadn't traveled to the country for the summer. Bored without the company of the rest of the *ton*, Malvina had declared Emmaline's arrival at Hanover Square "heaven-sent."

"How are you feeling today?" Emmaline asked, casting an awestruck glance at the lady's bursting waistline.

"Dreadful. Simply dreadful. Bother this child. I can't sleep. I have to use the necessary every half hour. And I swear some Seven Dials cutthroat made off with my ankles last night, replacing them with a pair of barrels." She plucked up her gown and revealed once-delicate ankles now ballooned in width. She sighed, then dropped her hem back into place. "But thank you for asking."

Emmaline laughed.

Malvina breezed forward, moving gracefully despite her figure, and wound her arm around Emmaline's. "Come invite me for some of Mrs. Simmons's tea cakes and tell me what *he* said."

"Who said?" Emmaline teased.

Malvina swatted her with her fan. "Sedgwick, you dolt. Tell me what happened last night when he got home. I want to hear all the details." She winked. "La! Rawlins retreated to a cot in the dressing room three months ago and I wonder if he'll ever return to my bed. So indulge a poor lonely woman—what happened?"

"If you know that he's home, then you probably know everything I could tell you."

"You dreadful tease," Malvina replied, leading her from the ballroom. "Now you must tell all. According to my upstairs maid, your servants were quite tight-lipped this morning. I've been in a state all day, waiting for Sedgwick to leave for his club so I could come over and have a good coze with you."

Emmaline shot a sideways glance at the woman. "How did you know Sedgwick would leave for his club?"

Malvina laughed again. "Emmaline, my dear Emmaline, how much you need to learn about marriage."

They left the ballroom and settled into the garden salon at the back of the house. The doors and windows had been thrown open and the roses growing in profusion beyond scented the room.

Emmaline rang the bell and ordered tea and cakes, and then settled down on the chair across from Malvina.

"So? What did he say about the house?" the viscountess asked. "More to the point, what did he say about you? Obviously he didn't toss you into the streets for beggaring him with all your redecorating." Malvina laughed at her jest, and Emmaline joined in, though for different reasons—mostly that she wasn't in Newgate or on her way to Botany Bay.

"No, luckily for me, he didn't," she said. "Though I thought he might for a moment there."

Malvina shook her head. "Men! They haven't the least idea the work and effort we undertake to make their lives infinitely more comfortable."

The tea and cakes arrived, the maid leaving them on the low table between the ladies. Emmaline poured a cup for her friend and offered her a plate of cakes.

As Malvina happily munched through several, avowing that they were all for the baby and chatting away about nonsensical gossip she'd picked up from her servants, Emmaline found herself silently recounting Sedgwick's entry into the ballroom.

She'd caught sight of him out of the corner of her eye and been too nervous to do anything more than cast furtive glances in his direction.

Emmaline's only hope had been that the blush she felt heating her cheeks wasn't noticeable across the room. Gads, what was it about him that had her turning as pink as the roses outside?

Oh, she knew what it was. The memory of his kiss. His scorching, devastatingly passionate kiss. The very thought of it took her breath away . . .

And yet Sedgwick had appeared so unaffected. So demmed indifferent. And then their gazes had met, and she swore that she'd seen that heat flare to life in his green gaze. A memory shared, a memory that now bound them together, until they could find a way to douse that flame.

She'd glanced away then, unable to continue looking at him and not have her knees melt beneath her. But her curiosity, her need prodded her to spare a peek in his direction again, only to find his gaze had roamed upward, cast in the direction of the ceiling.

Holding her breath, she wondered at his thoughts—until

she'd been rewarded with a look of complete awe and then appreciation for the painting that was being done.

She'd followed his gaze as he'd looked around the room, and she just knew he'd understood what she was trying to accomplish. He'd known, and he'd approved of it.

And when Hubert had come in, like a weasel, wheedling up to Sedgwick's elbow with his penny-pinching comments, she swore she'd heard Sedgwick defend her work.

Defend her? Oh, what was it that he'd said?

From what I've seen, she's done nothing but improve the house.

Emmaline could only wonder what had induced him to say that. Let alone agree to take her to dinner at Lady Oxley's, though she suspected Lady Lilith's sly comments had something to do with his change of heart.

A London dinner party. She took a deep breath. However would she manage to pull that off?

It wasn't that Emmaline didn't understand the workings of society. She'd made a study of them, for heaven sakes, made her living aping noble manners and taking advantage of their rules and needs to support herself.

But country gentry and the London leaders were two different ponds. Coming to London was like navigating the ocean in a punt.

Without the pole.

". . . And then I hear tell that Lady Tisbury had twin goats yesterday," Malvina was saying. "Much to the earl's delight."

"How lovely for them," Emmaline said, considering what she would wear, let alone how she'd make it through a formal dinner. For what the devil was she going to do if she

actually knew someone there? Worse, what if someone recognized her?

"Emmaline Denford," Malvina said, leaning forward and
snapping her fingers. "Are you listening to a word I've
said?"

Sitting up, Emmaline nodded. "Yes, you were saying . . .
um, I do believe you were . . ."

Malvina shook her head. "What has you worried? You sat
through my perfectly delicious story about Lord Templeton
without even batting a lash. You are woolgathering like my
great-aunt Mary and I want to know what has you so distracted. Is it Sedgwick? Is there anything I can do to help?"

"No, it isn't him. It's just that . . . well, tonight . . ." Emmaline felt guilty enough about her less-than-honest relationship
with Malvina, but having to ask her for help—make that more
help—just didn't set well. "'Tis nothing. I'm perfectly fine."

"Bother that," Malvina declared. "There is something
wrong and I will have it out this moment and I shall not
leave until I do!" She plopped her swollen ankles up on the
sofa and folded her hands over her belly.

"Really, there is nothing wrong," Emmaline assured her.

"And I am the Queen of Persia," came the reply. "I would
hate to think what this new sofa would look like if I were to
have this child here. Not to mention Lord and Lady Tottley's dismay that their first grandchild wasn't born on hal-
lowed Tottley property. Of course, I shall blame you
completely." Malvina's lips twisted with a wicked smile.

Emmaline grinned back. "Well, if you must know—we
are to dine at Lady Oxley's tonight."

That ended her friend's high spirits. A great groan
erupted from the sofa. "And you didn't refuse it?"

"How can I? She's Mrs. Denford's mother."

"Relations! I confess, I find them such a bother." Malvina sat up and frowned at Emmaline. "If only we could marry and not collect more family."

By now Emmaline was quite familiar with Malvina's acrimonious relationship with her in-laws, the Earl and Countess of Tottley. Lady Tottley was considered the bellwether of society and it drove Malvina to the point of fits that she had to live in her mother-in-law's constant scrutiny, if not social shadow.

"When Rawlins inherits," she had said on more than one occasion, *"I swear I shall not be such an old cow, tromping about town pronouncing who is important and who shall marry whom. I will bring a refinement and sense of dignity to the name Tottley."*

"As it is," Emmaline was saying, "I must go tonight, but I'm—"

"Don't say another word. You poor thing, I'd be blue as May if I had to suffer through yet another of Lady Oxley's evenings. Lady Tottley adores her—and that in my mind is no recommendation."

Emmaline cringed and wondered if Newgate was such a bad place. Surely there were some cells with a view, or ones that could use a bit of new paint.

Malvina, however, wasn't through. "We got an invitation, purely because Lady Oxley and Lady Tottley are such bosom bows, but I declined. Rawlins insists I stay close to home. But in truth I think he was relieved to have the excuse."

"Who will be there?" Emmaline asked, knowing full well Malvina would have a complete reckoning. Her knowledge of the social maneuverings of town life was astounding.

And of course, Malvina did know. "The Mabberlys," she said, "because Oxley is marrying Miss Mabberly. Lady Jarvis—awful woman that she is. Lady Pepperwell. Poor *ton,* but you can't exclude her—she's a terrible gossip. Templeton. The Earl of Lamden and his daughter. Most likely the Marquis of Westly."

Emmaline's gaze swung up. "Who?" she asked as innocently as she could.

"The Marquis of Westly. Rawlins mentioned seeing him the other day. I suppose he's in town for that piquet game of his. I wish someone would beat him and be done with it. His tedious crowing all year as to how he can't be beaten is decidedly unbecoming."

Emmaline suppressed a smile. *Malvina, you are closer to your wish than you realize.*

Now her reasons for succeeding at this dinner rose. She had to meet Westly, at least to get an introduction so that when she arrived at his challenge, her entrée would be assured.

"Malvina, can I tell you something?"

The viscountess smiled. "Of course. You are my dearest friend."

"In confidence?"

At this, Malvina's eyes widened, then her features took a serious turn. "Unlike my mother-in-law, I do not gossip."

That wasn't quite the truth, but Emmaline had no one else to turn to. "I've never gone to a formal dinner."

"Never?" Malvina's hand went immediately to cover her gaping mouth.

Emmaline shook her head.

"Why, of course you haven't," Malvina replied. "What with that unorthodox upbringing of yours. I don't think there would be much call for a formal dinner in Africa. And then with your illness . . ."

The one thing about the *ton,* Emmaline had learned, was that everyone knew everyone else's business. Sedgwick's wife's "unorthodox upbringing," as most everyone liked to call it, made Emmaline a point of curiosity and went a long way toward explaining her less-than-perfect manners or knowledge of London society.

She had to give the baron credit, when he'd invented a wife, he'd chosen wisely. Lord Haley and his wife had left England twenty-nine years earlier to investigate the wilds of Africa. Lady Haley had perished in that inhospitable land and there had been no word of Lord Haley for close to fifteen years. Emmaline, their daughter, was apparently Alex's own invention, and it worked perfectly, for who was there to dispute such a thing when Lord Haley was the last of his lineage?

Malvina struggled off the sofa. "Gracious heavens, Emmaline, why didn't you say something earlier? You can't go to Lady Oxley's unprepared. She and Mrs. Denford will be lying in wait like a pair of lions. The Christians had better odds in Rome. And the last thing you want to do is embarrass Sedgwick." Malvina paused. "I suppose you know Lady Oxley had plotted for Sedgwick to marry Lilith."

Emmaline shook her head.

"Oh, well, that is long past. But it doesn't bode well for you. Lady Oxley will want to make sure she shows your husband what an ill choice he made. No matter that! Anyone with sense and a pair of eyes could see how much better suited you are to be his wife." Malvina caught her by the hand and dragged her up from her chair.

Pregnancy was no deterrent to the viscountess when there was a social battle at hand.

"I intend to see that you carry the night and be the envy of all," Malvina declared, forefinger raised in the air. "But first we need to pick the type of gown that will ensure whatever rift is between you and Sedgwick is well healed by the evening's end. A night he'll remember forever." Malvina winked.

Forever? No, that would never do. Yet she could hardly tell Malvina that all she needed was a fortnight.

"Sedgwick! Fancy seeing you so soon," Jack called out from a billiards table as Alex entered White's. "Looking for another round of fisticuffs?"

Alex glanced around the great room. It was nearly empty except for a few fellows deep in play at a card table in a far corner. With the Season over, White's was more a quiet oasis than a social hub.

Jack glanced at his pocket watch. "That has to be a record, even for you, in removing the Denfords from your house." He grinned. "And am I to assume you have also evicted your other unwanted guest?"

"No. On both counts."

Jack froze, his hand in midair about to wave down one of the waiters. "What do you mean, no?"

"Exactly that—no." Sedgwick ran his hand through his hair. "I came looking for you because I need help. Hubert refuses to leave town—apparently Lilith's brother is getting married."

"Oh, yes, I heard. Oxley is set to marry that Mabberly

chit. Demmed heiress. My brother is furious I didn't make an effort there." Jack heaved a sigh. "Have heard that Lady Oxley is dead set against the match."

"Yes, well, that may be, but it doesn't get the Denfords out of my house."

Jack nodded. "And once they've gone packing, so shall Emmaline."

"Exactly. Which is why I need your help."

The waiter arrived and Jack ordered a bottle. Then he sat back in his chair, arms folded over his chest. "How can I be of assistance?"

Alex grinned. "Well, it seems to me you would have some expertise in removing an unwanted houseguest."

Jack's eyes narrowed. "You know I don't have a house."

Alex cocked a brow. "I really wasn't referring to you as the host."

"Now, that's uncalled for." Jack sat up, his features set in indignant angles. "I've never been called unwanted. At least not to my face."

Alex said nothing, just sent him a withering stare.

"Perhaps I've overstayed my welcome . . . once, maybe twice."

Alex's gaze rolled toward the ceiling.

"Do you want my help or not?" Jack asked.

"Desperately."

The waiter arrived with the bottle.

"You paying?"

Alex nodded. The man put the bottle on the table and then left. Once the fellow was well out of earshot, he leaned forward and said, "Now, I think the first thing I need to do is establish who's divulged my secret."

Jack heaved a sigh. "Who could have been so bird-witted?"

Instead of being blunt, Alex tried a more polite response. "You haven't told any of your ladybirds, have you?"

"Me?" Jack's hand went to his heart. "You wound me. I've been the epitome of discretion."

Alex shot him a hard look.

Jack held up one hand in a pledge. "I have far better things to do with a mistress than exchange *on dits* about your dull affairs."

Alex wasn't so convinced, but then again, of all the things his friend was, being indiscreet usually wasn't one of them.

Jack shrugged off his hurt feelings by helping himself to a healthy measure. "Well, to start off, how many people know the truth about Emmaline?"

"You—"

"I think we've already established my lack of motive there," he said, rubbing his swollen nose.

"You," Alex repeated. "Simmons. My solicitor, Mr. Elliott, and Mr. Elliott's wife."

Jack shook his head. "Any chance of anyone else discovering the truth? Accidental slip to a mistress? Drunken ramblings in front of your grandmother?"

Alex shook his head. He'd considered all this, but in truth, he hadn't had a mistress in some time and the handful of times he could recall getting foxed were all with Jack.

"What about Hubert? Could he have discovered the truth? He's a sly fellow."

"No. Besides, he'd have nothing to gain by divulging the truth." Alex paused. "Though that wouldn't stop him from capitalizing on the fact if he knew."

"Oh, aye," Jack agreed. "He'd make you pay through the nose."

"Exactly. Besides, Hubert wouldn't spend the money to perpetuate such a ruse—or let his decoy run my finances into dun territory in the process."

"Spent all that, has she? Then I've learned my lesson from your example—an imaginary wife is well beyond my meager purse."

Alex laughed. "Yes, she's quite the whirlwind. You should see what she's done to the house."

Jack chuckled. "Suppose that has Hubert in fits. Would like to see that." He took another drink. "Still, my money is on your cousin, despite what you say. Never trust a man who won't buy a round or two."

"No, I don't see how it could be him," Alex countered. "Besides, Emmaline's nonexistence was always a boon for him, for it leaves me without the opportunity to produce an heir."

"Not anymore," Jack said, tipping his glass at him.

"What the devil do you mean?"

"Remember I've seen your Emmaline and she's a tempting piece. Now there's opportunity, if ever there was." He paused for a second. "Too bad real wives don't look like that. Marriage wouldn't be such a sorry state if one got to marry the pretty and beguiling ones."

Jack had the right of it there. Tempting was the word for Emmaline. Now that he'd tasted her lips, he knew the memory of her kiss would plague him for some time to come.

And opportunity was what made it worse—for she was under his roof. Sleeping in his bed—with her perfume scenting the sheets, the impression of her lithe form leaving a reminder behind in the soft confines of the mattress. All he could envision was her there, in some lacy bit of silk, with her hair falling loose and . . .

"Alex, are you listening?" Jack's question shook him back to the matters at hand. "Gads, I haven't seen that look on your face since you were smitten with that opera dancer our first year in town."

"I was not smitten." Alex poured himself a drink and avoided Jack's gaze.

"You were besotted. And you had the same vacant look on your face for a week after you . . ." Jack's words faltered to a stop and his eyes widened. "You've been with this Emmaline."

"No. Absolutely not. When would I have had time to—"

Jack leaned back in his chair, a sly smile on his lips. "Perhaps not. Truthfully, that would have been fast, even for me."

"Well, I haven't," Alex said, crossing his arms across his chest.

"Fine, have it your way," Jack said, his eyes alight with merriment. "Have you considered that she wasn't hired by someone, that she found out on her own?"

"The thought had crossed my mind, but I don't see how that could be the case."

"Then we have to go on the supposition that someone discovered the truth and hired her." Jack appeared to be relishing his role as investigator. "I suppose you can't just rattle the truth out of her?"

"Like a bill collector?" Alex shook his head. "No, I daresay that wouldn't be all that honorable." Besides, it would involve taking her in his arms again, and that temptation was more than he wanted to consider. One glance from her melting blue eyes and he'd be lost again. "I think the better course of action is to get rid of her. But how am I going to do it?"

"Well, she's been ill all these years. Why can't she become ill again?"

Alex thought of Emmaline, rosy and pink, in the finest of health. Soft and supple in his arms.

There wasn't anything unhealthy about her. Save the way she ignited his blood.

"I don't know—"

"Women can take ill at a moment's notice. No one will think twice about it."

That made sense. When his grandmother felt put out over some slight she sought her bed, and his Aunt Imogene was known to take refuge in her room for weeks with some ague or infirmary—*malades imaginaires,* his grandmother liked to call them.

"Take a lesson from my brother," Jack offered. "When he and my esteemed sister-in-law deem that I've overstayed my welcome, he opens his wallet and sends me on my way—a nice fat draft in my pocket and a mutual agreement that I not return for a good six months. Pay Emmaline off and be rid of her."

Alex frowned. "I don't like the idea of giving this woman a farthing."

"Then keep her," Jack suggested.

"No—she'll spend me into debtor's prison. I'd rather keep you as a friend."

Jack grinned, with pride, no doubt. "I'm immune to your insults."

"Well I know." Alex poured another drink and tossed it back.

Not to be outdone, Jack leaned forward. "There is always your lack of charm. A few hours in your company and she'll leave town voluntarily."

Alex laughed. It never worked on Jack, and he suspected it wouldn't work on Emmaline.

Besides, he wasn't all that convinced he wanted her to leave.

Which was, in itself, another sign that she had turned his life upside down.

Alex returned to Hanover Square with the resolution that he would open his wallet and remove Emmaline with a healthy bribe. Then, once he determined who had hired her in the first place, he would extract that amount from the fiend.

When he got to the house, he was met on the front steps by a very pregnant Lady Rawlins. He'd always thought Malvina Witherspoon a saucy handful, and Rawlins a fool for marrying her. But seeing her like this, so full of child, cumbersome and almost helpless, he felt a twinge of something he'd never felt before.

Something akin to jealousy.

No, it couldn't be, he told himself almost immediately. It was just the usual discomfort he felt around women in that state. There was something altogether too disconcerting about a woman with her belly pushing out like the prow of a ship. And right now Lady Rawlins bore a startling resemblance to one of Nelson's mighty warships.

"My lady," he said, bowing over her hand.

The cheeky chit had the nerve to wink at him. "Sedgwick. Nice to see you home at last. Emmaline is waiting for you. The Denfords went ahead without you. If it was me in there I'd have your hide for being so late, but your wife is much more forgiving. Along with other things."

Demmit. Lady Oxley's dinner. He'd completely forgotten about it.

Lady Rawlings squeezed past him and teetered her way down the steps. "I hope you have the good sense to admire my handiwork. I spent the last two hours getting her hair just so. But don't admire it so much that it becomes mussed before you arrive at Lady Oxley's." She winked again and made her way to the Tottley residence across the square.

He was met at the door by Simmons, who seemed as put out by his late arrival as Lady Rawlins.

"Milord, there you are! I have your dress clothes laid out in the second bedroom. You'd best hurry or else your late arrival will arouse comment." That pointed remark was followed by a not-so-subtle nudge toward the stairs.

Alex turned and stared at Simmons. He was unable to remember the last time the old family retainer had taken him to task. Probably not since he'd gone to Eton.

And before he could comment, remind the butler that the woman upstairs wasn't his wife, Simmons was calling for Henry to bring the carriage around.

Between Lady Rawlins's machinations and Simmons's apparent turn around the bend, he was starting to wonder if anyone remembered this was *his* house.

He made his way upstairs, bypassed the second bedroom and went straight to the master suite. He strode in without knocking and found no one about.

"Emmaline?"

"In here," she called out.

He crossed the room toward the connected sitting room, to find a screen had been set up in one corner.

"I'm here," she called out from behind it.

Alex came to a halt in the middle of the room and stared at the Chinese painting covering the partition.

He didn't dare venture any closer. The memory of her kiss was too fresh in his mind. And while he'd disavowed being besotted to Jack, there was a small part of him that was willing to acknowledge that she was a demmed tempting minx.

There was no need to go adding to his problems by venturing behind a perfectly good screen. One that right now he'd be more than happy to pay the bill for.

"I think we need to come up with a plan for the evening," he told her. "We will arrive, make an appearance, then just before dinner, I want you to claim an illness. I'll make our excuses and then we'll be done before any further calamities can strike."

"That will never work," she told him, with a confident air that took him aback.

Wasn't anyone in his household listening to him anymore? "Whyever not?"

"If I feign an illness suddenly, everyone will think I'm increasing."

With child? Alex stammered for breath. And he thought his life couldn't get any more tangled. "You aren't, are you?"

"Most certainly not!" she replied with enough indignation that he thought he ought to duck for fear her outburst would be followed with a flying hairbrush or some other not-so-blunt instrument.

"I meant no offense," he said.

"Harrumph."

Offense obviously taken. He didn't know why he should feel responsible for her ire—she was the one who'd broached the subject.

"So what do you suggest we do?" he asked against his better judgment.

"Go through with the evening."

Alex was shaking his head even before she finished. "I don't know if you realize it, but Lady Oxley is known to have the highest instep in the *ton*. One mistake, and she'll have you revealed as a fraud."

"That would be unfortunate for both of us," Emmaline replied. "But don't you think it would be better for your deception if I passed Lady Oxley's muster? Then there would be no more speculation. No more of Hubert's sly inquisitions."

So she knew about those. "Too risky a gamble," he told her, though he did see that her plan had some merit.

"Believe me," she said, coming out from behind the screen, "I know a thing or two about gambling."

And when he looked up and took in the sight before him, he realized there was going to be more at stake this evening than Lady Oxley's approval.

For even as his breath caught in his throat, he knew he was lost. And he wouldn't be alone. Every man at Lady Oxley's was going to be just as captivated, just as enthralled—with this all-too-tempting woman who wasn't even supposed to exist.

Chapter 6

At first, from the look on Sedgwick's face, Emmaline surmised he'd seen Signore Donati's bill for the ceiling mural. Shock and dismay stretched from the arch of his brows to the odd, tight set of his jaw.

Well, really, what did he think such an original design should cost?

But then it struck her that he was looking at *her*. In the same strained manner he had earlier in the day after they'd kissed. As he had in the ballroom. So as his gaze rose from her hemline up to meet hers, what she spied there shocked her right down to her satin slippers.

He desired her. Found her tempting beyond redemption.

She stumbled back and bumped into the dressing table.

Oh, she should never have let Malvina and her maid get her dressed for the evening. They'd gone too far.

And you let them, a practical little voice whispered. The one that usually told her to fold a hand and leave the table.

Yet that wicked, devilish part of her had wanted to prompt this response. To see if beneath his stony exterior he was bluffing.

"Take me," she said, without really thinking.

Or perhaps she was.

"I beg your pardon?" There it was again, that arch of his brow. That skeptical look that made her wish she'd let Malvina pin her bodice a little lower.

Really, before she took these jobs, she needed to find a better source of information than her mother's old copy of *Debrett's* and the *Morning Post*.

Not that the *Post* had ever had much cause to discuss Baron Sedgwick. Until now . . .

"I—I mean to say," she stammered, "think of what it would mean to you if you took me. Once I'm gone, you will be left to live without all these pestering questions about your unknown wife."

He tipped his head and regarded her. Then he closed his eyes and drew a deep breath, as if he were considering her suggestion. But his next words surprised her.

"Who are you?" he asked.

"Emmaline Denford, Lady Sedgwick," she said softly.

"No, I mean who are *you*?"

"Does it matter?"

"You have to ask? You want me to take a lady of questionable origins before one of the most discerning hostesses in England. I have every right to know who you are."

"I can do this, Sedgwick," she assured him. "No one will doubt that I am Lady Sedgwick, if that is what you are asking."

"No. Before this charade goes on for another moment, I want to know who you are and who hired you."

Oh, bother, not this again. "I told you, I'm Emmaline—"

He staved off the rest of her answer with a curt shake of his head. "Madame, I want answers and I want them now." He stepped closer, and his very physical presence, towering over her, would have been intimidating, if she didn't know the truth.

Steady, Emmaline, she told herself. *He's bluffing.* And then she realized the truth of it. He needed her. And if he didn't know it now, he was about to realize it.

Besides, Sedgwick was many things, but a bully wasn't one of them. His cousin, now, that was another matter, but not this man. If he hadn't any heart, he would have thrown her out by now. So perhaps it was time for them to come to an understanding.

She stood her ground. "You'll not rattle the answers out of me, if that is your intent, nor will badgering uncover what you seek."

"It won't?" He shot her another look—one that said he knew other ways to get her to answer his questions, his gaze falling to her lips, as if he were remembering the searing kiss they'd shared.

Perhaps she didn't know him as well as she thought. Emmaline tried to edge back a little farther, but she was trapped by the dressing table. That and Sedgwick's suddenly intimidating presence.

"How much?" he asked.

"How much what?"

"How much will it take for you to leave?"

Emmaline drew a breath of relief. Oh, he was in worse straits than she'd imagined. "You want to pay me off?"

"Yes," he said. "How much?"

"Fifteen," she said.

His gaze narrowed. "Fifteen pounds?"

She shook her head and jerked her thumb upward.

"Outrageous!" he sputtered. "I'm not about to give you fifteen hundred pounds."

Emmaline covered her mouth and yawned. "Who said anything about fifteen hundred pounds?"

"I would think not," he shot back.

"I meant fifteen thousand."

His eyes widened. "You're mad."

She shrugged, as if such a staggering sum were nothing more than what he carried about in his pockets. "Fifteen thousand pounds and I'll walk out that door."

"You thieving little—"

She waved her finger back and forth in the air. "Now, now, now, Sedgwick, that is no way to speak to your wife." She smiled at him. "Remember, you are besotted with me. Hubert said as much. I would think a man in your condition, and, shall we say, situation, would be quite generous."

"My cousin is a horse's ass, and you, madam, are a horse thief if you think you can wheedle fifteen thousand pounds out of me. Why, I ought to—"

"But you know you can't," she told him. "However, there is a way I can gain my reward without it costing you a single farthing."

His eyes narrowed and he said nothing.

Smart fellow, she mused. He was a better gambler than he knew. Good thing for her he had never taken to dissolute living; he would have made a formidable opponent at the tables.

"What would you say to a little wager?" she offered. Again, he said nothing, so she continued undeterred. "If I can pass for Lady Sedgwick this evening, convince everyone there that I am your loving wife, you agree to allow me to continue posing as your wife for another fortnight."

He shook his head. "No. Absolutely not. This is courting disaster. This is—"

Emmaline shrugged and sailed past him, making her way to the clothespress. After opening it, she rummaged around in the bottom until she found what she was looking for.

"Aha," she muttered, plucking her valise out and putting it on a nearby chair. She returned to the dressing table and started to retrieve her few possessions.

"What are you doing?"

"What does it look like? I'm packing."

"Packing?"

"Yes. One usually does pack one's belongings before one leaves."

"Good, and good riddance," he said with smug assurance, crossing his arms over his chest.

"Yes, and do give my kind remembrances to Lady Oxley tonight."

"Harrumph," he snorted.

"And my regards to Mr. and Mrs. Denford. I'm sure they will wonder why I left on such short notice. But really, I'm sure you will have a capable excuse that will dismiss *all* their inquiries."

He flinched ever so slightly. But it was a reaction nonetheless.

And so she continued, tucking her brush and comb into her valise. "And don't forget Lady Rawlins. She'll be bereft at my defection. Of course, she'll wonder why I didn't send word, not even a note, but then she believes you've been vexed with me of late, so she can come to her own conclusions as to my odd disappearance."

Sedgwick paled and she hid her smile by turning around

and surveying the room to see if she'd missed anything.

Not that everything she owned wasn't already inside the valise—for Emmaline had a strict rule: She never unpacked.

In her line of work, there were times when a hasty departure was required and precious moments spent packing were a luxury she could ill afford.

"This is blackmail," he sputtered.

"Then give me one night to prove I can pass for your wife. And if I succeed, then I can stay for a fortnight as Lady Sedgwick. At the end of that time, I'll depart."

His gaze narrowed, but she could see the interest flickering there in the dark depths. "Without a farthing?"

"You will owe me nothing," she promised.

He blew out a disbelieving breath. "You are mad."

"I'm not the one with the imaginary wife."

"Nor am I, if you continue packing," he pointed out.

"What have you got to lose?" she asked, fearing that he was going to let her leave. "If I make a cake of myself tonight, you can claim that my prior illnesses left me unsound and that you had to send me away. You'll be pitied, but at the same time applauded for standing by such a bird-witted wife. Therefore, if I never come back, which I assume is what you want, no one will be the wiser. You have nothing to lose and everything to gain."

Perhaps this wasn't the smartest bargain she'd ever proposed. But she needed her entrée into Westley's card game, and if she couldn't convince him to take her with him tonight, she may never be able to gain it.

His jaw worked back and forth and his gaze raked over her as if he were assessing just how likely she was to succeed. Then he said the words she'd longed to hear. "One night. You convince Lady Oxley that you are my dearest wife, and you can have your fortnight."

In her relief, Emmaline rushed to him and threw her arms around his neck. "Oh, thank you, Sedgwick, thank you. You won't regret this."

And then she realized just what a tangle she'd gotten herself into . . . for to be a lady, she certainly shouldn't be entertaining the thoughts that sprang to mind the moment she found herself in his arms.

He glanced down at her and his sharp green gaze cut into her, sending tendrils of awareness down her spine—the heat of his hands at her shoulders, the way her breasts were pressed to his wall of a chest.

"Regret this? Madame, I already do," he said. Then he carefully extracted himself from her grasp. "Now hear me well: There will be no more of your stories. No more bouncers about highwaymen or other such rot. I mean it, Emmaline. Not another of your ruinous Banbury tales, or I will toss you out and tell one and all you've gone around the bend."

"Yes, Sedgwick, no more stories," she promised. "After all, it is only for one night. How hard can that be?"

He looked at her again and closed his eyes, shaking his head. Well, so much for his confidence in her.

Then he started from the room, and she called after him, "Sedgwick?"

He stopped and turned.

"You never did say how I look. Do I look like your Emmaline? Like a lady?"

He shook his head. "No. Not in the least." And then he left.

* * *

Did she look like Emmaline? What a laughable question. In his mind, Emmaline had always been a mousy sort of a chit, a shy English violet, quiet and deferential.

He'd never imagined a wife so . . . so . . . well, like a blowsy, showy peony. Fragrant and full of life, demanding attention and closer inspection.

He glanced back at the door to his suite and shook his head. Never, ever had he imagined an Emmaline who could take his breath away.

Alex retreated to the solitude of the second bedroom and began to dress himself. Simmons came in a few moments later and stepped silently into the role of valet.

"Simmons," Alex said. "Have I gone around the bend?"

"You, my lord?" The butler shook his head. "Not in the least."

"I just agreed to a bargain with that minx across the hall that if she could convince Lady Oxley she is my wife, she can stay for a fortnight."

He could have sworn the man muttered, "Thank God," but he must have been mistaken, for Simmons glanced up at him and said, "Is that wise, my lord? What with the Denfords in residence."

"No, that's why I think I've gone mad."

Simmons handed him a perfectly starched silk cloth, and Alex began tying it around his neck. In about three turns, it creased and fell awry. He tore it off and Simmons immediately had a second one at the ready.

"I must be mad." Alex ran his hand through his hair. "I'm taking a woman who is most likely a light-skirt to Lady Oxley's supper party."

Simmons said nothing, but there was no mistaking the

frown on his face. Good, at least the fellow understood the seriousness of all this.

"Did you see her?" Alex asked. "She's all done up. And she's all . . ." He waved his hand over his chest. "All showing and . . . and tumbling all over. That's it. She looks well tumbled."

Again Simmons muttered something under his breath that sounded suspiciously like, *"About time to get on with it."*

"Get on with what?" he asked, assuming what the proper fellow meant was throwing her out.

"Seeing her tumbled, my lord," Simmons said, with the same serious intonation as if he were announcing an afternoon caller.

Alex coughed. "You think I should . . . should . . . with her?"

"She is your wife, my lord."

He stared at one of his most trusted employees and spoke again, lowering his voice. "Have you forgotten that there is no Emmaline?"

"I think the very lovely lady across the hall proves otherwise," Simmons said, his broad, sure hand smoothing out a wrinkle in Alex's coat.

Whose side was his butler on anyway?

"That lady across the hall is blackmailing me into keeping her for a fortnight," he pointed out. "That lady will give most of the men at Lady Oxley's apoplexy when she arrives, more so than a new dancer at the Revue." He straightened and sent a pointed stare at Simmons. "That lady across the hall, the one you are so ready to defend, has been shot. How many ladies of the *ton* do you know who have been shot?"

"None until today, my lord."

Alex ground his teeth together, and avowed that once this Emmaline nonsense was over, he was going to see Simmons properly pensioned and sent to live in some nice quiet cottage where he could perhaps regain some semblance of his wits.

"To Lady Oxley's, of all places," he muttered, since he knew he was going to get no support from Simmons. "I must be mad. Well, my only concession is that she'll never be able to pull it off. And when she fails to pass Lady Oxley's muster, I have an out. I'll declare she's ramshackle and pack her off and no one will be the wiser. Why, she'll be forgotten before next Season."

"If you think so, my lord," Simmons said.

He glanced over at his butler again. She would be forgotten. He'd put Emmaline out of his mind the moment she left London. Forget her billowy hair, her sumptuous curves, her radiant, infectious smile. The way she looked right now, spilling out of her dress like a walking temptation.

Demmit, he swore silently. How could he take her out tonight? Any man who saw her wouldn't forget her easily. Alex heaved a sigh.

"My lord?"

"Simmons, what do I know about taking a wife out in good society?"

"Just do what comes naturally, my lord."

Naturally? He didn't dare tell Simmons what natural thoughts he was having about the lady across the hall. It had nothing to do with taking her across town to Lady Oxley's elegant house, but rather dismissing the entire staff for the night and making love to her until dawn.

"Never fear, my lord," Simmons was saying. "Lady

Rawlins spent the entire afternoon preparing Lady Sedgwick. She'll be a credit to the household."

Alex gulped. "Don't tell me that flibbertigibbet knows the truth about Emmaline?"

Simmons frowned and shook his head. "Certainly not. Lady Rawlins believes that Lady Sedgwick's upbringing is the reason behind her occasional deficiencies."

"Her upbringing?"

"In Africa. With her father, Lord Haley."

Alex closed his eyes. "Of course!" That was why she was so sure she could convince them she was Lady Sedgwick— her failures and missteps would only lend more credit to her background.

Lies and cover stories he'd embellished over the years.

Egads, the little minx had known it all along. She'd outwitted him at his own gammon. *Again.*

"She tricked me," he muttered under his breath.

Simmons looked him in the eye and smiled. It was probably the first time Alex had seen the ancient man turn his lips in that direction. "As she will everyone tonight. Have no fear, my lord. She will be a credit to your name."

That was exactly what Alex feared.

Lord and Lady Sedgwick departed from Hanover Square fashionably late, but looking like the very first diamonds of society. There wouldn't be a more handsome couple at the dinner party, of that the Sedgwick staff was positive.

"Do you think he noticed?" Mrs. Simmons asked as her husband closed the door.

"He noticed," he assured her.

"Good. We need an heir around here," Mrs. Simmons

huffed, as she went to see to the long list of demands Lady Lilith had left behind.

While the staff was feeling sure of the impending success of their lord and lady, Emmaline didn't share their confidence.

Sedgwick didn't think she looked like a lady.

Which meant he thought she looked like a . . .

She pursed her lips and stared out the window. How many country houses had she stayed in over the last six years? How many of the people she'd met in her travels had ever thought of her as anything but a gentlewoman?

Well, perhaps there had been one or two, she conceded, who might have suspected she wasn't quite what she seemed. But besides those few sharp-eyed crows and country lotharios, she'd made a tidy living impersonating a lady, albeit one of limited means.

Not a lady, indeed, she thought, glancing over at Sedgwick's stony visage. Why, she'd like nothing more than to tell him a thing or two.

First and foremost, exactly why she *did* look like a lady.

Her gown had been purchased on Bond Street, while the shawl around her shoulders had come from a shop of very exclusive and expensive Huguenot weavers—both of which were of the latest fashion. Her hair had been dressed by Malvina's French maid, whom the viscountess had lured away from the Marchioness of Madley, who'd brought the girl back from France just before the outbreak of the Revolution.

She couldn't look more like a member of the *ton* than if she had been born the daughter of a duke and listed in *Debrett's.*

But that was the problem. She wasn't. The daughter of a duke, that is. There wasn't even the barest hint of a Right and Honorable in her lineage.

No matter the clothes, no matter the manners she aped with practiced perfection, beneath it all, she knew the truth.

She was nothing more than the daughter of a highwayman and a lunatic.

There it was. Her sorry past. She wondered what Sedgwick would say to that.

She knew exactly what he'd say. He'd recant their bargain and toss her out of the carriage without a glance back, wiping his hands of this entire wretched chapter of his life.

For he was right on all counts: She certainly was no lady. Ladies didn't roam about the countryside, conning and gulling respectable people.

She spared another furtive glance in his direction. And he was worried about how she'd appear! Why, if one didn't know better, one might mistake him for some brawler from the docks, what with his once-handsome face at half mourning. But dash it all, even with this new arrangement of his features, no one would ever mistake him for anything but a gentleman. He could forgo the perfectly tied cravat, the fashionably cut coat—it was in his bearing, his very stance that declared to one and all that he carried generations of noble blood in his veins.

Twenty-one, to be exact.

Emmaline sighed, and when he glanced over at her, she tossed her curls and stared out the window.

So why was she suddenly having these ridiculous fantasies of him ignoring centuries of noble tradition and declaring her his perfect baroness? Of being able to tell him everything about herself, and know that it would matter naught to him.

Oh, but it would. For Alexander Denford, Baron Sedgwick, would never see her as anything but . . . Demmit, what had he called her? *A thieving little—*

Emmaline closed her eyes and leaned her head against the carriage wall. If only he hadn't been so close to the truth.

"Are you well?" he asked.

He needn't sound so hopeful that she was about to fall ill. "Yes. I'm fine."

"Because if you want to—"

"No," she shot back. She'd prove to this handsome, stuffy fellow that she was every bit as much of a lady as his fictional, imaginary Emmaline could ever have been. Why, she'd—

Before she could finish that thought, the carriage came to a sudden halt, jolting her forward and throwing her into Sedgwick. He caught her with those oh-so-steely arms, even as she slammed into the wall of his chest.

They were nose to nose, their lips but a breath apart, and Emmaline thanked every one of her ignoble ancestors that she wasn't a lady.

Because she couldn't help but believe that ladies never had the scandalous thoughts that were assailing her this very moment.

He looked about to say something and she feared the worst. He'd deny her. Tell her again she was a fraud, even while the warmth of his touch scorched her bare arms, sent fiery memories through her limbs. Memories of how those fingers had burned as they'd caressed her earlier.

She couldn't breathe, she couldn't think, assailed by very unladylike desires to have him do more than just stare at her.

Then she knew she wasn't alone in her passion, for she was pressed intimately against him.

Very intimately.

Even through all the layers between them, she could feel that telling hardness, that very masculine length of unyielding and unrelenting promise of rapture.

"Hmmm," she purred happily, without even realizing she'd done it, or that she was leaning closer, her hips rocking toward him, as if to gain their own estimation of just what he had beneath all that wretched wool and silk between them.

Then just as suddenly she realized what she was doing. Heavens, she was acting like the worst sort of doxy. What was it about this man that had her so transfixed by desire?

"I—I mean to say, I'm so sorry . . ." she stammered.

"I'm not," he said, tipping his head until his lips caught hers, stealing the kiss she'd vowed never to offer.

Yes, well, she'd reconsider that vow tomorrow, because right now there was no denying him. Not when his lips caressed hers, when his teeth pulled at her bottom lip, suckling her, drawing her toward him with the same greedy temptation that her hips had found but a few moments before.

Emmaline opened herself to his heady exploration.

Certainly this was no time to be a lady.

Chapter 7

Alex should have known better than to kiss Emmaline. How had it happened? One moment she'd looked positively ill and the next thing he knew she was in his arms and gazing up at him with those innocent blue eyes.

Innocent, indeed! Her body had molded to his until it had been impossible to deny her—like a cat stretching and purring, waiting and oh-so-willing to be scratched.

From the scent of her perfume to the press of her full breasts against his chest to the provocative way her hips rode up along him, there was nothing innocent about this minx.

Just pure sensual intoxication.

And amidst this rising tide of passion, a chorus rang in his ears.

Well tumbled . . . you've had her . . . mussed . . . what comes naturally . . .

All the ill-gained advice he'd received during the day suddenly made sense. At least that was what he told himself as he lowered his mouth to hers and tasted what further devilment could be found in this wretched tangle.

Yet, the moment his lips touched her silken pair, he knew he was lost.

Bloody hell, a wife shouldn't taste so intoxicating . . . like fine brandy on the tongue. Neither should a woman fit to a man like she'd been measured and cut to his design.

But Emmaline did. She was all these things.

Alex continued to kiss her, drawing her closer, one hand cupped to the small of her back, while the other rose to cradle one of her breasts, full and rounded in the confines of her corset.

His thumb rolled over the nipple, and it hardened beneath his touch, reminding him of his own rampant arousal.

"Sedgwick," she gasped. Her back arched and her shoulders rolled back until it felt as if her breasts would spill from her gown, fall into his eager grasp like ripe fruit. As he stroked her anew, this time she sighed. "Oh, Sedgwick."

The sound of his name on her lips only made him want to hear her say it over and over, until she found her release with him buried deep inside her.

Lord, he should have tossed her out of his house the instant he'd arrived in London.

But there was something about Emmaline that kept him at sixes and sevens. Had him brawling in the streets. Had him kissing a woman he barely knew and wishing there was a way to stop time, to keep her in his arms forever.

"Ahem, milord," came Henry's discreet cough, followed by a knock on the carriage door. "We're here."

"Um, yes, thank you," he managed to say as he wrenched himself away from her, tossing her onto the other seat. He'd quite forgotten where he was, that he was in a carriage in front of Lord Oxley's town house. Then he glanced up at Emmaline, her lips swollen from his kisses, her eyes wide and full of passion. Her breasts rose and fell with her ragged breathing, while her once-perfectly-done curls fell down around her shoulders like those of some intoxicating nymph.

Gads, he'd done all that? Whatever had come over him?

"I . . . I . . ." he stammered. What the hell did one say to a woman who was supposed to be his wife yet whom he shouldn't be kissing?

She said it for him. Emmaline reached up, cupped his face in her delicate gloved hand and smiled at him, a sad, tired light in her eyes. "I know, Sedgwick. I know."

Then, with an elegant ladylike grace, she got down out of the carriage and walked into the Oxley town house like a duchess, leaving him in her wake.

Leaving him to wonder how the hell he was ever going to let her go.

Because letting her go was the only practical thing he could do.

Having dined with country gentry, baronets and even a few newly elevated peers, Emmaline soon discovered that none of it had prepared her for a London supper party.

The Oxley town house was a study in noble elegance. Italian marbles, damask and velvet curtains, rich gilt trims. The house was aglitter in all its splendor, a house meant to dazzle the eye and put the guest on notice that this was a higher realm.

She took a deep breath. *I am a baroness now, a member of this rarefied company.* If she wanted to continue being Lady Sedgwick she needed to comport herself accordingly.

Head up, shoulders back, a slight smile on your lips, she told herself as she handed her wrap over to one of the bevy of servants lined up to assist the arriving guests.

Now all she had to do was maintain this haughty, ladylike composure the rest of the evening and she'd as good as have won her bargain with Sedgwick.

Yes, that would be quite easy if her lips weren't still swollen from his kisses, her body not burning with the passion of his heated touch.

Bother! How was she ever going to maintain any sense of decorum if she had to live under the same roof as that man for another two weeks without . . . well, without! Oh, she was in worse straits than when she'd been shot and left for dead.

Certainly this wasn't her fault in the least, she reasoned. She'd been assured the baron was a predictable sort, overly honorable and rather dull. Certainly she'd been deceived on those accounts. Or perhaps it was Sedgwick who'd fooled the *ton,* gulled his family and servants for all these years, hiding his true nature behind duty and honor.

But who couldn't see that his eyes held a rare fire of intrigue, that he had the mercurial temper of a Greek god or that hidden behind all his stuffy manners was the passionate heart of a lover waiting to be discovered? If only she didn't see him so clearly, desire him so utterly.

As if on cue, there he was at her side, a model of noble composure and not a hint of the passionate man who'd nearly ravished her in the carriage. He held out his arm to her, warm and steady, and she placed her palm on his sleeve, ignoring the way her body thrilled in recognition.

Emmaline glanced up at him, even as he looked down at her. In that instance, their gazes met and she felt his confidence in her. Knew she had won before the evening had even begun.

All she had to do was smile and keep her opinions to herself. No meddling, no Banbury tales.

How hard could that be when there was so much at stake?

Everything went perfectly until the ladies left the gentlemen to their port and cigars and retired to the drawing room.

Emmaline continued to press her lips together and maintain her vow not to say anything untoward. All too quickly though, it became like the time she'd promised herself never again to play piquet. While her resolve was genuine, she failed utterly.

"You will not believe what I heard about Lady Bennett," their hostess, Lady Oxley, was saying. "She's gone and left her husband."

"No!" several of the ladies gasped, sounding properly shocked while their faces were as eager as a bevy of alley cats outside a fishmonger's shop.

Emmaline held her tongue. She'd once spent a week at the Lord and Lady Bennett's and knew for a fact that Lord Bennett was a beast. He thrashed his staff for the least little offenses, and when there was no one else left to discipline, he took the remainder of his venom out on his defenseless wife.

"'Tisn't surprising," Lady Oxley said. "Her mother was a Thorpe and that family is highly irregular." She said this with a pointed glance at Mrs. Mabberly and her daughter, who both sat like a pair of proper statues on the edge of the sofa.

As she said the word "irregular" Emmaline could see

Miss Mabberly flinch. It wasn't the first time during the evening that Lady Oxley had gone out of her way to send a pointed, but oh, so discreet barb at her future daughter-in-law. Miss Mabberly wasn't even married to the earl yet, and already Lady Oxley was putting her on notice that she didn't find his choice up to par.

Meanwhile, the ladies around them were already discussing the Thorpes and their propensity for flighty behavior.

"It comes from marrying beneath you," Lady Oxley was saying.

"Not all of us are lucky enough to escape such a fate," Lady Diana Fordham commented dryly, though Emmaline sensed the woman was in sympathy with Miss Mabberly.

"At least you discovered the truth about that awful Captain Danvers, my dear, before you wed him," Lady Jarvis offered. "Turned traitor," she explained in an aside to Emmaline.

"Still, it is unfortunate how haphazard marriage has become," Lady Oxley was saying.

Emmaline glanced over at Miss Mabberly and felt the girl's discomfort as if it were her own. It was on the tip of her tongue to point out to the countess that while Miss Mabberly's father was a *cit,* her mother descended from a noble lineage that went back to the times of Edward III. Her nobility far exceeded Lady Oxley's own heritage.

"Breeding will always tell, won't it?" Lady Jarvis was saying, adding her own snide comment in the direction of the future Lady Oxley.

"I couldn't agree more," Lady Oxley said.

Miss Mabberly turned a bright shade of pink and stared down at her slippers. Why, the girl couldn't be more than ten and six, Emmaline fumed, and hadn't the wherewithal or experience to defend herself. Someone really should stand up for her.

Leave well enough alone, Emmaline told herself. *This is none of your concern.*

Hadn't she learned time and time again that meddling in the affairs of others was the surest way to find herself out in the road with no roof over her head?

But she couldn't help herself—the girl looked to be on the verge of tears, and that would never do. It would give Lady Oxley fuel to make her daughter-in-law's life a living hell.

Emmaline glanced behind her at the double doors that led to the dining room. They remained shut tight, the men encamped behind them, probably knee-deep in cigars and port or whatever it was that they did when the ladies left them to their own devices, so therefore, Sedgwick would never have to know.

"I'm shocked you would say such a thing, Lady Oxley," Emmaline piped up, surprising all by suddenly joining the conversation. Surprising even herself.

In for a pence, out for a pound, she thought, digging into her resolve.

"Perhaps with your savage upbringing and poor health, Lady Sedgwick, you haven't the opportunity to witness the refinement that careful breeding brings to society." Lady Oxley's remark might have been enough to daunt most ladies, but Emmaline didn't fall under those restraints.

Goodness, not being a lady *was* a blessing.

She squared her shoulders and smiled at her hostess. "I just would think that someone with Thorpe ancestors would hardly be in a position to cast such stones at another relation, albeit a distant one."

Lady Oxley's eyes narrowed. "Are you implying that I am related to Lady Bennett?"

Emmaline smiled. "Not implying, just simply stating fact. Your mother was a Harris, wasn't she?"

Lady Oxley nodded, her lips too tightly drawn for the woman to speak.

"And her father was the Earl of Whitehead?"

She nodded again.

"The Earl of Whitehead's grandmother was a Hastings."

The sharp-eyed matron's brows knit together. "What has that got to do with the Thorpes?"

"Her father, Baron Hastings, inherited the title from his cousin, Reginald Hastings. That Hastings line was descended from Sir Reginald Thorpe. You and Lady Thorpe are cousins of a sort." Emmaline smoothed out the folds of her gown and then looked up and smiled. "I fear those sorts of cousinly distinctions leave me terribly muddled. But bloodlines are bloodlines, are they not?"

Lady Oxley went as white as her lace fichu. "That is impossible. I think I know my own lineage."

"Not at all impossible," Emmaline replied. "A copy of *Debrett's* will bear me out." She sat back on the sofa and sighed. "Breeding, Lady Oxley, is only one facet of a lady."

Lady Lilith rose abruptly, her face flushed. "I will fetch mother's copy immediately, and you shall see—"

"Lilith, sit," her mother ordered. "I am sure that Lady Sedgwick is just confused about the connection."

Not likely, Emmaline wanted to reply, but she needn't worry about her assertion. She'd bet her last farthing that every lady in the room was going to go straight home and spend the rest of the night poring over their copy of *Debrett's* until they found the wicked bend in Lady Oxley's family tree.

And find it they would.

But not before they got to witness Lady Oxley sharpen her claws all over Lady Sedgwick.

Emmaline could feel the woman's malice fill the room. But at least it was no longer directed at a defenseless young girl.

"Lady Sedgwick, how entertaining you are—tell me, how is it you are so familiar with *Debrett's*? I wouldn't think such things would matter in the deep reaches of the jungle."

"I learned to read with a copy left to me by my dear departed mother." Emmaline did her best to look woebegone for the loss of her saintly parent. After all, that much was true. Her mother's only possession had been the battered record of peerages that Emmaline still carried today. Though rarely in her right mind, the lady had taught her daughter to read from it and it was there that her talent for memorization had come to light.

By six she'd been reciting lineages like most children sang nursery rhymes. And her enterprising father had seen that this talent would be better served in a more economical fashion, by teaching his daughter to count cards.

But that was a skill for another time.

Emmaline drew her handkerchief up to dab at her eyes. "My dear mother gave so much to stay by my father's side. Her very life."

Several other women in the room nodded in agreement.

There, Emmaline thought, *let Lady Oxley cast stones at the virtuous and dedicated Lady Haley.*

"How touching," the countess said without a bit of sympathy. "Now here you are with us, quite recovered." Lady Oxley's eyes narrowed and Emmaline didn't doubt for a moment that the woman was moving in for her social kill. "How is that, my dear? How could it be that you've been so close to death's door for so long, and now, why to look at you, one could hardly imagine that you've ever been sick a day in your life."

All heads turned at this volley, looking to see how the newcomer in their midst would respond.

Emmaline rose to the challenge. "How right you are, Lady Oxley. It is hard to believe that I am the woman before you. But I can say with all honesty that I would not be here today if it had not been for the extraordinary lengths my dearest, beloved Sedgwick went to, in order to see that I lived."

"Sedgwick?" Lady Oxley asked. She shot sideways glances of disbelief to her cronies, who all tittered in agreement.

"Yes, my husband," Emmaline declared as if there could be no doubt to her statement.

Lady Oxley smiled at her allies, rallying her troops. "Are you telling us that Lord Sedgwick is responsible for your miraculous recovery?" She smirked again.

"Quite so." Again, the truth was such a strong foundation. If Sedgwick hadn't invented Emmaline, she wouldn't be there before them. He was all too responsible for her arrival in society.

"Let me guess," Lady Oxley said, tapping her fan against her thin lips. "It was his dearest devotion that worked this miracle." This time the titters and snickers were less discreet.

"Exactly," Emmaline said, the beginnings of a tale creeping up inside her. She glanced at the door again and saw there was still no sign of the gentlemen. Besides, it would only be a small bouncer, the tiniest of lies. Not hardly worth recalling.

At least not in front of Sedgwick.

"Harrumph," Lady Oxley was sputtering. "Sedgwick, indeed."

"You see, Lady Oxley," Emmaline said, ignoring the lady's disbelief, "up until three months ago, I couldn't even rise out of bed, I was so weak and ravaged by sudden fevers. Last winter the doctor wrote to Sedgwick to come immediately, for he feared the end was very close."

Lady Pepperwell gasped.

Emmaline lowered her head and shook it slightly. "Yes, I was very near death's door." Perhaps not death's door, but she'd certainly been in dun territory. Becoming Lady Sedgwick had saved her life. Quite literally.

"What happened?" ventured Lady Pepperwell. Despite Malvina's assertions that she was poor *ton,* Emmaline thought she was, if anything, a kindly woman with a tender heart.

The kind she had taken advantage of time and time again, she thought. Why was it that this had never bothered her before, but now . . .

"Yes, whatever did Sedgwick do?" Lady Diana asked, prodding Emmaline out of her reverie.

"S-Sedgwick?" she stammered. "Oh, yes, Sedgwick. He came at once, braving snowdrifts that could have buried him, so he could be at my side. When he arrived, cold and nearly frozen, his fears so clearly etched on his brow, I was overcome with guilt as to how much my condition had beset him."

Out of the corner of her eye, she spied one of the younger ladies pulling a handkerchief out and dabbing her eyes.

Emmaline continued, warming to her story, ignoring the fact that she shouldn't be telling it in the first place. "That night I overheard dear Sedgwick confiding to the doctor that he didn't know what he would do if I were to die."

"Perhaps remarry?" Lady Oxley suggested.

"No, I fear not," Emmaline told her. "You must know the Sedgwick barons are overly cautious when it comes to marriage, but to wed twice?" Emmaline shook her head. "No, I knew he would never marry again. And that was my worst fear. That Sedgwick would carry his love for me to the grave. That he would die without an heir—"

"Well, you know quite well he has an heir," Lady Lilith sputtered.

"Certainly Hubert would inherit," Emmaline told her. "But I know Sedgwick longed for his own son. *Several of them.* As much as he trusts and respects Hubert, a man wants *his* own stock to carry on." *Not some beastly shirttail relation,* was her implication. Ignoring Lady Lilith's outraged moue, she continued. "So right there and then, I resolved to live, and I told Sedgwick so. He was so taken with my determination that he spent every waking minute caring for me."

There was another "harrumph" from Lady Oxley, but her once-rapt audience was now paying her little heed.

"He carried me from my bed each morning, insisting that I take fresh air, even if it was just a chair by the window. He ordered delicacies brought from London for me to have with my tea." She glanced up shyly at her rapt audience. "He even brought me small bouquets of flowers for my bedside on the days when my health truly prevented me from arising. Yellow ones, for he knows they are my very favorite."

Now so caught up in her own fiction, Emmaline continued unabashedly, pulling her thread so taut it was hard to believe it didn't snap under the weight of her lies. "As it was, his heroism, his faith were a tonic to my soul. 'Emmaline,' he would say, 'Emmaline, my dearest Emmaline, live so that I may spend the end of my days with you by my side.' " She managed to force up a tear or two, perfect punctuation for her whopping story. "And at night, he would hold my hand and read to me from my father's letters, begging me to remember the deep love that had moved my mother to follow my father to Africa. To let her example of dedication and perseverance be my path." She bowed her head in reverence, praying that her story would hold together.

And so it seemed it did. Several of the ladies were crying openly, no longer worrying about risking Lady Oxley's ire.

"I can scarcely believe it," one of them said. "Sedgwick? He's always been so . . . so . . . What I mean to say, Lady Sedgwick, is that your husband has always been a bit of a—"

"Dullard," Lady Oxley interjected. "Lady Sedgwick, I can't believe you are going to lead us all to believe that the Baron Sedgwick we all know is a caring and overly compassionate man?"

Emmaline straightened. "Love, Lady Oxley, has a way of bringing to light what is of the utmost importance. And while the baron hasn't always been the most attentive of husbands, I can assure you, of late he has come to realize the importance of being a caring and devoted spouse."

A round of applause broke out behind her. Emmaline spun around to find the doors to the salon now open and the company of gentlemen filling the open space. One of them, the Marquis of Templeton, she thought, was leading the round of approval with enthusiastic clapping.

She didn't need to guess how long they'd all been standing there listening to her story.

One look at Sedgwick's furious features told her it had been long enough that she was about to suffer a very fatal reversal to her current state of good health and fortune.

Chapter 8

Alex flinched as first the Marquis of Templeton, then most of the ladies in the room, broke out in applause.

No more stories, he'd told her. *Absolutely, no more stories.*

And what had she done? Spun another sticky yarn from which he'd be forced to navigate an escape.

"Lady Sedgwick, I for one applaud your good health, and declare you a most welcome arrival in our midst," Templeton announced, wiping at his eyes as if they were as filled with the same tears as many of the other ladies exhibited.

Lady Oxley didn't look like celebrating—not in the least. The woman looked positively murderous.

So besides Emmaline's ridiculous tale about her miraculous recovery, what else had she been up to? She'd only been alone with the ladies for an hour.

He closed his eyes for a moment. *Only an hour?* It

wouldn't have surprised him to arrive in the room and find every social convention turned upside down in her unconventional wake.

"I wondered why Sedgwick was so keen to return to the ladies," the Earl of Oxley was saying. "And now we discover the truth—he fancies his wife." The man laughed, and was joined by several of the other gentlemen.

Hubert had the nerve to chime in. "Utterly besotted," he told them. "Just last night he was—"

"Mr. Denford!" Lady Lilith exclaimed, surprising Alex by coming to his rescue. Albeit only for a moment. She continued by saying, "I don't think that is . . . Well, there are young ladies present." She finished her admonishment with an arch of her brow that said more than if she had let her husband finish his lascivious tale.

Lady Oxley obviously took her daughter's cue and decided to toss some more kindling on the pyre. "Sedgwick, I can't believe all your wife has been telling us. Such remarkable tales of dedication and loving attention. Why, it seems impossible!"

Alex shot a glance at Emmaline, who sat demurely studying the tips of her slippers, the very epitome of feminine modesty. He knew better.

To his chagrin, Lady Pepperwell spoke up. "It makes me weep to think how your rare demonstration of affection saved this dear girl, Lord Sedgwick. And here I always thought you such a dull, stuffy fellow." She reached over and patted Emmaline's hand affectionately, while her watery blue eyes looked about to well up with more tears. "I for one shall laud your dedication to all who will listen." That comment was shot in Lady Oxley's direction.

There was a nod of heads from around the room.

Lady Diana spoke up as well. "Indeed, my lord. Constancy in one's affections is a trait to be admired. Your wife, envied."

No, no, no! Alex wanted to bemoan. The last thing he needed was a parade of champions for Emmaline. It was bad enough that Lady Rawlins had taken her under her wing and Simmons held her in favor, but now she was gaining the patronage of some of the most gossipy and influential women in society.

With them on her side, he'd never be rid of her. Not without hiring a team of Covent Garden playwrights to devise a convincing script for her exit.

"That really isn't necessary," he told them, forcing out the words to sound as kindly as he could.

"Not necessary? Of course it is," Lady Pepperwell declared. "If you were willing to walk through snowdrifts last winter to be by her side during our dear Emmaline's darkest hour, then I, sir, can use my poor influence for your sake, as well as hers."

"Snowdrifts?" Lord Oxley snorted. "You wouldn't catch me walking through a snowbank for my wife."

"Not unless someone had dropped a farthing in it," the Marquis of Templeton muttered under his breath as he passed by Alex on his way to the sideboard. When he got there, he poured two glasses of port and handed one to Alex. "Fortification, my good man. You look like you need it," he said quietly.

Meanwhile, Oxley had come to stand behind his betrothed, Miss Mabberly. "Marriage isn't about all that romantic drivel, Sedgwick. It is about making the right match." He dropped a meaty paw down on the poor chit's shoulder and gave her a shake, like one might a favored hunting hound. The girl looked terrified enough to jump out of her chair and bolt for the door.

"My lord, you'll find Miranda quite above all that nonsense," Mr. Mabberly declared. "Got a level head on her shoulders, our gel does."

"Oh, yes," her mother added. "Miranda is very much aware of the favor you've bestowed upon her, upon all of us with your choice, Lord Oxley."

The earl postured and preened behind his bride-to-be. "I'd think so. She's about to join the highest order of society. I'd say that's enough to keep most wives happy for a good ten or twenty years."

"Poor chit," Templeton muttered under his breath.

Alex took a glance at the man beside him. He didn't know Templeton all that well, for what he'd seen of the fellow hadn't ever recommended him—a frippery sort, always done in the latest fashions, if not setting the newest craze. His company ensured merriment and a litany of jests and jabs that would be repeated for weeks to come.

But there was nothing merry and light about the man's words tonight.

And even odder yet, when Alex looked at him again, he found the marquis' gaze lingering across the room on the unlikely person of Lady Diana Fordham.

The very proper Lady Diana and the outlandish Templeton?

The moment didn't last long, for the marquis glanced over, as if he had sensed being caught in some secret rite, a deeply private ritual. In that instant, Alex saw the man's heart in his eyes—a veritable Pandora's box of regret and sadness and envy.

Envy? Envy for what?

He soon found out.

Templeton raised his glass and said, "Then perhaps, Lord Oxley, I can give you this advice about marriage—a subject to which I have infinite knowledge and woeful lack of experience from which to draw upon." The room broke out in polite laughter. "I would suggest following Lord Sedgwick's example—for devotion to one's partner never goes out of style."

"Hear, hear," everyone repeated as they raised their glasses.

While a few others added their own toasts, Templeton turned to Alex and said in an aside, "Few men find a wife worthy of such devotion, and even fewer still are smart enough to keep her."

Alex felt himself at a loss amidst the wistful note in Templeton's words. No, he realized, what the man was offering was advice, to be taken to heart before he suffered some selfsame loss.

Around the room, the toasts and well-wishes flowed toward him, and Alex shifted from one foot to the other under the weight. He didn't deserve any of this praise, nor the envious and covetous looks from the ladies around the room. Especially when he knew the truth—he wasn't the man Emmaline had described in such glowing terms.

But as she'd sat there, describing this paragon of husbandly devotion, he'd found himself considering an odd notion.

Was it possible to love a woman so deeply? So utterly?

More so, could he be such a man? Be the man that Emmaline had described with words that rang from the depth of her heart?

He shook his head and set such thoughts aside. It was

nothing more than tomfoolery, ridiculous figments of her imagination, just as Emmaline had always been a figment of his.

But he couldn't shake the sense of shame that he wasn't anything like the man Emmaline had described.

No, he was probably more like Oxley than he cared to admit . . . like most of the men in the room, viewing marriage as nothing more than an alliance between two worthy families.

Except for the Marquis of Templeton. He seemed to possess a rare understanding as to what Emmaline had been saying. Suddenly Alex found himself envying the man. Envying the pain in his eyes, the heart-wrenching desire for a woman he couldn't have. For wasn't that what love was? The hope, the longing for something that was just out of reach?

And only a man brave enough to cross that chasm ever discovered the rapture that poets eulogized, that eluded common souls.

He wanted to tell one and all that he was just a regular coward. That it wasn't in him to have done even a fraction of what Emmaline had credited to him.

Yet there she was, so full of life, living and breathing, and so very much within his grasp. And the magic that she'd spun tonight, in her kiss and in her far-fetched tales, urged him to take that giant leap into the unknown and be that reckless, fearless man.

Much to Alex's relief, latecomers were announced—Sir Francis and Lady Neeley—cousins of Lady Oxley's who were obviously forgiven their tardy arrival for the diversion they provided.

Introductions were made all around, and in the resulting

chaos, Alex slanted a glance at Emmaline—only to find her eyes riveted on the arriving baronet and his belaced and fussy wife.

Any of the high color she'd gained from her sortie with Lady Oxley had drained from her face.

Then he looked again at the new arrivals and realized she knew them.

And in turn, they must know her.

From her deathly pallor, the acquaintance wasn't something she looked forward to renewing. She rose from her seat and moved slowly to the back of the room, putting as much distance as she could between herself and the Neeleys.

Short of leaping from the window, which right now she looked quite capable of doing.

Demmit, what had he been thinking, bringing her here? Her assurances earlier returned to taunt him.

No one will doubt that I am Lady Sedgwick.

No one, indeed! Apparently that wasn't so true. And now, to his horror, her mysterious past was about to be unveiled. In front of Lady Lilith and Hubert, in front of Lady Oxley, in front of the worst gossips in the *ton*.

Yet instead of feeling the kind of panic that came with one's social demise, oddly enough, all he could feel was that there had to be something he could do to save her.

Not himself, not his position. *Save Emmaline*. In a thrice, he crossed the room and took her hand in his, setting it on his sleeve and taking a casual stance, as if it were the most natural thing for him to do.

Lady Oxley turned to them last. "And cousins, you know Lord Sedgwick, but here is his wife, Lady Sedgwick, so long from town, but now blessedly in our midst," she said, though not sounding the least pleased about Emmaline's arrival. "Lady Sedgwick, may I present my cousins, Sir Francis Neeley, and his dear wife, Lady Neeley."

Emmaline made a polite curtsy and kept her face demurely tipped toward the floor.

"Now, aren't you a pretty little thing," Sir Francis said, coming closer. "Not hard to guess why your husband has kept you out in the country with all this illness nonsense—wants to make sure none of these rakish devils about town catch your eye and make you a cuckold, eh Sedgwick?" The old man laughed in a wheezy voice, with only the earl and a few others joining him.

The few, Alex noted, who had spent most of the evening eyeing Emmaline with just that same rakish glee.

"Now let me get a closer look at you, Lady Sedgwick," the baronet said. "You look familiar. I declare, have we met? Been to Nottinghamshire of late, have you?"

Emmaline pulled her lips into a polite smile, but all Alex could see was a ripple of panic cross her features.

"No, my lord," she said. "I don't see how we could have met. I've never been to the northern counties."

Sir Francis shook his head. "I'm never wrong on these accounts. We have met. Play cards, do you? I never forget anyone I take a few pounds from, or worse yet, those I lose to." He laughed again. "Perhaps it was at the Shackleford-Demsley house party last winter. Now, there was a full house, easy to miss someone in that crowd."

"No, it wasn't me," Emmaline told him, edging away from Sir Francis's close inspection. "I fear I haven't the talent for cards or travel."

"No talent for cards, eh?" Lord Westly piped in. "Then, madam, you are most welcome at my annual piquet challenge. As long as your devoted husband is willing to put forth your stake."

Everyone laughed at his joke, as did Emmaline, but Alex knew that what was at stake this moment was much higher.

And while Emmaline's disavowal and disclaimers might have been enough for most people, not so for Sir Francis. He wasn't Lady Oxley's relation for nothing—persistent and dogged.

"Letty," he said, waving to his wife. "Who does she look like?"

Lady Neeley spared Emmaline a squinting glance and shook her head. "I haven't the slightest notion." In an aside to Lady Jarvis, whom she'd taken a seat beside, she said, "My husband thinks everyone looks like someone."

The assembled company laughed, even Emmaline, though her performance sounded forced to Alex.

"I don't think that," Sir Francis protested. "I'm usually correct when I say I've met someone, and I swear I've met Lady Sedgwick."

"Oh, bother, Francis," Lady Neeley declared. "You won't be fit company until we get to the bottom of this." She glanced at her friend. "May I?" she extended her hand and Lady Jarvis placed her lorgnette into her palm. Flipping it open, Lady Neeley held it to her eyes and gave Emmaline a long, searching gaze. Her lips pursed together and her brow furrowed, then it was as if she came to some untold conclusion and snapped the glasses shut with a definitive click. "I daresay she—and please, Lady Sedgwick, don't be offended—bears a passing resemblance to that cheeky woman the Duchess of Cheverton keeps as a companion. The one the Shackleford-Demsley's took in last winter when the gel was robbed on her way back to rejoin Her

Grace. You remember her, Francis, the one who beat everyone at parmiel and then disappeared so abruptly."

Sir Francis slapped his knee. "Yes, so she does. Scandalous wench, that Miss Doyle."

"Not that horrid Miss Doyle," Lady Jarvis exclaimed. "My sister was taken advantage by that wretched gel three years ago. After Regina afforded her every comfort and consideration, the gel turned around and paid her back by convincing my niece to elope with the neighbor's *second* son." She paused, her brows drawn up in high arches. "It was well known she was intended for the heir." The lady heaved an aggrieved sigh. "And if that wasn't bad enough, she disappeared quite altogether without so much as an apology. Interfering, wretched woman. She quite ruined my niece with her meddling."

"I say, it is a shame Her Grace keeps the gel employed," Lady Neeley said. "I wrote to the duchess to inform her of her companion's scandalous conduct and she wrote me back and told me to mind my own business." She sniffed with indignation. "Mind my own business! Have you ever heard such a thing? The duchess is lucky the baggage hasn't robbed her blind."

Heads shook in dismay. A few others added what they had heard of the duchess's infamous companion, but Alex had stopped listening to their indignant chatter.

Well, now he had an answer to one question. Who Emmaline was.

She was this Miss Doyle, this parmiel-playing, reckless, meddling companion of the Duchess of Cheverton. The duchess most likely had finally grown tired of her employee's peccadilloes and dismissed her. And now this infamous chit was masquerading as his wife.

Alex ground his teeth, considering all the ways he was going to toss her into the streets. Damn Lady Lilith and Hubert, damn the ensuing gossip. He was done being gulled and certainly wasn't going to be clucked over by the gossips of the *ton* when her true identity came to light.

But even as he fumed and railed against the fates that had brought her conniving ways to his door, he glanced over at her.

He never should have looked.

For at that moment, she glanced up at him, and the look in her eyes, the fear and desperation there, stripped bare his pride, tore away his anger.

By God, she was terrified.

As she should be, he tried to tell himself with every bit of righteous offense he could muster. But that sentiment was hard to hold on to when he realized how pompous, how haughty the self-righteous jury assembled around her sounded.

"Why, I rarely lose at parmiel," Sir Francis was saying, "and that gel took me for twenty pounds. Ruthless at cards, she was. Without a bit of conscience."

Twenty pounds, Alex had to guess, was what Sir Francis probably lost every night at cards, so why was he so indignant? Was it because it was to someone he considered beneath him?

"Well, if I were ever to meet with this Miss Doyle," Lady Oxley declared, "I wouldn't offer her a moment of charity. I'd send her packing right back to her employer. I have always made it a rule never to offer aid to strangers and those less deserving." She sent a pointed glance toward Mrs. Mabberly and her daughter.

"Yes, quite so," Lord Templeton chimed in, coming to

stand by the pair of ladies. "Charity is best left to those whose heart is capable of placing the needs of others well above their own. Mrs. Mabberly and her daughter's attention to the poor widows and orphans of town make them such a delightful oddity."

"An oddity for sure," Lady Oxley declared. "Throwing good money after bad, if you ask me."

Her son swaggered to the forefront. "Never worry, Mother. There'll be none of that charitable nonsense from Miss Mabberly once we are wed."

Mother and daughter exchanged brief glances. Obviously this was news to them.

Oxley gave his intended another well-intentioned shake. "You won't see any of our blunt going into those foolhardy baskets for widows and orphans. No more of those soirees to aid education. Can't tolerate educated women. Makes them coarse."

Apparently, Oxley wasn't opposed to marrying one if she came with a tidy dowry.

"But I—" Miss Mabberly began to say, but was cut off by a sharp retort from her father.

"I couldn't agree more," Mr. Mabberly told the earl. "Never been all that comfortable with this Ladies' Aid Society myself." He turned such a hard look toward his wife and daughter, Alex suspected it could have stopped the French rabble from storming the Bastille.

No, if anything, Alex felt an uncharacteristic pang for Miss Mabberly. Yet why should he care if the young lady would have to foreswear her own interests for that of her husband's? That was how it ought to be.

Wasn't it?

But another glance at the misery written across the girl's

youthful features chided him in ways he'd never considered.

"I will strive to be the perfect wife," Miss Mabberly was saying as if she were repeating a hard-earned lesson.

"Yes, yes, of course you will try," Lady Oxley told her. "I've made it no secret that I am not pleased with this union, but my son tells me it is his sincere wish to wed you, and thus I must respect his decision." There wasn't anyone in the room who didn't understand what the soon-to-be dowager was saying. Respect her son's decision, yes, she could own to that. Make her new daughter-in-law welcome? Well, that was another matter. "I am sure that under my careful and diligent guidance," she said, "you may yet make a tolerable wife for him."

Such poisonous encouragement only served to make the poor chit pale even further. Alex couldn't help thinking the girl would be better off married to a spendthrift like Jack, or living her life as a lowly spinster.

Luckily for Miss Mabberly, one of the other matrons launched into a long complaint about her ill-bred daughter-in-law, drawing the attention away from her. The girl made a brief excuse to her mother, then fled the room. As she brushed past him, Alex could see the tears brimming in her eyes.

Oh, demmit, he cursed silently. He had more problems than he knew what to do with, without adding some Bath miss's tears to his burdens. He wasn't responsible for Miss Mabberly's fate. Yet as the minutes ticked by and she didn't return, he wondered if someone shouldn't go see to her. He certainly couldn't go—more scandal was the last thing he needed. But he knew someone who could.

He turned a pleading glance at Emmaline and found that she too was watching the door.

"Can I . . . ?" she whispered.

He nodded and Emmaline squeezed his arm, then wove her way gracefully through the room and slipped out the door.

There, Alex thought. He no longer had to worry about the situation. Emmaline was a woman. She could tend to the girl's problems.

The conversations drifted through the room, covering the usual topics of gossip favored by the *ton*: upcoming marriages, fashions, horse races, the latest scandals.

He glanced at the clock on the mantel and couldn't imagine what was taking Emmaline so long. Couldn't she just offer the girl some plaudits and be done with it? Really, she seemed to have a talent for meddling.

Then he recalled what Lady Jarvis had said about Emmaline, or rather, Miss Doyle.

She quite ruined my niece with her meddling.

He closed his eyes and nearly groaned. What had he been thinking, sending Emmaline after an impressionable young lady? One ripe for "meddling."

Egads, she'd have Miss Mabberly throwing off her parents' authority, calling off her marriage—not that he didn't disagree with that notion, but, well, it just wasn't done—not to mention that Miss Mabberly's defection would have Oxley and his mother cross as crabs, as well as put them in dire financial circumstances.

Knowing Lady Oxley, she'd blame Alex for the entire sordid affair, and prod her nitwit son into calling him out.

"I should see to my wife," he said, making a hasty exit

from the room. Once out of eyesight, he tore down the hall, hoping to avert the sort of disaster that only Emmaline could orchestrate.

Then the sound of weeping brought him up short. Usually a woman's crying was enough to send him fleeing in the opposite direction, but then he heard Emmaline's dulcet voice and his curiosity outweighed his reluctance.

He moved quietly up to the door and took a tentative peek inside. There stood Emmaline in the middle of a private parlor with Miss Mabberly. If she had been pale and shaken by the arrival of the Neeleys, apparently meddling was restorative, for she was once again the fiery, formidable woman he knew.

"You mustn't let her see you cry." Emmaline handed the girl a handkerchief. "Don't give Lady Oxley any further cause for comment."

"I know, I know," the girl said through a spate of sniffles and hiccups. She swiped at her tear-stained cheeks and watery eyes. "But I don't see how I can go through with this. Lord Oxley is . . . is . . . awful."

"I'd have to agree with you there," Emmaline conceded.

Miss Mabberly sniffed a few more times. "He's nothing like Lord Sedgwick."

A twinge of guilt rifled down Alex's spine again. He wanted to tell the girl he wasn't some bloody paragon of matrimonial bliss.

I'm more like your betrothed than I care to admit.

There were more tears from Miss Mabberly, and Emmaline put a steady arm around the girl's shoulders.

"Oh, Lady Sedgwick, how will I be able to bear it— being married to that awful man?"

Emmaline bit her lip—she certainly wasn't disagreeing

with the gel, but neither was she agreeing with the dis-traught bride-to-be. Good, she wasn't meddling.

Still, Alex found himself thinking, would it really hurt all that much if Emmaline *was* to talk Miss Mabberly out of her wedding?

"I don't want to marry him, I never did," the girl de-clared.

"Then why are you?" Emmaline asked.

"Father said I must or he wouldn't let Mother continue her charitable works."

"That's terrible," Emmaline said.

Alex was of the same mind. Someone should say some-thing to Mabberly, rattle the old *cit* into seeing what a wretched life he was consigning his only child to.

Call out Mabberly? What was becoming of him? He drew back and shook his head. What did he care if Miss Mabberly was being forced to marry Oxley? It would never have mattered to him a few days ago.

That is, before Emmaline had entered his life.

No, that did it. He needed no further evidence that it was time to be rid of her. Before she wreaked any more havoc on his life. A few more days and he'd be as interfering as Grandmère, or worse, Emmaline.

"Your father must have some good reason for wanting to see you wed," Emmaline was saying. "Surely he only wants to secure your future."

Miss Mabberly shook his head. "Oh, it has nothing to do with securing my future."

"So why would he want you to marry Lord Oxley?"

That wasn't a difficult question, Alex mused. What *cit* didn't want his daughter married into the *ton*?

Miss Mabberly let out an aggrieved huff. "There is a tariff repeal being debated in the House of Lords and Father needs support for it. Oxley agreed to help him, but for a price." The girl sniffed and wiped at her tears. "Father wouldn't stand for that. Wasn't going to give gold to someone he couldn't trust. Instead he figured I would be good collateral. If Oxley made me his bride, his support would be guaranteed, since what helps raise father's coffers will only help Oxley, since I am Father's only child and heir."

"Some way to treat one's child," he thought he heard Emmaline mutter. But she covered herself by saying, "Perhaps it could all come to some good."

"I don't see how," the girl complained bitterly.

Alex agreed with Miss Mabberly. He didn't see how the match would be of any benefit to the girl—what with Lady Oxley as her mother-in-law and her oafish son as bridegroom.

"Perhaps you will be able to effect some change in the earl," Emmaline suggested. "I've seen it many times, wherein wives have been able to gently guide their husbands toward a more mutual understanding."

Or nag them into an early grave, Alex wanted to add.

"I don't know," Miss Mabberly said.

Emmaline rushed in. "The only person who can change that man is you. Besides, he already holds some regard for you—"

"For my dowry, you mean."

"That may be, but it is up to you to foster some deeper regard within him. If Lord Oxley falls in love with you, you'll find him quite happily carrying baskets for the widows and orphans."

Miss Mabberly laughed. Whether it was from the unlikely idea of Oxley fostering an emotion resembling love for anyone other than himself, or the impossible notion of him visiting the poor, Alex didn't know. But one thing was for certain, Emmaline was easing the girl's immediate fears.

"Carry poor baskets, indeed," Miss Mabberly scoffed. "Now, your Lord Sedgwick, perhaps—but not Lord Oxley. The earl will never hold such a rare regard for me." The girl reached out and touched Emmaline on the forearm. "You are a lucky woman, Lady Sedgwick, for you were allowed to marry for love."

Emmaline winced. It was obvious to Alex that she was no more comfortable with the sham of their besotted union than he was. "Every marriage has its own ups and downs," she told her. "Don't share this with anyone, but earlier this evening, Sedgwick and I were having the most awful row over something quite trivial."

That you are impersonating my wife? He would have liked to point out that the matter was hardly trivial, but this was neither the time nor the place.

"You are teasing me, Lady Sedgwick," she said. "I can't imagine the baron ever raising his voice to you. He seems so . . . so . . ."

"Dull?" Emmaline offered.

Both of them laughed, much to Alex's chagrin. Dull? Emmaline thought him dull?

He would like to remind her that earlier she'd seemed quite enthralled with his company.

"So you see there is a perfect example of what I was saying earlier: Lord Sedgwick wasn't always the dashing and besotted fellow you might think he is—it was my influence, my guidance that helped him become the man he is today. If it hadn't been for my help, I fear he would have remained quite tiresome the rest of his life."

Alex felt his spine bristle. Her influence, indeed! He'd have her know that in some circles he was regarded as quite fast company.

On occasion. When the situation necessitated such behavior.

Egads, he realized, *I am dull.* A regular curmudgeon of boredom.

And always had been.

In truth, conjuring up Emmaline was the only imaginative thing he'd ever done—and he was deliberately ignoring the fact that she'd been Jack's idea to begin with.

And the other thing he certainly didn't want to acknowledge was that since her arrival at Hanover Square, her literal, living and breathing arrival, his life had been anything but ordinary.

And to his consternation, he had to admit all those changes were a result of this blowsy, bossy, bothersome chit.

He glanced up at the sound of Miss Mabberly laughing. "It cannot be so . . ." she was saying.

Demmit, he'd missed whatever Emmaline had been telling her.

Emmaline was laughing now as well. "Oh, yes, why I remember just the other day, Lord Sedgwick was being quite impossible and I suggested that he—"

Alex had heard enough. "Emmaline, are you in there?" he called out, announcing his arrival.

"In here, Sedgwick," she replied. "The man is utterly

bereft without me nearby," she said in a loud aside to Miss Mabberly.

The girl giggled, but then turned away, wiping at her cheeks and dabbing at her eyes, restoring her countenance before she turned and curtsied to him. "Lord Sedgwick, good evening. I fear I've been keeping your wife from you."

"Not at all," he told her. "Absence makes the heart grow fonder."

"Yes, so it does," Emmaline agreed. "Actually, I was just telling Miss Mabberly how impossible you are to live with. I hope you don't mind me tarnishing your perfect image." She moved to his side and laid her hand on his sleeve.

And he didn't even want to consider how right it felt to have her fingers resting there, as if she were drawing her strength from him.

What a farce, that. Her drawing strength from him. This woman seemed to possess a magical power all her own that left him pale in her glimmering wake.

One Miss Mabberly also appeared to have fallen under. "Lady Sedgwick, if I may be so bold," the girl was saying, "would I be imposing utterly if I asked you to . . . well, perhaps if you didn't mind, and if you had the time, would it be possible, that is to say . . ."

"What is it?" Emmaline asked, smiling at her with encouragement.

The girl blushed and said, "Would it be a terrible imposition of me to ask you to stand up with me at my wedding? It is only a fortnight away, and if you and Lord Sedgwick would be available, it would be my wish that you were both there."

Alex looked at the starry light in Miss Mabberly's eyes

and knew the girl had few pleasures in her life, and even fewer still to look forward to. As much as he wanted to revert to form and lay down an unequivocal denial, that her ladyship would certainly not be available (and with any luck would be about as far from London as a fortnight's travel would carry her), he took one glance at Miss Mabberly and then one at Emmaline.

"Sedgwick?" Emmaline asked, looking for his confirmation—or his denial.

Try as he might to harden his heart, he couldn't find the old familiar words that would have constituted his reply a week ago. Who was he to say no and cast himself as the most perfect curmudgeon who ever lived?

"Don't look at me so, either of you. I'm not some ogre. Of course Lady Sedgwick can stand up with you, Miss Mabberly, if that is your fondest wish."

"Oh, Lord Sedgwick, thank you," the girl exclaimed, catapulting herself into his arms and giving him a fierce hug.

He didn't know quite what to do. He'd never been the recipient of such a spontaneous act of affection, not even from one of his mistresses when she'd been presented with a particularly fine gift.

"There, there," he told her, patting her on the shoulder. He glanced over at Emmaline, beseeching her for help, but she was too busy grinning at his obvious discomfort.

With no aid forthcoming, he disengaged himself and set the girl aside. "No more of that now. What if Oxley came in and found you in my arms? He'd call me out and I'd be having grass for breakfast."

"Oh, Sedgwick, you are a tease," Emmaline said. "Everyone knows you are a crack shot and would most likely kill Oxley." She sighed, then winked at Miss Mabberly. "Think of the very scandal. Why, he'd make you a widow before you were even married."

"That would be no crime," Miss Mabberly pointed out, and all three of them laughed.

Just then Mrs. Mabberly arrived, looking utterly apoplectic. "Miranda! There you are. Come immediately. Lord Oxley made mention that you were taking an inordinate amount of time and your father is displeased." The lady caught her daughter by the hand, bowed her head slightly to Alex and Emmaline and then scurried back to the sitting room with Miranda in tow.

Alex turned to Emmaline. "What you did for Miss Mabberly was very kind."

"Not really." Her bitter retort surprised him.

"But you eased her fears," he said, glancing over at her, only to find all her kind smiles were gone.

"I convinced that girl to sell her soul into a marriage she has no desire to enter. I don't call that doing her any favor." She crossed her arms over her chest. "I should have—"

"No, no, no," he sputtered. "No more interfering."

Her hands went to her hips. "Are you telling me that you think it is wise for Miss Mabberly to marry . . . to marry—"

"Our host?" he offered.

Her gaze rolled upward. "Yes, *our host,*" she conceded.

He could well imagine what sort of colorful and imaginative adjective she might have chosen. "It's a good match for Miss Mabberly," he said, reverting to the safety of honorable intentions. "She is young and may not understand yet that she'll have a good position in society."

"Thus says the man who made up a wife to avoid matrimony."

Alex rose to his own defense. "My situation was entirely

different. It was a matter of self-preservation." And that had been the case.

"Bah!" Emmaline scoffed. "It was utter selfishness, pure and simple."

"I hardly see how. You obviously don't understand the difference between my situation and Miss Mabberly's. One must consider the nature of your alliance when contracting a match."

"Listen to you! You would think that you were hiring a new stable hand." Emmaline shook her head, a frown marring her fair brow. "I think I understand the situation more clearly than you would like me to. You have the means and power to avoid an unwanted marriage. However, Miss Mabberly does not." Emmaline pointed at the doorway that led to the salon. "For that dear child to be forced to wed Lord Oxley is a precursor to disaster, if not a moral crime. Would you align yourself so . . . so purely for financial and political gain? Without any thought of your future partner's happiness or feelings?"

Alex glanced away. Anywhere but in Emmaline's direction. He'd always thought of marriage as nothing more than a social union—with happiness, much less love, a matter of chance, only found by fools and professed by those of little wit.

Up until today, he would have been as blind as Oxley obviously was to his betrothed's sensibilities. The earl had no idea his bride loathed him, and most likely didn't care.

Suddenly such a marriage held little warmth for Alex. Perhaps it always had and that was the real reason he'd allowed Emmaline to come into his life, like a seawall against the unhappy tides he saw in so many marriages, arranged marriages, marriages of financial and political union. Up until now, he would never have admitted, even to himself, that he had perhaps always held a small dream that he would add his own romantic notation to the family annals, to live a life like that found in the sunny pictures of Sedgwick Abbey.

For sensible as he was, he knew that such a dream was hard, if not nearly impossible to find in the false world of the *ton*. In all these years, after watching glittering parade after parade of young eligible ladies waltz through their Seasons, he'd never once felt that stir, that elation that love promised as he watched the ladies go by.

Love was a miracle after all. His own parents had met in a roadside inn. His unspoiled mother on her way to her first Season, his father on his way home from London, fleeing the arriving onslaught of bridal hopefuls like one might the barbarian hordes. His mother never made it to London.

And hadn't his grandfather met Grandmère in Paris at a corner café, his grandmother fresh out of convent school, unsullied by the jaded ways of the world? Another chance meeting that changed the course of family history.

Yet Alex's life had always seemed so ordinary, so lacking in magic that he'd never thought such a wonder of happenstance would ever cross his staid path.

Emmaline stood there, her lips pursed, shooting him a wry look.

How was it that this woman who had known him for less than a day had spotted such a dream in him without so much as a by your leave? As if she'd known the truth all along and thought it was high time he realized it as well.

Who the devil was she?

Not your wife, was the haunting reproach that came springing to mind.

Well, that was a good thing, wasn't it? Who would want a wife who could see inside one's dreams, one's transgressions? One's soul?

And demmit, if she could see that much, she might also know that in the course of this evening, he suspected that his father's good fortune, his grandfather's rare luck may just have fallen into his lap.

Chapter 9

A few hours later, Lady Lilith and her mother stood in the bow window and watched the guests depart.

"I don't know what is to become of you, my dear," the countess lamented. "That woman will be the ruin of Sedgwick, and in turn, your husband."

"You should have let me refute her, Mother," Lilith said. "How dare she imply that we are related to the Thorpes."

Lady Oxley waved her hand. "That is of no conse quence." Her eyes narrowed as she watched Sedgwick hand his wife up into the carriage and then get in beside her.

"Goodnight and good riddance," she said under her breath.

"Mother?" Lilith asked.

Lady Oxley smiled and patted her daughter's hand. "You need to see that Lord Sedgwick and his wife return to their previous arrangement. *Apart.*" She turned her gaze back toward the retreating carriage. "A child from that union would be most inopportune."

"I don't see how we'll be able to get him to set her aside," Lilith complained. "You should have seen them last night." Her daughter clucked her tongue. "It was a disgraceful display."

Undoubtedly, Lady Oxley thought.

"Shameless pair," Lilith continued. "I had Hubert write his grandmother, demanding that the dowager come to London."

"Bother the dowager. She's French and they are never reliable. Given her flighty nature, she may declare that woman the perfect wife for Sedgwick and use her Gallic wiles to help his bride."

Lilith's eyes widened. Obviously she hadn't thought of that possibility.

Just then, Hubert came up behind them, his greatcoat and hat in hand, along with Lilith's cloak.

Lady Oxley had never thought much of her son-in-law, other than his likelihood to inherit the Sedgwick barony. But Hubert was about to surprise her, more so than she'd ever thought possible.

He glanced out the window at his cousin's carriage and shook his head. "Something not quite right about Sedgwick's bride."

"Mother was just saying as much," Lilith said. "She thinks we need to do something more than just summoning your grandmother."

Hubert nodded in agreement. "Never fear, ladies, I already have."

The Denfords and Lady Oxley weren't the only ones watching the Sedgwick carriage pull away. The Marquis of Templeton strode across the street toward the barouche he'd liberated from his grandfather's stables for the night, his thoughts filled with the events of the evening, of spending it so close to Diana, and yet . . .

He came to an abrupt halt before his borrowed conveyance, from which his driver had as yet to get down to open the door or even make an attempt to notice his arrival. "Ahem," he coughed.

Instead of making any attempt to act like a regular servant, Elton just sat in the driver's box staring down the street. "Who was that? In that carriage?"

Temple shot a glance over his shoulder. "That one?" He pointed at the vehicle turning the corner.

Elton nodded, his one good eye never leaving the carriage.

"Sedgwick. Baron Sedgwick," Temple told him.

"And the woman?"

The marquis cocked a brow. "Gawking after a married woman? At your age? Elton, I'm shocked. And you know demmed well that it takes a lot to make me scandalized."

"Who was that woman with Sedgwick?" Elton repeated, his voice deep with intent.

Temple stepped back and eyed his servant. "My good man, in all the years that you've been in my employ, this is the first time I've ever seen you look twice at a woman. Besides, it is highly irregular for servants to be dallying after a married noblewoman."

"You don't pay me regular enough to be considered a servant, so I'll ask ye again, milord: *Who is that woman?*"

Temple felt a chill run down his spine. He'd never seen this fierce side of Elton, and he wasn't foolish enough to cross the man given his dark past. "The lady is his wife. Lady Sedgwick."

"His wife?" Elton didn't sound like he believed a word of it.

"Now don't do anything foolish there," Temple said, giving up any hope that Elton was going to open the door to the carriage and doing it himself. He climbed in and leaned back in the seat. "Sedgwick is a dull sort, but I have a feeling that when it comes to his wife, let alone his honor, he wouldn't take kindly to being cuckolded."

"That woman isn't his wife," Elton said, spitting over the side of the seat and then picking up the reins.

"Not his wife? You're mad." Temple glanced up at the sky and wondered where his driver had found the blunt for drink, because he must be half pissed to think otherwise.

Elton turned around and shot him a level look. The kind Temple imagined he'd used when he'd been engaged in his former profession—as a highwayman.

Undaunted, Temple crossed his arms over his chest. "If she isn't his wife, then who is she?"

"My daughter."

Emmaline sat stock-still in the Sedgwick carriage. She knew her best course of action was to say nothing. Not a word.

She'd made a muddle of the evening. First she'd incurred Lady Oxley's ire by revealing a few unsightly branches in her family tree, then she'd broken her promise by telling that outlandish story and finally she'd come to Miss Mabberly's aid, when obviously no one else was going to stand up for the girl.

Of all her sins, that was the worst. She'd done the girl no favors. The meddling promise was the one she should have broken, and sent Miss Mabberly out in search of a worthy second son.

Then again, she still had two weeks . . .

Most likely not, she realized, glancing over at Sedgwick's arched brow and the cold, icy set of his jaw. She had to wonder if he was going to allow her even the courtesy of going inside Number Seventeen long enough to fetch her belongings.

No, best that she not say a thing.

Oh, bother, that was never going to work. "Sedgwick," she began. "If I could just—"

"Is it true?" he asked, interrupting her.

"What?"

"What Lady Neeley said. Are you this Miss Doyle?"

Emmaline flinched. She'd never thought that the discovery of her other identity would be the least of her problems.

"Are you this Miss Doyle? The Duchess of Cheverton's companion?"

She was in dun territory now.

"The truth, madam," he said, "or I'll haul you back to the duchess and damn the consequences."

"The truth?" she managed to quip. "Really Sedgwick, it was such a debatable subject." Then she glanced up at him and knew for perhaps the first time in her life, the truth was the only answer. "Oh, bother. Yes, that was me." She shifted in her seat, setting her reticule and fan down beside her. "However, I wouldn't recommend taking me to the duchess."

"And why not?" He had that tight, stuffy tone to his voice that she really abhorred.

"I've actually never met the duchess," she confessed.

His eyes narrowed. "But Sir Francis said—"

She smoothed out the folds of her gown. "Yes, well, perhaps he was slightly misled on that point."

"So how is it that you are this Miss Doyle, the Duchess of Cheverton's companion, but you've never actually met the woman?"

Emmaline wrung her hands. "It might have been implied that I was connected to the duchess and unfortunately it was a misconception that I forgot to rectify."

He groaned and covered his face with his hands, shaking his head back and forth.

"'Tis hardly as bad as all that," she argued.

"All that bad? From what I heard tonight, you've gulled the Shackleford-Demsleys, Sir Francis, and Lady Jarvis's sister. You're a *swindler*."

Emmaline straightened her shoulders. "You make it sound like I've done something wrong. I'll have you know, I never . . ." One glance into his stormy gaze and she faltered. "Never intentionally—" His dark brow arched again. "Fine then. It was me. I've spent the last six years posing as the Duchess of Cheverton's companion. But I am no thief."

"Six years?" he exclaimed. "I don't believe it. How is it that you haven't been caught?"

She bristled. "Because I am demmed good at what I do."

He couldn't deny that. Look how easily she'd slipped into her role as Emmaline. Still . . . "How can you say you aren't a thief?"

"Because I never took anything from anyone that wasn't freely offered."

He could believe that as well. Emmaline had a way about her that could charm the worst curmudgeon.

Well, nearly the worst one, he concluded, thinking of

Lady Oxley. Then again, he doubted a host of angels could turn that old battle-ax's heart. But that was beside the point.

"Why?" he asked.

"Why what?"

"Why did you pose as the Duchess of Cheverton's companion?"

She heaved another sigh and glanced out the window. "Because the alternatives were less appealing. I shouldn't have to tell you what choices are available for a woman alone in the world, without the protection of name or family."

Like any other nobleman, Alex did his best to ignore such chasms in society. Yes, there were few choices for women, but how could he be held accountable if they chose the wrong path? Besides, this was an issue of right and wrong. "While your choices may have been rather limited," he conceded, "can't you see what you were doing was dishonest, not to mention unlawful?"

"How so?" she asked, defiant in her defense. "I never took anything from anyone. I only accepted what was offered—a place to stay, food and, more often than not, a ride to the next posting inn." She folded her hands in her lap. "Have you never offered hospitality to strangers?"

She had him there. His grandmother was forever bringing home wayfarers and offering them the respite of Sedgwick Abbey before they continued on their way. And he'd never objected. If anything, the added company in the house diverted Grandmère from her other favorite occupation, nagging him.

"It is just that it seemed . . . I mean to say, from what Lady Neeley was saying—"

"Sedgwick, believe me," she told him, "I never took anything from those houses."

His gaze narrowed. "Just how many of those houses were there?"

Emmaline chewed at her lip.

"More than five?" he asked.

"Does it really matter?"

"Yes!" He had a well-known and well-practiced flimflam artist posing as his wife. He'd like to know how many more people like the Neeleys were out there.

She seemed to be considering her answer, counting on her fingers and gazing at the ceiling of the carriage as she came to her final total. "Twenty-eight, but without pen and paper that is merely an estimate."

Twenty-eight? He had a feeling that nothing about her was an estimation, that Emmaline could name the date and place of each of her transgressions.

He'd seen how she'd wrangled with the tradesmen. Twenty-eight households amongst the country gentry must have seemed like child's play.

And as the carriage pulled to a stop in Hanover Square, Alex knew there was only one thing he could do now.

"My lord, my lady," Simmons said, coming down the steps to greet them. "Thank goodness you've come home. And in time."

"Whatever is wrong?" Sedgwick asked him.

" 'Tis Lady Rawlins."

"Malvina?" Emmaline's hand went to her lips and she glanced across the square toward Tottley House.

"Yes, my lady. I fear the news is not good. 'Tis the baby." Simmons's mouth pressed tightly shut and he looked away, shaking his head. "She's been asking for you."

For me? Emmaline didn't know what to say. The sting of

hot and sudden tears burned her eyes. And without realizing it, she reached out and took Sedgwick's arm. "Please," she said quietly. "May I go to her?"

He glanced over at Simmons, and the butler shook his head again. "Has the doctor been summoned?"

Simmons nodded. "The man left an hour ago. He saw no point to staying when the midwife could handle such a thing. Sir, Lord Rawlins has been over twice. It seems that her ladyship would find Lady Sedgwick's company a comfort before . . . before . . ."

"Oh no!" Emmaline gasped. How could such a thing happen so quickly? To her dearest friend. Her only friend. "Please, Sedgwick."

"Yes, of course," he told her, turning with her and helping her down the steps.

To Emmaline's dismay, they were met by the just-arrived Lady Lilith and Hubert.

"I would have a word with you, Cousin Emmaline," Lady Lilith began, blocking their path, her nose pointed in the air. "I know you aren't familiar with London ways, but I must say your behavior tonight was simply appalling. Your conduct toward my mother—"

"Not now," Sedgwick told her.

Lady Lilith was not to be averred. "I disagree. I will not be so easily silenced. Sedgwick, you were not there. You didn't hear what—"

"Stow it, Mrs. Denford," he barked at her. "We are needed elsewhere."

Hubert wisely drew his wife back and allowed them to pass.

They made their way off the curb and continued into the street. Emmaline glanced up at the sky and wondered how it was that a night that had started so starry and full of magic now seemed so cold and empty.

To lose Malvina? Emmaline couldn't think of her illustrious friend as anything but full of life, full of her undeniable passion. The tears stung anew.

Not since her father's desertion, since her mother's death, had she let herself care for another person. Her very profession lent for a solitary life.

And then into her life had come Malvina. Like a hurricane, she'd forced her way into Emmaline's world and become . . . a friend. And now Malvina needed her.

Sedgwick marched along beside her. "Do you know anything of childbirth?"

Emmaline stumbled to a halt. "G-goodness, no," she stammered, staring in horror at the looming town house before them. All she knew of the process was shrouded in mystery. A mystery she had no desire to meddle in. Not even for a dear friend.

But there wasn't time to retreat, for the door burst open even before they reached the steps. A disheveled and distraught Rawlins rushed down to meet them. "Lady Sedgwick, you've come in time." He clasped her hands in his. "I thought . . . I feared . . . And now you are here for my Malvina. Bless you."

Before she could protest, Lord Rawlins was drawing her up the steps. Inside Tottley House, the staff was lined on either side of the foyer. Never had Emmaline seen such a collection of long faces.

And from upstairs came a dire scream. One of pain and agony that tore at the heart. She'd heard such cries once before—from her mother—and knew that they portended only one conclusion.

Emmaline felt the claws of panic rising in her gut. She couldn't do this. She couldn't watch the only friend she'd ever had die. But even as she spun around, she ran smack-dab into Sedgwick, and his arms folded around her like castle walls.

She gulped and stammered into his waistcoat, then turned her gaze up to him. "I can't do this. What if she—"

Another cry erupted from the upper floors, a piercing keen that could divide the stoniest of hearts. One of the maids broke down, weeping openly.

"You must be brave." Sedgwick caught her by the shoulders and gave her a shake. "Emmaline, you are the bravest woman I know." He drew her into an alcove and whispered in her ear, "You've been shot, for God's sakes."

"Yes, but I wasn't awake for most of that."

"That may be, but consider this. You crossed swords tonight with Lady Oxley and survived. What is childbirth in the face of such bravery?"

"Thus says the man who will never face such a trial."

"What—Lady Oxley or childbirth?"

"Either," Emmaline huffed.

"That may be, but that doesn't mean I can't admire the one woman I know who is brave enough to dare both the dragon and the fire." He leaned over and pressed a kiss to her forehead. "Emmaline, there is only one of you. I know it, and apparently so does Lady Rawlins. Now go and help your friend, for she needs you—more so than any of the other people you have helped so freely and willingly."

Demmit, why did he have to be so steady? Remind her of what honor and duty meant? She owed much to Malvina, and if she was ever to be proud of anything in her misspent life, she needed to do this. Needed to help her friend.

And trying to summon the bravery that Sedgwick seemed to think she possessed in spades, she went upstairs.

"Drink?" Sedgwick asked. He and Rawlins had retired to the man's library to await the evening's outcome.

Rawlins nodded.

They'd never traveled in the same circles. Rawlins, as the heir to the Tottley earldom, was toplofty indeed and his cool disdain and awareness of his position had always kept him far above just a mere baron. However, the unkempt man before him hardly resembled the smooth and well-turned-out viscount Alex knew.

He handed the drink to him right as another scream from upstairs pierced the night.

The man threw back the brandy in a single toss and shuddered. "What did I do to her? I should never have . . . I didn't know it would come to *this*."

Alex tossed his own drink back. He didn't know if he was brave enough for this sort of heart-to-heart conversation with a man he barely knew.

And, much to Alex's discomfort, Rawlins took his silence as permission to continue. "Malvina is my very life. She's the finest woman in England. Demmit, I don't want her to die. I love her, you know."

Alex tried his best to hide his shock at this emotional outburst. Certainly Viscount Rawlins and his wife were a prominent and well-made match, but he'd never suspected, never known that it had been a love match.

He, like everyone else in the town, had thought Rawlins had married the outspoken, madcap Malvina Henley for her ten thousand a year.

But for love? No, never.

"Yes, I can see it on your face, you don't believe me," Rawlins said. "No one does. But Malvina is the best woman I've ever met. Oh, don't get me wrong, she isn't the easiest woman to live with, but there is something about her that is undeniable. Something about her that makes me wild, something about her that makes me want to be a better man." He paused and looked away, and it was then that Alex realized the man's shoulders were shaking, his head bowed to hide his tears.

"I love her so very much," Rawlins managed a few moments later. "But you must understand how it is—given that you married for the same reasons."

"Th-the same?" Alex stammered.

"For love," Rawlins said matter-of-factly, as if he were admitting Alex to some wonderful and secret society. "You needn't be ashamed of it. It is a rare gift in our lot to find a wife you can love with all your heart. The real shame is that so many think it a crime to care for one's wife. How sad for them, don't you think?"

Alex just nodded. He didn't know what to say in the face of all this. Tell Rawlins the truth—that Emmaline wasn't his wife. That he wasn't besotted?

The viscount poured another glass for himself and held the decanter out to Alex.

He was of a mind to tell the man that he didn't think more drink was a good idea, for it seemed to be tearing down the walls of good manners which said one didn't discuss such things. But at the same time, Alex found himself curious. Rawlins loved Malvina?

This night was going from revealing to unbelievable.

Upstairs there was another wretched cry, a long, pained wail. The kind of sound that seemed to cut the night. Alex didn't envy Emmaline her place beside Malvina. That she'd gone at all said much of her character.

He doubted he would have been able to muster so much courage. But perhaps that was one of the qualities about women that a man had to admire, to envy. That when all was said and done, it was the women who tended to the two most important events in life—to bringing children into the world, and comforting those about to leave it.

The viscount having drunk his measure down, came over and filled Alex's glass again. Then his own.

Alex stared down at the brandy, the amber liquid swirling around the glass like a timeless mist, full of secrets, full of promise. The screams were coming closer and closer together, and each one was like a knife.

He decided another drink wasn't such a bad idea. *To dull the memory*.

"How can she survive this?" Rawlins was muttering.

"I was just thinking the same," Alex said, realizing that his words probably weren't all that helpful when the viscount's gaze swung up, alarm all over his wide-eyed features. "I meant to say," Alex told him, "your wife has a tremendous capacity for living—I doubt this is her end."

Rawlins nodded, catching hold of Alex's encouragement like a lifeline. "You'll understand it better when your time comes. When you're pacing about downstairs waiting for your child to arrive."

"My—" Alex shook his head. "I don't think that will—"

"I'm sorry," Rawlins said quickly. "I forgot that Lady Sedgwick's health isn't . . . demmit, I'm sorry."

"Don't concern yourself."

"But you've faced this, haven't you?" Rawlins asked.

"Faced what?" he asked, looking up at the ceiling. At the confinement above them.

"Possibly losing your wife. Malvina said Lady Sedgwick was desperately ill last winter. That she nearly—" He closed his eyes and shook his head. "I suppose I'm being too familiar. I know we aren't friends, but I feel like we have something in common."

"In common?" Alex repeated.

"Our wives. Coming close to death. Loving them."

Alex shifted uncomfortably. They had nothing in common. Really, they didn't. Other than the fact that Malvina and Emmaline shared a propensity to meddle.

"It was difficult," he said diplomatically. More so than Rawlins could ever imagine.

The man threw himself down on a nearby chair. He waved at the matching one for Sedgwick. "I knew you'd understand. Malvina changed my life utterly and completely when I met her. Turned it upside down."

Alex raised his glass to that point. Perhaps they did have something in common.

Now what was he thinking?

He glanced down at his glass and realized that the Tottley brandy was probably the finest and most illegal of French vintages. It was going straight to his head and making him as mad as Rawlins.

"I knew she was the woman for me when I saw her at Almack's. Coming across the room like a Venus."

Alex's gaze snapped up. *A Venus?* Wasn't that what he'd thought the first time he'd laid his eyes on Emmaline?

"And she led me on a merry chase. Had me at sixes and sevens with her flirtatious ways. Gads, she drove me mad, what with the way she charmed all who met her."

Alex might dispute the point that Malvina Henley had ever charmed anyone with her brassy ways, but Emmaline . . . now, that was another matter. She seemed to possess charm enough for a dozen wives.

"When you met Lady Sedgwick, didn't you just know? Know in your heart that there was something about her that would make your rather ordinary life complete, give you a reason to get up in the morning and see what mischief she was up to?" Rawlins sighed. "I knew all that within the first twenty-four hours of meeting Malvina. That there would never be another woman like her in my life, and that I would do anything, give up anything, to keep her at my side."

Fall in love with someone in a single night? Impossible, Alex wanted to tell his host. However, just then the clock struck one, and Alex realized his own twenty-four hours had come to pass.

One day with Emmaline. How could he deny that his life would ever be the same? Suddenly he knew exactly what the viscount was saying.

And Lord, how he wished he didn't.

Emmaline sat by Malvina's side, her own hand being crushed by the viscountess's tortured grasp.

The midwife was busy at the other end. "It's coming wrong," the plainspoken crone said. "Got to turn it. No way around it."

Malvina cried out again as another contraction wrenched her body.

"She can't push," the midwife said to Emmaline. "Nature is telling her to push, but you can't let her."

"No pushing," Emmaline repeated. How the devil was she supposed to accomplish that? She pried her hand free, and reached for the cloth beside the basin, soaking it in the cool water and wiping it across her friend's soaked brow. "Malvina, you can't push."

The viscountess ignored her, moaning and crying.

"Distract her, milady," the exasperated midwife instructed. "Give her something else to think about. Something that will really stick in her craw."

Malvina began to wail again, mindless of the people around her, of the midwife's words.

Emmaline took a deep breath and climbed into the massive bed, crawling up beside her friend and taking her face in her hands. "Malvina, Malvina!" she snapped. "Listen to me."

"I'm dying, Emmaline. I can't bear it. Tell Rawlins I loved him. I would have been proud to be his countess."

His countess. The Countess of Tottley.

Emmaline grinned. She knew how to distract Malvina.

"Malvina, don't you dare die. You would have this child raised by your mother-in-law? By Lady Tottley?"

The mention of Rawlins's mother caught Malvina's attention quicker than a new display of hats on Bond Street.

And as the midwife had asked, it stuck in her craw like nothing else could.

"Lady Tottley?" she managed to gasp.

"Yes, Lady Tottley. Who else would be left to hire the baby's nanny and tutors but Lady Tottley?"

Malvina's gaze narrowed. "No," she ground out. "Never."

"That's it," Emmaline told her. "Never mind an heir. What if your child is a daughter? Would you have that old harridan raising your daughter? Choosing her finishing school? Presenting her to the Queen?"

"Never!" Malvina said, rising up in the bed, digging her elbows into the mattress.

Emmaline wasn't going to stop there. "And you know the countess wouldn't rest until Rawlins remarried. *Properly this time.*"

Malvina's craw overflowed. Her eyes narrowed, her brow furrowed and she looked down at the midwife and said, "What do I need to do?"

The silence unnerved Alex more than the screams and it continued that way for hours. The viscount and the baron had fallen into a silent, solitary vigil, with only an occasional muffled cry or the sounds of movement from above to draw their attention.

And just as the fingers of dawn started to dance across the rooftops of Hanover Square, the door to the library finally opened and the Tottley butler came in.

"My lord, you are wanted upstairs."

Rawlins bolted for the door, then came to an equally hasty halt. "Sedgwick—I don't think I can—would it be too much of an imposition for you come with me?"

Alex wanted to shake his head and forgo the horrible scene that must surely await them.

But Emmaline was there. And he wanted to know that she—well, he wanted to see her. She might even need him.

That was, oddly enough, more a hope, he realized. That Emmaline, strong and resolute Emmaline, might need him.

He squared his shoulders and nodded to Rawlins.

As he followed the viscount through half-light of morning, the once-dark house seemed like it was holding its breath, just as the earth did as the first traces of light stole across the horizon, chasing the realm of night away and heralding the glory of the sun.

In that quiet, waiting time, they walked upstairs to see what the Fates had dealt during the night.

A few steps away from the door, a new noise reached their ears.

A cry. Not the cry of a woman in pain. But that of a babe. Lusty and strong, the cry told one and all that the night's endless travail hadn't been for naught.

"The child," Rawlins said, breathless wonder in his words.

"Your child," Alex told him, feeling a sense of pride and . . . envy for the viscount.

The housekeeper stood by the door, tears streaming down her face. "A bonny child it is, milord." She opened the door and revealed a scene that left both men with tears streaming down their cheeks.

For inside the room sat Lady Rawlins, ensconced in a queenly manner atop the large bed, holding a squalling bundle in her arms. "Come in, Rawlins, and see your daughter."

"My daughter?" he whispered, coming slowly and hesitantly into his own chamber as if he'd never been in the room.

Malvina grinned at him and patted a spot beside her. "I'm sorry it isn't a son."

Rawlins peeked at the child and smiled from ear to ear. "She has your disposition," he teased. "What more could I ask for?" Then he laid a tender kiss on his wife's head and sighed mightily, like he'd been holding his breath all night.

Alex glanced away to give them their privacy and his gaze fell immediately on Emmaline. She sat in a chair, her eyes glassy and dazed. Her color was gone, and she looked as if she had witnessed more than she could comprehend.

He knelt by her side and patted her hand. "Emmaline, Emmaline, are you well?"

"Oh, Sedgwick," she said. "You should have seen her. She did it. It was terrible, but she managed to do it. And the baby is well, and so is Malvina. Thank you for letting me be here."

Before Alex could say anything, the midwife interjected, "Her ladyship has you to thank, ma'am. Without you here, I don't think she would have come through." She turned to Alex. "I've seen my fair share of births, milord, and I aver that your wife is a credit to the happy ending you see here. She gave her ladyship a reason to live, the will to get through a difficult time." The midwife finished wiping her hands.

"I didn't do anything," Emmaline said. "I have no skill in these things."

"Modest, you are," the midwife said. "You gave her your strength and the will to live when she'd all but given up. I know these things, but when a woman gives up, she's lost for certain."

Emmaline shook her head again. "It was all Malvina."

"You go ahead and say that, but I know the truth." She glanced over at Alex. "When her time comes, send for me. It would be my honor." The woman finished gathering up her supplies and tucked them carefully into her woolen bag. Before she left, she paused and said to Emmaline, "If you don't mind me asking, milady, what was it you said to Lady Rawlins to help her pull through? Professionally speaking and all."

Emmaline blushed, and from the bed Malvina, who must

have heard the woman's question, laughed. "Don't you dare repeat a word of it, Emmaline Denford. Not one word."

Emmaline grinned. "Never, Malvina. I promise."

Rawlins glanced up at Alex. "Suppose that is a good motto all around."

Alex knew what he meant. What had been said during the night went the way of the night. "Decidedly."

They all four laughed in companionable merriment.

Rawlins tipped the blanket down to look at his daughter. "What name shall we give her?" he asked his wife.

"Lucinda," Malvina said, her forceful personality back in good order. "Lady Lucinda Emmaline Witherspoon."

Chapter 10

Alex offered Emmaline his arm as they walked home. Hanover Square was still and quiet, as was Number Seventeen when they entered.

Though the rest of the house still slumbered, there was Simmons, ever loyal and ever patient, waiting in the foyer for their return. "My lord, my lady, how fares Lady Rawlins?"

"Very well," Alex told him. "She delivered a fine daughter this morning. Lady Lucinda *Emmaline* Witherspoon."

This perked up Simmons. He bowed his head to Emmaline, very aware of the honor bestowed upon her and, in some regard, upon this newest addition to the *ton*. "And Lady Rawlins?" he asked.

Sedgwick laughed. "When we left, she was writing out Lady Lucinda's application for Miss Emery's Establishment. It seems choosing the right finishing school cannot be put off or left to chance."

Simmons laughed. "I am well pleased to hear it."

Alex turned to ask Emmaline for her account, but there was no sign of her. She was gone. He glanced around the foyer and then spied her trudging up the stairs, looking for all purposes like a condemned man walking up the steps of the gallows.

The butler beat Alex to the mark. "My lady," he said, "is there anything I can do for you?"

"No," she said quietly from the landing. "I won't take long. I have but to get my bags."

Simmons shot him a look of pure alarm that mirrored the exact thing Alex was thinking.

Get her bags?

"My lord—" Simmons began to protest.

He didn't stop to listen to the rest, for he was after her in all due haste, taking the stairs two at a time. She was already in the bedchamber, opening the cabinet where her valise was stowed, by the time he caught up with her.

"What are you doing?" he asked.

"Getting my things." She didn't even look at him.

So she thought that she'd failed! Lost their bet. She had, with her far-fetched tales but she'd redeemed herself in so many other ways that he didn't know where to begin. For she'd been more of a lady tonight than any of the other women in the room—coming to Miss Mabberly's aid when everyone else was merely contented to let the poor girl suffer her fate. Not to mention how she'd helped Lady Rawlins.

Emmaline hadn't lost their bet, she'd won it quite handily.

Won it? Egads, what was he thinking? Here he had his out. A way to extract himself from this mess. He'd have his life back. His ordered, predictable, staid existence exactly as it should be.

Suddenly that prospect wasn't as bright and golden as it

promised. For how could he know that happenstance would come his way more than once?

So perhaps there was another way to handle this mess . . . at least for the time being. Certainly if he was to let her stay, there would have to be some ground rules.

He was still the master of this house, after all . . .

"I don't remember giving you permission to pack," he said, utilizing his most pompous tones.

This brought her gaze wrenching up. "I beg your pardon," she sputtered. "I'm not allowed to take my belongings? While you may think me a thief, I'll have you know I've never taken anything that—"

"*Sit,*" he commanded, pointing at a chair.

She looked about to protest, but he wasn't the twenty-second holder of the Sedgwick title for nothing. He pointed at the chair again and cut her with his most direct stare. The one family legend claimed the very first baron used to send the infidels running while serving Richard the Lion-Hearted.

Emmaline looked to be made of sterner nerve than the Saracens, for she shot him an aggrieved look, yet it lasted only a few moments and she sat nonetheless.

Sometimes having a stuffy, no-nonsense reputation had its advantages. "I will ask this question again: Who are you?"

Her lips pursed. "No one of consequence."

"I disagree." He met her surprised glance with a level stare. Tonight had changed so much. To see Rawlins, the epitome of the untouchable Corinthian, opening his soul in such a manner, had left Alex questioning everything he believed in.

Could it be true? That one could fall in love with a woman in just a matter of hours?

There was no denying that there was something about Emmaline that tugged at his heart. And yet her deceptions as Emmaline and this Miss Doyle left him with no choice.

Unless . . .

"No, Sedgwick. You were right earlier. I am no lady."

He shook his head. "Emmaline, I was wrong to say that. Everything about tonight proves otherwise—your kindness to Miss Mabberly. The extraordinary service you lent Lady Rawlins."

"Sedgwick, don't—" she started to say, glancing away from his praise, waving her hand at him. Her hand stalled in midair, then came to rest over her mouth to cover a large yawn. "Really, I didn't—"

"I would like you to stay."

Now she did look at him. Wary and unwilling to believe she'd heard him correctly. "You want me to what?"

"Stay." He paced a few steps back and forth, some wild vestiges of a plan forming in his mind. "I would like you to stay for a fortnight."

"Why?" She folded her arms over her chest, her suspicions coming to the forefront.

"Because . . . um, well . . ." He glanced around the room, seeing anew the changes she'd wrought. "Because I would like you to finish your work here. I can't bear to see the house go unfinished. And between you and me, if you don't see the task done, Lady Lilith will step in." He closed his eyes and shuddered. And then opened them a bit to judge her reaction.

Sleepy as she was, she smiled at him. "I know I told that

story, and I'm not sorry I did. If you had heard Lady Oxley—"

He shook his head. "You needn't explain, Emmaline. You won the wager."

"I hardly see how I did." She rubbed her brow, her eyelids closing with heavy surrender.

What a night she'd had. He could scarcely believe she was still awake.

"Our wager was for you to pass as my . . . as my . . ." He was obviously having problems spitting out the words *my wife,* and finally settled on, "Lady Sedgwick, and you did that. I see no reason to quibble over your means."

"So you truly want me to stay?"

He nodded, then began to pace again. "But I have certain conditions. First of all—"

But when he turned around, he discovered that his conditions would have to wait.

The lady had fallen asleep, a happy smile on her face.

He sighed and knelt before her, brushing a few stray strands of blond hair away from her face.

Oh, what the devil am I going to do with you, Emmaline?

Well, until he had that puzzle solved he thought the best course of action was to let her sleep. So he picked her up and carried her to the bed.

She stirred in his arms, then nuzzled closer. "Thank you, Sedgwick," she whispered, as he lowered her to the mattress and covered her with the spread.

"No," he said, to her now-sleeping form. "Thank you."

And he meant it for so many reasons, most of which he dared not fathom.

Emmaline awoke hours later. Sunlight streamed through the gauzy curtains, casting the room in a warm glow. There in the comfort of the bed, still caught in the half sleep between dreaming and waking, Sedgwick's words echoed clearly through her hazy thoughts.

Stay, Emmaline.

He'd asked her to stay. She still didn't quite believe it, wondering if his request had been but a flight of fancy conjured by Queen Mab.

No, it couldn't be true.

"Yes, I did ask you to stay." This time the words were not imagined, but from the man himself.

She sat up and looked around until she spied Sedgwick leaning in the doorway between the bedchamber and the sitting room.

"How did you know what I was thinking?"

"You looked ready to leave again."

Perhaps she was still asleep, for she could swear that she heard a trace of trepidation in his words. Did he really want her to stay? Especially after all the trouble she'd wrought last night.

"You fell asleep before we could reach an agreement," he said, leaving his post at the door, moving closer to the bed.

Wearing navy breeches and a white shirt, he looked more like a highwayman than a nobleman. Especially since the bruises around his swollen eye were now a disreputable rainbow of purple, black and dark red.

Highwayman, indeed! She knew better than to fall in love with one. And she should be applying that same reasoning to her heart with concern to the baron. He was just as dangerous to her future plans as if he were riding along the North Road, pistol in hand, crying out "Stand and deliver!"

Why that spontaneous kiss they'd shared in the carriage

should have been warning enough. The very thought of his lips covering hers stole her breath, jolted her body awake with awareness, her nipples hardening as she recalled how it had felt to have his hands caress her there, her very private core becoming tight with an ache that cried out for that self-same touch.

Oh, if just having him near did this to her, she doubted she would be able to maintain a professional stance for an entire fortnight.

No matter what was at stake.

She glanced up at him, and spied that same recognition in his eyes. That he was sharing the very same recollections.

And when she glanced down at herself, she realized he might be having memories of a different encounter . . . one she certainly didn't remember.

"Where are my clothes?" she demanded. Demmit, she wore only her shift. If she was going to be honest, her anger was more from the fact that she didn't recall him undressing her than at the fact that he'd done so to begin with.

"I didn't do anything . . . I mean to say . . ." His brow furrowed. "I just thought you'd be more comfortable out of your gown. I assure you I was a gentleman about the situation."

Oh, bother Sedgwick and his wretched honor. He hadn't even tried to take advantage of her.

"Thank you," she finally said, tugging the sheets modestly up to her chin. Just then, the clock on the mantel chimed the hour, and her gaze flew there. "Dear heavens! Why, it is past three." She sprang from the bed, catching up her wrapper and heading to the cabinet.

"Where are you going?" he asked.

"To work. I have much to do," she told him, taking out her plain gown and a clean shift and stockings. She paused and glanced over at him.

He looked well rested and rather content. Too content.

She glanced down at herself again, wondering if he'd been as honorable as he professed. Truly, she'd had some rather intriguing dreams about him. "Where did you sleep?"

"Here," he told her, his brow quirked in a teasing arch.

"Here?" she asked, glancing at the bed and looking for a second indentation in the mattress.

"Madame," he said, crossing his arms over his chest, "I'll have you know that Simmons kindly set up one of my grandfather's old campaign cots in the sitting room."

She peered around him, spying the long, narrow bed tucked in there. "How long have you been awake?" she asked, as she slipped past him into the other room and dodged behind the screen to get dressed.

"Long enough to know that you talk in your sleep," he said, following her into the sitting room.

"I do not," she said, glancing around the side of the screen.

He shrugged. "I swore I heard my name coming from that room. Several times."

Emmaline felt a blush steal over her cheeks. "I would never be so indiscreet."

"So you admit you were dreaming about me?"

"Never," she told him.

"So you say. But we both know the truth, now, don't we?"

Incorrigible man. "What are you doing, lurking about in here?" she said, thinking it was the better part of valor to change the subject.

"Waiting for you to awaken."

She snorted, glanced in the mirror and sighed at the state of her hair. "Do tell the truth, Sedgwick. You are a terrible liar."

"Whatever do you mean?"

She came out and stopped in front of him. "Why are you here?"

"I'm waiting for you." He said the words with such determined force that she stepped back from him. "Emmaline, I was waiting for your answer. Will you stay?"

Stay and be ruined. Stay and have her heart broken. Oh, she shouldn't, but her reply came forth before she could stop it. "Yes, Sedgwick. I'll stay." She bit her lips and cursed herself silently. Now she was in for it. "But if I am to stay, there will be conditions."

"Agreed, for I have a few of my own."

Of course he would. This was Sedgwick, after all. She edged past him, feeling more than a bit uncomfortable standing so close to him, even now that she was dressed. "What do you require?" she asked, settling onto the settee on the other side of the room, folding her hands primly in her lap.

"First and foremost," he began from his post by the door, "I want you to finish the house."

"Carte blanche?"

"Your heart's desire," he offered.

She didn't dare tell him her heart's desire, but at least she could realize some small part of her dreams by turning Number Seventeen into *the house* she'd always imagined. "What else?"

"You must agree to stand up with Miss Mabberly."

She didn't think she'd heard him correctly. "At her wedding?"

"Yes," he said. "I think she would find some comfort having you there."

Emmaline felt her breath catch in her throat. His peers thought him dull and uncaring? Ridiculous! "Oh, Sedgwick—"

"Oh, no you don't. Don't look at me that way. I simply thought you were kind to her, and if the poor gel must marry Oxley, let her have some solace in the day."

"You want me to stay for Miss Mabberly's sake?"

"Yes."

"And for nothing else?"

"No." He paced a few steps. "Well, perhaps I have another reason. Your assertion earlier that having the *ton* see Emmaline and make their association to you makes sense. You should quell most of the speculation about my wife, if only . . ."

"If only what?"

"You quit telling these ridiculous stories about me."

She flinched. "I'm ever so sorry about last night. But you weren't there. Lady Oxley said the most insulting thing about you, and I felt that as your wife—"

His brow cocked.

"As the embodiment of Emmaline, it was my duty to defend your honor."

He shook his head. "I think I preferred the highwayman tale you told Hubert and Lady Lilith."

Emmaline tipped her nose in the air. "My embellishments on your character are exceedingly helpful."

"Helpful?' he sputtered. "You told the worst gossips in town that I walked through snowdrifts to be by your side."

"I was just giving you an advantage for later."

"How so?"

"When you decide to marry—marry for real, that is—

you should have no problems finding a bride. Every young lady in town will be vying for your hand."

"Yes, and her expectations will surpass my capabilities."

She glanced up at him. "You might surprise yourself."

"Now don't you go falling prey to your own romantic stories. Let me assure you, I'm not that sort. Snowdrifts, indeed!"

"Oh, Sedgwick, I would wager you would traverse more than that for someone you loved. For your Emmaline. In fact, I think you made up a bride simply because you couldn't find the perfect woman."

"Such a creature doesn't exist."

"Perhaps that is because you haven't looked for her." And this time, his gaze bore into her, as if he were looking to find one that moment. Feeling uncomfortable under his scrutiny, she rose and went to the mirror to finish fixing her hair. "What else?" she asked. "You said you had other conditions. What are they?"

"Before you depart, you tell me who brought you here, who else knows my secret."

She sighed. He deserved to know the truth. "Fair enough. But not a day before." Emmaline patted at her hastily done chignon, tucking loose strands back into the knot. "Anything else?"

"Yes. No more parmiel. No gambling, Emmaline."

She bit her lip. Well, certainly by the time she left for Westly's piquet challenge she would no longer be under these strictures. So she nodded. "Have you more to request?"

"No. That should be adequate for the time being," he told her. "And you?"

She closed her eyes and sighed, pushing the words past

her lips. "I insist . . . well, I think it would be best if we didn't repeat the mistake from last night."

"What? Going to Lady Oxley's?" he teased.

She shot him a wry glance. "That goes without saying. But what I meant was . . . I mean to say, in the carriage, when we . . ." She crossed her arms over her chest. "I might be posing as your wife, but that doesn't mean I will—well, I'm not that kind of woman."

That wasn't quite the truth, for his kiss could have tempted even the most virginal of hearts to partake in a bevy of sinful pleasures. Desires that now haunted her dreams, her very thoughts as she looked at him, standing there the very image of noble perfection, in his crisp white shirt and taut breeches.

"Emmaline, I'm not about to complicate this situation by demanding . . . marital rights."

I was afraid you'd say that, she thought.

"Excuse me?" he said, his brow quirked with a bemused knowing arch. "You looked like you had something to say."

"I'm glad to hear you agree," she said, turning toward the mirror again and making a hasty (and unnecessary) repair to her hair, neatly avoiding looking him in the eye.

"As long as you don't throw yourself at me," Sedgwick said, "I am sure we will be able to maintain—"

"Throw myself at you?" She stabbed another hairpin into her chignon and whirled around. "I did no such thing."

"As I recall, I was sitting on my side of the carriage minding my own business when suddenly you were in my lap."

"I was unprepared for the sudden stop. I wouldn't put it past you to have tipped your driver to perform such a subterfuge." She fired off her volley and then looked up at him.

His one good eye was alight, and she found herself caught in the spell.

"Emmaline, not even I could have thought of such a deception, but clearly I will have to speak to Henry." He turned to leave the room, and she caught him by the sleeve.

"Don't you dare," she said.

"Are you sure?"

Emmaline gulped. Oh, demmit, she'd tip Henry herself if she thought it would change things between them.

But the fact remained that he was who he was—a nobleman—and as such, his fate, his future generations couldn't be sullied by such an unthinkable union. Certainly there was the occasional errant earl who threw caution to the wind and married beneath himself, but Emmaline couldn't see Sedgwick taking such an irrational step. Not that he didn't possess the wherewithal (his current black eye and the mere suggestion that she continue posing as his wife were evidence of that), but there were other considerations that no amount of eccentricity or noblesse oblige could erase—that she was an imposter and, as he had so eloquently implied earlier, a common thief.

No, it was better not to tread any further into his arms and discover that, lady or not, she possessed a heart that could break as easily as any other.

"Yes, Sedgwick," she told him. "I'm sure."

He let out his own sigh. "Agreed. You are right that it is for the best."

"Yes, for the best," she said, glancing down at her fingers still resting on his arm. Quickly she pulled her hand back and edged away from him.

Certainly it would be easy to avoid such contact, Emmaline reasoned. There was too much at stake to be so diverted. Yet the stakes had changed somehow. During the kiss in the carriage, and through the long night, everything had changed between them.

And she would have been foolish to continue telling herself that it was going to be easy to avoid Sedgwick. Easy to ignore the clamoring in her heart.

"You never did say why you were up here," she said, looking for a hasty way to change the subject, cut the tie that seemed to keep pulling them together despite their best efforts to disavow it.

"I was going through some accounts," he said, nodding at the open books on the desk. "But in truth, I told Simmons to declare that I was sitting in vigil by your side, in recognition of your bravery and fortitude in facing last night's ordeal." He grinned at her.

She smiled back at him. If anything, his skill at prevarication was improving. "When you gave that excuse, were you referring to Lady Rawlins's lying in or Lady Oxley's supper party?"

They both laughed, and in an instant they were once again in that dangerous, tenuous place that had the power to draw them together despite any vow.

But luckily for them, there was a soft knock at the door.

"Yes," Sedgwick called out, turning toward it too quickly in Emmaline's estimation.

"My lord?" Simmons called from the door. "There is a disturbance in the ballroom that requires Lady Sedgwick's immediate attention."

"Oh, dear," she said, glancing again at the clock. "The draper must be here. I fear he and Signore Donati do not see eye to eye."

Alex watched her leave and let out a long sigh.

"Am I to assume that Lady Sedgwick will be staying a bit longer?" Simmons asked.

"Yes, for a fortnight."

"I'm glad to hear it, my lord."

"Was there anything else you wanted?" Alex asked, thinking that perhaps the real reason the butler had come up was to plead Emmaline's case.

"Unfortunately, there is. Mr. Denford is quite insistent about seeing you. He has some report he wishes to discuss and I fear he also wants to air Mrs. Denford's grievances."

Alex groaned. "I should throw them both out, bothersome pair."

"I am sure Mrs. Simmons and the maids would be more than happy to assist with any packing," the butler offered.

Alex had to imagine the entire staff would lend a hand to see Hubert and Lady Lilith tossed into the streets. "I fear we can't do that. Though I don't know why they don't stay at Oxley's. He is just as much family; more so, I daresay."

"I believe the food is better here," Simmons said.

Having eaten at the earl's just the night before, Alex couldn't argue with that. Perhaps the man's marriage to an heiress would improve the fare at Oxley House.

"Might I suggest an alternative to spending the afternoon with Mr. Denford, milord?"

"Gads sakes, yes, man, help me out."

"I think if you had a prior engagement, you would be able to put off Mr. Denford."

"Such as?" Alex asked, because clearly his crafty butler had a plan in mind.

"Perhaps a picnic, my lord. With her ladyship. I believe

she is rather fond of the countryside, and it would serve to keep you both out of the house and her ladyship well out of Mrs. Denford's path."

A picnic? He hadn't been on one since his youth, and the memories still warmed his heart. "An excellent suggestion, Simmons." Though after he said it, he realized he needn't sound too enthusiastic or it would only serve to encourage Simmons's matchmaking, so he added, "If only to keep Lady Sedgwick and Lady Lilith from coming to blows."

"Why, of course, my lord," Simmons said.

"Would it take long to arrange for a basket and the necessary items?" Alex was willing to bet that the man already had the carriage ordered, the basket packed with a bounty fit for a feast and the rest of his grandfather's military furniture tied to the back of the phaeton.

"Not long at all, my lord," Simmons demurred. "Actually, the Tottley chef sent over a hefty basket this morning as a thank-you for Lady Sedgwick's service last night." He paused for a second. "Is it true? That her ladyship saved Lady Rawlins's life?"

Alex nodded. "So said the midwife."

Simmons beamed. "I knew it. Especially since the child now bears her name. I should tell you that the entire staff is beside themselves with pride."

Despite his own feelings on the subject, Alex tried to lessen his butler's lofty regard for Emmaline. "Remember, Simmons, she will only be with us for two weeks."

Simmons pressed his lips together, but said nothing.

"It's how it must be," he told him.

"I don't see why—"

"Simmons—" Alex shook his head. "I fear it is how it must be."

Anything more than a fortnight and he doubted he'd be able to extract her from his life.

From his heart . . .

"If you say, my lord." Simmons bowed and went out the door. "And I'll see to your request immediately." He went to leave, then stopped at the door. "And Lady Sedgwick? Should I inform her of your wishes?"

"No, I'll go tell her."

Simmons nodded. "Very good, my lord."

"Simmons?"

"Yes, my lord?"

"How do you know that Emmaline enjoys the countryside?"

Simmons smiled. "One has only to look around this house to know that."

And as Alex followed the butler down the stairs and toward the ballroom, he looked again around his house and saw what Simmons thought so obvious.

The colors she'd chosen. A deep blue like the sky in June. The delicate yellow of primroses. Greens in all shades, from the first blush of spring to the rich, deep green of summer.

She'd banished the shimmer of gilt, the deep reds, the artifice of town to transform the house on Hanover Square into a pastoral oasis.

I wonder what she'd do to the Abbey, he thought, considering she'd most likely beggar the Sedgwick fortune redoing his ancestral home.

He strode into the ballroom, thinking it would be a pleasure to see her do it, if only to send Hubert into paroxysms of shock over the loss of his potential inheritance.

The large chamber was once again a beehive of activity, with the paper hangers competing for space with the painter and his assistants as they were putting the finishing touches to the ceiling.

Mr. Starling and Signore Donati were in the middle of the room arguing some matter, and Emmaline stood between them, her hands on her hips, her gaze cast upward in exasperation.

"Ahem," he coughed.

The tradesmen ceased their bickering at once and then practically fell over each other in an attempt to curry his favor.

"*Il mio signore*—"

"Lord Sedgwick, my apologies for making this disturbance, but my esteemed colleague here will not—"

Alex walked right past them, ignoring their groveling, his gaze locked on Emmaline.

As he drew closer, he spied a bit of blue paint on her nose. Leave it to her to get to the heart of the matter without delay. The woman was a veritable whirlwind.

"I am so glad you're here," she began without any greeting or preamble. "I can't seem to get these two men to work together. Mr. Starling claims he cannot risk his paper, what with the way Signore Donati and his assistants are slopping paint about, and I haven't the vaguest notion what Signore Donati is saying. I don't know a word of Italian, but what with the small bit of French he knows that I can understand, I believe his assistant who usually does all the translating was hired away by some scurrilous woman who wanted her boudoir painted with scenes of Naples. And then he keeps saying something quite unconscionable about using Vesuvius to rid the world of pompous English tradesmen."

Alex laughed. "Leave them to me."

He waded into the middle of the ruckus, speaking first to Signore Donati in his native tongue.

Emmaline's translation had been somewhat accurate, but apparently the assistant had also taken the signore's portfolio of drawings and now the man was without his renderings to finish the mural.

Emmaline was at his elbow, listening to the exchange. "You speak Italian?"

"*Sì*," he said, then explained the entire situation to her, including the name of the culprit.

"Lady Jarvis!" Emmaline crossed her arms over her chest. "She was quite interested in all the details of the signore's work the other night at Malvina's, but according to Malvina, she is far too purse-tight to pay for the master's work."

"Well, apparently she found another way to get her murals."

"My lord, if you please," Mr. Starling was saying, "can you make sense of this fellow's yammering? Because I would appreciate it if you would tell him to—"

"Mr. Starling," Alex said, interrupting the man's complaint, "I think you will find some compassion for your fellow artisan when you hear the reasons behind his 'yammering.' " He then went on to tell about Lady Jarvis's underhanded tactics.

"Well, I never," Mr. Starling said. "Scandalous. Now I see what has the fellow in such a fine state. Please offer my apologies to him and ask him how I can help. Don't like for him to think we are all so disreputable. Stealing apprentices!"

"Then perhaps, Mr. Starling, you could be a little more accommodating with the signore this morning. Perhaps you could work on the opposite side of the room and I'll ask the signore to move his paint pots well out of your way."

"A fine idea, milord. Yes, indeed, milord," he said, bowing. "You, there," he called to one of his own apprentices. "Move those ladders and give these foreign fellows some room."

Meanwhile, Emmaline had stripped off her apron and was starting for the door.

Alex caught her by the arm. "Where are you going?"

"To Lady Jarvis's to get those drawings. I'll not have my ballroom copied by the likes of that woman."

Alex glanced at her stormy countenance and laughed. "No, you don't. The last thing I need is another *on dit* being bandied about the *ton*. We've fed those gossipy cats enough tattle broth without you adding more hot water to the pot." He glanced up at the doorway where one of the footmen was lolling about. "Thomas! Come here!"

The footman rushed forward. "Aye, milord?"

"Go over to Lady Jarvis's and find an Italian fellow by the name of—" He turned to Signore Donati and asked him in Italian for the name of his assistant. With the information provided, he continued to instruct the footman. "Find this Luigi—discreetly, of course. And then offer the fellow twice whatever Lady Jarvis is paying him to come back here. Get a nice purse from Simmons to use as a lure."

"And don't forget to retrieve the signore's portfolio," Emmaline added.

Alex nodded. "With the portfolio," he told Thomas.

"And any drawings or copies," she added.

"I believe Thomas gets the point," he told her, grinning at her wrinkled brow. He rather liked this fierce firebrand side of her.

"I'll find this fellow," Thomas promised, making a cheeky wink, then leaving in all haste.

Alex translated his plan to Signore Donati, who all but wept with joy, that is after he was finished hugging Alex and kissing his cheeks.

"Grazi! Grazi!" he effused.

Mr. Starling shook his head at the display. "Foreigners," he muttered as he went back to work, redirecting his men to clear a section of the room for the painter.

Alex brushed his hands together and grinned at Emmaline. "Now, with that solved satisfactorily, I wanted to ask if you would—"

"Ah, cousin, there you are!" Hubert called out from the doorway. "If it isn't an imposition, I have a few matters of the utmost importance to discuss with you, if you would but—"

"Can't do it now, Hubert," Alex told him.

His cousin blinked once, then blinked again. "I don't think these matters can be put off. We need to settle accounts from last night—Lilith is still in high dudgeons over the entire episode and I think—"

"Not today," Alex repeated. "I promised Emmaline that we would go on a picnic this afternoon. Isn't that right, my dear?"

Her lips pursed together, while one of her brows quirked up. *No more tales, eh?* she seemed to be chiding him.

Please, Emmaline, he wanted to say to her. *Spend the day with me.*

Then her eyes lit with amusement and she played her part like the finest of thespians. "How forgetful of me!" she exclaimed. "Our picnic! I fear this crisis with Signore Donati quite overshadowed my memory. Will you forgive me, Sedgwick?"

"Of course," he said. He glanced over at Hubert. "Sorry, my good man. But duty to my wife calls. Perhaps tomorrow."

Hubert glanced from one to the other and then let out a wheezy "harrumph," before he marched from the room.

Once he was sure that his cousin was well and gone, Alex dug around in his pocket and produced a handkerchief. "You have some paint," he told her, pointing to his own nose.

"Oh dear," she said, taking the handkerchief and wiping at her nose.

He shook his head, took the cloth from her and, edging closer, wiped the remaining bit of paint from her face. For a moment they stood together, so very close that all he could think of was the night before when he'd held her in his arms in the carriage.

Oh, yes, his earlier boast about not wanting to exercise his marital rights had sounded good, but right now . . . well, that was another matter.

There was something about Emmaline that captivated him. Left him longing for something he couldn't quite put his finger on.

"Thank you, Sedgwick," she said, a faint hint of blush on her cheeks, as she moved out from beneath his shadow. "Do you really want to go on a picnic?"

"I suppose we have no choice now, do we?"

She bit her lip and glanced over her shoulder, considering the work still to be done. "I don't know . . ."

"You wouldn't leave me to an afternoon with Hubert, would you?"

She laughed. "No, I don't suppose I would wish that fate on anyone. But—"

"Never fear," he rushed to tell her, "Thomas will have

this Luigi fellow back in a thrice. Besides, you deserve a reward."

As if on cue, Simmons came in. "My lord, the carriage is ready and Mrs. Simmons has the basket prepared for you and her ladyship."

"A spontaneous invitation?" Emmaline slanted a glance at him. "You had this planned all along, didn't you?"

Alex shook his head, his hands rising upward. "I believe that Simmons is the culprit here."

"Too bad. For a minute I thought you were trying to charm me."

Chapter 11

Emmaline dashed upstairs to find a simple shawl to toss over her gown, as well as her straw bonnet, but then Mrs. Simmons came hustling in to help her, and protested her choices most vehemently.

"My lady, if Lady Rawlins saw you leave the house dressed so, she'd be over to ring a peal over my head for a good hour, laying in or no." Then the old busybody got a sly look on her face. "Besides, don't you want the master to see you in your new things?" With that, the housekeeper pulled out an exquisite buttercup carriage dress, a beribboned and flowered poke bonnet and an elegant lacy shawl.

Emmaline's protests that the dress was too fancy for a mere trip to the park were met with deaf ears as Mrs. Simmons pinned and tied her into it.

"There now, my lady," the housekeeper mused, like a shameless mother hen, pushing her toward the door. "You look as pretty as a picture. Won't you just turn his lordship's head."

Emmaline slanted a glance at her. Not Mrs. Simmons as well?

Still, despite the housekeeper's assurances, it was with some trepidation that she went out on the front steps and awaited Sedgwick's verdict.

He came forward, a wide grin on his face, taking her hand and bringing it to his lips. For a man who wasn't supposed to be charming her, he was doing a good imitation, as he led her down the steps with all the attention and respect a gentleman afforded his ladylove.

When she quirked a brow at him, he drew closer and said, "For Simmons's sake. I'd hate for him to be disappointed in us after he went to so much trouble."

Emmaline grinned at him. "Mrs. Simmons, as well."

A picnic, she discovered, at least a Sedgwick picnic, was no hastily produced basket of soggy morsels and stale treats, but a feast that could sustain a battalion.

Mrs. Simmons's basket was a huge affair that took up the entire tiger's seat, along with a long slender case, containing what, she couldn't fathom. In addition to all this was a stack of blankets and pillows, along with military-style furniture, folded and organized neatly, tied to the rear of the carriage. No doubt leftovers from the twentieth baron's military campaigns with Howe.

"Is there room for us?" Emmaline asked as she surveyed the overladen phaeton. Heavens, how long could a picnic take? It looked like he was packing for a trek to the wilds of Scotland.

"Of course," he said. "The afternoon awaits us." He led her to her side of the high flyer, the kind of expensive phaeton that only the dabbest hands drove.

Emmaline eyed the dangerous conveyance with suspicion. She'd never ridden in such a sporting vehicle. And when the horses started to prance and snort impatiently in their traces and the entire thing swayed dangerously, she wasn't too sure she wanted to get aboard.

"Do you know how to drive this . . . this monstrosity?" she said from the safety of the last step.

He turned to her. "Lady Sedgwick, never question a man's skill with his cattle."

"When my neck is involved I think I have every right to inquire."

"You are quite safe," he assured her. "Remember, I am a man besotted. I wouldn't let any harm come to you." Then he winked at her, his green eyes sparkling with amusement.

The devilish flirt.

"If you please," he said, holding out his arm.

She eyed the carriage and the horses one more time, then screwing up her courage, let him hand her up into the seat.

His hand lingered on her arm, and she found his touch unsettling. She tried telling herself that she was still overtired from her long night, but that wasn't the entire truth. She loved the feel of his muscled forearm beneath her fingers. The strength he lent her so readily, a feeling she told herself she had no right to claim.

But when he got in, she found that the narrow seat afforded them little room. Wedged in next to him, her thigh pressed to his, her hip to his. She could only grit her teeth and try her best to remember her vow.

Not to repeat their kiss . . . not to let him take her in his arms. She'd have to add no more rides in this blasted phaeton, for it was going to be tortuous to make even the short jaunt to the park.

"Ready?" he asked.

She nodded.

Simmons and his wife were gathered to see them off, while upstairs Lilith and Hubert watched them from a window. But she had little time to worry about their dour faces, for just then, Sedgwick tapped the ribbons, sending the horses forward and the lofty carriage rocking on its great springs.

"Oh, dear!" she cried out as she clutched for something to hang on to. The first thing she found was Sedgwick's arm.

"First time in a phaeton?" he asked, letting the horses take the carriage careening into traffic.

"I thought we decided not to ask each other questions," she said through gritted teeth.

He glanced down at her from beneath his tall beaver hat. "That would make the afternoon rather dull, don't you think?"

She wasn't too sure what to say, for she was still convinced this horrible carriage was going to be her death.

"Why not make it a game to pass the time?" he ventured.

Emmaline slanted a glance at him. Really, how many questions could he ask between Hanover Square and Hyde Park?

"But for each question you ask, I get one of my own," she told him. "And nothing regarding my identity."

"Agreed," he said. Little did she realize then, Sedgwick had no intention of going to Hyde Park. "Ladies first."

"Oh, no, my lord," she said, having regained her balance and folded her hands demurely in her lap, regretting that she hadn't an excuse to continue to hold him. "This is your game. You may have the first volley."

"Excellent!" he declared. "Where did you learn to decorate?"

At this, she laughed. "I've been to some of the nicest houses in England—"

"Twenty-eight, to be exact," he noted.

"Yes, twenty-eight," she replied. "And in those houses, I suppose I picked up a sense of what I like and what I don't like."

"Yes, and how lucky for me that this acquired taste of yours is so expensive," he teased.

"I prefer the word elegant," she told him loftily.

"What do you think about the words beggared, penniless and insolvent?"

She chose to ignore them and instead she jumped into her question, for now he was in her debt.

"Why is it that you aren't married?" Best to put him on the defensive quickly before he had another chance to pry.

"But I am!" he said smartly.

"Sedgwick!" she said, shoving her elbow into his ribs with a very unladylike nudge. "You know exactly what I mean, and I expect nothing less than the truth."

"Honestly?"

"Yes."

"I don't know."

She looked up at the sky. "If you won't take this game seriously—"

"No, that is the truth," he said in all earnestness. "I don't know. If I did, I assure you I would have wed, if only to end my grandmother's and my family's endless hints and suggestions."

Emmaline tried not to smile. "You do have quite an interesting family."

"That is an understatement."

She ventured another question. "Are they all like Hubert?"

Sedgwick laughed. "No. But don't let that ease your fears. The Denford clan is, shall we say, a rare collection of characters."

"Is that why the barons always marry so late? Afraid of continuing the line?" This time she was teasing.

"Something like that. My grandfather didn't marry until he was nearly sixty." He glanced over at her. "Do you have any family?"

She shot him a hot glance. "I thought we agreed that those sorts of questions—"

"Emmaline, I only wanted to know if you have any relations. Not who they are. I gave you my word."

She looked away. It was a fair question, but the answer was hard to give. "No."

"None?"

She shook her head. It wasn't completely the truth, for she thought her grandmother might still be alive . . . if the law and fate hadn't caught up with the old harridan.

"I'm sorry," he said.

She shrugged and asked her next question. "Tell me about Sedgwick Abbey."

At this he slanted a sideways glance at her. "Don't get any ideas. You'll not be sinking your brocade-loving, new-furniture and Italian-painting claws into my ancestral home."

"Oh, bother that," she told him. "Just describe it to me."

And so he did. Telling her with a voice filled with love and attention to detail all about his ancient family seat. Emmaline found herself so enraptured by his descriptions, that it wasn't until they were well past the park and headed out of London that she realized for the first time in a long time, she'd been gulled.

"Why, you had no intention of just a simple ride to the park," she sputtered, glancing over her shoulder at the city gates.

The smug man beside her just grinned.

"This isn't your way of getting rid of me, is it?" she asked. "Taking me out into the countryside and abandoning me along the way?"

He shook his head. "No, I leave those tasks for Henry."

"Well, thank goodness I know that now. If Henry ventures to ask me for a picnic, I'll be sure to refuse!"

They both laughed, and Sedgwick turned the carriage onto the main road. The way straightened out before them, so he gave the spirited pair of horses their freedom. The carriage picked up speed immediately, dizzyingly so.

When Emmaline caught her breath, she peeked up at the baron from beneath the brim of her bonnet. It took her breath away to look at him, he was so utterly handsome. His strong jaw, his chiseled lips, the deep cleft in his chin.

This close to him, she wondered what she'd been thinking to accept his invitation. Let alone how she'd found herself married to such a man.

Then she had to remind herself they weren't really married and that in a fortnight's time she'd have to put away the title, the armoire full of clothes, the elegant and newly redecorated house on Hanover Square and, worst of all, she'd have to bid farewell to this man who left her feeling at odds with everything she held dear.

Like her independence. How many times had she left a country house thankful that she'd never be trapped in some loveless marriage? Not with some overbearing man who liked to make demands and put his foot down at the least little thing.

She smiled a little. *Such as Sedgwick.*

But she had to admit that, while their first few encounters had been rather fraught with demands and bluster, suddenly he'd become . . . well, quite likable.

Take this picnic. Why, he'd practically begged her to come along with him.

Rather than spend the afternoon with Hubert, her jaded reason complained. A picnic with her was probably the lesser of two evils. But he hardly looked put upon at the moment. He actually looked quite content.

Content? Oh, no, that would never do. There was no room in their agreement for such a notion. No more than there was for her to allow his matchmaking staff to truss her up in some misguided notion that Baron Sedgwick would fall in love with her. Couldn't they see how that would never come to bear?

Besides, contentment on Sedgwick's part had never been part of this reckless bargain. A living, breathing Emmaline was supposed to be leaving him vexed and annoyed.

"Oh, heavens," she muttered under her breath. "This will never do."

"What now?" he asked. "Remembered another tradesman due by the house and ripe for you to harangue another few quid out of his profit?"

She tipped her chin up. "I'll have you know I've done a very good job of saving you quite a bit of money."

"While spending me into the poorhouse," he laughed back. "You are an incorrigible thief when it comes to those merchants. Why, you'll blacken the name of Sedgwick for generations to come."

"I'd rather fancy that they won't come to your house overcharging you for second-rate goods."

He tipped his hat back and grinned at her. "Do you have a ready answer for everything I say?"

"Of course."

"Then who are you?"

She planted her lips together and shook her head. "And you say I'm incorrigible? I thought we agreed that wasn't a subject we were going to discuss."

"Yes, I know, but you can't fault a man for trying. We are married, after all, and what am I to say to your legions of fans about town when they ask me about you? If I can't give them some hint as to your likes and dislikes, then they will start to doubt the veracity of our besotted union."

Emmaline tapped her chin with her fan. "I suppose you have a point there."

"So," he began, giving the reins a gentle toss, "what is your favorite color?"

"Green."

"Just like that?" he asked. "Green?"

"Of course. I think I would know what I like."

"Is that your favorite color or Emmaline's?" he asked, his eyes alight with mischief.

"Amazingly enough, we have very similar tastes," she told him. What a terrible tease he was. She would never have guessed such a thing about him.

"How convenient," he conceded. "So we have a favorite color of green, which will make buying flowers for you quite convenient."

"How so?" she asked.

"I can tell the florist to forgo the blossoms and just send you the greenery."

She nudged him in the ribs. "Some besotted husband you make. That wouldn't be acceptable in the least."

"Whyever not?"

"Because if you were my besotted husband you would know that I also like flowers."

"Yellow roses, I assume?"

"How did you know?" she asked, wondering at him anew. First the teasing, now this.

"You have a charming one on your hat," he pointed out.

Her hand went up to her brim until her fingers touched the silk flower pinned there. "A lucky guess."

"Not really," he said. "I have further proof—the gown you wore last night had yellow roses embroidered around the hem."

He'd noticed her gown?

"I didn't think you the type to notice such things." Dull, stuffy fellows didn't pay the least bit of attention to what a woman wore.

"A beautiful dress on a beautiful woman, I notice," he told her.

Emmaline tried to breathe. He thought her beautiful. How many years had she hid behind a severe chignon, spectacles and dull, oversized gowns, the costume of spinsterly companions hired by rich, bored matrons? Once or twice she'd had a sharp-eyed rake see through her disguise, but she'd never believed any of their honeyed compliments that she was truly beautiful.

And despite her best intentions never to listen to such

falderal, her heart skipped a beat and she found herself wickedly distracted with her own ruinous thoughts.

Of his kiss, of his touch. Of him finding more than just her face and gown beautiful. Of a dappled green meadow dotted with little daisies, and a blanket spread across the verdant lawn and Sedgwick drawing her closer, calling her beautiful and asking her to . . .

The carriage veered off the main road onto a country drive, and Emmaline's daydreams came to an abrupt halt as she bounced into his side, her hands scrambling to find something to cling to.

His coat, his sleeve, his thigh—as solid and muscled as the Elgin marbles.

"Demmit," she cried out, one hand clinging to Sedgwick, the other on her bonnet. "Have you gone mad?"

"I just wanted to see if you were awake," he said, his brows quirking at her rather unladylike curse. "You looked like you were woolgathering and needed to be roused."

"A simple 'ahem' would have sufficed," she told him, trying to regain her composure and set aside the tangled web she'd been weaving. "Where are we?"

"Clifton House," he told her, nodding up the drive at the residence ahead.

So it wasn't one of his houses, she realized, somewhat disappointed—not that she had any reason to be. Clifton House, she knew from her *Debrett's,* was the family seat of the Earl of Clifton. The lovely and ancient country manor looked like it had been a part of the landscape for centuries, sitting on a gentle knoll like a squat sentry. Down from the house spread an ample lawn that ended at the Thames.

On the river, a wherryman poled his boat downstream, heading toward the city.

It couldn't have been more picturesque—as dreamy as the watercolor scenes she'd found of Sedgwick Abbey in the attic.

"How beautiful," she declared.

"I thought you might find it so."

"Do you know the earl?" she asked. "Oh, never mind that question, you are related, are you not?" She paused for a second, recalling the correct passages in *Debrett's*. "Though distantly," she noted.

Sedgwick slanted a glance at her. "Is there anything about the *ton* that you don't know?"

She shrugged. Memorizing family lineage was one thing, but it didn't let one see inside the heart of a man. It didn't give the mercurial details of a family's quirks and idiosyncrasies.

"So are we to meet the earl?" she asked, not really in the mood for a social call. She had thought they were going to spend the afternoon together.

Alone.

Oh, bother, she told herself. *Stop thinking along those lines . . . because they could come to naught.*

Her disappointment must have shown, because he said, "Sadly, Clifton is not here. I'm afraid it will be just us."

Emmaline decided for once to say nothing. But perhaps the happy tip of her lips revealed her feelings.

They came to the end of the drive and stopped in front of the house. Sedgwick climbed down and was in the process of taking her hand to help her to the ground, when the front door opened and a plump lady in a lace cap and apron came bustling out the front door.

"Lord Sedgwick, is that you?"

"Mrs. Calliwick," he said. "Are you still here?"

"Wouldn't leave, not iffin his lordship tossed me out. Which he keeps threatening."

He bowed regally to her. "If that devil ever dares, you will always have a place in my household."

The old lady grinned, revealing a few missing teeth. "That's whats I tell 'im, and it straightens 'im right out."

They both laughed and Emmaline continued to stay in the background, that is until Mrs. Calliwick spied her. Without a moment's hesitation, the lady edged Sedgwick out of her way with a well-placed elbow. "Now, who's this? Your lady wife? About demmed time you brought her here to meet me."

"Emmaline, Lady Denford," Sedgwick said, "may I have the pleasure of presenting Mrs. Peregrine Calliwick, Lord Clifton's housekeeper."

"Very nice to meet you, ma'am."

Mrs. Calliwick's gaze narrowed. "Listen to her, all full of manners, and for me, of all people. She's much too nice for the likes of you, Sedgwick. And too pretty, to boot. Always thought you'd marry one of those sourpuss misses from London who'd have you a henpecked wreck afore a year was out."

Emmaline smiled at the outspoken woman. "I'm working on the leg shackles, madam, but I fear he's been rather obstinate about wearing them."

The lady cackled long and loud. "And she's got a right sharp wit to her. Have you got a sister, milady? A fine, tart-mouthed gel for my master?"

"Now, Mrs. Calliwick, no more matchmaking. You know Clifton doesn't appreciate your efforts."

She frowned and waved her hand at him. "Bah! Well, maybe your example will prove a tonic for my master, as well for that worthless friend of yours—"

"Lord John?"

"Oh, aye, Lord John. That fellow will end badly one day if he doesn't find himself a bride. Mark my words, his wild ways will ruin him yet." She brushed her hands over her apron, as if washing her hands of that problem. "Now, you didn't come all the way from town just to introduce me to your pretty wife, so how can I be of assistance, Lord Sedgwick?"

"I was wondering if we could have a picnic down by the river."

A sly look crossed her face, then she beamed at Sedgwick. "You are as besotted as I hear tell. Bringing her out here so you can have a cozy little nuncheon—you do my heart proud, Sedgwick. That you do." She wiped at a few stray tears that had sprung from her sharp brown eyes. "Why, of course you can use his lordship's property. Do you need a basket? I haven't much baked right now, but I could—"

"Never fear, Mrs. Calliwick, I'm sure Mrs. Simmons has outdone herself."

"Of course Betsy has," Mrs. Calliwick declared. "She's my daughter, she is. I taught her well how to run a house and keep a family in good care."

"And I appreciate your lessons every day," he told her.

Mrs. Calliwick beamed anew, before putting her hands on her ample hips and calling out toward the stables. Very quickly, a couple of lads came running.

"Grandsons," Sedgwick whispered.

"There you worthless lads are," she scolded. "Didn't you

hear the carriage come in? I did, and I was in the back of the house."

Now Emmaline knew where Mrs. Simmons got her uncanny ability to know when something about the house was amiss. She imagined Mrs. Calliwick had heard them when they turned from the main road.

No need for bellpulls for Mrs. Calliwick or her daughter.

The old lady was already directing the boys to unload the carriage and carry all the baskets and furniture and accompanying necessities down to the water's edge.

Then, before Emmaline could say another word, Mrs. Calliwick bustled her into the house like a tiny Banty hen, so she could "freshen up a bit" and have a good "coze."

Half an hour later, Emmaline ventured tentatively across the lawn Mrs. Calliwick had spent the entire time giving her marital advice, for it seemed the lady had buried three husbands.

"Let 'im wait a bit, milady," Mrs. Calliwick had told her. "Let 'im wait for you down by the folly. It will get his blood up."

Emmaline bit back the truth. How could she tell the woman that the last thing she needed to do was to get Sedgwick's blood up?

It was her blood that seemed to be fevered—for she could hardly contain herself once she'd escaped Mrs. Calliwick's clutches. She wanted to run down to the water's edge, barefoot and carefree, and throw herself into Sedgwick's arms like a besotted bride might.

Instead, she did her best to restrain herself and amble down to the water in a respectful, ladylike manner.

She failed utterly.

After a few steps across the rich lawn, she couldn't resist the temptation. She reached down and plucked off her slippers. It was a warm day, so she'd forgone stockings, and now she wiggled her bare toes in the velvet grass.

Across the lawn rose a hearty laugh. She glanced up to see Sedgwick standing before the folly Mrs. Calliwick had mentioned, wearing only his his shirt and breeches, having discarded his jacket and waistcoat.

So she wasn't the only one tempted beyond the rules of propriety.

She joined his laughter and skipped across the lawn, relishing each step. As she drew closer, she discovered Mrs. Calliwick's description of the folly hadn't done the lovely building credit.

Built in the classical style, it had pretty marble columns and a round roof. Situated beside the river, and surrounded by a flower hedge, it was delightfully private.

He bowed to her and then waved his hand for her to join him there. As she climbed the steps, she found the table and chairs set up for the occasion. A crisp white cloth covered the table, and atop that sat plates and cups, and a tray of breads, cheeses, meats and fruits, along with another plate of biscuits and sweet delicacies. And as she drew nearer, she spied in one of the cups a handful of freshly plucked buttercups, their sunny yellow faces bright and merry.

He'd picked flowers for her?

Her heart tripped unevenly.

"To your liking, Lady Sedgwick?" he asked as she slanted a glance over her shoulder at him. He stood nearby, his stark white shirt in such strong contrast to his dark hair and fierce mien.

"Entirely so," she said. "Though I still don't see how all this could be the work of such a spontaneous invitation."

He started to shake his head in protest, then just gave up. "I believe Simmons and his wife are trying their hand at matchmaking."

"Shameless pair," Emmaline said, edging around the table as he came closer. A bit of breeze whispered up from the river and playfully tossed the ribbons from her bonnet. "But it would be even more shameless if we were to let their good efforts go to waste." Then she realized how her words might have sounded and hastily added, "I meant the food, that is. It would be a terrible crime for this lovely meal to go to waste."

"Agreed," he told her, but the sly turn of his lips and quirk to his brow hinted that he liked the implications of her first suggestion better.

Now he was flirting with her. Whatever would this day bring next? But even as she wanted to revel in such attentions, she reminded herself that flirting hardly meant a thing amongst the *ton*.

Especially when it came to flirting with ladies of her ilk. Besides, it was a ridiculous notion—she and Sedgwick! Surely he was only practicing his image as a besotted husband.

And with that in mind, what harm was there in enjoying his attentions amidst a lovely sunny afternoon and a delicious meal?

He held out her chair for her, and when she sat down, her heart hammered to have him so close behind her, his hands just brushing against her as she scooted her chair in.

Then he sat down across from her and she filled a plate for him, then for herself. They chatted about the setting, and

Sedgwick regaled her with tales of the Clifton earldom and their checkered past—stories that never made it into the gilded annals of *Debrett's*. His family and the Cliftons had been friends, comrades and allies for centuries and at times had intermarried, so as she had said earlier, they were also relations in a distant and meandering sort of way.

They laughed and talked and ate their fill until Sedgwick leaned back in his chair and sighed. "I think I've had nearly enough."

"I might have thought that after your fourth helping," she said, folding her napkin and laying it neatly on the table.

"Can I help it if fresh air and such lovely company gives me a healthy appetite?" His smile took on a wolfish quality that sent ripples down Emmaline's spine.

So if the tarts aren't enough to appease him, what else could he want, she found herself wondering. Hoping . . .

Oh, Emmaline, she chastened herself. *Do stop these ridiculous whims and flights of fancy.*

Sedgwick is too toplofty and proper to see beyond blood-lines. Why, even his imaginary wife had possessed a spotless pedigree. And hers . . . well, her relations and connections were as checkered and tattered as a well-worn Scottish plaid.

Yet when she looked up into his eyes, she spied a dark, sensual light there, and she had to wonder if she was the only one this afternoon giving in to such implausible no-tions.

"Now it is time for the real diversion this afternoon," he said, standing up and winking at her.

"I don't know . . . I mean, if you think—" Emmaline be-gan, rising on shaky legs. What was she saying? This wasn't what she was supposed to be doing, and yet Sedg-wick was too handsome for words, too charming by half.

And when he smiled at her like that, she swore he had her muddled enough to toss aside even a perfect hand.

Because wasn't that what she was holding? The perfect hand. She had the connections now to get into the marquis' tournament, to win a fortune, and yet here was Sedgwick. This wickedly handsome and incredibly tempting man.

"Are you ready?" he asked, holding out his hand to her.

Without even a second thought, she placed her fingers into the warm grasp of his and followed him from the folly. Into a folly of a different sort.

Chapter 12

"Yes, there is nothing better after a picnic than this," Alex said, as they headed toward a blanket spread under a great oak. Emmaline's gaze was so fixed on that secluded spot, the soon-to-be site of her happy ruination, she almost missed that he was holding up the long, narrow case she'd spied earlier in the carriage. "Yes, this will just do the trick."

"That?" Suddenly she suspected that he wasn't about to seduce her.

"I suppose you are going to tell me you've never done this?" he asked. "Now don't be shy about it. Though my mother always abhorred it, my grandmother still finds it delightful."

She shot him a sideways glance. His mother and grandmother? Gads, she'd better have misunderstood him. "Excuse me?"

"Fishing," he said. "What else is there to do on such a lovely day?"

Fishing! He had brought her here to this secluded bower, this perfectly romantic spot, for an afternoon of fishing?

She didn't know whether to cry or to push him into the water. Before she could indulge herself further in a fantasy of him rising from the water like Neptune, shirt and breeches clinging to his muscled frame, he'd assembled one of the rods and was pulling out a second one.

"No, I think not," she told him. And she meant it.

"You won't be disappointed."

Care to make a wager? Truly, she'd had enough disappointment for one afternoon without some wily fish adding to her vexation.

Not that Sedgwick seemed to notice her ire, for he was too busy enthusing about the joys of fishing and the right bait.

He held out his hand again, "Come along, Emmaline, give it a try."

This time her legs stayed put and she remained rooted in place. Nothing like talk of grubs versus worms to cool one's ardor.

"No, thank you," she told him. "I think I'll remain here and just watch." *And fume.*

"Well, watch carefully," he shot over his shoulder as he climbed down the low bank to the water's edge. "And if you feel like joining in, just let me know."

She managed to smile at him, and then stretched out on the blanket and watched the sunlight as it danced and played over the lazy water. But her gaze continued to stray to the man before her, taking in the way his shirt stretched tautly at his shoulders, the way his brow crinkled as he concentrated on casting out his line.

From what she could see, fishing looked to be a lot of work (and cursing) for nothing. Clearly there was more to it than Sedgwick's professed expertise, for he wasn't having any luck.

"Are you sure you are doing that correctly?" she called down to him.

"Why don't you show me how it is done? Or are you afraid you'll be slighted by these fellows as I've been?"

Oh, bother, why not? she reasoned. *Might as well be snubbed by both man and beast.* That is, if a fish qualified for a beast. If not, she'd let Sedgwick stand in for both.

She made her way down to his side.

"Now stand here," he said, gently guiding her in front of him, then pulling her in close.

Suddenly fishing became much more interesting, as her back pressed into his chest, her body melded to his. If the summer's day hadn't been warm enough already, the heat sparking to life between them turned it into an inferno.

Her memory hadn't been playing tricks on her: His body was as long and hard as she'd recalled. And as she tipped her head back to look up at him, all she could see were his lips—the ones that kissed with such masterful skill.

Sedgwick's gaze met hers and she swore she saw the same recognition in his eyes that must be burning in hers.

How could it be possible that they affected each other so?

Her mother had always said that when she fell in love, she'd know it in an instant. As her mother had with her father. Not that she'd ever regarded her mother's advice about men as sensible—considering her idea of the perfect mate was a highwayman she often mistook for a nobleman.

She looked again at the baron and a chill ran down her spine. Demmit, this was not a good sign.

Closing her eyes, she prayed, *No, not Sedgwick.* She didn't want to fall in love with him.

Yet she knew with a certainty that she would never find another man who would make her feel so alive, so insensible, like she was falling, slipping away . . .

And that was because she was.

Slipping, that is.

For when she'd shifted in his arms, to get closer, to gain a chance at another kiss, she put her foot on a slick rock that suddenly gave way.

And sent her falling not into the arms of Alexander Denford, but into the cold reward of the Thames.

"Oh, no, oh dear!" she cried out, as she flew out of his arms and fell with a mighty splash into the river.

Luckily for Emmaline, the water wasn't overly deep. She landed on her backside in the muddy bottom. If anything, the cool water worked well at temporarily dousing her ardor—especially when she realized he still stood on the bank clutching his demmed fishing pole.

"Goodness, Emmaline, you almost lost my best rod," he called after her, a twitch of a smile on his lips.

"Bother the rod," she shot back at him. She rose up, drenched and covered in mud. "Do you know how much this dress cost? Now it's ruined!"

"It doesn't look so ruined to me," he said, tipping his head to one side as if to survey her claims. Whatever it was he found brought a wicked tilt to his lips and that hauntingly sensual light back to his eyes.

She glanced down at herself, only to discover the pretty muslin clung to her like a second skin, revealing curves that Sedgwick was eyeing with all the appreciation of a practiced rake.

"Lady Sedgwick," he declared. "How shocking that you've kept such a delightful form hidden from your husband for all these years."

"Demmit, Sedgwick, stop giving me the glad eye and get me out of here." Her feet were stuck in the muck and try as she might she couldn't pull either one free.

To her chagrin, he only laughed. Roared like he'd never seen anything so funny. "Why would I want to do that?" he asked. "I might never have another chance to see you thusly."

"I wouldn't be in this predicament if you had caught me before I fell," she scolded, trying to sound as severe as she could. His good humor was infectious, try as she might to be vexed with him. Really, where were his manners?

"Yes, but to save you I might have lost my best fishing rod in the bargain."

Oh, so that was his priority! Emmaline grit her teeth and used every bit of strength she possessed to pluck one of her feet free. It got her close enough to the bank to catch hold of his fishing rod and pull it and its precious owner into the water beside her.

Sedgwick landed with a mighty splash and came up sputtering and spitting.

Emmaline grinned down at him. "Having better luck fishing now?"

Sedgwick looked down at himself, then before she realized what he was doing, he caught hold of her ankle and up-ended her—right back into the muck beside him.

She came up splashing and laughing, for there was nothing else to do. They laughed and splashed at each other with abandon, forgetting everything and everyone.

"I do declare, madam," he said, affecting London manners and pretending to regard her though a lorgnette. "You look quite spectacular today. Quite smashing. Is that a new frock?"

Patting her dripping bonnet and sodden ribbons, she said in an equally haughty tone, "Why, yes, and I do believe this will be all the rage next Season."

They laughed again, and the companionable merriment stole into her heart, moreso than his handsome features and fine manners ever had.

Who would have ever thought that the oh-so-proper and starched Baron Sedgwick would find a dunking so amusing?

And it wasn't the only surprise Emmaline discovered in that moment.

She glanced over at him, his green eyes alight with amusement, and her heart quaked. It was like her mother had said, akin to spotting a falling star, a marvelous moment of happenstance, a moment to grasp.

How, she had always wondered, does one hold on to something as ethereal as a falling star?

She soon discovered how. Sedgwick reached out and caught hold of her. She struggled at first because she thought she was going back into the muck, but when she took another wild look at him, his gaze captured hers.

And as much as the kiss the previous night had changed the rules between them, in this fiery instant, the rules were completely rewritten yet again.

The merriment that had been there on his face was gone. She stared in wonder at him. *This cannot be.* But there was no denying it now. Sedgwick's smile had frozen and it seemed like he too was seeing her for the first time.

For a wild moment all she could think about was what an unholy sight she must be, like a dripping wet alley cat, but it obviously wasn't what he saw . . . that, or he had a soft spot in his heart for strays.

He pulled her into his lap and gathered her close. All his teasing, his high spirits were gone, now replaced by a look of pure intent.

Unspeakable desire.

Gently, slowly, he took her ruined bonnet off her head and sent it sailing into the middle of the river. Far and away, where it couldn't be retrieved.

Emmaline tried to utter a word of protest, but she couldn't even breathe.

He brushed back her sodden curls, his hand warm against her wet skin. It seemed like the entire world around them stilled; even the ever-flowing Thames paused for this magical, impossible moment.

This is *impossible,* Emmaline wanted to tell him. He couldn't, nay he shouldn't look at her like this, like he found her beautiful beyond words, like he held a regard for her that came anywhere near the burgeoning feelings hammering in her thundering heart.

His gaze seemed to be taking the measure of her every feature: her nose, her cheeks, her chin, her lips.

Then without saying a word, he leaned forward and stole a kiss from her lips. She melted closer to him as his lips teased hers. Then he drew back and looked at her. Looked into her eyes as if seeking some answer from her.

How could this be?

She didn't know, didn't care. Her life had been a series of lies and deceptions up until this point, so much so that the pure truth that seemed to be the essence of this moment left her staggered. Now she understood what it meant to follow one's heart.

Slowly, she tipped her head and ever so softly nodded at him, encouraging him to kiss her.

Not that he needed much prodding. A wolfish smile tugged at his lips and this time his mouth covered hers with a determined hunger.

That heat, that fire, while momentarily cooled by the river, sparked anew, unable to be dampened for too long. It flamed to life inside her, as she suspected it had ignited the desire behind his kiss. He kissed her deeply, his mouth devouring her as if he'd never get enough of her, enough of this heady, this wondrous joining.

But kissing wasn't enough, and they both seemed to know it, for his fingers tangled with her hair, the back of his hand stroking the column of her neck, his hands, warm and strong, winding around her shoulders, tugging her even closer still.

The sunlight sparkled on the water around them, the birds trilled and sang from the bushes and trees that grew in rich reward at the water's edge.

And all the while, Sedgwick kissed her. Kissed her deeply and thoroughly. Emmaline's body thrilled at his conquest, his exploration.

And just as suddenly as he had begun his kiss, he stopped. For a wretched, breathless heartbeat he took another long searching look at her, and she feared he was going to set her aside, as he had done in the carriage.

Then he rose from the river, hoisting her up with him in his strong arms, and carried her from the water.

"Sedgwick, I—"

He silenced her with another kiss, this one more demanding than the last. His lips covered hers, sending a river of another kind through her veins—passionate and teeming with desire.

He paused for a second and looked at her again, quirking a brow, as if daring her to protest, to say a word, say anything.

And when she didn't—for truly, she didn't dare—he carried her up the bank and knelt down in the thick grass within the secluded bower where the blankets and pillows lay.

And when he gently set her down and gazed at her, Emmaline knew without a doubt that fishing was the last thing on his mind.

He'd been struck with madness—for what he was about to do was utterly so.

He'd never desired a woman as much as he wanted Emmaline this very moment. He forgot that she wasn't his wife, that she was an imposter out to deceive one and all, he forgot the thousand and one reasons why this shouldn't be, for making love to her ran in the face of the careful planning and intelligence that he liked to lecture Jack about. The type of prudence and reserve that had kept Emmaline's existence a well-kept secret.

Yet all he wanted to do was continue this reckless course. To sate his desire for her, to discover that something about Emmaline that made him forget everything sensible.

For being sensible would never gain him her vagabond heart.

Alex thought he should blame Rawlins and his demmed French brandy for having turned his thoughts so. Though he knew that wasn't fair . . . The viscount's words had only given voice and meaning to what had sprung to life in his heart the first moment he'd beheld Emmaline.

He sought her lips again, and kissed her, wondering at her response. She melded to him, her body warm and supple. Like her mercurial temperament, she was like fire beneath his touch, arching to his hands as they explored her breasts, a throaty moan urging him on.

Beneath his palm, her nipples hardened, taut and eager for his touch. For his lips.

Secluded as they were in a bower of hedges, with no chance of being disturbed, Alex began to undress her.

"Sedgwick—" she managed to whisper, a soft protest.

"There is no one about—"

"No, it's not that," she said, giving him a saucy wink. "But the dress has to be undone in the back first."

She rolled in his grasp and glanced over her shoulder, a hot eager light in her eyes. "If you please."

"Very much so," he told her, tugging at the soaked laces and finally getting them free. Her gown came over her head, and then her shift.

There was a look in a practiced woman's eye when she first disrobes before a man. Alex had seen it with his mistresses and with a few other conquests, one that said that he was a lucky man to see such a sight.

But there was no such light in Emmaline's eyes. This was not a woman used to disrobing before a man, for everything about her was suddenly shy and hesitant.

Almost as if she feared he would be disappointed in what he found.

"Emmaline," he whispered as he nuzzled her neck, his teeth grazing her earlobe. "I know not where to start, for you are the most beautiful woman I've ever beheld."

She shook her head, as if she didn't believe his words.

So he let his body, his touch prove him true.

His mouth sought out one of her breasts, taking the rosy nipple with his lips and drawing it into his mouth, where he could lave over the pebbled peaks until she gasped.

"Your breasts are perfection," he murmured, now seeking out the other one, and giving it the same delicious inspection.

She writhed and rocked beneath him, her fingers clutching at his shoulders and holding him in place.

"Oh, Sedgwick," she whispered.

Even as he continued to explore and nuzzle, kiss and suckle her, his fingers were busy exploring her thighs.

Her skin, so soft and rich, was its own reward. His fingers grazed over the downy curls at her apex, and she gasped in response.

And when he did it again, teasing and parting a path toward a greater prize, she moaned, lusty and eager.

As he suspected, Emmaline was not a woman who took her pleasure with anything but complete abandon.

And so he explored a little further, gently unfolding the petals of flesh with gentle strokes, finding his way to the hot and wet center of her desire.

His finger slid over her, once, then twice, her hips rocking with his movements.

Even as she matched his cadence, he paused and then slid a finger inside her.

"Sedgwick," she groaned, her legs falling open to him, even as her hips rose to meet him.

He covered her mouth in a deep, hungry kiss, his tongue moving over hers, even as his fingers danced and teased her.

His own body felt so alive, so hard with need. He couldn't think of anything but filling her, uniting his fevered length with her tight and ready channel.

Alex drew back from a kiss and caught his breath, and in that instant her scent enticed him, drew him closer, and he left her lips to seek other forms of pleasure. His mouth trailed down her shoulders, stealing hot greedy laps from her breasts, then moving down past the flat plain of her stomach, until they nuzzled at her very sex. When he looked up at her, she was staring down at him, her eyes wild with desire, her mouth open as her breath came in ragged sighs.

"Whatever are you doing?" she gasped.

"This," he said, letting his tongue trace a new course over her nether lips.

"Oh, no," she gasped. "That's . . . that's . . ."

"Delicious?" he offered, tasting her again, this time taking her into his mouth and letting his tongue wash over her.

Her hips shuddered and he caught hold of them, holding her to him as he continued to draw her toward an unforgettable, undeniable release.

Emmaline wondered at her own audacity. She was naked on a grassy knoll with a man she barely knew.

Though right now that hardly seemed true, for he appeared to know every secret her body possessed and a few she would never have guessed at.

His lips had been teasing passion at her mouth, sweet torment on her breasts, but what he was doing to her . . . *there* . . . was unholy.

It was as if he'd discovered the very center of her desires and meant to pull them from her until she discovered her release.

Oh, she knew what a man could do to a woman, tempt her into believing with his kiss, with promises of pleasures unbidden.

But there were no promises in what Sedgwick was doing to her. Only his masterful intent.

And so when his tongue passed over her again, she felt her body tense with need, her breath still in her throat, for fear even the movement to take another breath would break this magic he was conjuring.

Emmaline's hips arched and wrenched as he drew yet another deep kiss from her sex, and this time it sent shuddering threads through her, portents of what was about to come.

Her hands fisted into his shirt, clung to him, and she gave herself up to his kiss, until her body tightened to the point that it had no other thing to do but burst free, rocking her into a world of pleasure.

"Ah, ah, oh," she managed to gasp, her hips rolling on an endless ocean of rapture. "Sedgwick," she whispered, as the surging waves began to give way to tender ripples.

He laughed and placed a trail of kisses from her thighs back up to her lips. "Don't you think it is time you called me by my given name?"

She let out a contented sigh. "Alexander."

"Still think I'm dull?"

She laughed and kissed him. "Anything but. What devilment was that?"

"Only the beginning," he vowed.

* * *

She had to admit that perhaps there was something to Sedgwick's honorable reputation. When he had promised her that her pleasures were only the beginning, he was a man of his word.

They made love in the bower, Sedgwick bringing her back to the brink of her release before he entered her, slowly and tenderly, stroking her fires to a heated pitch until her hips rose and pitched feverishly to meet his thrusts. Her climax had taken her by surprise, wild and tumultuous, shared as it was by his own release, which left him gasping and spent over her.

They'd lain tangled together, entwined as one, while the aftershocks and tremors continued to course through their bodies, leaving them adrift in a passionate storm.

If Emmaline thought he was finished then, she was surprised to find that Sedgwick was far from spent.

He cradled her in his arms, his fingers teasing the wild tendrils of her damp hair. "Emmaline?"

"Yes?" she said dreamily, her own attention caught by the dark triangle of hair on his chest. Her fingers toyed and pulled at the strands.

"Have you . . . do you . . . ?"

She glanced up at him, for she knew exactly what he was asking. Though it wouldn't be a question a man would ask of someone, say, like Miss Mabberly or Lady Diana Fordham, it was one asked of a woman like her. One who lived outside respectable society. One who wasn't a virgin when she'd tumbled into his embrace.

She wasn't insulted, only struck by his hesitancy in asking and his need to know. "No, Sedgwick. I don't. I haven't done this . . . well, in a long time."

He nodded and went back to toying with a strand of her hair.

However, Emmaline knew her answer wasn't fair. And Sedgwick too much of a gentleman to pry. Not that it mattered—her answer, that is—but it mattered to her to tell him. So that he wouldn't think too ill of her.

"There was someone once," she said. "I loved him and I thought he loved me." She glanced away, for she didn't like to look back, made it a rule not to dwell in the shadows of the past. "But until today, there was no one else."

And there wouldn't be another, she had to imagine. How could she ruin such a perfect memory? "I've always thought it was a matter of trust to take a man into my bed . . . or picnic blanket."

He said nothing for a great while, until he managed to ask in a quiet, steady voice, "And you trust me?"

The question held more weight than she dared consider. Gads, how had it come to this?

"Yes," she said, stunned by her own confession. Held tightly in her heart was one thing, but saying it aloud . . . She glanced up at him, into those slate-green eyes, and felt all her fears slip away. "I suppose I do."

The baron nodded, and then tugged her back into his arms, where she trusted him once again.

The hours passed, but only too soon it was time to depart. Sedgwick and Emmaline had tugged their sodden clothes back on and trooped hand in hand up to the house. Mrs. Calliwick greeted them at the door, her eyes at first wide with horror at the sight of them. Then she'd broken into a cackling laugh.

"My lord, you might claim to be Sedgwick, but you've got a healthy measure of Clifton blood in you, you do." She'd hustled them inside, where they found a hot bath set up for them in one of the bedrooms and a change of clothes laid out.

"Do you think she . . . ?" Emmaline asked, wondering if their secret bower was really as hidden as Sedgwick had vowed.

"No, she couldn't have," he told her, stripping off his wet clothes and getting into the bath. "But considering she's served the Cliftons for three generations, I imagine she finds such afternoon amusements to be quite commonplace."

They laughed and then he caught her by the hand and pulled her into the tub with him. They kissed and touched and washed each other. And before they dressed themselves, they took advantage of the Clifton hospitality one more time.

By the time they were back in the phaeton traveling home, long shadows lined the road. Emmaline cozied up against Sedgwick, her hand wound around his elbow.

She had no desire to return to London. She wanted this afternoon to continue forever. Not to let the reality of life intrude on her happy interlude.

But it did in a way she couldn't have expected.

At the crossroads, a woman with a passel of children at her skirts was hustling them like an old hen across the road. They pulled to a stop and waited for the carriage to pass.

The kids were clean and tidy, but it was obvious from their patched clothing and drawn faces that life was not so easy for the large family.

"Come along," the woman called to her children, waving her hands at them. "This fine gentleman and his lady have better things to do than wait for the likes of you sluggards."

It was then that Emmaline noticed what the lady held clenched in her hands.

Her bonnet. The one Sedgwick had tossed in the river.

She nudged Sedgwick and nodded toward it. His eyes widened and then he laughed.

At the same time, the youngest child, a boy of about four, broke free and ran back to stare at the horses.

"William, you're keeping the gentleman and his lady from their journey," she called out. "And yer brothers and sisters from their supper. What there is of it." The woman put on a brave face and pulled the youngster out of their way.

Emmaline glanced away, not wanting to count the children and determine just how hungry they would be by nightfall. Not after she'd spent the afternoon surrounded by all that wealth could afford. She'd lived her entire life bouncing between the disparities of English society. Sometimes she lived with pockets plump and ample, and other times not knowing how she was going to pay for even a tin of tea.

"Madam," Sedgwick called out after the lady. "A moment, please." He rose in his seat and handed the reins to Emmaline. Before she knew it, he'd climbed down and had tugged their still-laden basket out from the tiger's seat. "Would you do me the favor of lightening our load? The horses are tired, and we still have some miles to go." He held out the bounty to her.

The woman gaped, then recovered quickly, taking the offered feast. When she felt the full weight of it, her eyes filled with tears. "Lawks, milord. You'll make us all fat as kings. I am very much beholden. For the children, that is."

He nodded and got back in.

Tears stung at Emmaline's eyes as well. He'd made his

offer with grace and kindness, without embarrassing the poor woman as to her lowly lot.

As he took the reins, the entire family waved at them. The woman called after them, "It's me lucky day, it is. I found this here fine bonnet just floatin' along in the river, and now a feast for me family. 'Tis my lucky day, it is."

"Mine as well, madam. Mine as well," he said, looking not at her, but at the woman beside him.

Chapter 13

Even now, two days later, while running some errands for Malvina, Emmaline found herself warmed and confused by Sedgwick's odd confession.

My lucky day.

She didn't know whether it was just a passing compliment or a heartfelt confession. Whatever it was, he had continued to show his regard for her in a thousand ways.

That night, after the picnic, they'd come home, ignoring the inquiries as to their strange clothing, Hubert's protests for time and all the other questions—their eyes only for each other. They'd gone upstairs and fallen onto the great bed, a tangle of limbs and heedless desire.

They'd made love two, three times, the exact number even Emmaline couldn't remember, for the passion he elicited from her, the blinding arousal he drew from her with his touch, his lips, his kiss, left her senseless.

The next day had been no different. For she would turn

around to find him watching her as she supervised the work or met with the tradesmen, and then with a tilt of his lips, a glittering sultry glance, he'd lure her upstairs and again they would fall into each other's arms, heedless of the talk their besotted behavior was generating amongst the servants.

And when she had awakened this morning, the bedchamber had been filled with bouquets of yellow roses. The scent had been intoxicating, her appreciation unbounded as she'd thanked him well into midmorning . . .

They never once spoke of the future, of what was to come of all this at the end of their agreement. But then again, she had no desire to consider that day—not when there were ten more days and delirious nights before she would have to leave.

Thus lost in thought, she stepped off the curb on Bond Street nearly into the path of an oncoming carriage.

It pulled to a stop before her, her eyes level with the crest emblazoned on the side.

She hadn't memorized *Debrett's* for nothing, for she immediately recognized the herald before her. The Duke of Setchfield. She'd met his heir, the Marquis of Templeton, at the Oxley's supper party.

She glanced up at the open carriage—mostly out of curiosity to see the duke most of society regarded with an unholy terror, only to find the carriage empty.

Then she looked up at the driver's seat and her mouth fell open.

"You!" Her lips snapped shut and she juggled her packages back up into her arms. How could this be? He was supposed to be dead. And since he wasn't, what the devil was *he* doing driving about in the Duke of Setchfield's carriage for all to see him?

"Good to see you as well, Button."

Emmaline frowned. "Don't call me that." She looked left, then right, trying to determine which direction would be the best in which to flee. Yet when she started to walk away, the demmed fellow clucked the reins and followed her.

"Get in, Button. I need to have a talk with ye."

"I will not," she shot at him, then spun on one heel and headed in the opposite direction.

When she glanced over her shoulder, she realized he was not going to be deterred. And, worse, he was still a dab hand with cattle and had the unwieldy carriage quickly turned around, despite the thick traffic in the busy thoroughfare.

He rolled up beside her as she waited at the corner to cross the street. "Get in, Button, or I'll tell me master, Templeton, exactly who you are."

His master? She'd never known Elton to ever call any man master. And of course he would have to pick the Marquis of Templeton—why, the disclosure of her identity to the breezy and gossipy fellow smacked of blackmail. Oh, bother, it *was* blackmail.

Well, at least she could find some measure of comfort that some things never changed.

"Come on with ye," he told her.

She pursed her lips, then nodded. To her surprise, Elton started to get down to help her in like a proper driver, but she waved her hand at him. "Don't bother. I've come this far without your assistance, I daresay I can continue so." She flung open the door herself, tossing her packages onto the seat behind Elton.

Hiking up her hem, she climbed in. Once she was seated,

he glanced over his shoulder at her. "Hanover Square, mi-lady?"

He knew where she was living? Oh, this was worse than she could imagine. Then she realized he was still looking for her confirmation, so she nodded. No point in denying the truth to the likes of him.

"Hanover Square it is," he said, tipping his hat to her.

She crossed her arms over her chest and looked to one side.

He picked up the reins and very quickly had the carriage rolling into traffic. Emmaline cursed the fact that she'd taken a hackney earlier. But Sedgwick had taken the phaeton and Hubert the carriage, so she'd had no choice but do her shopping for Malvina with a hired conveyance.

At least she hadn't brought along one of the maids or Thomas—she could imagine what Sedgwick's servants would make of the fact that she knew the Marquis of Templeton's driver.

They drove in silence for some time before he spoke again.

"How've you been?"

"Well enough." Really, he wanted the truth? She'd been shot. Slept in the cold on more than one night. Survived for the most part by her wits and skill at cards, and he was making conversation as if she'd just spent the last month on holiday in Brighton.

"I tried to find you," he said. The words were softly spoken.

She flinched. *Liar.* "Well, it seems you have, though I might point out it is six years too late."

"Aye." He sounded none too pleased.

"I'm not giving you any money," she told him.

"I don't recall asking for any."

Not yet. "What are you doing here?"

"I could ask the same of you—posing as some toff's wife. Lady Sedgwick, you say." Again the disapproval in his voice pricked her nerves.

So he knew of that as well. She needn't ask how—he must have spied her leaving Lady Oxley's. If she hadn't been so distracted that night, she might have noticed him as well.

Sedgwick. She blamed him. He'd distracted her from her job. Distracting her in ways she could never have imagined. What she needed to do was disavow this illicit affair, leave him, keep her eye on what was at stake.

"Whatever are you about, Button?" Elton asked, breaking into her reverie.

"If you must know, I'm here to gain a stake. And you needn't be overly concerned, I'll be well and gone soon enough."

"A stake? Harrumph. Your mother nor your granddame would approve of how ye're doing it."

"Since old Mam was the one who taught me the finer points of piquet, I think she'd approve quite handily."

"Piquet?" he sputtered. "You don't mean to go to Westley's challenge, do you?"

She turned her head and stared at the passing shops and homes, deliberately ignoring his question.

"That fellow cheats—"

"That hardly matters," she shot back. "So do I, and you always said I was the best there is. I would think you, of all people, would approve of lightening the pockets of a nobleman."

He spat over the side of the carriage. "You'll lose your last rag and then where will you be?"

Rather than continue this subject, she changed it. "How is it that you aren't dead? I heard you'd been hanged."

And more's the pity they didn't finish the job, she wanted to add.

He snorted. "I can tell you mourned me, miss. Right and proper, I suppose?"

She bit her lips. She hadn't. And it was to her shame.

"If you are of a mind to care, I was given a chance to make a better life for myself—me master, he saw to a reprieve. I've a King's pardon, I do."

A royal pardon for him? Emmaline shook her head. Utter nonsense.

"Now, don't be lookin' like that. It's the truth. Himself, that is, me master saw to it. Saved me from the scaffold and set me free."

Emmaline stared at him. He wasn't free, he was mad. "You want me to believe that the Marquis of Templeton, that foolish tulip, plucked you away from the gallows and got you a pardon? A royal pardon?" She laughed. "I fear, Dah, you've lost your touch."

"So I'm your dah now. About time you remembered that fact," he said, sounding none too happy about her disbelief. "I would think you'd be happy to find that I'd cheated old Mr. Grim."

"Well, I suppose it is a comfort to know that Mother and I aren't the only ones you cheated."

He turned around and continued driving in silence. It was a few blocks before he spoke again, though he didn't turn around. "Button, I've gone straight since then. Facing a noose has a way of changing a man."

"Yes, and my name *is* Emmaline Denford."

"It's not like that," he told her. "I help the marquis. He relies on me."

"With what? His shopping? I met the man. He cares for nothing but the cut of his coat and his next quip."

"There is more to the man than those things—"

"So says the man who's lightened more purses than Dick Turpin."

"I don't do that anymore." Elton gave the reins a firm shake.

"Cats don't change their stripes," she said.

"Leave yer grandmother's sayings out of this. I'm a different man. And I mean to see you out of this devil's bargain you've got yourself into. Masquerading as a lady. You'll be the one at the end of a rope iffin you ain't careful."

"You stay out of my affairs."

"Whether you like it or not, I'm your dah, and I mean to see right by you. What would yer mother say if she could see you like this? She had high hopes for you. Claimed you'd be a right and proper lady one day."

A real lady, indeed! The daughter of a highwayman and a . . .

"Mother wasn't—" Emmaline's words stumbled to a halt and turned her head away so he wouldn't see the tears threatening to spill down her cheeks. Like her often absent highwayman father, her mother, though present in body, hadn't always been right in spirit—her mind wandering amongst the glitter of the *ton* as if she'd lived there all her life. And when she came to her senses and saw the true nature of her life, her grief replaced her madness. "She's gone now, and I don't like to speak ill of her."

A long silence passed before Elton spoke again. "I did come back," he said softly. "I heard she was sick and I came back as soon as I could."

"If you say."

"It was a nice marker you put up for her."

She looked up at this. He had come back, though not soon enough, and obviously well after her mother had died, for there hadn't been a stone there for many years, not until Emmaline had finally won enough one winter to see her mother's grave marked with a proper headstone.

For fear he might make more of these unsettling revelations, she asked, "How is Grandmother?"

He snorted. "Alive. Asks after you, regular-like. Well, more like bedevils me about you." He glanced over his shoulder. "She blames me for how you turned out."

She chuckled and almost felt sorry for Elton. His mother was a harridan of the first order, but really, it had been Old Mam, as she was known in some circles, who'd taught her to play piquet and parmiel. And how to ensure that Emmaline won nearly every hand she played through means no more respectable than the old girl herself.

They rode in silence, and finally Emmaline decided to end this charade of a reunion. "What do you really want, Dah?"

"To see you safely out of here. I can talk to his nibs. See that he finds you a position somewhere—a respectable one."

Emmaline rose up and caught the latch on the door. "I swear I will jump out of this carriage right this second if you dare—"

"Sit down, Button," he said, clucking at the horses so they picked up a bit of speed. "You always were a hot-headed one. I'll not mention ye to Templeton if that's what ye want. But I'll be watching ye to make sure no harm befalls ye."

"I am in no chance of harm." Not from Sedgwick—though that wasn't entirely true. Her heart was at great folly—but there wasn't anything anyone could do about that.

"Oh, your baron is a right enough bloke. It's those Denfords I don't trust."

The Denfords? Emmaline shook her head. "Hubert and Lady Lilith are an annoyance, nothing more."

"I wouldn't be so sure."

There was something about his statement that gave her pause. "What do you know of the Denfords?"

"Been watching them, I have. And I don't like what I've seen."

"They haven't any money, if that is what you are looking for. They depend on Sedgwick for their support."

"Will you listen to me, Button? I'm not looking for a mark, I'm looking after you."

She crossed her arms over her chest and let out a suspicious "harrumph."

There had never been a day in her life when her father hadn't been looking for his next mark. She'd learned her trade in his footsteps, made a living out of the lessons she'd gained at an early age from him.

"You are as stubborn as yer mother was, but you've got a right smart head on your shoulders, so you'll listen to me. That Hubert Denford is up to no good. Been skulking about the docks for the last few days. Down there right now. He's after something and he's demmed anxious about getting his hands on it."

Against her better judgment, she slanted him a glance in his direction. "What has that got to do with me?"

"Don't know, but the man is being cagey. He's a danger, Button, mark my words. He's got treachery on his mind, he does."

Oh, that does it, Emmaline thought. Hubert Denford, a danger? Certainly he was a sneaky fellow, but clever and treacherous were not words she'd ever associate with Sedgwick's dull cousin.

Elton wasn't done with his outlandish theories, for he continued by saying, "Me master said you riled up Lady Oxley. That her daughter was about ready to scratch yer eyes out." He laughed a bit, as if he expected nothing less from her. "The marquis thought you were a bonny one, he did. Told me straightaway, 'Elton,' he says, 'Elton, that was the finest evening I've ever spent at Lady Oxley's. That scrappy Lady Sedgwick put the old hen in her place.'" Elton smiled at her. "He called you 'scrappy,' he did. And coming from me master, those are high words of praise."

Emmaline didn't see how anything uttered by the foppish marquis could be held with such high value, but she listened to her father's advice as he went on.

"You've made an enemy of Lady Oxley, and in due course her daughter and, by that order, Mr. Denford. Nothing worse than a hungry and beholden fox living under your roof."

Emmaline glanced up at the sky. Heavens, not more of her grandmother's pithy country advice, never mind the fact that she often herself quoted her father's incorrigible dame.

But despite the country adages, Elton had a good point about Lady Lilith and Hubert. She was only too aware that the Denfords viewed her arrival with open dismay—especially since they thought Sedgwick and his wife were in a deliriously happy second honeymoon, one capable of producing an heir that would usurp Hubert's position.

That could very well make even a ninny like Hubert Denford dangerous.

"I see that crease in your brow, Button, and don't you go fretting none. I'll keep an eye on them. In the meantime, I want you to promise me to keep well away from Westly."

Emmaline started to sputter. "I will not be—"

"It ain't safe for you here in London, considering how many of them toffs you've bamboozled the last few years."

"What do you know of my . . . my . . . travels?"

"Been trying to catch up to you, if you must know. Find ye and make sure yer safe." He wiped his brow and clucked at the horses again. "But I've got me other duties for himself, so I haven't been able to do by you as I've wanted. But that doesn't mean I haven't heard about your flimflam." He spat over the side of the carriage. "The Duchess of Cheverton! That woman has the power to see you hang. What were you thinking, Button?"

This last comment came out with more worry than she'd ever dreamt of hearing from Elton. It plunged into her heart and burrowed in, taking root in a spot she'd thought long banished from her life. The part where she believed her father's promises.

She'd spent so many years listening to her mother lament his wandering foot, and eye, not to mention his haphazard source of employment as a gentleman of the road, that she'd never really been able to believe that he cared more for them than he did the lure of the road on a moonless night.

But here he was, concerned and caring. Checking up on her. Following Hubert about, if he was to be believed. And she wanted to believe him, believe that he regretted the lost time between them, but she didn't dare hope that such a foolish dream was possible.

Any more than Sedgwick would ever believe her a lady.

A lady worthy of . . .

She shook her head at such a thought. "I've done well enough . . . and been very careful."

Now it was Elton's turn to snort, and he did so with all gusto. "If you were careful you'd have never got shot in Surrey." He paused and stared down at her. "Didn't think I knew about that, did ye?"

She shook her head.

"Spent three months trying to find what happened to ye. Tore me heart out looking for your . . . your . . . well, never mind what I was looking for."

Emmaline didn't like the way her eyes started to moisten at the notion of Elton searching for her, nor did she want to hear the wrenching pain in his confession. He'd thought her dead.

"Was proud to know that you hadn't gone down without a fight. Though I can't say your aim was so fair. I taught you to aim higher, not at a fellow's parts."

Emmaline shrugged. "The room was dark."

He snorted. "Like your grandmam, you are. Like to put a man in his place when you gets the chance. Oh, Button, you don't know how I rejoiced when I heard there was a young gel playing a fair hand of parmiel about the countryside. Right there and then, I knew you hadn't died on me. No one

could play parmiel better than you. But I would have
thought that once you nearly found yerself done in, you
might be more careful. Might try to find a new life."

"I did," she told him. "And now I'm at the very end. I
have but this one last game. Then I'll put myself far from all
this. Put it all behind me."

Elton coughed. "So I told yer mother more times than I
like to confess. How I meant them words each time I promised her, but the road and the game, they always call you.
One last game. Those words will kill you one day, Button."

Oh, dear God. How many times *had* she heard Elton
telling her mother the same exact words? Making the same
promise that none of them had believed.

But her situation was so very different. This *was* going to
be her last game. Her last con. If not because of the money
she'd gain from Westly's piquet challenge, then because of
Sedgwick. He'd made her believe in something far beyond
that. That love and trust and faith could change a person.

Emmaline glanced up at Elton. *As perhaps coming face
to face with the noose had done for her father.*

But before she could say anything, he turned into
Hanover Square and came to a stop in front of Number Seventeen.

"Here you are, Button, just as I promised. Now all I ask is
that if ye get into trouble, ye send for me."

She nodded, though she had no intention of doing so. For
what if she did call for his assistance and the changes he
claimed in his life and intentions he offered were nothing
more than the gammon and cant that was as much a part of
him as that notorious patch over his eye?

Simmons had the front door open, and one of the footmen was coming down the steps to take her packages and assist her from the carriage.

"Thank you," she called up to Elton, and walked inside without looking back.

Toiling in the past won't put supper on the table, her grandmother always said.

Still, when she got to the top of the steps, she chanced a glance at him, but all she saw was the back of the elegant Setchfield carriage rolling out of the square. A wild impulse tugged at her heart, nearly had her fleeing after her long-lost father, when a voice from within the house stopped her in her tracks.

"Well, that was an enlightening sight," said Lady Lilith, coming down the staircase. "My, my, my. The virtuous Lady Sedgwick riding about in the Marquis of Templeton's carriage. I wonder, who will vouchsafe for you now? You've quite broken your fine reputation today, not to mention how it makes your husband look."

Emmaline stiffened. Sedgwick! How would she ever explain this to him? Perhaps she should just follow her instincts and race after Elton and be done with this entire crazy scheme—before it was her heart, not just her reputation, that was broken beyond repair.

But then something amazing happened. Simmons spoke up, with that patronizing, nobbish sort of tone that only a London butler could perfect. "Mrs. Denford, there is nothing circumspect about Lady Sedgwick's mode of transportation. She was left to use a hired conveyance for her errands for Lady Rawlins, because Mr. Denford had already taken the carriage and Lord Sedgwick was obliged to use his phaeton." Simmons sounded as put out as if it had been him left stranded. "Rather than see her ladyship have to ride in some questionable hackney on her return, I sent a note over to the Duke of Setchfield's butler to see if arrangements could be made for her to return in His Grace's carriage."

Lilith's brows drew together as she first shot a hot glance at Simmons and then at Emmaline. Then she turned on one heel and marched back up the steps, muttering a rather loud, "Well, we'll see about that."

Once she was well out of earshot, Simmons began his own scolding. "I hate to say it, but Mrs. Denford is right— what were you thinking, riding about in the Setchfield carriage? Everyone knows Templeton uses it, and with *that* man driving, it looks highly improper."

"He simply offered me a ride home because I had so many packages," Emmaline said, as she handed him her evidence, the bundle of purchases she'd made, followed by her pelisse and bonnet. "Besides, I don't think the Marquis of Templeton is exactly the most rakish fellow about town. Hardly the sort capable of compromising another man's wife."

"Madam," he said, "be that as it may, you cannot forget that a proper lady doesn't ride about in another man's carriage. Not even one as harmless as the marquis. People will assume . . ." He sent a significant glance upward. "Certain people will assume the worst and use it to their advantage. I wouldn't like to see her carrying tales to Lord Sedgwick."

Emmaline cringed. "I didn't know," she confessed.

"Now you do." He nodded toward the pile of packages. "Would you like Thomas to deliver Lady Rawlins's items to her?"

"No, he doesn't need to go to all that bother. Besides, I'll probably pop over there later to see how she's getting on this afternoon."

"Very good, my lady." He bowed to her and went about the tasks of putting away her bonnet and pelisse.

Emmaline continued through the foyer, then stopped and turned around. "Simmons?"

"Yes, my lady?"

"Why are you helping me?"

"I would think that is obvious," the man demurred.

She crossed her arms over her chest and shook her head at him. "Not especially."

Simmons heaved a great sigh. "You are the mistress of this house, and it is my honor and privilege to serve this family."

She crooked her finger for him to come closer. "Simmons, why are you helping me? And none of that flimflam about the honor of the household and such. Why are you helping *me*? Is it because I'm, well, offering some assistance with your piquet problem?"

"Madam, you insult me. Your assistance with that difficulty is only one of your unique charms. But if you must know, I am helping you because—"

Upstairs, Lady Lilith started bellowing for a maid to attend her. *Immediately.* As her strident cries pierced every corner of the house, Hubert strode into the foyer from the back hallway, muttering to himself.

Emmaline knew from the pinched expression that arose immediately on Simmons's face that Hubert had come into the house via the mews and through the kitchen. Again. Making one of his surprise inspections of the staff, to ensure that they weren't robbing his good cousin blind and to make recommendations for economies on any derelictions he spied.

"Simmons, there you are," he called out. "That Thomas fellow changed out the candle stubs again. I don't see why they have to be replaced so often. Someone is making a tidy profit behind the scenes, eh?"

Emmaline's mouth fell open. One of the privileges of being a butler was that he received all the candle stubs— which could be sold on the side for remelting. It was a common enough practice, but what Hubert was saying was as good as accusing a longtime family retainer of theft.

Simmons stealing, indeed! Well, one good deed deserved another, and there was no doubt she was in Simmons's considerable debt.

"Cousin, it was I who asked Thomas to replace the candles," she said. "Lord Sedgwick doesn't like them sputtering on him halfway through the evening."

Hubert pursed his lips, then stomped off in the direction of the library.

"Off to count the volumes again, I daresay," Simmons muttered.

Emmaline barely suppressed a grin. "I thought you said you served this family."

"I do," he said adamantly. "But my lady, there is family and then there is *family*."

Emmaline understood that one only too well. Her father was the perfect case in point. Still, she needed to understand why the butler was risking so much to help her. "But Simmons, why me? Especially when you know . . . well, you know that I'm not . . ."

"Not without your charms, my lady," he told her, bowing his head slightly.

Upstairs, Mrs. Denford was still shrieking at the top of her lungs for a maid to come attend her. *Now.*

Simmons closed his eyes and shuddered. When he opened them, his gaze fell on her and a smile rose on his usually stern lips. "This house needs a mistress. And more importantly, an heir."

Emmaline shook her head. Had she heard him correctly? An heir? Was he mad?

Oh, no, she thought as the truth hit her harder than if she'd been run down by a mail coach. Simmons didn't care who she was, had most likely been overjoyed at her arrival. He'd risked all this in order to see Sedgwick truly married. Married and besotted. Married and producing an heir so the Denfords' hopes of inheriting wouldn't be so . . . so obvious. The bride could have been plucked from Newgate, or Bedlam, or right off of the nearest convict ship, and Simmons wouldn't have cared, as long as he could be rid of the Denfords for once and for all.

"But I'm not . . . I couldn't . . ." She shook her head at him. As adamantly as she dared without ruining the riot of curls that Malvina's maid had arranged for her earlier in the day. She leaned closer to him and spoke in a whisper. "Simmons, I'm not going to be here long enough to solve *that* problem."

"Madam, that remains to be seen."

She shook her head again. "Sedgwick doesn't want a wife, which is why he made one up. And he certainly doesn't want me."

Simmons smiled again. "Doesn't he? Madam, you underestimate yourself. And while I'll deny to my death that I've ever agreed with anything Mr. Denford has said, I do believe you have Lord Sedgwick besotted."

Chapter 14

"**B**esotted," Jack said, leaning back in his chair. He had joined Alex at a corner table at White's. "'Tis on everyone's lips that you have gone around the bend for your wife. So is it true?"

Alex cringed. He never wanted to hear that word again. He'd come to his club to seek some peace from the painters and paper hangers and the Denfords . . .

And his desire for Emmaline.

Whatever had he been thinking, making love to her? The press of her lips, the silk of her skin were now like a fever he couldn't shake. One he couldn't resist. So he'd fled the house before he spent another afternoon whiling away the hours in her magical company, in her arms . . .

Much to his chagrin, his club was offering no respite. Every fellow who arrived had to come over and wish him happy returns as to Emmaline's much-improved health. It seemed Lady Pepperwell had made good her promise to tell all of Emmaline's miraculous recovery. Giving every rake, Corinthian and would-be blade an excuse to slap him on the back and make some jest about his being besotted over his bride. Including Jack, who had not only wished him "happy," but ordered a bottle of Madeira (on Alex's account) to celebrate Sedgwick's good fortune.

"Can't let this besotted image of yours come under scrutiny," his friend had said.

"I am not besotted," he told Jack as the fellow poured the expensive wine into a pair of glasses. "Why, it was utterly ridiculous."

Jack snorted. "So explain to me why you drove her out to Clifton's for an afternoon of . . . now, how shall I phrase it? Marital privacy?" He laughed. "Don't try to deny it because I saw you driving home wearing Clifton's bottle-green jacket and your Emmaline sitting beside you looking all pretty and mussed. Now, if that isn't telling, I don't know what is. Though I would like to know—"

"Jack . . ." Alex warned.

The rascal had the audacity to grin. "Now, don't get your cravat in a knot, I was only going to ask if they have another bottle of this stuff in the back," he said, waving his hand at the dusty bottle. "Besides, it wouldn't be gentlemanly to pry." He glanced around for the waiter, then signaled the fellow to bring another bottle.

Alex was all too happy to pay if it kept Jack diverted. But even the Madeira failed him utterly.

"But since we both know I am no gentleman," Jack said. "I demand a full accounting." Then he launched into a rapid-fire litany of questions. "Who is this paragon? Did you find out who hired her? And if you don't mind me saying, what the devil are you doing bedding her? Never mind that question, she's a pretty chit. I'd worry about you if you hadn't found a way to tempt her into your bed."

"I have you to blame for all this," Alex told him.

"Not this again," Jack said, reaching quickly for the newly arrived bottle, lest it be nudged out of his reach.

"I'm in over my head with all this Emmaline business," he confessed.

Jack studied him for a moment. "You don't look the worse for it. And if you don't mind me saying, Lady Sedgwick wasn't the only one looking contented the other afternoon."

For a time, the pair sat in silence, Alex musing what to say, and Jack having the good sense to keep quiet and drink the Madeira.

This was what came of all his smug boasts about careful planning and intelligence—look where it had gotten him. Tangled up with a woman who wasn't supposed to exist.

"Demmit, Jack, what am I going to do?" Alex threw up his hands. "This is more your territory than mine."

Jack laughed again. "Oh, aye. Not like you to go off without weighing all the consequences, considering the finer points of propriety. What *has* this chit done to you?"

Alex considered all his answers and then offered the honest one. "She makes me laugh."

His friend's gaze narrowed, then he shook his head. "Never thought you'd say that. Lord, you are in deep."

"You don't know the half of it," Alex said, then explained what he did know of Emmaline's past—that she was a con artist who made her living gulling old ladies by cheating at parmiel.

"A cardsharp?" Jack sputtered. "You've gone and married some Captain Sharp?"

"I haven't married her," Alex protested.

"Not yet," Jack muttered, topping off Alex's glass and then his own.

"Don't you see," Alex said, "that is exactly the point? I certainly can't marry her."

Why hadn't he just cast her out that first night, found some reasonable explanation for her departure and then washed his hands of this entire affair?

But now he couldn't. Not now that he'd made love to her, listened to her plans for the house as they lay before the warm embers in the fireplace, naked and content. Spent nights with her cradled in his arms. Taught her to drive in the park. Done a thousand things that married people took so much for granted.

She'd become more than Emmaline in these all-too-short-lived days. She'd become a . . .

"Sedgwick?" Jack was saying, snapping his fingers at him. "You're woolgathering. I'm going to have to cast my lot with the rest of London and declare you besotted if you don't get that look off your face."

"I have no such look," Alex complained.

Jack used what little discretion he did possess and said nothing. Instead he took a long draught. "I don't see that you have any other course but to keep her."

"Keep her? Are you mad?" Alex sputtered, as if such a thing could be done.

Could be dared.

He shook off that notion. No, he couldn't do it. "Can you imagine what my forebears, let alone my family, would say if it became known that I'd married a woman of questionable breeding?" Alex said. "Never mind the fact that she has a decided lack of morals when it comes to cards."

"Demmit, Sedgwick, don't be so dull-witted. Half the *ton* cheats at cards. And I've never understood why one had to, when choosing a wife, consider the opinion of one's ancestors. Stodgy, stuffy fellows who have long since gone aloft. It's not like any of them are going to turn up and complain. And if they did, they'd have to first get past that ridiculous grin you get on your face each time the chit is mentioned. Why, I've ordered two bottles of this Madeira and you haven't even noticed, let alone complained."

"I noticed," Alex told him. "And I will concede that Emmaline is an uncommon lady. But I can't let my heart make this decision. Marriage is about duty and obligation—not personal feelings."

"If you really believed that," Jack said, "then why haven't you just married some dour-faced heiress and been done with this entire business years ago? You can go on and on about 'making a good match,' but you and I both know what a good match means. Your cousin Hubert marrying Lady Lilith. This Miss Mabberly leg-shackling Oxley. But that isn't what you want. Never has been, I daresay."

"I have a title and a legacy to consider," Alex said. "I can't just choose any bride I want."

"Why the devil not?" Jack argued. "I would think that a title and fortune such as yours would buy a fellow a measure of eccentricity now and then. Marry the chit and spend the rest of your life grinning at all the naysayers."

Alex drew a deep breath and shook his head. How could he?

Jack shrugged. "Do with it as you will. Demmed waste of a title and fortune, if you ask me. But what do I care? As long as it means you continue to pay for my drinks."

* * *

Alex arrived at Hanover Square some time later. Jack and his cheeky suggestions! Keep Emmaline, indeed! Why, such a notion was ridiculous.

Yet that stodgy sentiment didn't slow his pace as he took the steps up from the curb two at a time.

He could only wonder what mischief Emmaline had gotten into while he was gone, and demmit if he wasn't curious to hear about her exploits—harassing tradesmen, gossip she'd collected from Malvina, Lady Lilith's latest complaint. Alex couldn't help but grin. Why, even Lady Lilith's complaints were amusing when it was Emmaline relating them to him.

He paused for a second at the door and glanced over his shoulder at Tottley House. Once again he realized that Rawlins's words from the other night were haunting him.

. . . Know in your heart that there was something about her that would make your rather ordinary life complete, give you a reason to get up in the morning and see what mischief she was up to.

What the devil would he do when Emmaline was gone?

He pushed open the door and decided not to dwell on that notion. "Emmaline?" he called out as he walked into the empty foyer. "Emmaline, are you here?" The gloomy silence that greeted him was as desolute as a Scottish moor. A cold reminder on a warm June day of the dull routine his life would return to when she was finally gone.

"Emmaline?" he called out again. "Simmons?" No one returned his greeting, but his moment's pause revealed the sound of laughter coming from the back of the house.

Her laughter.

Now what is she about? his curmudgeoning side growled, but Alex did his best to banish such thoughts. Wouldn't it be a fine hour, to know that all his dull days were well behind him? To always have Emmaline about?

As he made his way down the hall, he heard the shuffle of cards and her voice again.

"No, no, Thomas. That's not at all proper," Emmaline was saying.

Not proper. What the devil was that cheeky footman doing with his wife? Not my *wife,* he reminded himself. *She is not my wife.* Still, he picked up the pace and strode into the kitchen.

Inside sat Emmaline at the great table, with Thomas and Simmons across from her. There wasn't anyone else about the large room.

She bounded to her feet. "Sedgwick! What are you doing here?"

Something about the entire scenario didn't set well. What the devil was she up to? "This is still my house," he said, glancing at Simmons and Thomas. They both looked as if they'd spent the day pawning the silver. "I should ask the same of all of you."

She glanced at her two companions, then frowned. "Cards," she said hastily, snapping up the deck on the table. "I discovered Simmons and Thomas playing cards." She shook her finger at the guilty pair. "As I always say, cards are the surest way to find yourself damned for all eternity. I am surprised at both of you. Not to mention what Mrs. Simmons would say!"

She pocketed the deck and sighed. "Sedgwick, I shall leave them for your justice. I fear the sight of such licentious behavior has made me quite dizzy." She beat a hasty retreat, her curls bobbing in merry denial to the stormy line of her brows.

"What the devil was that about?" Alex demanded of the guilty-looking pair before him.

"Her ladyship has an aversion to card games," Simmons suggested.

"So I gathered." He glanced back in the direction she'd gone and shook his head. Perhaps he'd misheard her laughing a few moments earlier, for, apparently she was taking her vow to give up playing parmiel quite seriously. "Just see that she doesn't find out about your Thursday night games." No need to put her back onto the path of temptation.

"Of course, my lord," the butler said.

"Aye, milord," Thomas added.

He turned and went to leave the kitchen, but then stopped and glanced over his shoulder. There was something not quite right about the scene he had just witnessed, but he doubted he was going to get the truth from these two, and he knew it would take the fires of hell for Emmaline to divulge a word, so he'd have to trust she wasn't up to her neck in yet another coil.

He left the kitchen to follow her, but when he came back down the hall, he heard Lilith and Hubert both talking at once.

"But you must go, cousin," Hubert was saying. "You'll quite ruin our party if you don't."

"Yes, Mother will be extremely vexed to find a vacant seat in her box," Lilith added. "Besides, Sedgwick agreed to accompany us to the opera this very morning, isn't that right, Mr. Denford?"

"It is," Hubert said.

The opera? With Lady Lilith and Hubert? And Lady Oxley? He froze in his footsteps. Was that what Hubert had been nattering on about at breakfast? He also vaguely recalled agreeing to whatever his cousin was saying just to get him to stop talking.

Demmit, he had agreed to go with them tonight. He grit his teeth. He could hardly explain his true desires for the evening to his cousin. There were only so many nights before Emmaline . . . well, before he had to give her up and it just didn't sit well that he'd have to share her tonight.

So keep her . . . keep her always.

Alex shook his head. He was going to have to give up drinking with Jack. It muddled his reasoning and left him susceptible to all sorts of impossible notions.

Then, much to his relief, he heard Emmaline saying, "I just don't think I can go." Her voice was thin and reedy. "I think my shopping trip might have been more strenuous than I thought, for I believe my fever is returning . . . I feel ever so hot, and terribly dizzy."

He peeked out from behind the corner and spied her standing in the foyer with her hand on her brow and wavering on her feet like she was about to topple over. Though she was flanked by Hubert and Lady Lilith, neither appeared ready to jump in and stop her from pitching over.

And knowing Emmaline, as Alex thought he did, the chit would be willing to dash herself onto the marble floor just to avoid an evening out with Mr. and Mrs. Denford. Not to mention Lady Oxley.

He certainly couldn't blame her. He'd be more than happy to have his other eye blackened right now if it would provide him a convenient excuse. Perhaps if Emmaline was willing . . .

Really, he needn't go to such depths just to keep them home. Her illness should be enough to keep them out of Lady Oxley's clutches.

"Emmaline, are you unwell?" he said, coming forward and catching her just before she did indeed topple over. He hoisted her into his arms, relishing the warmth of her skin, the scent of violets in her hair.

"Sedgwick, dearest, is that you?" Her lashes fluttered, while her head lolled against his chest. That pair of kissable, rosy lips parted ever so slightly.

How he wanted to forget this was all an act and kiss them anew. To watch her go from this feigned illness to a fever of another kind. And he would, once he got her upstairs.

"Aye, my love, 'tis me," he said. He shot an apologetic, indulgent glance at Lady Lilith and Hubert, whom he was positive had never shared an endearment between themselves in their entire marriage. "What is it? Are you unwell?"

She sighed and snuggled closer. "No, I fear it is so distressing. I don't think I will be able to attend the opera this evening." Glancing up at him, she gave him such a woeful look that if it hadn't been for the ever so slight twitch of her lips he would have thought she was truly ill.

He shook his head and looked at his cousins. "Emmaline is too sick to attend this evening."

"No, do not say so," Hubert said. "Lady Oxley is most particular about her seating arrangements."

"Yes," Lady Lilith declared. "The box will be quite ruined with an empty seat. Mother will be completely put out."

What she really meant was that the parsimonious Lady Oxley would be vexed by a seat for which she had paid going unused. If anything, the dowager countess liked to get her money's worth.

"I fear she will be more than unhappy," Alex told them. "For I cannot leave my wife in this condition."

At this, Emmaline's eyes popped open and she glared at him. And just as quickly, she regained her composure and went back to her state of semiconsciousness, moaning softly at her accursed state.

Once again he felt that suspicious twinge that she was up to something more than just this charade to escape the Denfords—but what it was, he couldn't fathom.

Not that he wouldn't find out the moment he got her alone.

"No, cousin, you must come along," Hubert was saying. "Wouldn't do for you not to be there as well."

"Two unused seats would be unpardonable," Lady Lilith declared.

Then, to his complete surprise, Emmaline rallied and added her support to the Denfords' cause. "Sedgwick, dearest, you must attend this evening. I would be bereft to be the cause of so much unhappiness. Please, attend for my sake and give Lady Oxley my sincerest apologies. That way perhaps she won't be as aggrieved."

"But I—" he protested.

"There you have it, cousin," Hubert said, pointing at Emmaline. "You heard your brave wife. You must come along now."

Lady Lilith was nodding, and demmit, so was Emmaline.

He was of half a mind to drop her right there and then and lend her illness a more authentic ring.

"Perhaps you could have Lord John stand in my place," Emmaline suggested. "He called earlier looking for you."

Just then, Mrs. Simmons came out from the back of the house and saw Emmaline in his arms. She let out a howl of indignation that her ladyship was "dying again," and prodded Alex up the stairs with her.

Once there, the housekeeper forbade him from entering the room and hustled him out of the chamber like a mother hen protecting her chick.

Before he could give Emmaline a piece of his mind for getting him caught in the evening's entertainment, the door was shut in his face.

I am the master of this house! Let me in! he wanted to bellow, but he doubted anyone was going to listen.

This, he decided, was what came of marriage.

Well, when she left, things would go back to the way they should be. He'd be the master of his house once again. And his life would be . . . well, it would be . . .

And there was only one word he could think of . . .

Incomplete.

The evening at the opera was far worse than even Alex could have imagined. Especially with Emmaline comfortably ensconced at home while he suffered alone and in silence.

To his chagrin, Mrs. Simmons had stood guard outside their door like a Beefeater at the Tower. Her ladyship's health was too precarious for his "attentions," she'd declared. And so he'd had no choice but to accompany Lady Lilith and Hubert, since he'd given his word and hadn't Emmaline's flair for the dramatic.

Along with the Denfords, Mr. and Mrs. Mabberly were part of the party, as well as a miserable-looking Miss Mabberly and, of course, the always pompous Lord Oxley sitting beside the poor chit, oblivious to her discomfort.

Lady Oxley had also invited the newly-arrived-in-town

Duchess of Cheverton, for she was so very desirous of seeing Emmaline "properly introduced," as she told Alex.

Properly skewered, he thought, for the Duchess of Cheverton had the sharpest tongue in the *ton*. Few dared cross her or cross paths with her.

Emmaline had chosen her fictitious employer well.

Her Grace's arrival also had the effect of raising his suspicions about the Denfords and Lady Oxley as being the masterminds behind Emmaline's arrival in his life. Could they have hoped the public setting would make for a good scene to discredit her, as well as him?

After all, Lady Oxley had given her blessing to her daughter's marriage to Hubert because she believed (like most everyone else in the *ton*) that it was unlikely that Sedgwick would ever wed, thus leaving the barony to Hubert or his offspring to inherit. Even his marriage to Emmaline hadn't dampened the countess's hopes, given that Alex's bride was sickly and never seen.

Still, a living, breathing Lady Sedgwick—especially *this* Emmaline—would have cost them too much just to see his marriage discredited. And one thing Alex knew for certain—neither the penurious Lady Oxley or his miserly cousin Hubert would have hired such a spendthrift, such an unpredictable minx.

And to top it all off, Jack, who had agreed to come along—if for no other reason than to take another gander at a new dancer he had his eye on—had yet to make his bow. So Alex was alone to face the duchess's ire at not getting to meet Emmaline and Lady Oxley's vexation at having a seat in her box go unused.

He glanced at the empty seat and thought of who should be sitting there. Emmaline. What the devil was she about?

He just couldn't shake the notion that she was up to something.

He tugged at his cravat and glanced around the crowded theater again. There was more to Emmaline's feigned illness than avoiding the Denfords. He'd be willing to bet the last vowel he'd signed for Jack on it.

"I have heard much of your wife, Lord Sedgwick," the duchess said in a loud whisper, pointing her fan in his direction. "And I've only been in town for a day."

"I don't doubt that," Lady Oxley huffed. "The gel is quite of her own mind."

"She must be quite extraordinary to have gained the attention of society so quickly, not to mention gained your favor," the duchess said. "From what I've heard, you barely leave her side. She must be extraordinary, I do say."

"She is that," Alex told her, trying to be polite.

"He's besotted," Hubert said, leaning over from his chair.

Alex flinched. He was becoming convinced that was the only word his cousin knew how to utter of late.

The duchess waved her fan at Hubert. "Well, it has been my experience that when a Sedgwick baron finally gets around to seeking a bride, he usually marries because he is besotted. Never caring a fig for propriety—marrying for love, and damn the consequences." If it was possible to believe it, the Duchess of Cheverton smiled. "Keeps the line interesting, I say. And I wish you all happiness, Sedgwick. It appears your wife has put a twinkle in your eye. Much like your grandfather possessed when he returned from Paris wed to your grandmother. I never saw the need to shun her because she was an opera dancer, but—"

"A wha-a-at?" Alex and Hubert both sputtered at once.

"An opera dancer," the duchess said, as if such an outrageous notion were common knowledge.

"Your Grace," Lady Oxley said hastily, "you must be mistaken. The dowager was from a long line of French nobility. She was even related to the old King."

The duchess snorted. "Genevieve Denford may be able to claim royal blood, but it was from a relation born on the wrong side of the blanket. An opera-dancing blanket, I would guess."

Lady Oxley's mouth opened and closed several times, as if the words just couldn't get past this unbelievable revelation.

The duchess ignored her stammering and instead turned to Alex. "Your grandfather loved your grandmother passionately. There wasn't a woman in London who didn't envy her his attentions. Give your wife the same measure of love, and you will die a contented man, like your grandfather before you, and I daresay your father did."

Alex could only nod mutely at this sage advice. Besides, the duchess had turned her attention back to the stage and dismissed the stunned crowd around her.

Grandmère had been an opera dancer?

That explained much. Her reluctance to come to town wasn't born so much out of her grief for her husband, but her fear of having her past revealed, of being shunned before her family.

Instead of the outrage that appeared on Hubert's face, the duchess's revelation had an opposite effect on Alex. He wanted to laugh aloud.

He understood perfectly what his grandfather had done—more importantly, he understood why he'd done it.

He'd married the woman who captured his heart. The one he couldn't live without.

Couldn't live without her . . . Like Rawlins had asserted.

Meanwhile, Lady Oxley, Lady Lilith and Hubert were all trying to explain to the duchess how she must be confused about the dowager. To regain some negligible piece of family honor that had obviously mattered not to his grandfather.

And suddenly Alex saw the two choices before him. To live like Hubert and Lady Lilith and Lady Oxley, clinging to the good opinion of society no matter the cost, or live as Jack had urged him—on his own terms, and damn society.

He glanced up at the duchess, and the old gel had the audacity to cast him a saucy wink, as if she knew of the revolution that was going on within him.

He'd marry Emmaline. Marry her tonight if he could. And damn society. Damn propriety. He'd have the woman who left him utterly besotted, and not care a whit what anyone had to say.

No, the intermission couldn't come soon enough, for then he'd make his apologies and explain that he couldn't enjoy the evening while his wife was so ill. He'd use his besotted reputation to its advantage and be home in a thrice.

And when the act ended and the curtain closed, he bolted to his feet. "My apologies, Your Grace, Lady Oxley," he said, bowing to the pair of matrons. "But I fear my concern for my wife prevents me from staying."

"Harrumph," Lady Oxley snorted, her brow arched with skeptical regard. "Your wife is well enough, I suspect. Lilith was saying earlier that she was in fine enough health this afternoon to spend you into debtor's prison on Bond

Street and ride about in Templeton's carriage. Why, I think . . ."

But Alex wasn't listening. Emmaline was riding in Templeton's carriage?

His old stodgy sense of family duty rose to the forefront. *You don't even know this gel and you want to marry her? Madness! Folly!*

He tamped down his doubts and clung to his new resolve. Dull no more, he was a new Sedgwick. A man of daring and dash.

All because of her . . . If he knew Emmaline, she had a reasonable explanation, and if she didn't, she'd make up a bouncer that would be just as delightful.

The duchess eyed him through her lorgnette. "Bring this wife of yours around to visit me, Sedgwick, day after next. I would like to meet the woman who has so obviously captured your heart."

He bowed again. "I fear that may not be possible," he averred. "Her health—"

The lady drew herself up in her seat. "Day after next, Sedgwick." It was an order, not a request.

As he turned to make his apologies to the rest of the company, he found he wasn't the only one beating a hasty retreat from the Oxley box.

Miss Mabberly was leaving, her mother behind her and, from the way the lady's tongue appeared to be wagging, reproaching her daughter for not being more attentive to the earl.

He wanted to point out to Mrs. Mabberly that he doubted the earl even noticed her daughter's disinterest, nor did he think the man would care that his bride finds him offensive—she was bringing a small fortune to the Oxley coffers with her dower, and for a boor like Oxley, Miranda Mabberly's opinion on the subject of their marriage was naught to him.

Making his goodbyes and ignoring Hubert and Lady Lilth's protests that Mrs. Simmons would take good care of Emmaline, he departed.

Hurrying down the crowded aisles, he nodded to acquaintances and friends, until he quite literally ran into Jack.

His friend stumbled heavily. "I do say, watch out—" he said, his words thick and followed closely by a cloud of brandy. Blinking his rummy eyes, he appeared to struggle to focus them. "Alex!" he finally called out. "Been looking all over for you. It's a demmed disaster, it is. I'm done for. Ruined."

Passersby shot shocked glances at them, probably assuming they were both in their cups.

Rather than add further to his already *au courant* state of affairs with the *ton,* he caught his friend by the arm and steered him to a secluded alcove.

"What the devil is wrong with you?" he asked, giving the man a thorough shake for good measure.

"Ruined. I'm absolutely ruined," he complained.

"You will be if your brother hears about this. You know what a stickler Parkerton is about public drunkenness."

"Yes, well it matters not now," Jack said woefully.

"Why? Whatever has happened?"

"'Tis all your fault," Jack complained. "Your bloody fault. Went and got yourself a bride."

Alex lowered his voice. "If you recall, *you* made her up."

"Yes, so I did," Jack said. "But I never thought the chit would put me into such a fix."

"What has Emmaline got to do with this?"

"My purse-tight, moralistic brother has decided that if my good friend Lord Sedgwick has found his felicitations in marriage, then so should I."

Oh, I haven't got time for this, Alex thought, glancing around the crowded halls to make sure no one was listening to their conversation. "Then make up a bride."

"I would," Jack said, "but my brother is one step ahead of me and has already found one. Some right and proper vicar's daughter." Jack groaned as if he were being dragged over a spiked wheel. "Did you hear me? A *vicar's* daughter."

"So don't marry the chit."

Jack shook his head. "If I don't marry the gel, Parkerton will cut me off. Not another farthing."

"Jack, my advice is to go home, sleep this off and in the morning . . ." He paused and eyed his friend. "Make that the late afternoon when you arise, I'll go with you to your brother and help you plead your case."

"Won't do any good," Jack said. "He's told me to post the banns immediately . . . or I must leave the London house. He ordered Birdwell to start packing my bags if I hadn't seen the archbishop by tomorrow."

Alex doubted Birdwell, Parkerton's proper butler, would be so happy to see Jack tossed out of the nest. The man had always seemed to have an indulgent and soft heart for the duke's rapscallion brother.

"Come now, let me see you home," Alex offered.

"I think not," Jack said. "If I'm to be married off like some *cit*'s daughter, I'm going to have some fun before I go to the gallows. One last night to frolic between the sweet thighs of a—"

"Oh, no, you don't," Alex said, catching him by the arm.

But Jack shook him off. "Going backstage and see if my Giselle is free. My pretty little redhead, my heart's desire. Demmed fond of redheads," he declared. "I shall enchant her with my kiss, with my charms until I am leg-shackled and banished to the far reaches of Northamptonshire." Before Alex could stop him, his friend pushed his way into the crowd and disappeared from sight.

He shook his head and considered going after Jack, but his desire to wed Emmaline drew him out into the night and toward Hanover Square.

Jack stumbled away, blinking his eyes, trying to focus on his plan of attack.

Find that little dancing angel and . . .

Just then he spied a slight figure at the end of the hallway, near the door that led backstage.

Sly minx, he thought. Lolling about during the intermission in hopes of . . . He glanced back at the main hallway and saw there was no one about, for most everyone was in the process of retaking their seats.

He took another gander at her and shook his head. *Odd costume, that,* he thought, looking at her prim muslin. But then again, perhaps there was a dramatic reading during the second act and she was going to be in the chorus.

"Giselle, my dearest goddess, how glad I am to see you," he said, taking her by the hand and spinning her around. She flew into his chest and without hesitating he closed his eyes and caught her lips in a searing kiss.

She writhed in his arms, her hands coming to his shoulders in tight balls. She pounded at him, as if she didn't want his attentions.

Ah, Giselle, she did like to make their interludes athletic.

He pulled her in closer, then pressed her against the wall, pinning her in place with his hips, his hardened state riding against her. All the while, he continued to kiss her, teasing her tongue to come play with him, tugging at her bottom lip with his teeth, then deepening his kiss until he heard a soft moan come from her.

It never took long with Giselle, he mused, as his hand traveled up the length of her hip, rising along her waist until it came to cup her breast. His fingers rolled over the nipple, and like a virgin miss, she gasped, as if she'd never been touched so.

He had to give her credit, she was a fine actress, because she was starting to struggle again under his attentions, so he decided to end her complaints as he had the night before—his fingers prying her bodice down until her breast came free and he was able to explore it completely.

His hand roamed over her soft, silken flesh, delighting in the way her nipple hardened and puckered, her knees buckled beneath her. Now that he had his little firebrand teased and hot, it was time for the backstage tussle she'd promised him.

"So my sweetling, show me where we can have a few moments alone," he whispered into her ear, "and I'll make good my promise to see you well completed before the curtain arises."

"Leave me be!" she sputtered, her hands once again pounding at his chest.

Was it the brandy, or did the minx just sound different? Jack opened his eyes and blinked, trying to focus, and to his horror realized the woman he'd been making love to wasn't his Giselle.

It was then that the screaming began.

* * *

Alex arrived at Hanover Square not long after, though he had made two important stops: at Rundell and Bridge—waking the poor shopkeepers in the middle of the night—to obtain the perfect ring, and the archbishop's office to obtain a Special License.

He'd explained to the man that there were some incongruities with his original marriage to Emmaline and that he wanted to ensure his pending heir's rightful succession. The archbishop, sensible both to the moral implications of such a state and Sedgwick's reputation as a generous man, had written out the document and advised Alex to bring Lady Sedgwick before him and have the ceremony completed quickly and quietly.

He'd hastened toward Number Seventeen intent on seeing the task completed posthaste. But when Alex arrived at home, he found the house in chaos. A traveling coach sat at the curb, and every candle in the house appeared to have been lit.

He took another glance at the coach and realized it was his grandmother's berline.

Grandmère? Impossible. She never came to town. Ever.

But here was her carriage, which could only mean—

"My dear boy, there you are!" she called out from the front steps, her bevy of pugs barking happily at his arrival.

Alex closed his eyes and groaned.

"Grandmère," he said, kissing her cheeks and forcing a smile to his lips. "What a surprise!"

Never had he meant a greeting more. And as he looked at her, seeing her anew, he loved her all that much more. *Grandmère an opera dancer?* It explained so much.

"I don't see why," she declared, picking up one of her

cherished dogs and giving it a scratch on the ears. "I decided to come meet this wife of yours. I couldn't stay away any longer. I was letting my grief for your grandfather keep me from being a guide and champion for your beloved Emmaline. Why, after you left I realized the poor girl was left in town with only Hubert's wife and mother to introduce her to society." She glanced around and then steered him into the house. "You know I detest speaking ill of family, but Lady Lilith and her mother would be more likely to feed your innocent Emmaline to the gossips than to see her well situated. I knew right there and then that it was up to me to screw up my courage, face my dear memories and return to this house." She wiped a solitary tear from her cheek, then glanced back at his carriage. "But where is Emmaline? Isn't she with you?"

"No," he said without thinking. "She's—" He came to an abrupt halt and glanced up the stairs. Emmaline wasn't home? No, of course not. She was up to something and had deliberately wanted him gone for the evening.

Against his better nature, Lady Oxley's gossip plucked at his heart. *Riding in Templeton's carriage.*

No, he thought, he was letting the lady's malice eat at his better judgment. If Emmaline was out, it was for a good reason. At least it had better be. "I mean to say, where is Simmons?"

"It's Thursday," she said, shushing him like a child. "He's probably at that card game he likes to think no one else knows about." Leave it to his grandmother to still have her finger on the pulse of a home she hadn't set foot in in over fifteen years. She was smiling indulgently at him, then said, "Now, where is your wife?"

He ignored her inquiry. "You are probably exhausted

from your travels, Grandmère," he said. "Why don't I see you up to your room and in the morning you can meet Emmaline?"

"Bother that," she said. "I didn't come all this way to be put off for another twelve hours. Now tell me straight, Alexander, where is your wife?" Like the Duchess of Cheverton's earlier request, his grandmother's question was no polite inquiry but held the weight of a general's order. But as luck would have it, when she entered the house, Emmaline's changes distracted her. "Oh, my goodness, where did you find those paintings?" she asked walking toward the stairs.

"My lord, if I could have a word with you," Mrs. Simmons said in a whispered aside. "In private."

Alex nodded, and with his grandmother engrossed by the newly hung watercolors, he tipped his head toward Mrs. Simmons.

"Lady Sedgwick is not at home."

"Not home?" he asked. "Then where is she?"

At this, his grandmother glanced up. "Is there something wrong, Alexander?" From the look on her face, Alex knew this wasn't a conversation to be had within earshot of the dowager.

"Grandmère, I'll be with you presently," he called out. "Mrs. Simmons has need of my assistance."

His grandmother eyed them both skeptically, then went back to examining the new furnishings, the pugs seated on the steps around her like china figurines.

Alex followed the housekeeper back to the kitchen. It was empty save for a deck of cards on the table.

The image of Emmaline in the kitchen earlier with Thomas and Simmons flashed into his head. The cards. Emmaline had been holding cards.

The card game.

He looked at Mrs. Simmons and found her crying. "I begged them not to take her along, but her ladyship promised me no harm would come. I've never liked Simmons's penchant for cards, but a man has to have a vice or two or he isn't happy. And what with all the money that's been lost, it seemed she was our only hope."

Alex shook his head. If what she was saying was true . . . Egads, no. He'd rather have her riding about with Templeton. At least then he could shoot the marquis and flee the scandal with his honor in tact.

"It's all that Duchess of Cheverton's fault," Mrs. Simmons was saying. "She let them hire that sharp, and he's gone and stole all our money."

"A sharp?"

"Yes, the new footman at Cheverton's has been playing for high stakes and winning all the wages from every house servant in Mayfair. And her ladyship, well, she said—"

Alex knew what Emmaline had said. How she'd leapt in and decided to help his staff. But it stung. Not the fact that she'd broken her vow not to gamble, but that she'd lied to him. Betrayed his trust.

Hadn't trusted him enough to tell him the truth.

Then again, if she'd come to him and said she was going to go cheat at cards before all the servants in Mayfair, he would have locked her in the cellar.

"Where is the game tonight?" he demanded.

"The Queen's Corner," Mrs. Simmons said. She burst into another spate of tears. "They are playing at the Queen's Corner around the square and near the public stables."

He started for the door, then turned and said, "Keep my grandmother occupied until I return."

"Milord?" she called out.

"Yes, Mrs. Simmons?"

"If it is any consolation, Lady Sedgwick is going to return the honor of the game to this house," she told him, like that put everything to rights.

Alex knew the only way to save the family honor was to fetch Emmaline home without delay.

Chapter 15

The Queen's Corner, though located in Mayfair, wasn't the most reputable of establishments. Located next to the public stables, it tended to draw a clientele of drivers and carriage lads, street cleaners and chimney sweeps.

And on Thursday nights, the servants from the great houses throughout Mayfair. Butlers and footmen, pot boys and valets, even a few housekeepers and maids who had a fancy for a fellow from another house.

They came one and all to play piquet and commerce, whist and *vingt et un*. While the stakes were nowhere near what their masters and mistresses tossed down ever so haphazardly, the risk was no less.

And so it was that Simmons, Thomas and Emmaline arrived at the pub just after ten. Emmaline had spent the entire walk over to Queen's Corner explaining what she needed them to do.

"Thomas, do stop grinning," she said. "This isn't the

278

time for smiling. That will come when we leave with all their quarterly wages."

The footman furrowed his brow and did his best to look serious, but the sparkle in his eyes would surely give them away.

She brought the heel of her boot down on the top of his foot.

The man howled in pain, hopping about. "What the—"

"Now remember how that feels," she told him. "For I'll do worse if I catch you looking like my grandmother's cat in the cream."

He nodded, this time his face a mix of pain and serious intent.

"Cards are not to be trifled with, gentlemen," she told them as they paused on the corner opposite their destination. "But tonight, may lady luck smile upon us."

Then they crossed the street and entered the pub.

There were greetings all around, for it appeared that Simmons and Thomas were both popular and frequent visitors.

"Eh, Simmons, who's the new gel?" an older man called out to them as they waded their way through the crowded room.

"Miss Trotter, her ladyship's maid," Simmons replied.

Emmaline bobbed her head shyly, then from beneath her mobcap began taking stock of her competition. The tall narrow man holding his cards close to his chest. His hands shook as he picked up the cards dealt to him, but as he put them into his hand, the shaking eased.

Must have got the cards he wanted.

One by one she catalogued the players, filing away their mannerisms and sorting them out by the game they favored.

Simmons continued through the room and didn't pause until they got to the table hosted by the Duchess of Cheverton's servants.

"There he is," Thomas whispered. "The rascally one with the blue vest."

Emmaline glanced over at the Captain Sharp who had become the dread of Mayfair's serving classes.

She hadn't quite believed that a true sharp would be found playing ha'penny stakes with servants, but as she glanced at the piles of coins on the various tables, she saw there were plenty of brads and even a few crowns being tossed about.

Why, the right player *could* gain a stake in such a place, and from the looks of them, these servants were ripe for the picking. It was a wonder someone hadn't come along and plucked them all clean years ago.

At the table before them, their suspected enemy was dealing cards and, for the uninitiated, appeared preoccupied with his task.

Oh, he did his best to look like a fair to middling player, but to a trained eye the man was a sharp, no doubt about it. He did a good job at hiding his skill by dealing the cards awkwardly and smiling overmuch at passersby, but Emmaline didn't trust any of his maneuvers.

She hadn't played against some of the best not to spot one of her own. So, the true test would be being able to conceal her skill from him.

"Gatehill," Simmons said in greeting to a man about his own height and age.

"Simmons," the man returned in the same proper London tones.

Emmaline knew, from quizzing Thomas and Simmons about who would be there, that Mr. Gatehill was the Duchess of Cheverton's butler.

"Brought someone to win back your losses from last

week, eh?" Gatehill asked, chuckling a bit and nodding at Emmaline.

The Sedgwick butler squared his shoulders. "I wouldn't let her play against your lot, she hasn't the skills or the money to spare."

"But that's not true, Mr. Simmons, sir," Emmaline piped in. "Her ladyship gave me a little something for luck." With that she held out her hand and opened it up for all to see the gold guinea that just begged to be won from her fair hand.

Gatehill nudged a young, pimpled man from their table, then wiped the seat with his handkerchief. "Miss Trotter, you will find no finer men of service in Mayfair with which to spend the evening. Lay that coin down, and I suspect you will win not only your heart's desire, but our hearts as well."

Smug bastard, Emmaline thought, though she smiled as innocently as she could and did her best to muster up a blush as she sat down in the proffered chair.

Simmons played his part as well. "Miss Trotter, I would highly recommend you try your hand at commerce with the other maids." He pointed across the room to one of the other tables.

"But I've always wanted to try my hand at a new game," she said, placing her coin down in front of her. "My grand-mam taught me to play parmiel, but lawks, that was years ago. Do you gentlemen know the game?"

"There now, Miss Trotter," the sharp replied, "I believe you have brought Lady Luck to our table, for I am quite fond of parmiel. An old and venerable game." Two more servants from Cheverton House who knew how to play were re-cruited to finish out the table and the cards were dealt.

You are about to discover, she wanted to tell them as she picked up her first hand, *that Lady Luck has fled in my wake.*

* * *

Alex pulled his collar high and his top hat down low, and kept his face well hidden from each and every carriage that rolled past him.

Demmit, didn't she realize the risk she was taking? Not only chancing revealing her deception as Emmaline, but her own safety.

The Queen's Corner was no place for a lady.

No place for his wife.

Alex took a deep breath. She wasn't his wife, he tried telling himself. But that wasn't quite true. Not anymore.

Not once he got done proposing. Then she would be his lawful wife, and there would be no more of these elicit card games, no more of these surprises.

What was he thinking? He was marrying her for exactly those reasons. So he wouldn't spend the rest of his life in dull routine.

Demmit, Emmaline, he cursed under his breath, *don't let any harm come to you. We've a life together to discover.*

He entered the pub and found the place was crowded hip to jowl. No one paid him any heed, but with his hat dipped low and his collar up high, he was confident that, even if they did take a second look, they wouldn't recognize him.

From what he could see, most of the crowd seemed to be around a large table in the back of the room. Pushing and pressing his way through, he was finally able to see what was garnering so much attention—a large pile of coins sat in the middle of the table, probably enough to pay the monthly wages of every man in the room.

Alex shook his head. No wonder no one was paying him any heed, for every eye seemed riveted on the two players squaring off for the final hand.

The man he barely spared a glance, but the lady across from him gave Alex pause. *Emmaline*. And yet not Emmaline.

His fashionable, striking wife was hidden beneath a gray mobcap, a pair of spectacles and a dress that made her appear as if she'd gained two or three stone in a matter of hours. Her skin no longer held the rosy bright color, but looked pale and gray.

She'd done a fair job of disguising herself. No wonder she'd been able to pass herself off as a hired companion for so long—she certainly looked the part.

Then he glanced up and found Simmons at her shoulder, ever at guard. And not far from him, Thomas and two other of his footmen, along with the pot boy and several of the maids, all of them gazing in rapt adoration at Emmaline.

"More cards, Miss Trotter?" the man across from her asked.

Emmaline bit her lip and eyed her hand. "I don't know."

The spectators around the table all seemed to draw a deep breath, as if they too were in the same quandary.

So she did indeed hold the honor of the house in her hands.

Then she shook her head. "I believe these cards will do." Then she smiled at the man who held the deck. "That is, unless you need more cards?"

The man appeared to be considering his next move, adjusting the fit of his cravat and staring at his hand. Finally, he looked up and smiled. "No. For, I believe you are beat, miss."

Emmaline pushed her remaining gold coin in front of her. "Care to match your confidence?"

"Don't do it, Tuffrey," the Duchess of Cheverton's butler urged. "You'll leave us flat broke."

The man ignored the plea and slid his final coin into the pile.

Emmaline held her cards for a few more seconds, drawing out the tension in the room, before she laid her hand down. "I believe I win."

"Merde!" cursed the duchess's cook, who continued to rant in French to all who would listen.

However, his laments were quickly replaced by cheers from Alex's servants as well as those from the other houses.

"Three cheers for Miss Trotter," Thomas called out.

A chorus of "Huzzah, huzzah, huzzah!" rang through the room.

"She's won back our wages, she has," Alex heard one of his footmen say to another fellow. "She's put an end to that fellow's cheatin'."

Alex glanced at the footman, then back at the table. He didn't know whether to be furious with her for the chance she took or let the feeling of pride that was welling up in his chest have its day and join the others as they cheered her.

She rose from her seat and threw her arms around Simmons. His usually composed butler hugged her, then, realizing himself, set her aside to start counting out the coins and redistributing them to the Sedgwick staff, as well as to the servants of the other houses.

"She cheated," complained Gatehill. "It's the only way she could have—"

"Beaten that cheat you brought to our games?" Simmons asked, rising up and facing the other servant nose to regal nose. "These games were just for us, just a friendly way to pass our evenings out, but you had to bring your Captain Sharp there and cheat your fellow servants out of their hard-earned pay."

Gatehill colored. But he didn't deny the accusation, which was more telling. "This isn't the end of this, Simmons," the man blustered. "Not by a long shot." Behind him, the Cheverton servants and their ringer stood dejected and, more to the point, surrounded.

The room now stood divided, and Alex stood at the ready, keeping a sharp eye on Emmaline.

"Harrumph," Simmons replied with all the imperial airs of a foreign dignitary. "Be gone, all of you. You are no longer welcome here." He pointed to the door, and to the jeers and cheers of their former peers, the duchess's servants were escorted out of the Queen's Corner.

The rest of the Sedgwick staff encircled Emmaline, lending their support and loyalty to the woman who had regained their losses. And it wasn't just his house, but the staffs and help of nearly every other house in Mayfair, those who served the lofty Tottleys down to the most insignificant lordling, one and all came up to pay her homage.

From the loyal light shining in their eyes, Alex knew, knew in his gut, that not one of these servants would talk if they knew or suspected who she was.

He made his way to the bar and nodded to the owner. The man came over and Alex slid his purse across the bar. "Let them all drink until this is gone." If anything, several rounds of brandy and ale would make their memories a little more hazy as to the events of the evening.

As for the duchess's staff, not only did they have their cantankerous mistress to contend with, he doubted they would want their misdeeds bandied any further about town.

The innkeeper hefted the purse, then he looked inside as if he couldn't quite believe it, and what he saw made him grin. Then he climbed up on a stool and called out, "Drinks for all!"

There were more cheers, and the servants rushed forward, while Alex eased himself back from the crowd and out the door. There in the night air, he took a deep breath and considered all he'd seen.

She'd done it once again. Meddled and risen to the surface unscathed. Was there nothing she couldn't do?

It took his breath away as he realized how little he knew about this woman.

His Emmaline—a cardsharp. Certainly, he had known that she played parmiel against old ladies and their companions, and the rummy likes of Sir Francis, but he'd never imagined her playing with stakes up to the roof against a man who looked more familiar with the South End hells than the rarefied air of Mayfair. The life she'd led that had brought her to him, he couldn't imagine.

So he had to wonder how he would ever be able to convince her to stay.

Stay with a dull curmudgeon like him.

Emmaline grinned as she watched Sedgwick's staff retrieve their wages. Demmit, it had been a close call to get them back, until she'd finally been able to figure out her opponent's methods and get the better of him—switching cards and cutting the deck twice for a better deal.

Tricks her grandmother, old Mam, had taught her at an early age. Disreputable old slattern that she was, no one could cheat at cards better than old Mam.

"Miss Trotter," Simmons said in a low whisper, "I think it would be best if we saw you home—the hour draws late and I wouldn't like to have his lordship return home and find you gone."

"No, that would be disastrous," she agreed, catching up

her cloak and throwing it over her shoulders. She didn't feel good about lying to Sedgwick, but how else would she have been able to help Simmons and the rest of the servants regain their lost wages?

Simmons waved for Thomas to join them, and the footman came immediately. They exited the pub and started for home.

"You did it, milady," Thomas said. "Thought we were goners for sure when he laid down that queen. However did you get the king?"

"Yes, Emmaline, do tell," came a familiar voice from behind them. "How did you conjure that card?"

All three of them came up short.

Sedgwick.

"M-my lord!" Simmons stammered.

Emmaline glanced over her shoulder and looked Alex straight in the eye. Now was no time to show fear, no matter that her legs quaked beneath her. "I didn't have to conjure anything. I always win."

"Yes, I can see that now."

"Milord—" Simmons began.

The baron cut him off. "I will deal with you later, Simmons. This is between her ladyship and me."

"Perhaps if we all just went home . . ." Emmaline suggested.

"You can't go there," he said, cutting her off as well.

"Because of this?" Her hands balled into fists and stuck to her hips. This was exactly the reason why she hadn't confided in him to begin with. "If it's because I helped the staff regain their stolen wages, I'll have you know I was only—"

If she thought she knew him, he surprised her completely by laughing and tugging her into his arms. "No, my little spitfire. It has nothing to do with the fact that you just outcheated probably the best sharp in London." He laid a kiss on her forehead. "You can't go home because my grandmother would be rather upset to find the current Lady Sedgwick looking like a scullery maid."

"Your wha-a-at?"

"My grandmother."

Simmons hadn't been standing as far away as he might have, and was obviously eavesdropping. "The dowager has arrived? Impossible!"

Alex glanced over at him. "Very possible, Simmons. She landed on our doorstep not an hour ago. And in a fine fettle at not being able to meet my wife."

Emmaline tried to breathe. Lady Sedgwick? Oh, she had gone too far in her deception if she'd drawn *her* to London. Alex was one thing, but his grandmother?

"Sedgwick, this is a catastrophe," she said.

He nodded in agreement. "But I might have an idea of how to get you back home," he told her. "Simmons, I need you and Thomas to go to the house and very discreetly do the following . . ."

He explained his plan to them and Emmaline stared at him in wonder. Who would have thought that under all that starch, Sedgwick could be so devious?

Of course, she reminded herself, this was the man who'd managed to make up a wife.

Then with Thomas and Simmons dispatched, Sedgwick caught up her hand and began leading her in the opposite direction.

The warmth of his fingers lent her the hope that she'd find a way out of this latest wrinkle. And she clung to his grasp with more tenacity than the purloined king she'd held earlier.

After a block or so, Sedgwick finally spoke. "Am I to presume you overcame your aversion to cards?" He slanted a wicked glance in her direction.

Emmaline flinched.

"As well you should cringe," he told her. "Just tell me you won that fortune fair and square."

She said nothing. What could she say? Really, it was more a question of moral ambiguity than right or wrong.

"Demmit, Emmaline," he shot at her. "Do you realize the danger you were in back there? That man you were playing against was no footman or callow youth. He had every marking of a cardsharp. You risked too much. You risked *us*."

Us? Whatever did he mean? Emmaline's gaze shot to his, only to find him looking straight ahead, as if seeing a future he had no right to dare.

Of them, together.

No, she was just imagining this. Imagining that he cared enough to find a way to let them stay together.

But didn't he know, didn't he realize that it was out of the question? No matter that it was what she wanted more than anything.

"So do tell," he began. "How is that you were able to beat him, when you have confessed to merely a passing skill at parmiel?"

She heaved a sigh. Perhaps it was time for the truth. *All of it.*

Oh, heavens no. Emmaline didn't dare. For to tell him the truth would put an end to any notion that they could stay together.

"I have a slight talent for cards," she said. That wasn't quite the truth—her skill for cards was legendary, to the point where she'd been unable to play in the regular circles of sharps and gamesters who made the rounds through the inns and byways of England.

Sedgwick came to a stop at a corner, and they waited there as a carriage passed. "And let me guess," he said. "This skill of yours was how you came to make your living."

Why did she think she could continue to gammon him? She took a deep breath and nodded.

"Before you were shot or after?"

"Both," she confessed.

Sedgwick groaned. "Is that what Lady Neeley meant when she wrote to the duchess about your indiscretions— you cheated Sir Francis at cards?"

"I didn't have to cheat to take his money," she shot back. "I beat Sir Francis fairly. He's a terrible player."

"And were all the players you encountered as terrible as him?"

She glanced away again.

"Oh, demmit, Emmaline, don't tell me you went about the country, not only posing as the Duchess of Cheverton's companion, but gaming your way through the most gullible of the country gentry?"

"Well, when put that way, it sounds quite disreputable," she said. "But that is hardly the case. I never played against anyone who couldn't afford to lose . . . or didn't deserve to."

Sedgwick gave a snort of disbelief.

Oh, bother the man and his pompous aristocracy. She loved him with all her heart, but sometimes . . .

" 'Tis easy for you to stand there so high and mighty, but not everyone has your position in society or your fortune," she said. "I daresay you wouldn't be so toplofty without your fat accounts and scraping servants about."

"My servants do not scrape," he said, his shoulders straightening with noble indignation.

"If you say so," she said, "but the world outside your protected sphere isn't the tidy and orderly place you would imagine. In fact, it can be quite dangerous. Especially for a woman alone."

Oh, demmit, she'd said too much. For his gaze narrowed, and then focused on her brow.

"You were shot for cheating," he said, his words more of an indictment than the concern he'd shown earlier. "That's how you became injured."

"No, Sedgwick, that's not why I was shot. If you must know, I was shot because I objected quite vehemently to being raped. Raped by one of your peers who thought it was his right and privilege to have any woman not of his class."

"You weren't—"

"No." Emmaline's voice was tight and closed off. He'd strayed too far into her secrets again and now she was pushing him away. But this time he wasn't going to let her.

"Tell me what happened," he said as he led her down a quiet, empty street.

She shook her head.

"Emmaline, have you ever told anyone?"

"No one has ever really cared to hear the truth," she said, as if she were daring him to do just that. *Care*.

Care about her.

"I want to know. Know everything." His words rang with a sincerity that she'd never expected. Like Elton's confession earlier in the day, Sedgwick's request burrowed into her heart and took root.

Where it had no place to even hope. That Sedgwick wanted to know the truth about her could only mean he wanted no more lies between them.

And yet once she told the truth, the entire truth, the admiring lights he saw in his eyes tonight would go dark forever.

She was sure of it. Yet how could she not tell him? She owed him that much.

Emmaline heaved a sigh, and stared down at the cobblestones. "If you must know," she told him, "the night began well enough. We were at the Drake in Surrey, with Hawthorne choosing the marks and me playing the hands."

At this point, he interrupted her. "Who is Hawthorne?"

Hawthorne? He would want to know the details. But this was Sedgwick, and he did deserve to know. Everything.

"My husband."

"Your what?" he erupted, coming to an abrupt halt.

"You heard me. My husband." She tried to get him to continue walking, but he stood his ground.

"You're married?"

Emmaline glanced heavenward. "Yes, but it isn't what it seems—"

"Not what it seems? When one's wife confesses that she is already married—"

Her hands went to her hips. "But we aren't, Sedgwick. We aren't married."

"But if you're already married, that means we can't—"

Can't what? She looked up at him and saw the truth. Saw his thoughts, saw his heart as if it were emblazoned in the very shock she spied in his eyes.

Oh, dear heavens he meant for them to marry. She didn't even want to hear such a thing. They couldn't marry, and that was just the way it was. For a thousand reasons beyond her own small impediment. And the foremost one being that proper barons did not marry cardsharps.

Oh, but if they could . . . She shook her head. "Do you want to hear my story or not?"

"Yes, but—"

"No more questions. I'll indulge you with this story, but no more questions. That was our agreement."

He made a noise in the back of his throat that sounded mostly like a growl, but she had to assume he was going to acquiesce.

After all, Sedgwick was a patient man, in the bedroom and out, so she knew he'd listen to her sorry tale, but the entire truth could not be forestalled much longer. Especially given the dowager's arrival in their midst.

"Go on," he bade her.

"Thank you," she replied. "Now, where was I?"

Chapter 16

"The Drake in Surrey," Sedgwick told her.

"Ah, yes. Hawthorne had found—"

"Your husband, this Hawthorne, approved of your cheating?"

"Yes, Sedgwick, my husband approved. Gads, he was the finest mace cove in three counties. 'Twas why I married him. If you can't beat them—" she started to say.

"I don't believe marriage is part of that maxim."

"It was at the time," she told him. "So, do you want to hear my story or not?"

He grit his teeth together, as if biting back an objection, then nodded for her to continue.

"As I was saying, there were two perfect marks. Local gentry, young and in their cups. However, they wouldn't play against a woman, so Hawthorne joined their table, much to my objections."

"I thought he was a good cheat."

"He was good at cheating, terrible at cards. I'll have you know that not all cardsharps cheat by sleight of hand or other such methods. Many work with a partner to spot cards from across the room or act as a distraction."

"The serving girl back there. The one with the . . ." he fumbled over the right way to describe her.

"The one with the spilling bosoms? Yes, but she was to distract Gatehill. Actually, the young pot boy from the Tottleys' was paid to distract—" Emmaline glanced over at Sedgwick and he looked about to be ill. Really, the man needed to get out more. She heaved a sigh. "Shall I continue?"

He took her hand in his. "Yes."

The warmth of his fingers curled around hers, reassuring and full of something she dared not even consider.

Well, once he'd listened to her entire sordid past, he wouldn't be so forthcoming, but she owed him the truth, especially after she'd lied to him about tonight.

"At first," she said, continuing her story, "he was winning."

"At first?"

"That was always the case with Hawthorne. I knew the night would most likely end with us being evicted, so I went upstairs to our room to pack and perhaps get a few hours' sleep. Besides, the public room had emptied out and it would have become obvious that Hawthorne and I were working as a team if I stayed. I had to cross my fingers he would be able to continue his lucky streak." She paused for a second.

"But he didn't," Sedgwick said, prompting her into the darkest part of the story.

"No." Emmaline closed her eyes. She couldn't do it. She'd never told anyone what had happened in that room.

Sedgwick, dear and wonderful Sedgwick, must have sensed her hesitation and gathered her close. "If you don't want to continue . . ." His strength surrounded her.

Then it struck her. She had to imagine she could dare anything enveloped in Sedgwick's arms. Even this, the nightmare that still brought her wide awake at night.

"I awoke to find Hawthorne coming into the room," she whispered. "Then to my horror, his two gulls came in as well."

Sedgwick took a deep breath. She felt his arms tighten, as if ready to launch himself into the coming calamity.

"Hawthorne had lost more than he had, more than we had. More than I had that I hadn't told him about."

Sedgwick let out a small laugh. "You held out on your own husband?"

"I may have been young when I married him, but not completely insensible to his deficiencies. I have to confess I had some coins hidden where not even he would find them."

He tousled her hair lightly. "So what happened next?"

Emmaline heaved a sigh. "Hawthorne had offered my services for the night. To both of them. When I protested, he knocked me on the bed and told me to shut up."

"Shut up, you little conniving bitch." Hawthorne turned to his companions. "You can have her, gentlemen, do with her what you will. She's a lively piece if you rough her up a bit."

She lay on the bed struggling to find air. He'd hit her so hard it had knocked the very wind from her.

Hawthorne? she wanted to gasp. Certainly he'd betrayed people in the past, but she was different.

But hadn't that been her father's protest when she'd run off and married Hawthorne?

Button, my lass, he'll not be true to you. He'll leave you in sorry states one day, mark my words.

Now her father's prediction was coming true, if the lascivious gleam in the two young men's eyes was any evidence. Yet, hadn't she always known that one day, somehow, Hawthorne would lead her to something so terrible that there might not be a way out of it?

Even worse, when she looked up, she spied the man she loved in the process of plucking up her hairbrush and slipping it into his pocket.

Gads, no. He knew about her stash, her hiding place in the handle. He knew and he was stealing everything she had saved.

"Goodbye, my dear," her once-beloved husband said as he made his exit.

Beloved no more. *The wretched bastard.*

But as much as she wanted to spit and curse at him, she was in a sorry state indeed. Then she remembered the one bit of advice from her father she still could put to good use. Better than one of her grandmother's pithy sayings.

Keep it close and keep it loaded.

And thankfully, she always had. Her gaze sped to her valise under the window. So very close, yet too far away to help.

With Hawthorne now gone, the first man said, "Come on, wench. Show us how you fight for it." He reached out, caught hold of her gown and tore it from her body.

As she started to struggle, began to scream, the other man slapped a meaty paw down on her mouth, pinning her to the mattress. His other hand wound into her hair, so she couldn't struggle.

"Don't be doing that," he warned her, whispering into her ear while his large paw of a hand cut off her air. "The innkeeper has had more than his fair share of trouble of late, what with the excise man and the magistrate breathing down his neck. He'll not want to be awoke by your cater-wauling."

The other fellow was fumbling with his pants. "Not to mention the ruckus we caused last week with that gel he brought in from London for us."

She didn't wait to find out what sort of trouble they had caused with that poor wretch. She could well imagine. She kicked the largest of the two in his swollen groin, sending him sprawling backward, howling in pain and swearing a blue streak.

His friend released her, only long enough to clout her in the head. He hit her so hard, she flew from the bed and lay in a heap on the floor. Dazed and confused, she shook her rattled senses, struggled to stop the room from spinning. But this time, luck was on her side. She looked up and realized she'd landed under the window, and within reach of her valise. She shoved her hand inside and managed to grasp her pistol.

Now all she had to do was to be able to see straight enough to find her target and to make good the one shot she had.

In the path of moonlight streaming through the window, she thought she spied a looming figure coming toward her. She certainly heard the black, ugly promises he was spewing and knew there was only one thing she could do.

She raised her wavering hand and pulled the trigger.

The pistol exploded to life and the bastard fell aside.

"Did you kill him?" Sedgwick asked. His question wasn't filled with condemnation, but rather wry hope.

Emmaline shook her head. "No. I only winged him. But it was enough to fell him for the time being." She paused, pulling together the last vague threads of her story and not telling exactly where she'd nicked the blackguard. "I don't remember much past this. I got up to run, but I had only taken a step or two, when I was shot."

She could hear Sedgwick's jaw working, then his terse, anguish-filled question. "How did you survive?"

"Luckily for me, the innkeeper was in dire straits. He was under a cloud of suspicion by the local authorities, and the good citizens of the town had been making a hue and cry to see him closed down. The last thing he needed was the squire's son being shot under his roof, never mind a woman of questionable reputation dying in one of his upper rooms. There would have been an inquest at the very least. So they hauled me out of the village and down to the main cross roads, throwing me to one side of the road, assuming that I would perish before morning, well away from the inn, leaving them free of suspicion."

"How did you learn all this?"

"I found out later." Without thinking about it, she touched her forehead. It pained her still, but it had been a lesson in duplicity that she'd never forgotten.

"The next thing I knew, I was in a gypsy's wagon," she told him. "They had happened by in the wee hours and one of the children spied my arm sticking out from the bottom of a hedge. The leader wanted to leave me be, saying it wasn't their concern, but his mother, a woman of some power, decried such a notion and said it would bring ill fate to their family to ignore my plight. She claimed that one day I would be able to repay her family in kind." Emmaline smiled. "Whatever the reason, I have her to thank, for she also had considerable skill as a healer. She cleaned my wound, stitched it closed and gave me a draught to sleep."

"And you remember all this?"

She shrugged. "Bits and pieces. I remember her face, the smell of herbs, and the voices, low and in their own tongue. I learned the full story later, when I was a bit more awake."

"Then what happened?"

"The caravan continued for a week or so until they came to a small village high up in the hills, and the old woman declared this was where I needed to go. They left me with a kindly vicar and his wife, who took me in without even blinking an eye. The old gypsy woman intimated that I was quality and it would do them well to help me. So they cared for me and I followed the old woman's lead and let them continue to think that I was a well-to-do victim of terrible circumstances. Slowly I recovered, but eventually my stay came to a crisis."

"How so?"

"A heavy snow fell and stranded a large party in the village. The Duke and Duchess of Harringworth. There was no room at the inn to house all their servants, so the vicar and his wife were pressed to offer rooms as was everyone of some standing. I overheard the vicar, a singularly devout man, telling his wife he knew not what to do. They needed my room but hadn't the heart to oust me."

"However—"

"Yes, however, when faced with the opportunity to house the duchess's companion it was more than even he could pass up. He needed a new roof for the parish, and perhaps if the duchess's companion was well pleased with her accommodations, she would recommend his case to Her Grace."

Emmaline paused. "You see, I was in the best guest room and they could hardly offer the duchess's dearest companion the attic."

Sedgwick nodded. "I see their dilemma."

"So you can imagine who was moved to make way for their well-connected guest."

"A lesson you heeded," he noted.

"Most decidedly," she confessed. "But the lesson didn't begin until later that day when the duchess wanted to play parmiel but enough players couldn't be found."

"And let me guess . . ."

Emmaline grinned. "In a single evening I discovered an entirely new quarry—rich and bored matrons."

Sedgwick laughed. "I assume you took ample advantage of the situation."

"Not at first," she said. "The duchess was the most over-bearing, frightening woman I'd ever met. Besides, I was stunned that people played with so little thought to the out-come." She glanced up at him. "Though my amazement wore off quickly when I realized there was a stake to be had."

He laughed. "And so you gained one."

"Yes. But better still, because I learned to read with my mother's copy of *Debrett's,* I possessed a working knowl-edge of society."

"I take it that's how you knew so much about Clifton and Lady Oxley."

She flinched. "You heard about Lady Oxley?"

"How could I avoid it? Hubert recounted Lady Lilith's grievances in detail this evening on the way to the theater."

"I'm sorry about that," she offered.

"Actually, I'm quite impressed. It sounds like you have the entire thing memorized."

"I do."

"Prove it," he demanded.

"Ask me something," she challenged back. "Anything."

"Fine. Lady Pepperwell, for instance. Who was her mother?"

Emmaline glanced toward the night sky. At least he could have tried a little harder. "Lady Pepperwell's mother was Miss Mary Trippley, the second daughter of the fourth Baron Nocton. I believe the current baron resides at Nocton Park, which adjoins Sedgwick Abbey. Isn't that so?"

Sedgwick's mouth fell open.

"Care to try again?"

He shook his head. "I'd say your lessons were put to good use. Can you really recall it all?"

"Everything but for the pages I'm missing," she told him. "As my grandmother would say, everything has a purpose. And my ability to recite those entries allowed me to converse quite readily with the duchess and her companion. Meanwhile, the duchess was a wealth of information about the inner workings of society. The sort of *on dits* that aren't on the venerable pages of *Debrett's*."

"Ah, the bread and water of the *ton*—gossip."

"Exactly. And when I left the vicar's I had a new purpose—"

"And a new identity," he added.

She nodded. "Yes. I saw how the vicar and his wife nearly fell over themselves trying to coddle the duchess's companion. So after a little time spent probing the duchess's extensive connections, I was able to winnow out who would make the best employer—"

"Or rather the most convenient," he noted.

"Exactly. The Duchess of Cheverton rarely if ever comes

to town. But when she does she is known for cutting a wide swath with her biting and blistering comments."

"A woman to be feared," he said.

"Yes, and one that most everyone would like to curry favor with. While her disdain is dreaded, her favor is regarded as a social *compli,* for occasionally she takes pity on some young lady and sees to it that she secures a fabulous match. So by posing as her companion, everyone would want to come to my aid—"

"And at the same time, perhaps gain the duchess's largesse."

"Precisely." Emmaline glanced around and shivered.

Sedgwick took her by the hand and led her around the corner, stopping before a regal-looking house, the columns and bow window speaking of rich elegance.

"Who lives here?" she asked.

"Jack."

She glanced at the house again. "Seems a little fine for your friend. Aren't his pockets a bit thin?"

"Jack barely owns a pocket," Sedgwick said with a laugh. "The house belongs to his brother, the Duke of Parkerton, but the two of them have a tacit agreement that Jack can live here so long as he keeps himself out of scandal."

"And he still retains use of it?" she said in jest.

"With a fair amount of groveling," Sedgwick told her, walking up the steps and pulling the bell.

A beleaguered-looking butler came to the door with two footmen in tow.

"Lord Sedgwick?" the man said. "Thought you were the master, come home drunk again." He turned to the other servants and nodded at them to go back to their posts. "Sometimes Lord John needs a bit of assistance in seeking his bed."

"I can well imagine," Sedgwick said.

"I fear the master is out and I don't know when he'll return." He was about to close the door, but Sedgwick shoved his boot into the crack.

"I'm not here to see Lord John," he told the butler. "But I have need of your parlor for about an hour." He stepped aside and let the man catch sight of her.

Emmaline saw the old servant glance first at her and then at Sedgwick.

"There will be no doxies in this house, milord," he said, shaking a finger at Sedgwick. "If His Grace heard of such goings on in his house, he'd have my hide, not to mention what he'd do to the young master."

"Birdwell, you are an admirable man, but this isn't what it seems—"

"Should I remind you that I work for Lord John?" Birdwell frowned. "I know exactly what it looks like."

Sedgwick caught her by the hand and pressed her forward, even as Birdwell was trying to close the door on them again.

"My good man, I want you to meet my wife, Lady Sedgwick."

"My lord, if you think I am going to believe that this is your wife—"

Now that she had clear sight of the man, she took another good look at the butler. It wasn't just his voice that was familiar, but his face as well. Emmaline grinned at him. "Proper and reputable, now that's a fine one, if ever I heard one," she said in a broad country accent. "But then again, I don't suppose the duke would be all that happy to know he's got Dingby Michaels as his trusted and faithful servant."

Birdwell's brows rose in alarm. Then he let the door ease open a little farther, letting a single narrow shaft of light fall onto her face.

"Button?" he asked. "Button, is that you?"

She grinned and nodded. "Now let us in, you demmed codger, or I'll have Bow Street down here to nick your nob."

Birdwell, aka Dingby, shook his head but then swung the door open wide. "Get in here, both of you, afore anyone sees you. The servants on this street are more gossipy than their mistresses."

Sedgwick followed her inside. He leaned over and whispered in her ear, "Button?"

She waved her hand at him. "Don't think it will get you any closer to finding out what you want. 'Tis an old name."

"And we've a code to keep, now don't we?" Birdwell was saying. "Come along, down the hall and to the garden room. It's got a nice set of doors to the back and there's mews to the right if you need them."

Emmaline nodded. Once a highwayman, always a highwayman, she thought. She held no doubt that her father's former partner knew every route out of London, and then some that even a weasel wouldn't be able to wiggle through.

Elton had always said that there wasn't a hangman's knot tight enough to keep Dingby Michaels from slipping through it.

"You two know each other?" Sedgwick asked.

"How much does he know?" Birdwell asked Emmaline.

She glanced over her shoulder and winked at Sedgwick. "Not near as much as he would like."

The butler laughed. "Button, you always were a sharp one. What are you doing here in—" The man came to a halt and spun around, pointing a bony finger at her. "It was you. You were the one down at the Queen's Corner tonight! I should have known it when I heard that some wench had cleaned out that cheat who'd been playing fast and loose down there the past month." He reached out and put a hand on her cheek. "'Twas a good thing you did."

"Oh, on with you," she told him.

The butler laughed again. "Still modest to a fault, but that's your mother's touch, I daresay."

Sedgwick edged into their cozy reunion. "I don't mean to be rude, but we came here for a reason."

"Nobs," Birdwell said to her in an aside.

"He's not so bad, as toffs come," she confided.

There was a loud harrumph from the toff himself.

"How can I help you, Button? For you know I owe your dah my life more times than I can count." Dingby hung his head. "God rest his soul."

Obviously he hadn't heard about Elton's continued good health, and she didn't see any need to enlighten him. While they had been thick as thieves, literally, she didn't think either man would want to renew their past association.

"Dingby," she whispered, "I need a place to change my clothes, clean up a bit."

"Like I thought, on the run, are you?" He nodded sagely. "The parlor will do you fine."

Sedgwick stepped forward. "One of my servants will be arriving with her clothes in a few minutes. Can you see that they are brought in here directly?"

"Yes, milord," Birdwell said, returning to his role as London butler, leading them down the hall to the elegantly appointed salon. He limped slightly and his shoulders were stooped with age. Apparently there were some things even

Dingby Michaels couldn't steal—his youth and vitality having been long lost.

He paused at the doorway and eyed Emmaline's disguise anew. "I'll fetch you a pitcher of water, some good soap and clean towels. Be back right smart," he told her, his words hinting at his Yorkshire roots.

He set the brace of candles he'd been carrying on a sideboard, then turned to leave. He started to close the door, but then with a second glance at Sedgwick left the door slightly open, as if he wanted to ensure she was going to be safe.

"Button?" Sedgwick repeated.

"A nickname, nothing more," she told him, pulling off her mobcap.

"Dingby Michaels," Sedgwick said. "Dingby Michaels, where have I heard that name?"

Emmaline shrugged. She'd said too much in front of Sedgwick as it was, but there had been nothing else she could do but reveal herself to her father's old friend, in order to gain them the help they needed.

Sedgwick needed, actually. She still wasn't convinced she shouldn't turn tail and run.

Lady Sedgwick at Hanover Square? Why, she never came to town.

She glanced over at Sedgwick and it appeared he was still trying to recall why the butler's real name sounded so familiar. And about then his mouth fell open, and Emmaline knew he'd made the connection.

"Dingby Michaels? That man is Dingby Michaels?" He pointed at the door, his head shaking with disbelief. "The Gentleman from York, the Scourge of Norwich?"

"Don't forget the Thief of Virtue," she offered. "He always thought that was his most illustrious claim to fame."

Sedgwick shook his head, his finger pointing at the doorway. "But that man is a dangerous, notorious criminal!"

Emmaline shook her head. "I don't think he could still get up into the saddle, let alone fire a shot. At least not a straight one."

"That doesn't excuse what he's done," Sedgwick began, his lips drawing into a tight intractable line. "The law is quite clear in these situations."

Her hands went to her hips. Sometimes Sedgwick's sense of right and wrong was wound so tight it became overly tiresome. "So you are going to report to the law that you believe the Duke of Parkerton's aged butler was once the most notorious highwayman between London and Gretna?" She shook her head. "Setting aside the resulting scandal and ruin you would bring upon the duke and his family, I must ask, who is going to believe you? And secondly, when the authorities ask you how you came upon this remarkable piece of information, what are you going to tell them? That Dingby Michaels is an old friend of your wife?"

He tossed his tall beaver hat on a nearby settee. "Emmaline, there are rules and order in this land for a reason. Demmit, I'm a magistrate, sworn to uphold the law."

She could see the conflict in his eyes. As much as she didn't really agree with him, how could she not admire his moral fortitude? With Sedgwick, the world was so very neat and orderly. Right and wrong.

And she'd spent a lifetime dancing over that line, sidestepping it at will and outright ignoring it when necessity and an empty purse required it.

And as much as she wanted to pull Sedgwick out of his pompous sanctuary, and take some of the starch out of his perfectly tied cravat, a part of her wanted to be able to climb into his ivory tower and never leave. To tip up her nose in noble indignation that such an outrage could be living not three blocks from Hanover Square.

A highwayman in Mayfair!

And from her lofty tower, high amongst the clouds, she wouldn't spare a second thought for Dingby, with his limp and rheumy eyes as the constable dragged him off to some cold cell, then dangled his broken and aged body from the end of a rope while crowds jeered.

But as much as the lure of Sedgwick's life held, as much as she'd spent so many years envying the gentry with their beautiful homes and endless servants, she couldn't forget where she'd come from, the life she'd lived.

The debts she owed.

Nor could she forget the man who'd brought her peppermint candies and ribbons for her hair, and remembered her birthday when her father had forgotten the day and her mother was so lost in her ravings to notice.

Meanwhile, Sedgwick had taken to pacing back and forth on the Turkish carpet. A very nice Turkish carpet.

Distracted, Emmaline bent down to examine it.

"Whatever are you doing?" he asked.

"I think this would look perfect in the library," she said over her shoulder, as she turned up one corner to inspect the quality. "I wonder if the duke would mind if I brought over Mr. Saunders to show him what I want him to weave? This is utterly perfect."

"Have you gone mad?" His pacing came to an abrupt halt. "There is a dangerous criminal in this house and all you can do is inspect the furnishings?"

"Leave poor Dingby alone," she told him, as she got up from the carpet and started eyeing the sideboard. It had nice lines and the carving was exquisite. "I doubt he's robbed anyone in a good fifteen years," she told him. "And you're a fine one to talk. You and your Emmaline. Did it ever occur to you, Lord Magistrate, that making up a wife might be unlawful?"

His jaw worked back and forth. But he said nothing, just looked at her with his brow all wrinkled and his teeth clenched. She hated it when he looked at her like that. As if he couldn't wait to get her and her bothersome past out of his life. So much for all his care and concern.

"Fine, I will forget Birdwell's past, if you will stop fingering the duke's possessions."

"Bother, Sedgwick, I'm not going to steal anything. Why should I when I have your money at my disposal?"

His brow furrowed at her jest.

She ignored his ill humor, and despite his protests picked up a vase she'd been looking at, turning it over to see who'd made it. Unimpressed, she put it back. "Counterfeit."

"What do you mean, counterfeit?" he said, walking over and taking his measure of the *objet d'art*. "I'll have you know the Duke of Parkerton is a very discerning collector. His eye for quality is renown."

"Then he should have his eyes checked. That is a fake. Not a Wenley."

"How would you know?" he said, picking it up himself and taking a look at the potter's mark. "The mark is right there—Wenley."

She shook her head and pointed to the inscription. "And do you see the ivy leaf to the left of the name?"

"Yes."

"On an original, it is right side up. Whoever made this was not only inattentive, he was outright lazy."

He stared at her openmouthed, and very carefully she took the piece from his hands and replaced it on the mantel. "I wouldn't like to see you drop that. Even if it is a fake, we would be hard-pressed to prove it if it was in pieces." She sashayed past him and went to look at the sconces nearby.

"How do you know these things?" he finally managed to ask. "That this isn't a true Wenley, or that Mr. Starling's chinoiserie wallpaper came from Cheapside?"

"Or that Lady Neeley's gems were paste?" she offered.

"They were?"

"Most decidedly." She shrugged. "When you were learning Greek and Latin from your tutor, I was learning the fine art of appraising goods." She paused and met his questioning gaze. "Stolen goods, Sedgwick."

His hand went to his temple and he rubbed his wrinkled brow as if to take away a sudden pain.

"My grandmother was a fence, and Dingby one of her finest . . . suppliers." Dingby *and* her father, but she wasn't going to tell him that. At least not now. He looked about ready to fall over.

She went to his side and led him to the settee. "If anything, consider what my rather unorthodox education has saved you with these London tradesmen. Why, it is shocking what they try to pass off as quality."

"Demmit, Emmaline," he managed to say, "every time I think I've discovered your worst secret, you shock me anew. Is there anything left or dare I risk apoplexy and learn all your darkest secrets?"

She slanted a sly smile at him. "That depends on the state of your health. It would be a shame to have my past be your undoing. I doubt very highly that Hubert would be very generous to your widow."

This time they both laughed, and then something magical happened: Sedgwick reached out to touch her cheek.

His touch sent tremors through her. Unbidden, her gaze drew up to meet his.

"You shouldn't have risked so much tonight."

Her heart thumped in a wicked beat. Had he truly been worried for her welfare? Not just for the risk to Emmaline, but for her? And then he told her as much.

"Emmaline, why? Why are you already married?"

She looked away. "There is nothing we can do about it now."

"We'll see about that. I'm not about to give up on ... ." He paused and looked at her. "I intended for us to be married tonight."

She looked away, tears stealing into her eyes. "Oh, Sedgwick."

"I thought we agreed you would call me by my given name."

She shook her head. "I have no right."

"You have every right," he told her. "And you'll call me that soon enough. When we are married."

"But how?"

"Perhaps this Hawthorne is dead, and you are free of him."

"An answer to many a prayer, that would be," she told him, laying her head on his shoulder.

"If not, there must be some incongruity in your marriage that could be used to have it annulled. Elliott, my solicitor, is a master for finding just the right hole in any coil."

Emmaline looked up at him. "You'd do all that for me?"
He nodded. "That and more."

"But my past, it will forever haunt me. There will always
be people like the Neeleys who remember Miss Doyle, or
like Dingby . . . There will be no escaping the scandal. Let
me leave now, Sedgwick. It is for the best." Her words,
bravely spoken, tore from her heart. She didn't want to
leave him, but to stay would be his ruin. She loved him too
much not to flee.

"Emmaline, I have no intention of letting you go. Besides, I've never been overly fond of London, and I think
you'll find the rooms at Sedgwick Abbey will keep you well
occupied for many a year." He toyed with one of her curls.
"So let there be no more talk of your leaving. Do you hear
me?"

She nodded, but wasn't as yet convinced.

Go. She should go, leave him and let him live his life
without her. And yet, what if he was correct and there was a
way for them to be together?

Dingby returned just then, and Emmaline's head
snapped up.

The former highwayman eyed her first, then the baron,
standing so close as they were, his brows furrowing with
something akin to paternal displeasure. And she knew what
that meant. She moved out of Sedgwick's shadow.

Grand! All she needed was Dingby coming to the wrong
conclusions. He might not be able to shoot straight, but that
didn't mean the fellow had forgotten how to fire a pistol.

"Your man brought this around," he said, coming between
her and Sedgwick. Handing her the bundle of clothes, the
cagey old man shot the baron a pointed look. "His lordship
and I will leave you to get yourself done up, Button."

She winked at Sedgwick, and said to her old friend, "Have you anything to drink around here, Dingby? I believe Sedgwick could use a drink. He's had quite an enlightening evening."

"That and something else," the old man muttered. "This way, milord. The duke keeps a rare port in stock, and though I'm under strict orders not to let Lord John know about it, I don't think he'll mind you having a glass of it."

Sedgwick looked from her to Dingby and back to her. "You'll stay here?"

Was it hope she heard in his voice? That he wanted her to stay? She'd rather thought her offer to leave might be met with relief.

"I'll be here," she told him. As much as she was tempted to flee into the night and avoid coming face to face with his Grandmère, she'd given her word.

"Come along then, milord," Dingby said in his best butler tones.

Emmaline pulled off her costume, wiping her face free of the ash and talc mixture she'd used to dull her coloring. There was a mirror over the mantel, so she was able to put her hair in some semblance of order, using the few pins she had at hand.

Luckily the dress Thomas had retrieved was one of her more simple gowns. Obviously he'd gotten one of the maids to help him. She pulled it on, but realized she needed someone to help her with the laces in the back.

She went over to the door to see if there was a maid about, when she heard Dingby's gruff voice.

"What are your intentions with her, my lord?"

"My what?"

"Your intentions, I say. Button is right important to me, and I won't see her being . . . being—"

"Mr. Birdwell, rest assured the situation is not what you think. Emmaline, or rather Button, is my life. In fact, I intend to see that she is protected and cared for."

"Harrumph," Birdwell muttered. "See that you do. I owe her father my life. Why, there was this time on the North Road when he and I were—"

Egads, no, Emmaline thought. That was the last thing she wanted Sedgwick to find out. She pushed the door open and put a bright expression of surprise on her face, as if she hadn't expected to find them there. "Heavens, I fear I need some help." She might have fooled the baron, but Dingby was anything but—he gave her a dark glare, the one that had gained him the nickname the Scourge of Norwich. She ignored him and blithely smiled at Sedgwick, then tilted her head toward her shoulder. "I can't reach the ties in the back. Could you help me?"

She turned her back to Sedgwick and shot Dingby her own hot glance.

The old man shook his finger at her. "Button, I'll have my say on this."

"Not and live, Dingby Michaels."

"Bloody hell," he muttered. Then he glanced up at Sedgwick. "Never should have taught the gel to shoot a pistol."

"So I have you to blame for the hole in my wall," Sedgwick said.

Birdwell snorted. "Be thankful that hole isn't in your breeches, milord."

Chapter 17

Alex and Emmaline entered the Sedgwick town house via the kitchen, but just as she was about to make her way quietly up the back stairs, a distinct voice rang out from the hallway beyond.

"She is not upstairs and neither is my grandson. Now, I intend to search this house from top to bottom until I get some answers." The door to the kitchen swung open and Genevieve, Lady Sedgwick, made her grand entrance. She stopped short and Simmons nearly ran into her as he came to a blustering halt. Around their feet, her dogs trotted obediently, looking from one person to another to see if anyone had remembered their midnight snack.

"Grandmère, there you are," Sedgwick said, as if he'd been searching her out.

She held up her lorgnette. "And where have you been?"

"Fetching me, your ladyship," Emmaline said, rushing in as usual.

316

Alex flinched, and said a hasty prayer that Emmaline's spontaneous explanation would have nothing to do with highwaymen.

He'd had his fair share of cardsharps and gentlemen of the road this evening.

"I am so sorry, but the confusion is all my fault," she said. "Lady Rawlins wasn't feeling well earlier and I left in a hurry to go sit with her." Emmaline leaned forward. "She's been rather weak since her confinement."

"As well she should be. Wretched business, childbirth," his grandmother announced. "But here you are, our Emmaline." She gave her a quick once-over and then drew her into her arms for a hearty embrace. What she whispered to Emmaline, he couldn't hear, but from the smile on his grandmother's face, all was forgiven. She took Emmaline's arm and began to pull her from the kitchen. "Now we can see about a good coze. I have so much to learn about you—"

"Grandmère, I believe that can wait for morning," Alex told her.

"Nonsense," she replied. "I've waited all these years to meet your dearest Emmaline and I am not going to be put off now."

But before she could make good her threat to spirit Emmaline away, the door opened and in came Lady Lilith and Hubert.

"There you are—" Lady Lilith said, her face flushed and angry, her finger pointing accusingly at Emmaline.

The pugs responded by barking wildly and growling at Mrs. Denford.

The tall, narrow woman shot a black look down her long nose and snapped down at them, "Be still, you ruinous pests."

The pugs turned their tiny tails and ran behind their mistress's wide skirt.

Lady Lilith barely broke stride as she spun her ire back at her original victim. "I blame you for all this, Emmaline Denford." She drew herself up. "Too sick to attend the opera with my mother. Utter rubbish! You rudely avoided my mother's kind invitation and sent that wolf, that debaucherous—"

"I beg your pardon," Alex began. "I am not—"

"Oh, do be quiet," Lady Lilith snapped, completely forgetting herself. "This isn't about your rudeness, but I'll get to that in a moment." Before he could say another word, she was off and running again. "I blame you for this evening's disaster," she said, her narrow finger stabbing the air again. "I wouldn't doubt it if you had planned this all along, sending Lord John in your stead, if only to ensure that he ruined my brother's one chance at happiness."

"Lord John?" Emmaline asked. "I only suggested—"

"Of course you did. How innocent it all appeared when you conveniently fell ill this afternoon and were able to beg off going. Sending that viper into our midst."

Alex narrowed his gaze at Lady Lilith, a sneaking feeling overcoming him. "What did Jack do?"

"What did he do? What didn't he do?" she cried out, nearly hysterical. "He ruined Miss Mabberly, that's what he did."

"He what?" Alex and Emmaline both exclaimed at once.

Hubert intervened and finished the story. "Right after you left, Sedgwick, Lady Oxley went out to find Miss Mabberly, only to discover her in a compromising position with Lord John. Apparently he had his hand—"

"Hubert! Do not say it!" Lady Lilith protested. "Don't force me to relive that awful moment."

"Unfortunately, Lilith saw it as well," Hubert whispered loudly in an aside.

"Yes, I did," his wife sputtered. "When Mother started screaming I immediately went to her aid. There was Lord John, in a terrible state, drunk, with his hand upon Miss Mabberly's . . . Miss Mabberly's . . ."

"Breast," Hubert finished.

Lady Lilith shot him a dark glance. "Her person," she corrected. "Mother found them kissing. If only that was the worst of it, for however can my poor brother marry her now? Not when her true nature has been revealed to all. Wretched, awful girl!" She turned again on Emmaline. "This is all your fault, your influence. You told her to do this, you told her to throw off Oxley by—"

"That is quite enough," Alex said, stepping between Emmaline and Lady Lilith. "My wife did no such thing. I heard every word of what she said to Miss Mabberly the other night and never once did Emmaline suggest that Miss Mabberly 'throw off' your brother."

"Harrumph!" Lady Lilith sputtered. "I still hold you responsible, Cousin Emmaline. If you had gone tonight, done your duty as Sedgwick's wife and appeared with him at the opera, none of this would have happened. Oxley is bereft over his loss."

Bereft for his loss of Miss Mabberly's dowry, Alex thought. "Perhaps not all is so dire," he suggested instead. "I could go talk with Jack. Perhaps there was a misunderstanding, and it could be smoothed over."

"A misunderstanding? He had his hand on her breast!" Lady Lilith exclaimed. And once she realized that she'd said the word aloud, in front of both him and Hubert, she colored a dark shade of red.

"That does sound a bit dire," Alex agreed. Oh, damn Jack and his drunken ways. What the devil had he been thinking, kissing Miss Mabberly? Then he remembered his friend's words. *Pretty little redhead.* A pretty little redhead?

Oh, demmit, he must have mistaken Miss Mabberly for his dancing light-o'-love.

"I will see to this in the morning," Alex promised. "I'll call on Jack and have him apologize to Miss Mabberly. I believe he might have mistaken her for someone else. Quite an honest mistake, and surely when Oxley hears the explanation and Jack compensates him for the situation, he can see his way clear to carry on with his marriage to Miss Mabberly."

"Marry that tart? Never! Mother was right about her all along. I say good riddance to her and her tawdry dowry."

With that Lady Lilith turned to her husband. "Come, Mr. Denford, I am all but worn to a fray." Then she marched upstairs, but not before shooting Emmaline one more haughty and aggrieved look.

Hubert shrugged his shoulders, then followed his wife to their room.

Once they were well and gone, his grandmother launched right back into her litany as if they'd never been interrupted. "Come now," she said, wrapping her arm around Emmaline's and starting to draw her toward the sitting room.

Just then the clock chimed the hour, and Alex used it to his advantage. "Grandmère," he said, quickly cutting in and separating the pair of them. "Can you not see that Emmaline is already in a weakened state? You wouldn't be so cruel as to keep her from her rest at this late hour? I would hate to see you be responsible for setting off another of her relapses."

His grandmother's gaze narrowed. "She looks well enough to me. In fact, I think—"

"Oh, I disagree," he interjected. "Emmaline is quite fatigued. Aren't you, dearest?"

Emmaline glanced from him to his grandmother, and for a moment he almost doubted that she was going to join in his fiction. She looked torn—but how could that be? Surely the last thing she wanted was this interview with his grandmother, and certainly not before he had a chance to finish briefing her on the letters his solicitor's wife had written over the past three years.

But then to his relief, she sighed heavily and sagged against him. "How right you are, Sedgwick. I feel terribly dizzy."

Alex played his part of doting husband by hoisting her into his arms. "Play along with me," he whispered into her ear, "and I shall make it up to you for the rest of the night." Then he glanced up at his grandmother. "As you can see, Emmaline is in no condition for your interview. Tomorrow will suffice."

At which time, he would have Emmaline spirited away, well and far from his grandmother's prying.

"Goodnight, Grandmère," he said as he began carrying Emmaline up the stairs.

Much to his chagrin, his grandmother followed. Right on his heels, like one of her pesky pugs looking for a sweet.

"What are you thinking, Alexander?" she protested. "Where are you taking her?" as he turned off on the second landing.

"Our suite," he said over his shoulder. He would have thought he'd told her that he was going to toss Emmaline from the window by the way she reacted.

"You can't do that!" she protested. "That is entirely inappropriate!"

Alex stopped, and suddenly a hint of suspicion niggled at him. He glanced down at Emmaline and she quickly closed her eyes, feigning a swoon. Not that he expected Emmaline and her cardsharp ways would give anything away.

So he turned around and faced his grandmother, who looked ready to panic.

"And why, Grandmère, is it inappropriate for my *wife* to spend the night in my *bed*?" He made sure he emphasized those words, and for good reason—she flinched at both of them.

"Well, because . . . because . . ." she stammered. "She's ill!" she said, pointing her gnarled finger at Emmaline. "She'll never get the rest she needs with you there. Place her in the Rose Room, where she belongs."

"But Grandmother, that has always been your room, and Emmaline and I wouldn't think of forcing you from your favorite chamber. Isn't that right, darling?" he asked Emmaline, giving her a good heft to rouse her.

She opened one eye and used it to gauge his intent. She didn't even dare look at the dowager. "Um, yes," she said. "We couldn't do that."

He smiled at his grandmother. "There you have it. Now my wife and I are going to bed. That is, unless you have something else to say, Grandmère?"

"I—I—" his grandmother protested, then snapped her lips shut and shook her head.

Alex nodded to her and marched into the master suite. He made a great show of tossing Emmaline onto the bed and then turning to face his grandmother. After shooting his shocked relation a saucy wink, he said, "Goodnight, Grandmère. Sleep well." And then he closed the door firmly and threw the bolt so there would be no interruptions.

If she had any further protests, he cared not, not now that he knew exactly who was behind Emmaline's arrival in his life.

"Why don't you tell me," he said to her, "when it was you met my grandmother and what inducement she used to convince you to come to London and play my wife?"

The dowager stood in the hall and gaped at the closed door before her. Whatever had just happened?

"Grandmother?" Hubert called out from the end of the hall. "Are you well?"

He came to her side and looked down at her, concern knitting his brow.

He was a doltish clod, but he was her grandson (though she blamed his father for marrying Baron Nocton's youngest daughter—the gel had brought a less-than-alert nature into the bloodlines). Still Hubert was family, and when there was trouble about, who else did you have to turn to but family?

"Grandmother, should I call Mrs. Simmons? Have one of the maids come to help you to bed?"

"Oh, leave off, Hubert, I'm not so in my dotage that I can't tend to my own needs." But still she let him lead her down to her chamber, albeit reluctantly. "It's just that I was a bit distressed to see Alex and Emmaline so . . ."

"Fond of each other?" Hubert offered. "Yes, it is disconcerting to see a man so agog over his wife. Not natural, if you ask me."

"He's agog?"

"Utterly besotted," Hubert confided.

Besotted? No, that couldn't be.

Hubert wasn't done with his tattle. "I fear they've been quite content to spend all their time in there of late. Sedgwick practically keeps her a prisoner to his whims. You should have heard the racket coming from that room last night. Why, it went on for hours!" He clucked his tongue. "Disgraceful."

"Hours?" his grandmother said weakly, slanting a glance back at the door.

"Hours," Hubert confirmed. "Really, something should be done about it. He'll kill her in the end."

"How so?" she managed to ask. Sedgwick had always seemed, well, so dull. Hardly the type to be so . . .

"How, you ask? I'll tell you. Though this is Lilith's theory, not mine. She says that given Emmaline's ill health, a child would surely kill her. She was most distressed by the thought."

"A child?"

Hubert nodded. "Perhaps you can speak to Sedgwick. Urge him to send her back to the country before it is too late."

"Never fear," Genevieve, Lady Sedgwick, told him, rallying her rattled senses and gathering up several of her beloved dogs in her arms. "In the morning, I'll see to just that very thing."

Emmaline scrambled up from atop the coverlet. "Wha-a-at?"

Sedgwick stalked toward her, shrugging off his jacket, his cravat and his waistcoat. They fell to the floor in a negligent heap. "I said, when did you and my grandmother cook up this little scheme?" His boots followed.

She shook her head. "I don't know what you mean."

Demmit, why had Lady Sedgwick come to town? She was about to ruin everything with her meddling—and Emmaline was an expert on just how much trouble unchecked meddling could cause.

Without a word, Sedgwick caught her by the ankle and plucked off her shoe, tossing it so it hit the wall and fell behind a chair. "How did she discover the truth?" he asked, his fingers running up her calf until they came to her garter. With a quick flick of his fingers, he had her stocking free and was rolling it down her leg.

"Sedgwick, you have it all wrong—"

He dropped her ankle and caught her other foot, giving it the same attention.

"She was doing well," he said as he caught hold of her and flipped her on her stomach. "Until I mentioned going to bed." He climbed atop her, his thighs on either side of her, and he quickly undid the laces of her gown, pulling them free.

"I didn't notice—"

He leaned over and placed a hot kiss on her shoulder, then whispered into her ear, "Are you sure?" His hands found either side of her gown and tugged it down to her waist. His fingers ran over her bare skin, his lips leaving a trail of hot kisses, teasing her desires awake.

Emmaline gasped. Egads, what was she to do? She shouldn't let him do this, not with his grandmother in the house, but damn the man, he knew just how to get her body seething with passion.

He caught hold of her, rolling her again so this time she faced him.

"I don't think we should be—" she started to say.

"Whyever not?" The passionate light of his eyes, the telltale bulge in his breeches, left her transfixed . . . for it all called to her own needs, left her only too aware of what was to come. Of what she desired . . .

"I'm . . . um, married," she offered.

"Prove it." He leaned over and kissed her stomach, her breasts, her shoulders. Then he paused and looked up at her. "Let me be very clear," he said. "Tomorrow we are going to have a long talk with Grandmère and there will be no more secrets between us." He reached out and cupped her chin. "And from this night forward, you are *my* wife. For now and always."

He said it with such force, with such intent, that all she could do was nod, mesmerized by the passion in his voice.

"Good." He pulled off his shirt and tossed it aside.

The sight of his bare chest left her breathless. Perfectly sculpted, the musculared expanse called to her hands to touch him, to run her palms across the steely plains.

"Hmm," she murmured, shocked as she always was by the way her body responded to him. Her breasts grew heavy, her stomach tightened and that ache, that delicious ache that only he could ease, spread through her limbs like quicksilver. "Sedgwick, this is wrong."

"Isn't it, now," he said, grinning. "Yet, it wasn't wrong yesterday when I did this . . ." He lowered his mouth to hers and kissed her deeply. "Or when I did this . . ."

Her gown came off in a tangled heap, and his hands slipped from her hips up to her breasts, fanning over them until he found the pebbled points, the hard evidence of her desire for him.

"Very wrong," she gasped, her hips arching and rocking in anticipation.

"Especially when I do this . . ." His lips covered one of her nipples, drawing pure pleasure from her with his kiss.

She couldn't take it any further without touching him, holding him, stroking him.

Her fingers trembled with desire as she found his waistband and tugged his breeches open, then down and off, leaving him completely naked for her.

"Emmaline," he groaned as she took his manhood in her hands and began to caress him. She eagerly explored the length of him, the silken head, now moist and ready for its own tempestuous travail.

His lips lay a trail of hot kisses up her body, along her neck, until they came to her mouth, where they arrived greedy and hungry, as if he wanted to steal her very breath. It made her weak and delirious all at once, and so very hungry for something more.

In the space of a heartbeat, he nudged her legs apart and entered her.

She sighed and arched up to meet him. How was it he always knew when she was so ready, so eager for him?

He filled her completely, soothing some of her cravings, but the ache, the desire to find her release, made her writhe beneath him, searching for the rhythm that would take her there. And just as she found it, she looked up at him and found him watching her.

His hand wound around her waist, and he spun them around, so that she was atop him and he beneath her. At first she tried to catch her breath, her balance, but as she shifted in place, testing her own movements, sliding on and off of him, teasing him with her motions, she discovered that such a position offered its own advantages.

Delicious, wicked and so wonderful.

"This is wrong," she told him, shaking her hair free, so the pins fell down around them.

"Then make it right."

So she did, riding him hard and fast, mindless that she shouldn't be doing this, only desirous of finding her release, of feeling him reach the same peak. Just before she did, he spun her again, pinning her to the mattress and stroking her hard and fast until she was but a breath away from her climax.

He paused there, and her eyes flew open. "You are mine, for now and forever more." Then he filled her anew, buried himself within her, and she cried out in joy with a shattering release. He joined her quickly, coming with a mighty thrust, his breathing ragged and thick.

The waves of rapture enveloped them both. The restive desires, the needs that had coiled inside her exploded and she called out his name. "Alex! Oh, Alex!" Her body rocked and heaved against him, seeking every last bit of glorious release that was there to be found.

And when those raging tides began to slowly ebb, Emmaline lay wrapped in Alex's arms and wondered at such contentment, such a feeling. There in the dark, with him still filling her, still holding her, she sighed and wished for a lifetime of such nights with this incredible man.

Neither of them said anything for a long time, each spent and languid, letting the quiet realm of dreams steal in around them.

And as she began to drift to sleep, he kissed her softly on the forehead. The last thing she remembered were the words she longed to hear again. Longed to believe.

"Forever, Emmaline. There will be nothing less between us."

Chapter 18

⌒◯◯⌒

When morning came stealing through the curtains, Alex was already awake. In truth, he hadn't slept much at all. He'd held Emmaline through the night, letting her sleep in the sanctuary of his embrace, and vowed a thousand different ways that he would have her thusly always.

But she was already married.

No, it couldn't be true. Yet for all his vows the night before, in the light of day he wasn't as confident he would be able to find a way for them to be together.

With any luck, this bastard Hawthorne was dead, but finding that out might take months, even years.

And what if the fellow was alive and learned of Emmaline's new life? She was right—there wouldn't be enough money to still his wagging tongue.

No, he had to rest his hope that her original marriage held some incongruity that would leave it null and void.

Demmed inconvenient time for Elliott to be gone. Especially since his solicitor was a wily enough fellow to be able to tap holes in the most ironclad of agreements.

Inconvenient, he realized, or convenient for someone who wanted to ensure that Alex hadn't had his crack solicitor on hand to untangle his current state of affairs?

Then he recalled the fellow's letter, the once-innocuous phrases taking on new meaning.

Odd inheritance . . . never knew the uncle . . . apologies, but we must go in person to Scotland . . .

Someone had wanted Elliott out of town, and badly enough to dangle a valuable property before him.

He raked a hand through his hair and groaned. He could just imagine who that might have been, recalling that his grandmother possessed a house and some property across the border.

Would she have forfeited it just to force his hand?

He needed to ask? This was Grandmère, bothersome and meddlesome to her very core. She'd tipped his life upside down—without any regard to the consequences. He couldn't be too mad at her, though. It was her secret past that had let him see his own future so clearly. Then he glanced over at the other meddlesome creature in his life and smiled. And after all, his grandmother's grand plan had also brought Emmaline into his life.

Alex eased out of bed and walked to the window, stretching his muscles and flexing his shoulders to pull the kinks and knots from them.

Taking a tentative peek out the window, he saw that the morning was dawning bright and rosy. Another fine day.

Perfect for a picnic, he mused, glancing back at Emmaline's sleeping form. And if they had been married last night, he would be ordering a basket from a grinning Mrs.

Simmons right this very moment, and they'd spend the afternoon at Clifton House, making love in the grass.

Alex smiled. That would give his grandmother apoplexy for certain. Well, she'd wanted him married and producing an heir, and now she had her wish.

An heir.

He stopped in the middle of the room. Gads, how could he have been so thoughtless? He stared at Emmaline anew.

She could be with child. The night with Rawlins suddenly took on a new meaning, chilling his blood right down to his bare feet.

What if a child came of this? He couldn't bear to think of his firstborn being declared a bastard. Or Emmaline being subjected to the ridicule and scorn of the *ton*.

No, he had to resolve this marriage issue immediately, even if he had to send Henry with the traveling coach to Scotland to fetch Elliott home.

Downstairs, the front door opened and closed. Alex glanced at the clock, where the hands pointed to half past six. Who could be leaving the house at this hour? It was early even for the servants, and besides, they never used the front door. He tipped the drapes open ever so slightly and spied Hubert walking briskly across the square.

Hubert? What the devil was his cousin doing up and about at this time in the morning?

Just then a hired carriage rolled into view and Hubert nodded to the fellow and got in. The driver tipped his head toward the hatch, listened to Hubert's instructions and then slapped the reins. They left with some haste, Alex staring after them, wondering at this mystery with a sense of foreboding.

Then the puzzle became even more baffling when a few

moments later another carriage rolled through the square, a dark unmarked vehicle following his cousin at a discreet distance. If that wasn't enough, his surprise knew no bounds when he spied the driver of the second carriage.

Elton, the Marquis of Templeton's infamous servant.

Whyever would *he* be following Hubert?

Suddenly he recalled what Lady Oxley had said the night before. That Lilith had seen Emmaline riding about "in Templeton's carriage."

Alex shot one more glance at the departing carriages to gauge their direction and then caught up his breeches, boots, shirt and jacket.

Casting one more glance at Emmaline, he blew a kiss in her direction, then said under his breath as he left her, "If you won't give me the answers I need to know, I believe I've found someone who might."

At the London docks, ships came and left with the tides in orderly shifts. Nothing could alter the rise and fall of the water, so that was why Hubert had come to the dock so early in the morning—to be the first to greet the ship now tied up to the wharf.

He'd been watching for its arrival for weeks, first with the papers, and now that he was in London, in person, waiting patiently for the day the *Bountiful Miss* returned home.

"Better be him," he muttered under his breath. "Better be him."

If it wasn't, he didn't know what he'd do next. A few more months of her in the house and he'd be standing by and smiling as his cousin announced the pending arrival of an heir.

Why couldn't Sedgwick's bride have just stayed ill, instead of showing up so robust and alive.

And of course his cousin *would* have a wife that kept him well entertained, a wife that was a sight to behold, a wife whose sweet voice was like a balm on a stormy day.

Never mind the fact that Sedgwick also had the title, the lands, the wealth, while he, Hubert Denford, just had the Denford name.

All his life, as his father before him had, he'd held out hope that one day some misfortune would befall the current titleholder and their branch of the Denfords would be restored to their rightful place atop the family tree.

Well, he wasn't going to spend his life waiting, as his father had. No, he was going to ensure that Sedgwick never had the chance to secure an heir. There was something not quite right about all this Emmaline business and Hubert was just the man to get to the bottom of the mystery.

Aboard the ship, the sailors were scurrying about, and finally the gangplank was put in place and the passengers began to disembark.

Had he gotten Hubert's letter? Was he even aboard?

Then a tall, slender man of about the right age came ashore.

Hubert took a deep breath. This was it. His great gamble. If this was the man, then Lilith would never again look at him like she did when *cits* dared venture into proper society.

"Sir?" Hubert said.

"Mr. Denford?" the man replied, and held up Hubert's letter. "I'm so very glad to meet you."

"And I, you," Hubert told him, shaking his hand enthusiastically.

* * *

When Emmaline awoke, Alex was gone. Disappointed to find the empty space beside her on the mattress, she tried to tell herself that perhaps it was for the best. As much as she wanted to believe in all of his promises, that he'd find a way for them to be together, she knew that such fairy tales never happened to women like her.

There was no denying what and who she was, and it was time she started to remember that.

Thus sobered, Emmaline pulled herself out of the comfort and warmth of Alex's bed—not hers, not theirs, but *his* bed—and got up.

She stood before the wardrobe filled with pretty gowns and sighed. They weren't hers. Never had been. Taking one last reluctant glance at the silks and satins, she reached for her plain old muslin and pulled it on.

A knock at the door caught her attention, and she froze. The dowager? Lady Lilith? She was surrounded by enemies, of a sort. Mustering her courage, she said, "Come in."

Mrs. Simmons breezed in, a large package in her hands and a smile on her face. When she spied the rumpled state of the bed, her smile turned to a grin.

Emmaline on the other hand, blushed. Did the entire household know what went on inside this room?

Apparently so.

"A present from his lordship. Just came. Thought you might like to open it."

Emmaline shook her head. The last thing she wanted to do was see one more thing that she'd have to leave behind. One more memory of Sedgwick's generosity . . . and her own duplicity.

"Milady, you must open it."

Emmaline shook her head again, and Mrs. Simmons

clucked her tongue and pulled the strings from the package and let the brown paper fall away.

"Oh, my!" Mrs. Simmons said.

Emmaline turned to look and wished with all her heart she hadn't.

It was a duplicate of her gown from the picnic. The one she'd ruined when she'd fallen in the water.

"There's a note," Mrs. Simmons said, plucking it up and pressing it into her hands.

She glanced at the words and felt the hot sting of tears.

For our next outing in the country. May it meet the same demise.

Sedgwick

But there would be no more picnics, no more afternoons spent in idleness and passion.

Mrs. Simmons, romantic soul that she was, already had the dress out of the paper and was shaking and smoothing the wrinkles from it.

"Well, you'll be putting it on right now," she said, in that no-nonsense tone she must have inherited from her mother.

"I can't—" Emmaline began to protest.

"You can and you will," Mrs. Simmons said, spinning her around and starting to tug the laces of her muslin gown. "Listen well, my lady, they forget right smart how to turn your head in the years to come, so you'll make sure you do your part to encourage his thoughtfulness by wearing his gift."

She knew from experience that arguing with Mrs. Simmons was futile.

Wear the dress, a small voice urged her. *Take it with you.*

Her fingers went out to touch the muslin, the embroidery around the hem. Emmaline couldn't help herself—she smiled at memories the look-alike gown evoked.

Of riding in the phaeton pressed to Alex. Tripping across the grass barefoot. Alex's arms around her . . .

She sighed. It had been a perfect day.

The housekeeper took Emmaline's dreamy expression as acquiescence and began to remove her old serviceable gown and replace it with the new one.

"He'll be ordering a basket when he comes home and sees you all pretty and ready for him."

Emmaline didn't have the heart to tell the woman that she wouldn't be here. She couldn't stay any longer. Not even the lure of Lord Westly's piquet challenge could keep her.

She could just hear the gossip now.

Did you hear of Lady Sedgwick? She played fast at Westly's, then ran off with the money. The baron is ruined. Ruined utterly.

The only thing she could do was to leave, and then "perish," as she'd planned all along. Then Alex would be free to seek a real marriage, secure an heir.

Leaving now was the right thing to do. And after a lifetime of not always being on the up and up, Emmaline wanted to do this one thing right.

But oh, how she wanted to stay. To see Malvina's daughter grow up. To see the ballroom finished. To finish teaching Simmons the finer points of parmiel.

To be Sedgwick's Emmaline forever more.

Mrs. Simmons had finished with her laces, and took a step back to survey her handiwork. "Hmmm." She tapped her pursed lips, apparently not yet satisfied with the results. "I'll send Jane up to see to your hair."

"There's no need—" Emmaline started to say, but turned around and found the ever-efficient housekeeper had bustled off to find the maid.

Emmaline knew there was no time to dawdle now—the best thing to do was duck out the back and be gone.

She fetched her ever-at-the-ready valise, tucked her old gown inside and turned to leave. Only to find Lady Sedgwick standing in the doorway.

"Just where do you think you are going?" the lady demanded.

Emmaline gulped. No need to leave now. From the murderous glint in the dowager's eye, she hadn't long to live as it was.

"What do you have in that valise?" Lady Sedgwick asked, pointing a bony finger at the battered bag.

"Nothing," Emmaline told her. "Nothing that I didn't already have when I arrived."

The dowager glanced at the bursting armoire and then back at the small and well-worn valise. An odd light twinkled in her brown eyes. One of understanding, Emmaline thought. But of what? How could she be acquainted with such a dilemma?

But before any more could be revealed, Emmaline's momentary reprieve came in the unlikely form of Lady Lilith. She poked her nose in the room and glanced first at Emmaline—her gaze raking over the new gown. She made an aggrieved sniff, as if the expense of it had come from her pockets, but then she seemed to remember her manners and made a begrudging greeting.

"Good morning, Cousin Emmaline." Lady Lilith may have lost her temper the night before, but in the light of day she must have remembered who was the current mistress of the house. No matter how much of an affront it was to her sensibilities. And with that bit of required hospitality completed, she smiled at the dowager.

"My lady, how wonderful you look! Are you coming down for breakfast? We'll have a lovely chance to catch up since it seems Hubert and Sedgwick won't be joining us."

"Sedgwick is gone?" Emmaline asked without thinking.

Lady Lilith shot her another one of her assessing glances. "Yes. Simmons said he left quite early. I would think you would know something of his plans, considering how . . . how attached the two of you seem to be." Her disapproval of such a marital relationship rang with each word.

"Actually, Lilith," the dowager said, "Emmaline and I were about to take a ride in the park. Care to join us?"

"A ride? In the park? At this hour?" The lady looked as scandalized as she sounded. "But, my lady, it isn't—"

"Fashionable? So I hear. But the morning is lovely and the air is still fresh and I've convinced Emmaline to come along with me." The dowager smiled at her. "Isn't that right, Emmaline?"

All she could do was nod, and hope that Lady Sedgwick's driver wasn't being well tipped to dump her in Seven Dials, or some other stew.

The dowager wrapped her arm around Emmaline's and led her past a gaping Lady Lilith. "Come along, my dear girl. We have much to acquaint ourselves with."

Emmaline wondered if this was how the poor French queen had felt on her last day as the lady of the realm.

"My lady—" Emmaline began after they were settled in the dowager's open coach and were riding away from Number Seventeen.

At least it was in the direction of Hyde Park . . . for now.

"Don't say a word, you duplicitous girl, until we are well away from the house."

"If you would but—"

Lady Sedgwick raised one finger and halted any further words.

Emmaline sighed. None of this was turning out as she had thought when she and the dowager had first concocted this scheme.

And all her current troubles were because she'd played one too many hands of parmiel at Lady Sedgwick's sister's house.

Joslin Park
Two months earlier

"Do tell us more about the duchess," Lady Joslin urged the young woman across the table as she dealt out a new hand of parmiel.

"Yes, do tell what she is like," Lady Sedgwick urged.

With such an eager audience, Miss Doyle did her best to regale her listeners with tales large and small as to every one of the Duchess of Cheverton's preferences and dislikes, while winning a tidy sum at parmiel. Another fortnight with these ladies, and she'd be able to take the summer off.

If only all the households she stayed at were as comfortable and easy as this one. These two dowagers, sisters by marriage, were delightful company and were lavishing every comfort upon her, if only to hear more about the Duchess of Cheverton.

Miss Doyle obliged them by launching into her favorite *on dits* about the infamous noblewoman. The secret behind Her Grace's buttermilk face cream. Her particular choice of modistes in London (not too trendy, but extremely competent), her favorite menu for Sunday dinner with the vicar, her favorite devotional readings.

To her dismay, the touching advice about devotional readings, which had always been a choice piece of information, brought gales of laughter from the two ladies.

"Are you telling us the Duchess of Cheverton has taken to reading devotional books?"

A con always knows the moment when the gig is up, and right then and there, Miss Doyle knew she'd stepped into a mire.

She immediately went to her secondary plan. Make a speedy and undelayed exit from Joslin Park. If she could reach the inn outside the village before eleven, she might make the northbound mail coach and be long gone by morning.

"Oh, dear, oh, my, I fear my megrims are returning. Would you ladies mind if I . . ." Hand on her brow, she struggled up to her feet but didn't get any farther.

"Sit," Lady Joslin ordered, pointing at the chair she'd just vacated.

Miss Doyle did as she was bid. There were some things she'd learned in her years conning the gentry. The first and foremost rule of thumb was never to cross a dowager.

"Really, you were quite convincing until you got to the devotional piece," Lady Sedgwick told her. "But my dear girl, the Duchess of Cheverton never reads anything but gossip columns and the shipping news."

"The shipping news?" Miss Doyle said, tucking away that tidbit for future use—doing her best to ignore the fact that her future was probably quite limited.

Then she looked up to find her hostesses in gales of

laughter. Then it hit her—they hadn't just discovered her duplicity—they'd known for some time. "When did you . . . ?"

"When did we what?" Lady Joslin asked, wiping her eyes.

"When did you realize that I am not . . . not, well, you know."

"Employed by the Duchess of Cheverton?" Lady Sedgwick prompted. "Since I offered you a ride in Upper Alton."

"Oh," Miss Doyle said. "Then why have you let me natter on for the last two weeks?"

"We were testing you," Lady Joslin said in a direct and no-nonsense tone.

"Testing me?" Miss Doyle didn't know if she liked the sound of that.

"To see how good you were at fooling people."

"Whatever for?"

"We want you to impersonate someone," Lady Sedgwick told her. "Her name is Emmaline Denford, Baroness Sedgwick, and you are the perfect woman for the task."

"Emmaline," Lady Sedgwick began once they were well away from Hanover Square, "when I overheard Sedgwick bragging about how he'd made up a wife, I swear I wanted nothing more than to punish him for his duplicity. You were supposed to be a rather unpleasant surprise to force him out of his complacency and move him with some haste toward his duty and obligations." She shook her head. "Making up a wife! Whoever heard of such a thing."

"I did everything you told me to do," Emmaline told her. "The clothing, the house, the public appearances."

"Oh, yes, I know," Lady Sedgwick said, brushing aside

her words. "But you've done a little more than we discussed. You weren't supposed to . . . Emmaline, you assured me and my sister that you were not a woman of loose morals."

"And I'm not!" Emmaline protested. "I . . . I . . ." She didn't know what to say, but rather burst into tears.

Lady Sedgwick sighed. "Oh, dear." She plucked a handkerchief from her reticule and handed it to Emmaline. "*Ma chérie,* why the tears?"

"I blame you, Lady Sedgwick!"

"Me?"

"Yes, you and Lady Joslin," Emmaline said, sniffing into the handkerchief and swiping at a few more errant tears. "You never told me Sedgwick is so . . . is so wonderful."

"Alex? My grandson?" The dowager sounded incredulous.

Emmaline nodded and burst into a new spate of tears. Oh, demmit, she never cried, but now . . . Oh, bother the man. Bother them all.

"But my dear, he is really quite dull."

"Well, he's not!" Emmaline told her. "He's kind and generous, and he's very good in—" At this she colored, as did the dowager.

"Oh, my," was all the lady was able to muster. Then she took another long, hard look at Emmaline. "This isn't more of your playacting, is it? For I won't be gammoned. We had an agreement. There will be no stake for your piquet challenge if you've—"

"I don't want it," she told the dowager. "I'm not going to play."

"But you said with the money from Westly's piquet challenge, you would be able to start a new life."

"I can't now," she said, glancing away.

"Why not?" the dowager asked.

"For if I were to play and then disappear, it would ruin Sedgwick."

"Yes, yes, we discussed that, but you'll fall ill and then die."

Emmaline shook her head. "I can't."

"Can't die? Of course you can, and you will, that was our agreement."

Emmaline began to cry anew.

"Oh, dear," Lady Sedgwick sighed. "Whatever is wrong?"

"I love him."

"You wha-a-at?" The dowager sat back in her seat and gaped at Emmaline.

"I love Sedgwick. I love him with all my heart. I don't want to leave him, but I must . . ."

"You love my grandson?" the lady whispered.

She nodded and sniffed loudly.

"And what are Sedgwick's feelings for you?" The dowager waved her hand at Emmaline. "Don't tell me. I saw him with you last night. Hubert was right, he's besotted with you."

"He wants to marry me," she wailed.

The dowager's eyes widened. "He does?"

Emmaline nodded again.

The lady reached across and took her hands. When Emmaline looked up into her brown eyes, she found delight and joy there.

"Then marry him. With my blessings."

"You'd want me to marry Sedgwick?" Emmaline couldn't quite believe her.

The lady nodded. "Yes. The only thing I ever wanted was for him to find someone to love, someone who brought him joy. And you obviously do that. Marry him, Emmaline. Stay with us always."

"I can't," she told her.

"Whyever not?"

"We come from such different backgrounds. I am no lady. I'm not worthy of him."

"Not worthy! I saw you; you were packing your bags to leave, and you hadn't taken anything that you didn't bring with you. I think you worthy."

"But my father, my mother . . ."

"Oh, is that what you are concerned about?" The dowager tipped her head. "Who were my parents?"

Emmaline sighed. "The Comte and Comtesse St. Hilaire."

The old lady shook her head. "My mother was an opera dancer, my father drove freight wagons."

"But in *Debrett's*—" Emmaline began to argue.

"Lies. Made up to ensure that there was no talk after we wed. My Alexander didn't care a whit about my humble origins. He met me at the Revue where I was a singer and he proposed three days later. We were married and my pedigree invented one night on our honeymoon." The lady sighed dreamily, as if recalling a most likely passionate night. "So you see, Emmaline, while there are those who find bloodlines so very essential, I have always believed it is a person's heart and character that matter most. And I think you have an abundance of both."

Emmaline started to cry anew, for she didn't know how to tell the lady that even with her blessing, a marriage was still impossible.

"Milady," the dowager's driver called out, then nodded at the road ahead.

"Botheration," the dowager said, looking up at the carriage approaching them.

"Who is it?" Emmaline asked, not able to discern the person's identity.

"The Duchess of Cheverton."

Emmaline sank into the seat and wished for all her heart the dowager's driver had taken them to Seven Dials.

"Genevieve?" the duchess called out. "Is that you, and in town? I am quite put out by Sedgwick. Why, I saw him last night and he didn't mention a word of you. Probably knew I'd call first thing in the morning."

The dowager put on her best smile. "Your Grace, how wonderful to see you again. But you mustn't be cross with my dear Alex, for I just arrived last night as a surprise."

"Bah! You've come to town to see that wife of his." The duchess peered into the carriage. "Is that her?"

Lady Sedgwick elbowed Emmaline to sit up and she did, albeit reluctantly.

The introductions were made and the duchess offered her advice on several points as to Emmaline's choice of tradesmen.

Apparently the duchess knew all about the renovations taking place at Number Seventeen, and as a neighbor felt it her duty, nay, her obligation to come over and see that the work and quality were being done to the standards one expected in their part of Mayfair.

Before Lady Sedgwick or Emmaline could demure, Her Grace made an appointment for tea with them at three o'clock, and then instructed her driver to continue on.

* * *

The Duchess of Cheverton let out a loud breath. "Well, Sedgwick's bride is nothing like I expected." She said this to no one in particular, but as her staff was used to her odd outbursts, no one offered a reply.

Save the footman in the tiger's seat. The fellow was new and therefore thought he should return her conversation.

"Isn't she rather old to be married to the likes of Baron Sedgwick?"

The duchess turned a regal eye on the man. "Did you say something?"

He hadn't been in her service long enough to realize this was another of her questions that really didn't need an answer.

"I said, Yer Grace, that the lady looked old to be Sedgwick's wife. I thought he was a young sort of toff."

Really, she needed to talk to Gatehill about these footmen he was hiring in her absence.

"The older lady was his grandmother," she told him. "The *other* woman was his wife."

The man had the cheek to shake his head at her. "Oh, no, that wasn't his wife, but her maid. Though she looks a fine sight better in daylight than—"

"What are you blithering on about?" the duchess demanded, turning around and casting a cold eye on him.

The fellow gulped. "That woman isn't Lord Sedgwick's wife, but his wife's maid."

"And how do you happen to know this?"

"Because she was at the Queen's Corner last night. Recognized her by the ring on her hand. Cleaned out every one of us, playing a mean hand of parmiel, she did."

"Parmiel?" the duchess demanded, shooting a glance at the Sedgwick carriage. "She plays parmiel?"

"Like a regular sharp, she does," he said, an air of regret to his words.

The Duchess of Cheverton was for once truly flabbergasted, her mouth falling open and her hand floundering to the side of the carriage for support. *Parmiel?*

Her driver dared a glance over his shoulder. "Are you well, Your Grace?"

"Rogers, turn this carriage around. Take me to Number Seventeen, Hanover Square right this very moment."

Sedgwick stood outside the bachelor lodgings of the Marquis of Templeton for most of the morning waiting for Elton to return.

He hadn't been able to catch up with either him or Hubert and without any idea of where they were headed, he decided his best course of action was to go to the next place the marquis' driver-cum-valet was likely to appear.

"Sedgwick?" came a droll voice from the doorway. "What are you doing about? Don't tell me that lovely wife of yours evicted you already and now you must seek new apartments?" The marquis came down the steps. "For I would warn you, these apartments are fine enough, but the landlady smells of garlic and vinegar most of the time." He waved for him to come up the steps. "But then again, I assume you've come to see Elton, not me. Been waiting for you to arrive since Lady Oxley's dinner, so I must assume you finally discovered the truth."

Sedgwick didn't know quite what to make of the odd fellow. At times the *ton*'s favorite clown, and at others spot on with his observations. It was impossible to know who the man was for certain.

"Knocked me over, most decidedly," Templeton was saying. "Your wife . . . well, you must know now, for here you are."

"My wife?" Alex repeated, his eyes narrowing.

Templeton watched him carefully. "So you don't know, and this was just a reconnaissance trip. You have commendable instincts, sir. I should introduce you to a friend of mine. Pymm, his name is. He's always on the lookout for a man of intelligence and wit."

The clip-clop of hooves broke into the man's words and he looked up. "Good enough. Here is Elton himself. We'll see what he has to say about your arrival. I bet him you wouldn't be here before tomorrow. So, you see, I've lost a crown to the man, but don't remind him, because I haven't a farthing to my name right now, and I'm behind on his wages again."

Elton stopped the carriage before the house. He jumped down and gave a passing nod to his erstwhile employer. Instead he stopped and met Alex's gaze with his own level and deadly stare. "You've come about Button."

Alex nodded in reply. "So you do know her, know who she is."

"Of course I do," Elton said, spitting at the cobbles in the street. "She's my daughter."

Of all the things that Alex had expected to hear, this was not one of them. And here he'd been almost foolish enough to think she hadn't any secrets left.

He must have looked as taken aback as he felt.

"Demmit, Elton," Temple cursed, "you can't keep telling people like that, just dropping it like a French cannonball.

Did the same thing to me the other night and I nearly fell out of the carriage." He nodded toward the door. "Come inside and have a drink, Sedgwick. You look like you could use it. Besides, I don't suppose you would like your wife's history being aired in public, even this poor public."

Alex nodded and followed Temple inside, with Elton bringing up the rear.

Once settled inside the infamous marquis' apartments, Alex was struck by their spartan, almost military decoration. A map of England hung on one wall, while another of France was tacked to the opposing one. Hardly the lodgings one would expect of the future Duke of Setchfield.

"You are Emmaline's father?" Alex asked Elton once Temple had poured all three of them drinks.

"Yes," the gruff man replied. "I can see you don't approve, but her being my gel shouldn't be the worst of your concerns."

Temple laughed. "I don't know. If I found out my bride was a highwayman's daughter, I might be a little disgruntled."

"Well, we both know that won't happen," Elton muttered.

Whatever undertones, whatever the story was behind the man's statement, Alex hadn't time to fathom. "Are you saying Emmaline is in some sort of danger?"

Elton didn't answer, he just handed Alex a folded sheet of paper. Then he nodded at him to open it.

It was a manifest from a ship, the *Bountiful Miss.*

He wasn't too sure what this had to do with Emmaline, so he looked up at Elton.

The man heaved an aggrieved sigh and pointed halfway down the page. Alex looked, as did Temple, who peered over his shoulder.

"No!" Alex managed to sputter as he read the passenger list.

"That ain't the end of it," Elton told him. "The fellow was met at the docks by your cousin."

"Hubert," he muttered under his breath. And there was only one place his double-crossing relation would take the gentleman—Hanover Square. He rose and headed straight for the door.

"Hubert?" Temple said as he followed them both out the door. "But I thought the name on the list said Howard. Howard, Lord Haley."

Chapter 19

Emmaline and Lady Sedgwick arrived back at Hanover Square not long after, the dowager having argued with Emmaline the entire way to stay with Sedgwick. Even after she confided the truth: that she was already married.

But the lady was undeterred. She believed that Emmaline should trust that Alex would find a way to muddle through the seemingly insurmountable difficulties ahead. Even as they pulled into the square, she confessed, "I should never have sent Mr. Elliott chasing after that property, but he's Scottish and such a thrifty fellow, I knew he would rise to the bait and leave London to secure it."

They were greeted at the door by a dour-faced Simmons. "Ma'am, my lady," he demurred before he shot a glance over his shoulder.

"What is it, Simmons?" Emmaline asked.

"Trouble, madam. Hubert has—"

"That will be enough, Simmons," Hubert called out from

351

the doorway of the sitting room. "I will take over from here. Ladies, if you please, come in here."

Lady Sedgwick shot her grandson an annoyed glance. "Hubert Denford, what do you think you are doing? I will not be ordered about—"

"Madam, come inside and sit down, or we can discuss your companion's lineage right here."

Emmaline gulped. Oh, dear heavens. Hubert had discovered the truth.

Just then an elderly man came tottering out of the back library. "You were right, Mr. Denford, the baron has an excellent collection of first-edition Billingsworths. I look forward to discussing my scientific finds with him, since you've said he would be—" He stopped when he spied Emmaline and Lady Sedgwick. "Oh, pardon me, where are my manners. Howard, Lord Haley, at your service." He made a low bow, which was a good thing, for both Lady Sedgwick and Emmaline gaped in a most unladylike manner at the man.

Lord Haley? Emmaline's father? It couldn't be!

"Wh-what did you say your name was, sir?" Lady Sedgwick stammered.

"Howard, Lord Haley, ma'am. Not surprised no one recalls me. Been in Africa for nearly thirty years. Out of society for far too long and, sadder still, away from the company of such lovely ladies." He made another bow, yet as he arose, his gaze strayed over Emmaline, his brow furrowing as he examined her features. Then he shook his head and took Lady Sedgwick's hand and brought it elegantly to his lips.

Emmaline glanced up at Hubert and found him grinning

like a cat. The wretched bastard had brought Lord Haley here not for the noble scientific ideals that the man thought, but to ruin Sedgwick once and for all.

"Lord Haley," Hubert said, with all the oily charm of a rag merchant, "would you excuse us for a moment? I must speak to my relatives. I do believe you will find the view of the garden in the back salon quite refreshing after your long voyage, and my wife would be more than happy to see to some refreshments."

The man smiled, completely unaware of his role in this Machiavellian farce. "Sounds lovely," he said.

Lady Lilith came forward from the hallway most willingly. "Lord Haley, this way. I shall ring for tea. When was the last time you had a nice fruit tart? Our cook is tolerable, but I believe the Earl of Tottley's chef sent over a fine selection just the other day."

Lord Haley followed her, while Hubert pointed toward the front sitting room. "If you will . . ."

Lady Sedgwick and Emmaline surrendered to his request, if only because they had no choice.

Once inside the room, Hubert closed the door with a confident slam. "Now, now, now, whom do I have the pleasure of addressing?" he asked Emmaline.

"Don't be an ass," Lady Sedgwick sputtered. "That is Alex's—"

He shot her a withering stare. "That will be enough. The charade ends now. I know, you know, we all know this tart isn't Emmaline Denford. There is no Emmaline Haley Denford, never was and never has been, and that man," he said, pointing in the direction of the rear of the house, "has no offspring."

"Hubert, don't do this," Emmaline said, coming forward to lay a gentle hand on his sleeve. "You don't want to do this to Sedgwick."

"Sedgwick!" he sputtered. "I should be Sedgwick."

"Oh, not that infernal rot," Lady Sedgwick muttered as she collapsed into a nearby chair.

"Yes, and it isn't rot," he said, his voice rising. "There is no reason to believe that I am not the rightful heir to the Sedgwick title."

Lady Sedgwick rolled her gaze upward.

Emmaline glanced from her to Hubert and asked the question, "Why would you be the baron?"

"Ask her," he said, pointing at his grandmother.

Lady Sedgwick blew out a noisy breath. "That was fifty years ago—and I am convinced I picked the right heir."

Picked the right heir? What the devil could that mean?

Hubert paced in front of his grandmother. "You mixed them up! You didn't even know which baby was which and then you just picked, helter-skelter, which child was to be the heir and which was to be surrendered to obscurity."

Emmaline glanced over at her, shocked by this revelation.

The lady shrugged with typical Gallic nonchalance as if she'd merely spilled the tea. "Alex and Hubert's fathers were twins," she explained. "A few months after they were born, I was with them while their nurse was out and somehow I got Alex's father and his uncle mixed up. I couldn't tell which baby was which. The heir or the second-born."

Emmaline stared at her. "Oh, heavens no."

"Her own children," Hubert scoffed. "Couldn't tell them apart."

"They were twins, for heaven's sakes. Identical in every way. Not even their nurse could tell which was which. So my dear Alex was summoned and he was quite cross with me. He ordered me to pick which one was the heir and which was to be the spare."

"And so she did, with no real proof either way," Hubert said accusingly. "There is no reason to believe that I am not the rightful heir."

Emmaline could think of a thousand reasons, but that was the least of her concerns. Sedgwick's place as baron was assured, but his future was anything but glowing.

Not with Hubert plotting his social ruin.

"What do you want, Hubert?" his grandmother asked.

"I want her to leave," he said, pointing at Emmaline.

"That's all?" she asked, incredulous that such a thing was the extent of Hubert's price.

"Yes, you are going to leave Sedgwick. Desert him," Hubert told her.

Now she saw the real prize he was after. But couldn't he see that it would never work?

The dowager saw the flaw in his plan as well. "Hubert, you fool, Sedgwick will never stand for this. You could send Emmaline to the ends of the earth and your cousin would find her. You cannot separate them."

"I can and I will," Hubert said, folding his hands behind his back and beginning to pace pompously about the room. "With his wife gone, Sedgwick will be unable to remarry. Unable to secure an heir, assuring the barony will pass to me, where it rightfully belongs."

"That is, if you survive him," his grandmother muttered under her breath.

* * *

Sedgwick, Elton and Temple arrived at Hanover Square at the same time as the Duchess of Cheverton's carriage came to stop in front of Number Seventeen.

"Your Grace," Sedgwick said, bowing low. Temple and Elton followed suit.

"Sedgwick, I must speak to you. There is something about your wife that has come to my attention . . ." She glanced over at the other two. "Temple," she said with a nod in his direction. "This matter doesn't concern you." Thinking him properly dismissed, she wrapped her arm around Sedgwick's and towed him up the steps.

"Please don't believe it gives me any pleasure to be the one to tell you this," she said, "but your wife was playing cards in a most disreputable inn last night." She paused and glanced at Alex, as if assessing his reaction. "She was gambling with servants. And I have reason to believe she isn't who you think she is."

Alex wanted to beat his head against the wall. First Hubert's duplicity, and now the Duchess of Cheverton at his doorstep. He didn't think there was anything left that could surprise him today. "Your Grace, I'm sure that there has been some sort of misunderstanding," he said, hoping to mollify her. "But I fear this isn't a good time to call." He took her arm and tried steering her back to her carriage, but the lady would not be naysaid.

"Sedgwick, we can discuss this inside like civilized members of society, or we can discuss this in the street like a gaggle of fishwives," she said in a loud, imperious voice that most likely could be heard in Hyde Park, if not Cheapside.

"She does have you there," Temple said over his shoulder.

The duchess turned her infamous cold stare on the marquis. "Temple, be gone, or I will have a word with your grandfather as to your disrespect."

"You will find him a sympathetic ear, Your Grace," he said, paying no heed to her glare. "For he says the same of me daily."

The duchess made an indignant "harrumph" and marched up the steps of Number Seventeen, entering the house as if it were her own.

Alex, Temple and Elton had no choice but to follow her.

Simmons was nowhere in sight, but there was an older man standing on the stairs studying the watercolors Emmaline had hung there.

"Fine work," he said, looking up at Alex. He adjusted his spectacles. "Lord Sedgwick, I presume?"

Alex nodded.

"I am—"

"Lord Haley?" the duchess exclaimed. "Howard? Is that you?"

"Your Grace," he said, making a courtly bow. "I am honored you still remember me."

"How could I not? Your lectures at the Scientific Society on aboriginal peoples had me in a swoon for a good six months afterward."

Lord Haley puffed up. "You flatter me. That was years ago."

"Whatever are you doing here?" the duchess asked. "Oh, foolish me, of course I know what you are doing here. You've come to visit your daughter."

"My what?" he asked.

"Oh, you! As absentminded as ever," she said. "Sedgwick's wife. Emmaline Haley Denford."

His brow furrowed. "Your Grace, you must have me confused with another, for I have no daughter."

Even as the Duchess of Cheverton's gaze narrowed on Alex, the study door came open, with Hubert backing out. He was followed by their grandmother, who, brandishing a parasol, was in the process of beating Hubert black and blue.

"You wretched boy," she was saying. *Whack! Whack!* "Your parents should have drowned you at birth, you unnatural whelp." *Thwack! Whack!*

"Grandmother! Please stop!" Hubert was crying out.

Emmaline was right behind the dowager, offering her encouragement and directions. "Again, my lady. For Sedgwick!"

As they came into the middle of the foyer, chaos erupted from all sides.

"A daughter?"

"There she is—Emmaline!"

"A fraud."

"The barony is mine!"

The cacophony continued unabated, with everyone shouting at once. The only one, Alex noted, who wasn't in the midst of it was Temple.

The marquis had taken a seat in the alcove, his long legs stuck out in front of him and his arms folded over his chest. He wore a grin that went from ear to ear.

"My word, Sedgwick," he called out. "And I always took you for such a dull fellow. I don't know how I could have been so mistaken."

Sedgwick stood in the middle of the sitting room, arms crossed over his chest, feet planted like the Colossus of

Rhodes. "I will remind each and every one of you that I am the master of this house and I will have order immediately. Mark my words, I will cast out anyone who disobeys me."

"Harrumph," the duchess sniffed.

He shot her a withering stare and the lady closed her lips tight.

Emmaline had to imagine it was because she didn't want to be forced out and miss one moment of this impending scandal.

"Sedgwick," Lord Haley began, "I find it unforgivable that you used my name in such a manner. The memory of my wife . . ." The man faltered to a stop and his gaze fell on Emmaline. "That is to say, I regard this as an insult to my Eleanor."

"Eleanor?" Emmaline and Elton gasped.

Haley shifted in his chair. "Yes, Eleanor." He adjusted his spectacles and looked at Emmaline again. "Though it is rather uncanny, for she had the same fair hair and blue eyes as you do, madam."

The duchess looked over at Emmaline as well. "By gads, Haley, you're right. The gel is the spitting image of Eleanor."

Emmaline felt a raft of goose bumps run down her arms. "My mother's name was Eleanor."

Lord Haley looked at her again and paled. "Tell me about her."

"I don't see that—" Emmaline said, always uncomfortable talking about her mother.

The man rose and sat down beside her. He took her hand and repeated his request. "Tell me about her."

Emmaline bit her lips and considered her words. "We shared the same coloring, but I always thought her hair and eyes were more vivid. And she loved flowers. Roses, especially."

He nodded for her to continue, prompting her with another question. "Where did you live?"

"In a cottage, near Upper Alton."

The man closed his eyes, his hands going to either side of his head. "Whose cottage?"

"It was my grandmother's, I believe. Not that I ever knew her, for she died just before I was born." She paused. "It was just outside the village and had a pretty stream that ran through one corner of the yard."

Lord Haley looked away, his eyes misting. "Tell me of your mother's character."

Emmaline looked at him, suddenly suspicious. "She was of the highest character, but she was unwell."

"How so?" he pressed.

"She was mad," Elton said in a low, quiet voice that stole through the room. "But you knew that already, didn't you, milord?"

Haley nodded, his eyes misting with tears.

"Her mother was a lunatic?" Lilith interjected. "Some surprise there."

"Do shut up, Lady Lilith," the Duchess of Cheverton said. "Your own mother doesn't exactly set the Thames on fire."

Lilith's mouth fell open at the insult, but she said nothing further.

In the meantime, Lord Haley was staring at Emmaline with wide eyes, in disbelief. "You're Eleanor's child?"

Emmaline nodded.

"My daughter?"

She hated to be the one to tell him. "No, my lord." She nodded to Elton. "He's my father."

There were more gasps around the room, mostly from Lady Lilith, who took this news with a triumphant smile that seemed to herald Emmaline's demise.

But it wasn't to be so.

Elton heaved a sigh. "Oh, Button, I loved your mother with all my heart. Raised you like my own. But Eleanor was far gone with you when I discovered her in that cottage." He nodded to Lord Haley. "That's your real dah, not me."

There was a stunned silence in the room. Emmaline backed away from Lord Haley. "This isn't true." Her gaze flew wildly to Elton, her hands over her heart. "I'm your daughter."

"Oh, how I wish it were so, for I've never been prouder of anyone in me life as I am of you." The old highwayman knelt before her. "But I'm not yer father, lass, and that I've always known."

"How can this be?" Emmaline looked from Elton to Lord Haley.

"I suppose I am to blame, my dear," Haley said. "I should never have married your mother, knowing that she wasn't of sound mind, but I loved her. When she was sensible, she was the most golden of women, loving and passionate. But then she would fall into her spells, and there was no way to reach her."

Emmaline nodded. That had been her childhood. Times when her mother was the most caring of parents and others when she was distant and vacant, barely recognizing her own daughter.

"The spells were coming closer and closer together and

they were getting more difficult to hide from society. My family urged me to have her sent to an asylum, and then tell everyone she was dead." He shook his head. "But I couldn't see her being put away, so I took her to Upper Alton and hired a woman to look after her. At least there she would be able to enjoy the flowers she loved. To hide her illness, I announced to one and all that she and I were going to Africa. And then I left without her. I left my Eleanor because I couldn't face the inevitable end."

He hung his head in shame.

"So you just left her?" Elton asked. "Just like that? If you loved her, how could you have done that to Eleanor?"

Lord Haley looked up at him. "And what have you to do with my wife, sir?"

"I loved her," he said. "And I only left her when I had to, to keep food on the table." He glanced around the room. "I had a different profession then. And from time to time had stayed at that cottage when I was in need of discreet shelter."

No one asked the reason for this, for Elton's past was well known, and Lord Haley was astute enough to guess the truth.

"I arrived one night to find the old woman dying and her being cared for by the most beautiful woman I'd ever spied." Elton smiled. "She was a rare one, Eleanor. In the morning, the woman was gone, and Eleanor helped me bury her. By evening, I discovered why it was that Eleanor was taking shelter there as well. She went from an angel to a madwoman in a matter of hours."

Elton bowed his head. "But by then, I couldn't leave her. Her being so far gone with child and all. I stayed, as best I could."

Emmaline felt the hot sting of tears in her eyes.

Lord Haley turned to her. "When were you born?"

"June 1773," she said.

The man closed his eyes. "Dear God, what did I do? I left my wife, I left her carrying my child." He made a strangled sound, so filled with anguish and guilt that it tore at the hearts of all who heard it. Well, all but two.

"I don't believe any of this," Hubert said. "You expect us to suppose that this imposter is in truth, your daughter?" He shook his head. "I for one will never believe it."

Lady Sedgwick picked up her parasol and whacked Hubert over the skull.

"Grandmother!" he protested, rubbing his head.

"Don't be so thick, Hubert," she said. "I for one don't need any further proof."

"The word of a . . . a . . ." he sputtered, pointing at Elton, who glared at him so darkly Hubert's mouth snapped shut. A few moments later he finished by saying, "A man of questionable character?"

Lady Sedgwick responded by hitting him again.

Emmaline shot a furtive glance at Lord Haley. *Her father?* She didn't know if she could believe it herself. She looked up at Sedgwick and found him grinning from ear to ear. He believed it. Utterly.

So, it seemed, did everyone else in the room, with the likely exception of Hubert and Lady Lilith.

But she still had her doubts. "Why didn't you come back sooner?"

"I wanted to, but when no letters arrived from the lady I hired, I just assumed Eleanor had . . . had gone on to her reward. And I couldn't bear to come back to England and not have her here." He paused. "But then Mr. Denford wrote to me. Said his cousin would be interested in financing my scientific works if I was willing to return to England, so I decided to overcome my guilt and return."

More than one hot glance turned in Hubert's direction. "I had every right," he complained. "I saw Lord Haley's name listed in the Manchester paper as part of a scientific report, and so I wrote to him." His mouth drew into a thin line. "I had hoped . . ."

Everyone knew what he had hoped.

Lord Haley continued his story. "It was not an easy decision to make. For how could I return and not have Eleanor there to offer her accounts of the *ton,* of society? Your mother loved London and all the glitter. Why, she could recite from *Debrett's* like some women can play a concerto."

"*Debrett's?*" Emmaline said.

"Yes, *Debrett's.* Had an old battered copy. Called it her bible. When I left, she tore out the page with the Haley lineage and told me to keep it safe and bring it home to her in one piece." He patted his jacket pocket. "I've carried it with me all these years."

"May I see it?" Emmaline asked, her heart hammering in her chest. *It couldn't be . . . it just couldn't be.*

He smiled and reached inside his jacket, pulling out a worn and frayed piece of paper. The ragged edge showed where it had been ripped from the volume, and the corners were worn, but it was still whole.

Emmaline's breath caught in her throat. "Just a moment," she managed to whisper before she excused herself and ran out to the hall. She caught up her valise where she'd left it and brought it into the room. Fishing out her copy of *Debrett's,* her mother's legacy, she opened it to the *H*'s and showed Lord Haley a sight that made the man burst into tears.

"What is it?" Lady Lilith complained, as everyone crowded around to see.

Lord Haley took his page and placed it inside the volume, the ragged edge matching perfectly to the missing page in Emmaline's volume.

"Eleanor," Lord Haley whispered to no one in particular. "I've come home, my dear."

There was, for some time, more confusion and laughter and hugs than even Sedgwick could contain. Everyone wanted to add their own congratulations to this miraculous reunion.

"Be this all as it may," Lady Lilith said, her strident voice rising above the merriment, "that doesn't explain how this woman came to London. If she didn't know she was Lord Haley's daughter until this afternoon, I would like an explanation of who she was before."

This stopped the chatter in a moment and all eyes fell on Emmaline.

"How very astute of you, Lady Lilith," Temple commented, though no one was listening to him.

But it was the Duchess of Cheverton who provided the answer. "Lady Lilith, I dislike your impertinence. Everyone knows that Emmaline was under my care. She's been my dearest companion for lo, these past six years. Haven't you?"

Emmaline gulped. She didn't dare disagree with the lady, so she nodded. But she had to wonder if the lady was of a sound mind to come to her defense.

Lady Lilith turned on this information in an instant. "Miss Doyle? That woman is your infamous companion?"

The duchess's brows rose. "The best hired companion I've ever had in my service." She winked at Emmaline. "She's kept me entertained like no other, and her wages were a bargain."

"I never!" Lady Lilith declared. "Why, this is ruinous!" Then as she looked around and realized that all her dreams of Hubert ever being elevated were past hope, she fell back into her chair and began to cry.

Wail, was more like it.

"It is all for naught. Now we shall be relegated to obscurity forever," she complained, weeping loudly and not caring who heard her.

Hubert knelt before her. "There, there, Lilith. Don't cry, my dear."

"All is lost," she continued to sob.

"Hubert," Sedgwick said, his voice commanding.

"Yes, cousin?" Hubert said, rising from the floor and facing his fate with a fortitude that was uncharacteristic of him.

"I have a proposition for you," Sedgwick said. "While I should throw you out on your ear for plotting behind my back, your efforts have produced a happy ending, so I feel the need to reward you."

"A reward?" Hubert's eyes widened as if he couldn't quite believe it.

"I have a plantation in the West Indies. I want you and Lilith to take it. But on one condition. That you not return to England for some time, and that what has been said in this room will never, ever be repeated."

"Never?" Hubert said, sounding all too disappointed.

"Oh, Hubert, don't be such a ninnyhammer," Lady Sedgwick said. "Take the property and go. You'll not get another chance like this."

Hubert looked to Lilith. "We would have to leave your mother, your family."

"For good?" she asked with a noisy sniffle.

He nodded.

She brightened immediately. "Take it, Hubert," she told him. "Sign whatever Sedgwick demands. I'll pack our things." She pursed her lips. "I must own that my mother is a bit overbearing, and this way there will be no worries that she'll come to live with us once Oxley weds. Whenever that might be." She forced a smile on her lips. "While I had hoped to one day be a baroness, I thank you, Sedgwick, for your kindness."

He nodded to her.

"Lady Lilith," Temple said, "don't dismiss the notion of elevation so quickly. Have you ever considered serving your country?" He took her by the arm and was saying something about her "sharp mind" and introducing her to "Mr. Pymm. I believe he has need of a new contact in the West Indies."

Hubert trotted along behind them, like one of Lady Sedgwick's ever-present pugs.

With Lady Lilith and Hubert gone, the Duchess of Cheverton turned to Emmaline. "Miss Doyle?"

Knowing there was no use denying it, Emmaline nodded.

"I knew it," the old woman snapped. "When that new footman declared that you had won a fortune last night playing parmiel, I knew you had to be her." Then, to Emmaline's shock, the woman came forward and hugged her like a long-lost daughter. "You don't know the hours of amusement you have brought me!"

"What?" Emmaline asked. "You aren't angry?"

"Angry? How could I be?" The lady took her and led her to the settee, sitting down and patting the seat beside her. "My husband was the last Cheverton. When I die, the title and all will revert back to the crown. For nigh on thirty years, I've lived a lonely life. I may have the Cheverton title, but it carries no power with it, not like it once did." She sighed. "That is, until Miss Doyle arrived in my life." Her eyes sparkled. "Oh, the letters I've received on your account, the visits I've entertained. How I have loved hearing of your escapades, defending your character to those outraged fools you've gammoned. I'd be a lonely and bitter woman if it wasn't for you and your Miss Doyle. I thank you, my dear."

To Emmaline's shock, the old lady began to cry and hugged her anew.

Then, when the duchess regained her composure and looked around the room, as imperious and haughty as ever, she announced, "Here me well. From this day forth, Lady Sedgwick's character is never to be questioned again. Or the bearer of such tidings will have my displeasure to deal with."

With such an edict, there was no doubt that Emmaline's future was assured.

If only . . .

She looked up at Sedgwick.

"Hawthorne," he said quietly.

Elton's head spun at this. "That bastard," he replied. "What has he got to do with this?"

Tears stung at Emmaline's eyes. She was Lord Haley's daughter, she was Emmaline. But she couldn't take the one last step that would make her happiness complete.

"Elton, as long as I am . . ." She leaned over to him and said softly, "Married to Hawthorne, I cannot wed Sedgwick."

"That foul bastard," Elton said in a voice so cold, it chilled the blood to hear him. Then his lips turned in a devilish tilt. "Never fear, Button, I believe I can relieve your mind on that account."

"Old Mam paid to have his throat cut?" Emmaline had tears in her eyes at the very thought of it. Elton's mother was more tight-fisted than Hubert, and for her to have made such a gesture . . . well, it was heartwarming.

"Oh, aye, lass. But then again, you were always her favorite," Elton said fondly.

"And he's?" Emmaline didn't like to sound hopeful that Hawthorne had met such a grisly fate, but really, the man was the devil's own.

Elton relieved her mind by saying, "Dead. Dead as they come, Button."

Lady Sedgwick gasped, her hands going to her throat.

Elton glanced over at her and shook his head. "No, ma'am, it wasn't like that. Before Blighty could do the rotter in, a freight cart ran over him. Blighty was awful mad for losing his fee, but your grandmother was ever so delighted to have saved her money that she went so far as to buy a round that night, to toast his soul into hell." He turned a sentimental eye on Emmaline. "And I'll have you know, we all offered a few up for you that one day you'd find your way home."

"And so I have," she said softly, looking from the father she loved to the one she had yet to get to know. Then the truth of the matter hit her. "I'm a widow?"

"As merry as they come," Elton told her proudly.

"Sedgwick!" she said, rushing to his arms. "Do you know what that means?"

"Yes, I'll have to have your name changed on the special license. I don't know how I'll explain this to the archbishop. Do you know how much it is costing me to marry you?" Then he grinned and kissed her, deeply and thoroughly.

After much congratulations and well-wishes, Emmaline settled back into the comfort of Sedgwick's arms, her dreams now paving her future.

"Wait until I get to Sedgwick Abbey," she told him. "Grandmère tells me it is in dire need of improvements. Forty-two rooms! I don't know where I'll begin."

"I know where we'll end: debtor's prison," he moaned good-heartedly.

"Oh, do stop sounding like Hubert," she chastened him. "Do you want to marry me or not?"

"Oh, aye, I do," he said, gathering her into his arms and placing a resounding kiss on her pert lips. He'd marry her, today, tomorrow, every day. For there would always be something about Emmaline to discover, something that he had to imagine would happily take all the days of his life.

And just as importantly, he thought as he drew her closer, her body melding as it did to his, the path to discovery would take all the nights in between.

Epilogue

"**S**edgwick, you let me go back in there," Emmaline demanded as he all but carried her down the steps of the Marquis of Westly's town house. "He cheated, I tell you. There is no way that man could have beaten me at piquet."

"Suffice it to say, he did," Alex replied. "And there is no use crying about it. Elton and I both warned you not to go."

"Well, I am not going to stand for it," she said, doubling back and taking the steps two at a time.

Alex caught her before she could grab the bellpull and give it an angry yank. He hoisted her over his shoulder, and without a care for what it may look like, Baron Sedgwick carried his protesting wife down the steps and tossed her into his waiting carriage.

Damn the wagging tongues, he thought, his dull reputation gone forevermore. Especially with Emmaline at his side.

To his wife's credit, she wasn't about to give up so easily.

Something he'd discovered all too quickly in the sennight they'd been wed. Truly and irrevocably married.

"That man cheated," she complained loudly. "And I for one will not stand for it."

Sedgwick nodded to Henry, who sat grinning up in the box. The man started the carriage even as Alex jumped in, if only to keep her ladyship from leaping out.

"Emmaline Denford, you are the poorest loser I have ever met," he said, sitting across from her glowering figure.

She sat on the seat with her arms folded over her chest and her bottom lip stuck out. "That is because I am quite unfamiliar with the feeling. I never lose."

"You did today," he couldn't help teasing.

She sputtered something, but what it was, he didn't hear, for he reached across the narrow space between them and caught her up in his arms, dragging her into his lap and covering her mouth with his in a deep kiss.

Emmaline protested, but only out of a sense of leftover indignation, then eventually gave in to his seduction, winding her arms around his neck and pulling him closer.

"I promise, Sedgwick," she whispered, "from this day forth, I will never play piquet again."

He laughed, and then kissed her once more, for he knew something about Emmaline—she had a passion for living that would never make life dull. She'd play piquet again, and was most likely plotting anew right this very second how to gain her stake for next year's challenge.

"Bother, that man," she complained between kisses. "For the life of me, I can't see how he did it."

"Are you still thinking about Westly?" Alex asked.

"Yes," she complained. "I was going to use the money I won to redecorate Sedgwick Abbey. I've already contacted

Signore Donati about coming north this winter. And I have no idea how I'll pay for all the furniture I've ordered."

"You should have considered that before you spent the money your father gave you."

Lord Haley had given Emmaline a thousand pounds as a wedding gift, urging her to use it toward decorating the Sedgwick nursery. Apparently the man was of a mind to become a doting grandfather, since he had missed Emmaline's childhood.

"Rest assured," Alex told her, "there's money enough even for your extravagant tastes." He kissed her again, this time taking the liberties that a man so besotted with his wife was expected to take.

"The king!" Emmaline sputtered. "It was the king. He palmed it before the last hand. I wondered about how he had it at the end, for I was sure ''

Alex shook his head. "Will you forget about Westly?"

"No, for I swear I'll see him—"

"I am not doing this properly," he muttered, so he slid his hand up her leg, beneath her gown and began to tease her flesh.

She moaned and her eyes closed under his ministrations.

"That's better," he said, as it appeared she had all but forgotten her loss. He kissed her anew, and for a time it looked like the drive home was going to be a very pleasant end to the day.

Not so.

Emmaline sat up on the seat and smiled at her husband. "I have it! Next year I'll make sure to palm the king early in the game. That ought to vex that miserable Westly."

Alex laughed. And he'd wager she'd be plotting her revenge for the rest of the year and drive him to distraction in the meantime. Apparently it would be up to him to keep her sufficiently diverted . . . so he got to work on the problem immediately.

Oh, the labors of a besotted husband, he thought as he covered her with his body and did his best to help her forget.

For the time being . . .

Author's Note

Before you write and ask me, let me just say there is no such card game as parmiel. At least not that I know of. It is one of those delightful things we authors get to do—make up devices to fit a story line.

And before you write on another matter, let me assure you that Miss Mabberly will not be left out in the cold to face her ruin alone. Besides, I think Jack needs to learn a few lessons in gentlemanly behavior. Or then again, maybe not! After all, maybe Miranda would prefer a handsome rake? For that matter, who doesn't? Watch for their story coming soon.

In the meantime, you're welcome to visit my website at *www.elizabethboyle.com* for updates and more information. Until then, many happy hours of reading and my best wishes always,

Elizabeth Boyle